Page 99, by Joe Bancroft

Martin O'Neill

Copyright © Martin O'Neill, 2022
All rights reserved
ISBN 9798837848551

For my Dad

Page 1

Boldness, confidence, social skills. Joe Bancroft lacked all three. Hardly a great start for a kid whose dream was to become a world-renowned press photographer. And yet here he was, face to face with the captain of Manchester United on his very first day in the job. It's a powerful thing, is ambition.

"Ladies and gentlemen, Mister Martin Buchan .." The footballer smiled wryly as he lined up for his shot. He'd never seen a crowd this small - not since since he'd transferred to the first division, anyway - but, hey ho, the money was good and he'd still make it to the golf if he got a spurt on. He licked his lips, bent forwards and, in one deft movement, snipped a bright red ribbon that stretched across the two glass doors before him. Joe's camera flashed and a girl called Debbie (Branch Manager • Happy to Help - according to her name badge) let out a squeal and began to clap as if her life depended on it. "Well, that's that and there we arre," said Buchan, rrolling his rr's in a gentle Scottish brrogue. "I now declarre the new Stockporrt brranch of Hampson's Paint and Wallpaperr Shop .. open!" He put down a pair of shiny, over-sized decorators' scissors and turned to the photographer. "Was that alrright, laddie?" he asked. "Want me to do it again?" Joe swallowed hard and tried to hide the tremble in his hands. He looked down hastily and checked the settings on his camera. 400 ASA, 1/60th of a second, f8 with bounced flash (set to auto, of course!) "No, it'll be fine, thanks," he stammered, face red. "Thank you very much, sir. Thank you."

There was a shout from the eager huddle of onlookers. "We love you, Marty," yelled an over-excited man in a United away-strip and, as Debbie proudly pushed apart the matching heavy doors, he and the entire audience - all fifteen of them, all squished into the entrance to the shop - gave the footballer one last ripple of applause and surged into the store, passed the halves of ribbon, passed the perfect stacks of anaglypta and gloss emulsion, *passed Martin Buchan* .. and headed straight for the free sausage rolls and the Blue Nun.

Joe stifled a giggle as he packed away his equipment. "I can't believe it," he sputtered. "First day on the job, too." (Truth be told, he'd rather have photographed Bobby Charlton or, at the very least, Stevie Coppell but, hey ho, Buchan wasn't bad for starters.) He slung a small camera bag over his shoulder and laughed out loud. "I'm a bloody press photographer!" he wheezed. "At last!" Grinning broadly, he turned right as he left the shop. This is it, he thought, Fleet Street here we come. Just turned eighteen and I'm .. ah! He'd forgotten his motor-bike, parked up by the door of Hampson's. Bright green and brand new, it had been bought, just for him, by his newspaper, that very morning. He tutted loudly and brushed a greasy chip paper off its seat. "Right, what's next?" he muttered, and pulled out a typed sheet of photographic 'jobs', his initials scrawled in red by the ones he'd been assigned.

2 pm: Hampsons Wallpaper shop opening/United player/Chase Street, Stockport. (JOB)
2.30 pm: Presentation of Women's Institute crocheted blanket to Children's Ward/Trafford Hospital. (JOB)

Two thirty? Bloody Nora, it was already quarter to three and the hospital was *at least* twenty-five minutes away. On top of that, Joe was scared to death of the motor-bike and .. *what?* .. the presentation of a *blanket?*

-

He was pulsing with excitement when he arrived home that night. "Dad," he yelled, slamming the front door loudly. "I've just had to photograph Martin Buchan." His Dad looked up, distractedly. He was picking his nose and scanning that evening's 'paper, trying to select a horse for the following day's 2.15 at Haydock. "Oh yes?" he said, circling Stringent Nancy in green biro. "Who's he?"

Joe wished he could tell his Mum too, but he hadn't seen her for almost two years.

Page 2

Joe was working class. Not that he knew it, or even that such a class existed. He ate his dinner at lunch time and his tea when he got home from school and, in winter, slept in a coat and balaclava, blithely scraping his initials in frost on the *inside* of his bedroom window. Come summer, he never went away on holiday, but always returned to school with a tan thanks to Mum's insistence on basting her offspring in a slime of olive oil and vinegar that fried them at gas mark five in the erratic August sunshine.

He grew up on a council housing estate, five miles from the middle of Manchester. (He could get to 'town' in an hour on the 67 bus, if only he'd had reason to go.) He was shy and thin, with brown, curly hair; black, National Health glasses and annoyingly unpredictable skin. He wasn't the brightest button in the box but he got along alright, all things considered. He lived with a Mum and a Dad and two younger sisters, and they all smoked like chimneys. (Alright, maybe not the sisters - at least not yet - although they *would* by the time they were thirteen and fifteen.) Mum was small and solid, with jet black hair and a pale, white face made all the smaller by a pair of wide, funky glasses in the shape of cats' eyes. Dad was wiry and just as small, though he seemed

taller thanks to a big frizz of springy, salt and pepper hair atop his red, weather-worn face. Two wide, twiddly sideburns - his lifelong pride and joy - grew down all the way to his jawline. The sisters just looked like sisters.
(Oh, there *was* an ugly bitch called Donna too but, luckily for her, she didn't know that, seeing as she was only a dog. Fortunately, there *were* other dogs on the estate that *did* find her rather attractive, especially when she was on heat.)

The house they called home had been built in the 1950s and, like that of many a good God-fearing Catholic household, had an illuminated crucifix on the wall in the hallway and a little font of holy water by the front door, into which Joe would dip his fingers every time he left the house, smearing a slimy sign of the cross onto his forehead as insurance from The Almighty against calamity. The garden was full of rose bushes, carefully-tended scarlet explosions that lit up an otherwise street-long strip of cloned, weedy lawns and unkempt privet hedge. Mum loved roses. She loved her new house too, having moved there in 1966 - when Joe was just six - from a grotty Victorian terrace with an outside loo and no hot water. The new house had an inside loo *and* an electric immersion heater. If only she'd had the money to switch it on. As a kid, Joe cleaned his teeth with soot and table-salt (for flavour), and thought nothing of standing on an empty cardboard cornflakes box, drawing around the shape of his foot and using that cut-out as an insole to cover the ever-present holes in his shoes. He didn't know what ground coffee smelled like (or was!) or what it was like to eat in a restaurant. Spaghetti and peas came in tins and salad was only *ever* eaten on a Sunday, drowned in Heinz salad cream. (Anything to liven up all that bloody cress!) They had peaches for afters, too. A tin of peaches and some evaporated milk. Bloody delicious. His school shirt had to last five days, and a hair wash and one bath a week was the norm, even if he didn't actually fancy one. (Third in after your sisters was never going to appeal, and he'd check the tepid, grey water for wee before he got in.) His life revolved around school, television and playing out in the street, although there *was* a brief flirtation with the Cubs, which he packed in after the Sixer in Wolf pack pulled off his woggle and threw it in the brook. A normal evening for eight year old Joe was homework followed by telly - Blue Peter, never Magpie - sitting on the floor with his sisters under a fug of Mum's cigarette smoke, her push-down ashtray stacked high with Players No. 6 fag ends. Dad was never there, because Dad was always at work.

Saturdays in the 70s meant sixpence to spend on 'toffees' at the newsagents and watching 'The Generation Game' with Bruce Forsyth and his drool-inducing conveyor belt of desire. Life .. is the name of the game!

"Why can't we get a toaster, Mum?"
"Why haven't we got a decanter, Mum?"

Mates were many and varied and there was never a shortage of pals to play football, though an older kid at the end of the road was to be avoided as everyone said he was prowling for 'bum-chums', whatever *they* were! They were always nice to the blue-faced lad though, the one with the hole in his heart, who they'd begrudgingly allow to score and always made sure he was on the winning side in any game. Shame when he died. (Fourteen, Joe thought.) And Gaffer? Well, everyone wanted Gaffer on their side. The only black kid on the estate, brilliant in nets. Would let you touch his black if you asked him nicely.

It was a beautiful bubble of life, growing up back then. It seemed to Joe his family wanted for nothing. (What *is* a decanter, anyway?) He could have sugar butties whenever he wanted, and tomato sauce ones if there was ever any left in the pantry. He even got a custard yellow Raleigh Chopper bike for his eleventh birthday, the first kid on the street to possess such an object of desire, although he wouldn't find out for years - long after the frame was rust and the tyres had popped and perished - that it had taken his parents thirty-six months to pay off the Hire Purchase agreement.

He was constantly dirty, constantly being scolded for ruining his trousers/blazer/shoes and constantly sporting a cut or a bruise or a scab. 'In the wars', as his Mum used to say. It was great.

The day I met Joe Bancroft ..

I got there as soon as I could. The gaffer let me off work early, so I dashed home for a hurried wash and one of the lads gave me a lift to hospital in his Dormobile. We were there by ten past seven.

"He's got your chin," a nurse announced. A huge, bulky woman - bonny, you'd say - she stretched out a thunderous wide arm and aimed it at a cot, double-parked alongside a hospital bed in which lay my darling wife, looking white and drained and forcing herself to smile. I nodded at her, oddly embarrassed. Being embarrassed embarrassed me more. Ach, I didn't know what to do, did I? I'd never been in a maternity ward before. Or seen my beautiful wife looking so spent and wrung-out. Do I go ahead and kiss her, I wondered .. in front of all these *people??* .. or should I just head straight to the baby, my brand-new first born child?

Holy Mary, Mother of God, I'm a *father!* A rush of blood made my head spin. Or was it the sickly smell of the ward? The overpowering heat? In all honesty it was more the shock of seeing all those nightie-clad ladies, all snoring or groaning or farting, although some, I could tell, were feeding. I felt like an interloper, a pervert almost. I managed to smile at my wife and she half-raised a hand in return. She looked so young, child-like herself, and she looked exhausted, like she'd just swum over to the old country and carried our new baby back over her head, keeping it dry, keeping it safe, bringing it home. A caesarian will do that to you, apparently.

My *chin*? Is that it, after all we've just gone through? Nine months of vomit and cravings for gherkins and chalk, and all I've passed on is my *chin*? Still, my wife loves my chin. Rugged, she'd said it was, soon after I met her, just after her eyes lit up when I told her I was an engineer. "Ooh, *you've* got prospects," she'd cooed at the dance. And then, aye, "You have a rugged chin, Mr. Bancroft," and the way my knees folded when she said it told me she'd soon be taking my name. They almost folded again as I walked round the foot of her bed. It should have been a thrilling moment but I was petrified, weighed down with the knowledge that, from that moment on, I held the responsibility for two peoples' lives instead of one.

"He?" I said to the nurse, my own voice making me jump. "You said 'He's got your chin.'"
"So I did," nodded the nurse. (I think she was a Dubliner.) "You have a son, so you do. A lovely, healthy, seven pound son .. with a beautiful chin."

I looked over the top of the cot and tears fell as I saw him for the first time in my life. Now, I'm not good with words but at that moment, I swear I felt my heart grow physically in my chest. It swelled. Expanded. Opened wide. Wide enough to take in this new addition to my life. I was in love. The boy looked up at me through bleary, far-focussed dish-water eyes and I'd have sworn he was thanking us for bringing him into the world. Thank you, Mummy, he seemed to say. I will always be grateful. And thank you Daddy, I will be a good son, I promise.

Sorry, have you a tissue? I'm a sentimental old fucker when I get going.

We'd agreed - my wife and I - that if we had a son we'd call him Joseph, after my Pa and *his* Da and the patron saint of all workers. (Bella, if it was a girl, after her Mother.) Joe Bancroft. It had a nice ring to it. It should have been my name too but Father Hoolihan must have been on the potcheen when he baptised me and the eejit went and put Joseph in the middle.
"Hello, Joe Bancroft," I said. "Welcome to Manchester. (I told you words weren't my thing.) "Now don't you worry your wee head about anything," I said next. "I'll look after you, son, you just watch." But I tell you now, I can't remember a thing after that. I don't think there was capacity left in my brain to make any more memories, coping as it was with all the joy and the wonderment and pride. Apparently the nurse ticked me off, worried that the factory-filthy fingers I wiggled at Joe would soil the woolly, white blanket that covered him, and my wife laughed when she told me later I'd said Joe would make a great accountant. She also reminded me that I'd cried. Of *course* I did. I'm such a soppy old bastard, see? And look, here I am, eyes moist again as I

think back to that wonderful, heaven-sent August day, the day I met Joe Bancroft.

Page 3

On his first ever trip to the seaside, just turned six with arms and legs on the stretch, Joe was dredging the busy shoreline with a net on a long pole, 'fishing' in a foamy water so shallow it barely troubled his shins, when he blundered into a dug-out castle-moat hole in the sand that had been covered by the incoming tide. He disappeared head first beneath a rotting, wooden boat-launch and, feeling terror for the first time in his life, began to bubble and thrash as his lungs filled with an opaque Blackpool brine. Blissfully, he passed out after twenty horrendous seconds and was a goner until he was pulled back into the land of the living by a lanky teenager who, in a bizarre coincidence, had just moved into the house at the back of their own. (As grateful reward, Mum bought him a 99 ice-cream and gave him sixpence.) The next day, she booked Joe in for swimming lessons, but the fear was in him now and the boy was bloody useless. He *did* eventually gain his 'length certificate', but only after six months of panicky gasping and a ridiculous kiddy-style doggy paddle, much to the derision of his classmates. No, the damage had been done and Joe was forever afraid of deep water. It really shattered his confidence. As did passing the Eleven-Plus exam, the only pupil in his year to do so.

-

School had been blissful up to that point. Joe had just enjoyed seven years of friendship and belonging, with playtimes full of marbles and football cards, conkers and British

Bulldog, and hours of playing Batman and Robin with his best pal John Dayne. (Arms linked tightly, they'd bomb around the shoe-shredding cinder playground in a ten year old's version of the Batmobile, John always Batman, Joe forever Robin.) But now he had to go to the Grammar School. The *Protestant* Grammar School, forty-five bus-ride minutes away in a strange new part of Manchester. He was delighted at first. Naturally. As were his parents. Of course they were. They even bought him an expensive Parker fountain pen and a bottle of dark blue Quink ink so that he could write 'properly' at the 'Big School'. But, as his first day there grew nearer, things began to change. Whilst he was taken to one shop to buy his new uniform, his friends all went to another. The textbooks he bought weren't the same as theirs, his stationery requirements all different. And his autumn term started three days before his friends' too, by which time he'd already noticed they weren't treating him as he'd normally expect. He was excluded from their excited 'new school' gossip, ignored when they went to the 'chippy' for a bag of scratchings, wouldn't have the ball passed to him when they played football. His exam mark marked him out, and he was no longer the same as his peers. A seed of insecurity had been sown, and its roots spread quickly. By the time he approached the school's huge Victorian edifice that bright September morning, any lingering sense of optimism had been knocked right out of him. He felt immediately that he wouldn't fit in, right from the moment he walked through the ominously large double doors and under the 'Facere optimum' coat of-arms. He'd know soon enough what the motto meant, when he had to start learning Latin. (Latin? Oh, quid est iocus.)

It was loud in that grand, dusty hall as rows of fresh-scrubbed first-years chattered excitedly, friendships formed already. They'd all come from the same nearby primary schools - exam-passed en masse - and were simply carrying on where they'd left off at the start of their summer holidays. Joe sat alone and stared at their smart haircuts and shiny new satchels. He couldn't quite put his finger on it but these kids, they seemed so .. different. They had an 'air' about them. A confidence, an arrogance, a certainty. *Posh people!* He shrank back, chin down, timid. And then he caught the smell. The alien aromas of humus and garlic, cigars and Chanel, leather car-seats, chickpeas, cricket-pads, airports, coffee beans and Beaujolais. The air was infused with their moneyed, middle-class lifestyles and Joe felt all at sea. He'd never experienced any of these smells in his *life*.

He got barred from religious instruction. "He can't be taught *Protestant* ways," Father Sheehan had huffed, his crimson face inflating dangerously. "Not one of *my* boys!" (Joe had served as an altar boy at St. Matthew's RC Church.) The parish priest insisted that, to avoid being 'dragged down' into heathen 'proddy-dog' ways, Joe should be kept out of the school's RI lessons and instead, spend meaningfully quiet 'study periods' on his own, to which end a desk was placed on the high stage at the end of the hall and Joe sat, alone and silent, for two hours every week. He was then made to attend one-to-one *Catholic* religious teaching in the priest's sacristy every Friday evening. It was boring as fuck! Years later, Joe told one of the reporters on his newspaper about those glum, depressing days. "Did the priest ever touch you up?' the florid journo asked, keen for a tasty exclusive. "Just the once," Joe replied. "But it was only for a quid and he gave it me back the next day!"
(He liked that one!)

The bullies never actually punched or kicked him, but it *did* get a bit rough. On a regular basis, Joe would be yanked from the playground and dragged into the cold, brick outdoor toilets for a spot of 'scare the shit out of the first-year weirdo', and his optician became rather bored of replacing or bending back into shape the arms of Joe's black National

Health glasses. (One time, the old fart handed him back the straightened specs without realising he'd got his thumb through the space where a lens used to be. Oh yes, it got a bit rough.) Being locked in the dingy underground cloakrooms brought terror to Joe's young life for a second time, and he would foreverafter hate the smell of burning matches. The fourth-years who rejoiced in his whimpering would slam shut the subterranean cellar's metal doors and flick the little burning javelins at him through its grills. His schoolbag got scratched and his precious new fountain pen bit the dust on the day John Howard used it as a dagger, bending the nib all cock-eyed as he stabbed Joe in the hand during Tech Drawing. Joe panicked for days he'd die of 'blood-poisoning'. He got his first nickname when the smart-arse next to him in Biology decided to call him 'Specimen' - Joe's specs and unruly 70s hairstyle lending him the air of mad scientist - but that quickly changed on the day he became 'Mince'. Stupid, stupid Mince. (To be pedantic, it should have been pronounced 'mance' - as in dance - because it came from the French word meaning slim, slender, slight or small. All adjectives that so accurately applied to Joe. He really was a skinny bastard.) The oiks in his class laughed out loud when they read out the word in their flat west Manchester accents, and stuck Joe with the derogatory moniker until he eventually left the school.

"Pass the ball, Mince."
"Done your homework, Mince?"
"What you having for tea, Mince? Mince?"

At least there was 'Peter and The Wolf', poured soothingly over his stress during a music lesson one wan, November morning. Strings, french horns, kettle drums? How stirring. The nearest he'd come to any of this was tooting out 'Frère Jacques' on the recorder as a seven year old. He asked for the LP for Christmas and Santa delivered it with The Peter Fairley Space Annual and 'Slade Alive', a 'live' album that was the nearest Joe would come to an actual gig for another six years. Small glimmers of joy in all the Grammar School gloom.

Another glimmer was Simon Parkinson, the lad Joe sat next to in those Tuesday period three classes. St. Simon (bless him) took pity on poor, put-upon Joe (as he liked to describe him) and invited him back to his house, just around the corner from the school, to listen each week to the new Radio One top twenty. He would show Joe off to his mother - who would sit knitting as a cleaner hoovered around her feet - like a six-year-old who'd just rescued a starving puppy. That all ended three weeks into Joe's second year at the school, when Si was hoiked off to Hemel Hempstead with his parents. (The cleaner got a really good reference.) For the best part of that next year, Joe would burst into tears during woodwork lessons, 'pretend' to miss the school bus on frosty January mornings and stand shivering by the sidelines when his class played rugby in the rain. "I don't even *like* rugby," he'd whine, clatter skidding across the playground to the 'rugger' pitch and standing in line as the class was divided into teams. The two captains - it was always the same two, the tall blond and the gorilla with the sprouting chin bristles - would stand in front of them all and choose their sides.
"I'll have Smith."
"I'll have Jones."
And on they'd go until Joe was the last one left.
 "Ok, *you* can have Mince," Blondie would say.
"No, it's alright," Whiskers would answer. "*You* have him."
"Oh, don't bother yourselves," Joe would pout. "I don't want to play anyway," and he'd sidle off to the furthest reaches of the school field to pop spots and make daisy chains until the teacher blew the final whistle. At the start of his third year his unhappiness was finally noticed and, despite his parents' disappointment at the 'downgrade', he was trans-

ferred to the Catholic Secondary Modern, the school to which his parish priest had wanted him to go to all along.

It was the school to which his Primary School friends had gone, two years prior, where they'd formed bonds that Joe could not, and would not, break. Trevor Walls made sure of that. The 'cock' of the school, he took an immediate dislike to the perceived 'posh' boy and spent the next three years filling in where the Grammar School yobs had left off.

It was the school that organised a field-trip to Llandudno, for which his parents couldn't afford the fare. In an echo of his recent past, Joe spent the entire day alone, revising in the school hall as his classmates hiked the Great Orme and threw up on too much candy floss and hormones.

It was the school that incongruously employed an Irish priest to teach sex education to the boys. "Right lads," he'd once said, rubbing his hands together enthusiastically. "Who can tell me another name for masturbation?"
"Wanking, Father," said one cocky smart-arse, smirking to his pals.
Wanking farther? thought Joe. How far? And what's masturbation, anyway?

It was the school that started a camera club.

The days of my youth ..

We lived by the sea on a diet of dulse, flatfish and seaweed soda bread. (I'm surprised I didn't grow fins, so I am.) We swung with the moods of the Lough; playing - on the good days - in its ever-shifting dunes and avoiding its tantrums on the bad, but I cannot tell you how much I hated the sea. Not that I swam in it much. (I can't swim at all, to be honest.) Oh sure, I had the odd splash-about when we fooled around the harbour, but that's about all. It just wasn't in my blood like it was for my pals. Their fathers were all fishermen, mine a self-employed gravedigger. Fastest spade in the east, he used to say, though he didn't really get much practice. There were only about two deaths a year in our wee village.

As a family, we were poor, but close. God love us, nine wee 'uns in a two-bedroomed house will always guarantee that. In our 'leisure' time - as they call it these days - my seven sisters would sit at home and copy make-up and dress fashions from months-old Woman's Own magazines, whilst my brother Eugene and I would take off after Mass for fags and a ride on Declan Docherty's BSA Road Rocket. Good-looking bike, that was. And a good-looking lad, was Declan. Taught me the Teddy-Boy quiff, he did, and told me once he'd gone all the way with Vonnie Reardon. Vonnie the vixen, he'd called her. A real funny guy, Declan, even for a Protestant.

The Troubles? Well, we didn't know them by that name back then, or even see much in the way of 'conflict', although I did get roughed up at a youth club once after calling a guy a heathen gobshite. Other than that, nothing. No, wait a minute, Declan's bike was stolen in Belfast and they found it burnt out off the Falls Road. Ah yes, I remember now. After that, our whole family took to praying things would calm down again, just as soon as we got to Mass at St. Nicholas's. And then again during our bedtime prayers. And then at Benediction, and at Stations of the Cross, and during Grace before and after meals. (I always said The Troubles would've never happened if every Ulsterman had just stayed on his knees and blathered to The Lord Above. There wouldn't have been any bloody *time* left for all of that hatred.)

I tried it on myself with Vonnie, once. After she'd got back from a trip to England. (Rumour had it she'd gone for some kind of 'treatment', but all I know is she looked awful pale when she got back.) Anyway, "Take a hike, Bancroft," she spat, but it was nice she'd actually spoken to me, wasn't it? Of course, I still had Molly Haveron to have a go at, and Frances Doyle and .. ach, listen to me, harping on as if I was Gary bloody Cooper. No, there was none of that 'how's yer father' back then. At least not for me, and probably just as well. Me Da would have reddened my arse with his grave spade if he'd caught news of any of that shenanigans.

It was my old man that spotted my way with machinery. Sure, I was always taking that Road Rocket to pieces, so I was. Here son, he said, you've an interview at Harland and Wolff and, four years later, there I was with an apprenticeship in the bag and a life in the shipyard ahead of me. Then, here son, he says again, you've an interview for a job in England and, four weeks later, there I was, walking off the boat in Liverpool and hitchhiking my way to Manchester. Getting there was the furthest from the sea I'd been in my life. I suddenly missed it like hell.

1973 and, on a damp, dull afternoon in October, a moment that would change Joe's life forever. Pinned to the school noticeboard, a hand-written sign heralded the launch of a new camera club. Open to fourth and fifth years it said but, despite the fact that he was still only a thirteen-year-old third year - and despite the fact he had never given photography a single thought in his *life* - Joe had begged, *pleaded,* to be allowed to join. "Please sir," he'd beseeched the science teacher, a bearded George Best lookalike with an unexpected Brummy accent. "Please??"

The school had just commissioned a new-build teaching block, which boasted a small but well-equipped darkroom between its biology and physics classrooms. Having finally got a reluctant 'ok' from the teacher, Joe would crowd in there with a handful of older pupils and watch in awe as 'Comb-over' Kellett took them through the intricate and mysterious process of film and print development. He was hooked from day one, from the moment he was introduced to photography's magical, chemical wizardry; seduced by that cliché photo-moment when an image appears unbidden from an otherwise blank sheet of paper. (That, and the exotic smell of the fixer!) As well as learning darkroom techniques, the club members were given simple Kodak Instamatic cameras and sent off to photograph 'assignments' over their weekends. Trees, frost, friends, fruit bowls. Joe threw himself at the projects with gusto, took to them like a duck to water, even sneaking out of school for a bit of 'extra-curricular' when he heard the Queen's Rolls-Royce would be going past on the M62. (It was a very blurry shot and he decided not to show it to anybody!) His fellow clubmembers weren't as keen though, and every one of them had left within the first three weeks. Even Kellett called it a day after a month. "Here Joe," he drawled. "Look after this, will you?" and he handed over the one and only key to the darkroom. And so, whilst his class studied the physiology of the common toad, Joe would lock himself in the darkroom and develop FP4 in D76. As they tackled algebraic constants, he taught himself dodging and burning from a musty school library book. Nobody noticed he was gone.

During a fourth-year careers lesson, Joe and his classmates were discussing with the teacher what they wanted to 'be' when they left school. Slouched in a circle around 'Virgo' McVine, they took it in turns to prophesy their futures.

"Nurse, sir."
"Welder, sir."
"Sailor."

McVine sighed and rolled his baggy eyes. For the love of God, can't *one* of them *ever* mention university?

"Typist, sir."
"Hairdresser, sir."
"Mechanic."

"Press Photographer, sir .."

The teacher sat bolt upright and coughed out loud. "Be realistic," he barked, his expression incredulous. Joe went puce with indignance. "Thanks for the encouragement, *sir*," he huffed, and sulked for the rest of the period. Press photographer? Where the hell had *that* come from?

Victor Blackman, that's where.

Vic was a press photographer who'd written a book about his wonderfully action-packed Fleet Street life. 'My way with a camera' had started as a weekly column in Amateur Photographer magazine, which Joe had taken to reading from the age of fourteen, having swapped it - very maturely, he thought - from his 'Look-in' music and telly comic. He'd bring home each week's new edition, make himself a nice cup of coffee and flick immediately to the old pro's latest article. Once the book had been published, Joe worshipped it like the Bible, absorbing himself into a world he'd never imagined, never heard of, never even *thought* of, in which Victor got to photograph royalty and pop stars, exotic locations and fighter jets, Arsenal, Miss World and Gina Lollabrigida! (Whoever *she* was!) Despite (or perhaps because of) having the sum life-experience of a boiled-ham sandwich, Victor's exotic lifestyle was absolutely thrilling to young Joe. A few years later, the book would be joined on his shelf by 'Flash, Bang, Wallop', a collection of rather more lurid news stories from the Daily Mirror's Kent Gavin. It had naked breasts on the front cover - phwoar - and dripped with exotic jet-set travel, foreign war, topless totty and footballers .. usually with topless totty. Now that *was* a long way from the life Joe lived on the housing estate. But Vic came first. As well as his enthralling 'real-life' stories, his book was full of useful advice to a rookie like Joe. It even had a chapter at the back called 'Breaking into Press Photography'. Handy! On a practical level, Vic wrote things like 'when taking portrait photographs, always focus on the eye of the subject nearest to the camera' and, 'in readiness for any fast-changing action, practice putting a new roll of film in your camera whilst walking down the street.' Joe had to improvise a little on that one as, even with a Saturday job on a bread round, he was only ever able to afford one roll of film at a time, but he felt it was a valuable exercise and practised as best he could. He certainly wanted to be ready if he ever found himself in the midst of any 'fast-changing action'. It was another piece of the old pro's advice that gave Joe the bigger problem ..

'Wear a white shirt when shooting portraits'.

Vic's thinking was this: if a photographer stood close enough to his subject he could illuminate their face with the light reflected off his shirt. All very clever, Joe thought, but he was so bloody shy he'd inwardly shudder at the thought of getting 'close' to another person. He knew only too well though, there was no place for timidity in the rough-tough world of press photography. He couldn't be breaking into a cold sweat every time he needed to take a photograph of someone - white shirt or no. This needed working on.

Page 5

He wore white on his first day as a press photographer. Sensible tie. Nice new pair of flared slacks. It was October 1978, damp again, still dull and near as damn it five years to the day since Joe had joined the camera club. And now here he was, at a Manchester motor-cycle dealer's, just two hours into the job, being asked to choose a bike from what, to him, was just a bewildering array of wires, wheels and shiny chrome.

The acceptance letter he'd received from the newspaper was framed and hanging on his bedroom wall. 'We look forward to welcoming you to our team', it said, and promised him forty-five quid a week and a company car. (A company car? At eighteen? Oh, yes please!) Unfortunately, as Joe was still only half-way through his driving lessons, that much-coveted prize would remain on hold until he could pass his test. As a stop-gap - and much to his horror - he was bought a motor-bike, helmet and a full set of water-proofs. (A lockable rear-mounted box was generously thrown in for his camera bag.) His new boss - the self-designated 'Chief Photographer' - a bald, jowly, fifties fatso in a

shiny, five hundred year old suit, drove him to the local bike dealer and waved a sweaty hand over the massed ranks of glittering Kawazukisakis.
"Take your pick," he said. "Which one do you want?" I don't want *any* of 'em, Joe thought, having never been on a motor-bike in his life. His obvious panic was only assuaged when a fidgeting member of staff put his fag down and stepped in to help. Spotting Joe's anxiety, the greasy shop assistant - a lank-haired anorexic in a Harley T - helpfully suggested a safe, bright-green Honda 50 'step-through' that "couldn't do forty downhill in a fuckin' 'urricane." The boss left the two of them together as Joe was given a cup of tea and a run-through of the bike's basics. It took him thirty-five edgy minutes to cover the four mile journey back to the newspaper office (in a calm south-westerly breeze), and his bright blue waterproofs squeaked liked mice as he walked into reception.
"Where the bloody hell have you *been*?" asked his boss. Joe's voice was muffled inside his new brown crash helmet. (He looked like he had a profiterole on his head.) "I was just getting used to the .."
"Take all that off and come with me." Joe followed the boss the one hundred yards to 'Focus', the town's one and only photography shop, where a new camera and a pair of prime lenses were out on the counter, alongside a Mecablitz flash gun and a light beige Billingham shoulder bag. He screwed up his face at the Olympus OM1. Although light and compact, it was built completely differently to any camera he had ever used, its shutter settings placed awkwardly and unnaturally on a dial around the lens instead of on the top plate. It was all arse about face and Joe hated it. "We all use them," the boss shrugged, sheepishly. "You'll soon get used to it."

A much-needed lunchtime burger set Joe fair for his first afternoon as a professional 'snapper'. (There was a Wimpy Bar only four doors down from the office. Oh yes, this town had it all.) He threw a 'deluxe' version of the Manchester A-Z into his bike-box, stuffed a brand-new spiral notebook into his jacket pocket, 'suited up' and headed off to the wallpaper shop, only stopping every three minutes or so to check directions on his new street map. (He'd never been to Stockport before. Talk about exotic locations!) He photographed Martin Buchan (*Martin Buchan!*) and then he (eventually) photographed Mrs Jayne Packenham-Walsh, the President of the South-East Manchester Women's Institute, as she handed over a multi-coloured crocheted blanket to Staff Nurse Cathy Dragisic in the Trumpton ward of Trafford General. (Thank God she'd stayed on for tea and Victoria Sponge.)

Returning to the office - and still not used to the bike - Joe bashed his metallic stallion into the front bumper of a sleek red Datsun 280Z, owned by the newspaper proprietor's 'bit of stuff', and his heart was still pounding when he hit the sack that night.

"I can't believe it," he squealed, pumping the air like Mohamed Ali. "I'm a bloody press photographer!"

Page 6

Day two was a bit of a shocker. Scheduled to start at half-nine, Joe had started up 'The Frog' - as he'd nicknamed his new green motorbike - and set off nice and early for work. He only lived fifteen miles from the newspaper office but, as he hadn't taken any kind of motorcycle proficiency test (or, of course, even *ridden* a motor-bike until the day before) he was unable to use the motorway that would have sped him there in less than twenty minutes. (Not to mention the fact that his new wheels weren't actually fast enough to *go* on a motorway!) So Joe had no choice but to use A roads, B roads, back lanes and a short cut through an industrial estate to get to his new place of employment. Along the way was the swing-bridge over the ship canal. And the traffic lights that hit red every forty yards. And the fire station that seemed to get a call-out every five minutes. And the two level-crossings. And the school-crossing patrols. (Bloody lollypop men.) And the roadworks (Bloody diggers.) And the three busy junctions that merged onto main roads. And the fact that, as it was only his first real day on the bike, he took a wrong turn off the bypass and ground to a halt down an overgrown cul-de-sac littered with beer cans, a broken stiletto shoe and enough used Johnnies to re-float the Titanic.

9.35 am. "Where the bloody hell have you *been*?" (The same opening line. At least the boss was consistent.) Joe struggled to remove his helmet and squeaked as his scarf squeezed his neck. "I got lost, and the traffic .."
"Take all that off and come with me."

The newspaper was housed in a nondescript end-of-terrace building that, for over thirty years, had been an oil-cloth and carpet shop. On his first day, Joe had been shown its tiny, makeshift darkroom, tucked away under a central staircase and sporting two doors - one leading from the reception area at the front and the other to a kitchen at the back. The boss knocked on the front door and a muffled voice yelled "One minute!" There were several scraping sounds, the click of an electric light, the swish of a heavy curtain and then, as the door swung open, Burt Reynolds stuck his head into the light. At least, the best impression Joe had ever seen. (Not that he'd seen many! Now *that,* he thought, was a moustache.) "Andy," said the boss by way of introduction, and the handsome lookalike - about five years old-

er than Joe - held out a slippery, dripping hand and shook Joe's with an enthusiastic "Hello, mate. Delighted!"
"What time did you get here this morning, Andy?" said the boss. Andy's moustache curled at the corners as he stretched out his bottom lip. "Er, dunno. Seven? Quarter past? You know I'm always in early after my day off." The boss looked back at Joe and raised his eyebrows. (There was a lot of facial hair action that morning!)
"But I'm on a nine-thirty start," whined Joe. "It says so in the contract." The boss smiled - a smug, patronising smile that doubled the size of his gobbly, gouty neck - a gurn that Joe would get to know well - and said "So when are you supposed to develop your photographs?" It was his way of telling Joe that his contract's 'hours of work' meant nothing, and not just because the news didn't stop when his shift did. Nine thirty 'til five? Forget it. One o'clock until 11pm? No chance. Joe quickly realised he was expected to work until there was no more work to do and then stay late or come in early the next day to develop and print it all. No-one had thought to include 'processing time' within the hours of a normal shift, so it had become an accepted 'norm' that the 'paper's photographers would devote their own 'free' time to develop and print the photographs they'd taken. (It was just as well Joe was in his element!) And at least working from seven (or earlier!) did have one advantage. It meant that Joe's light-sensitive work wouldn't be ruined if Della, the sweet little front office receptionist, decided to burst through the darkroom door to make a brew. The seventeen year old would try to use their workspace as a short-cut to the kitchen whenever she made coffee for the reporters and tele-sales staff that worked up the stairs. Lord knows why she never thought to knock on the door. Lord knows why the doors weren't fitted with locks. Lord knows why she never asked the photographers if they fancied a cup of tea!

Joe soon got used to the extra hours. Truth be told, he'd have done them even if he wasn't expected to. Almost three long decades before digital photography told a hold, the desperation to see his latest pictures meant he just *had* to get into the darkroom to develop his film and, after a busy day's shooting, he'd be itching to see just what he'd got on his rolls of black and white HP5. It was second nature to shut the darkroom door, switch to complete darkness and, by touch alone, load his film into a spiral holder and make it light-tight in a developing tank. It was then only a matter of minutes before, processed and fixed, he'd hurriedly unwind the film, water dripping down his arms, to get his first expectant glimpse of the work. The thrill of that first look never left him. In fact, the 'magic' of the entire photographic process still amazed him but, despite the books he'd bought himself, and a three month night-school course, the technical side of photography remained a complete mystery. Silver halides? Sodium Thiosulphate? *Gelatine*? "Film is made from *cows*?" he'd once asked the night-school tutor, having learnt of the base quality of film. Boiled bits and bones? He wasn't a vegetarian but, ugh! Nothing, however, was going to spoil the joy he felt when he unspooled a liquid ribbon of newly-processed 35mm film and cast his eager eyes over its deliciously inverted images for the first time. Drying the wet film was another matter. There was no professional drying cabinet at the office for Joe to hang his film. He had to use a hair-dryer. The boss kept it in the same drawer as his porno magazines and hair oil.

Page 7

In the years to come, Joe would look back on his childhood with bewilderment. Just *how* had he known how to grow up? It had just .. happened. He knew of course - of course he did - that it was all the work of his parents but now, as he touched base with adulthood, he realised he'd retained so few memories of it all and, of those he *could* drag out, very few of them actually featured his Dad. It was Mum who dominated his past. Taking him shopping for shoes, combing his hair for nits, giving him 5p after going to buy paraffin for the heater. Joe could still picture her, sitting at the dining table, meals going cold as, glasses down her nose, she would lose herself in a novel that she'd prop against the sugar bowl for ten minutes of escapism. (Lord knows, they were the only moments of peace she ever got to herself.) Her radar was always on, though. "Stay away from those Sladdens," she'd shout, as Joe snuck from the house to play out. "They're bad 'uns, those Sladdens," she'd bellow. "Stay away from them, Joe. I'm warning you." But, of course, you couldn't say that to a seven year old and expect him to obey you, could you?

Every street had them. The 'rough' family that all the mothers feared. Sadly for them the Sladdens were like magnets, pulling in the kids around them like a black hole sucks in stars. Scruffy, piss-poor chancers, two of the older brothers already in the nick and fifteen year Sandra the proud mother of twins, their 'non-conformity' was exactly what made them so attractive to everyone under fifteen on Foxton Street. Joe was drawn to Mark Sladden, two years older yet a good two inches shorter than he was. (Perhaps smoking *did* stunt your growth, after all.) "Hey, Bangers," Mark said to him one day. (Joe hated being called 'Bangers' but you didn't argue with a Sladden. Especially when he'd just spoken to you *personally*.) "Get yer bike and come with me. I want to show you something." They cycled to the end of the road, little Gordon Horrocks pedalling furiously behind, to where a busy railway embankment brought a dramatic end to Joe's long street, its sheer size an abrupt physical cessation to any further progress. Towering forty feet above them, a constant stream of trains hammered along its tracks. Manchester to Liverpool. Liverpool to Manchester. The train that took Joe's Dad from the sea.

"Don't go near the railway," Mum would scream. "Stay away from the train tracks, Joe. I'm warning you."
"Let's go over the train tracks," said Mark.
"I .. I can't," said Joe, squeezing the one working brake-block on his bike. "My Mum won't let me go near the 'banking'."
"Aaaah, you sissy," hissed Mark, already half way up the slope. "Come on, Horrers," he added, dragging Gordon by the sleeve. "Leave the mardy here, with his mummy."
"Oh, alright then," said Joe, suddenly brave. "Wait for me", but his daring dissolved as he got to the top of the rise. He'd never been up there before and it was scary. So high, so purposeful, with hard metal rails that took his breath away. He squinted at the tracks off to his left and to his right and, when he turned back, he actually gasped out loud. Mark was lying on his stomach with his head resting against the cold, shining steel.
"What are you *doing*?" Joe yelped. "You'll get your head chopped off, you dumbo."
"Shhh .." shhd Mark, a finger to his lips. "I'm listening out for trains."
"Why don't you just look?" said Joe, instantly regretting it. (You didn't say flippant stuff to a Sladden.)
"All clear," Mark pronounced importantly, thankfully ignoring Joe's comment. He nodded assuredly and dragged his bike across the tracks, little Gordon behind, and the pair of them stopped to look back at Joe. "Come on, you big bloody baby."

"Aw, you said 'bloody'," said Gordon, mouth open. Mark thumped him on the arm and waved for the bloody baby to follow. With a last look left and right Joe high-kicked over the rails and almost let go of his bike as he dropped onto the other side. The other side. A whole new world. And it was rubbish. Miles and miles of it, in giant, vibrating mountains, with paper blowing everywhere and seagulls dive-bombing like gannets at a bait-ball. "It's the tip," said Mark, which would have been stating the bleeding obvious except for the fact that Joe had had *no idea* a tip existed there. So close to their homes too. (Although he did wonder sometimes why their evenings hummed so much in the summer.) "Ace," he said, his bravery fading again. "Thanks for showing me, Mark. See ya." He stuck up two thumbs and turned away.
"No, no," said Mark, grabbing Joe's handlebars. "That's not what I wanted to show you. Look at *this* .." and he wheeled his bike down towards an enormous electricity pylon, its wires fizzy crackling with invisible airborne moisture.
"Oh .. I'm not going near that," said Joe. "I might explode."
"Ha ha ha ha .." Mark and Gordon almost wet themselves. "Come on, you softie," said Mark, and he dropped his bike and dived into the long grass that flourished, smugly out of reach of the council mower, between the thick, grey struts of the pylon. He rummaged at the foot of a girder and pulled up a plastic bag, well-used, wet and muddy. "This is what I wanted to show you," he said, and Joe couldn't resist. He dashed into the grass and sat down just as Mark pulled a porn mag from the bag. "Look at this," he squealed, his voice rising an octave. He flicked open two pages that weren't stuck together and paused at a picture of a luscious, mega-breasted centre-fold, shot from above in what looked like a large, pink paddling pool. "Look at the tits on *that*," he slathered. "Aren't they fantastic?"
"Fantastic," repeated Joe, excitedly. "Er, tits?"
Mark dropped the mag and looked at Joe, incredulously. "Yeah, you know, tits," he beamed, fingers curling descrip-

tively at his chest. "Bazookas! Boobies! Busters ..!" Joe's face was blank. "Oh well, never mind that," said Mark, wafting a dismissive hand. "Have a look at this instead." He fiddled in the bag, pulled out another well-creased magazine and triumphantly prised open the pages. "What do you think of *that,* Bangers?"

"Look at the size of that sausage!" Joe gasped. "I've never seen a sausage like *that* before. But why's she eating it with her hands? Where's her knife and fork?" Mark did actually wet himself then. Just a little drop of wee, because he'd never heard anything as funny in his life. "Knife and fork?" he screeched. "Agghhhhhhhahaha .."

Joe and Gordon left Mark rolling around under the pylon where, two hours later, a council driver sat and wondered how his stash had ended up all over the grass. "He's daft, that Mark, isn't he?" said Joe, as the pair dashed nervously back across the train tracks. (They'd waited five whole minutes before they were *sure* there wasn't a train coming.) "What's he so excited about, anyway?"

"Sex," said Gordon, flatly. "That's called sex, that is. Our Tracy's had a go. She told me."

"Sex? What's sex?"

"It's when a man puts his willy in a lady's divider," said Gordon, eager to impart his knowledge.

"His *willy*?"

"Yeah, that's what the sausage was," Gordon nodded. "'Cept, it wasn't a sausage, it was his willy."

Joe's jaw dropped. "But why was she eating his *willy*?" he squeaked, eyebrows flying north. "Eeeuuw! And how come his willy was so *big*? I'd wee on the ceiling if my willy was that big." They giggled all the way home and, as they got off their bikes, Gordon put his mouth to Joe's ear. "If you want to see more of those tit things .." he lisped " .. your Mum's catalogue's full of 'em." Intrigued, Joe dropped his bike in the back yard and ran into the house, yanking Mum's John Myer's shopping catalogue from the front room bookcase. He flipped through until he came to a fifteen-page underwear section and shrieked out loud. "Oh yes, tits! Waheeey! Oooh, any sausages?" A whack round the head knocked him flat to the floor. "What the bloody hell do you think *you're* doing?" barked his Mum, a rolled-up newspaper in hand. "Put that back and get to your bedroom, right now. There'll be no tea for you tonight and you just wait 'til I tell your Dad what you've been up to." Joe rubbed his thick ear and crept off up the stairs. Tits? What was the big deal about tits? At least Mum didn't know he'd been over the train tracks. Now *that* had been an eye-opener.

The day it came up ..

Listen Joe, I said, your Mum's told me what you've been up to. (Have a word with him, she'd said. Just put him right, will you, love?) My son looked up at me wide-eyed, but his blushes gave him away. "How did she know?" he said, in a tiny, whining voice, and I immediately felt so sorry for him, the poor wee thing. I'd taken him into the garden for a chat, the evening still light and warm after I'd got back from work but, if you want to know the truth, I was terrified, having absolutely no idea what I was going to say to him. The 'episode' made me wonder if *I'd* ever had an introduction to the 'birds and the bees' but, try as I might, I had not a single recollection of anyone, at any time, ever telling me a single thing about them. Fat lot of use I was going to be!

I'm sorry, Daddy, he said. I won't do it again. That's all well and good Joe, I said, but we still need to have a wee talk, man to man, as it were. I remember giving him a playful thump on the shoulder just to drive the point home. I *did* look both ways before I went over, he said, his face open and urgent. I made sure ..

Went over? I said, not understanding. Over what? What are you *talking* about, Joe? The train tracks, he said, lowering his head. I looked very carefully before I crossed them. Honest! And Mark had already listened with his ear to the rail, so I knew it was safe to go ahead.

Ears? Rails? What the hell was he talking about? I made a mental note to tell him off at some future date. (I didn't want to confuse my messages.) I'm talking about those rude pictures you were looking at, I said. My voice tailed off. What *about* them? Outraged as I was, I was glad that he'd broken the ice, so to speak, by looking at them so soon. Saved me a far harder talk in the future. (Wouldn't tell the wife that, of course. Good God no, she'd have throttled me.) I tried to think of a way to explain the wrong he'd done. But *was* it wrong, I wondered? Was it *wrong* for him to look at pictures like that? Surely, as a Catholic, it *must* be, I thought, and I racked my brains, trying to remember what the church had to say about pornography. Stay there, I told him, and went off to dig out my Catechism.

Pornography - it said - *perverts the conjugal act, the intimate giving of spouses to each other. It does grave injury to the dignity ..*

I gave up on that approach and went back into the garden. Erm look, I said, it's not very nice of you to look at pictures of people when they're having .. er .. I couldn't say it. Gordon says it's sex, said Joe, ever so helpfully. His sister's done it, he told me. What? I shouted. Oh, for the love of God, Tracy Horrocks is fourteen if she's a day. (This was much worse than I'd thought.) Oh Joe, Joe, I wailed, Tracy is far too young to be doing that sort of thing. Sex .. I forced the word out .. is for Mummys and Daddys, not little boys and girls. Now you must promise me that you won't look at dirty pictures like that ever again, and if anyone asks you about .. it .. you just tell them that Daddy says no and you'd have to go to Confessions because God would know all about it. Promise me? He nodded and looked relieved. I actually think he'd switched off when he realised he'd got away with crossing the railway tracks. Alright Daddy, he said. I promise. I led him by the hand to the house and, as the sun went down, he looked up into my eyes and said Daddy, have you got a big sausage, too?

Page 8

At five on Friday evenings, the boss would sit down with the photo-department's well-thumbed WH Smith diary - one day to a page - and designate a photographer to cover each of the 'assignments' listed for the coming Saturday and Sunday. The diary was a compilation of photography requests from the reporters on each of the company's various titles. The free-sheet - launched just five years earlier by a very successful middle-eastern entrepreneur - had expanded to six titles, and photographic requests flew in thick and fast from its twelve journalists, all requiring imagery to go with their stories. It was these weekend 'jobs', on Joe's first Friday, that the boss went through now, scribbling his own initials, and those of Joe and Andy, alongside the events each photographer was selected to cover.

"Hey look," chuckled the boss. "When I write Jo B next to a job, it spells JOB. How funny. Ha ha ha .." There's a bloody 'e' in Joe, sighed Joe, before almost passing out when the boss handed him a photo-copy of the listing.
"What?" he frowned. "How?" His initials appeared eleven times down the page.
"And here's Sunday," said the boss, pulling a second sheet from the copier.
"I don't understand," Joe huffed, counting nine more jobs.
"And look at this! My name's down for five jobs at 2 o'clock on Saturday. How can I do five different jobs at the same bloody time?" The boss smiled the gouty-chin smile again and snorted down his nostrils. "You'll have to prioritise, won't you?"

Five jobs at 2 pm meant that five reporters from the group's various titles had all requested a photograph from an event in their area that started at that time. Given that the furthest distance between two of the 'papers was over thirty-five miles, reaching both at the same time was an obvious physical impossibility - especially on The Frog - but Joe quickly learned that the key was to check out *what* the event was, and work it back from there. If the event *happened* at two, it took priority over an event that *started* at two. Thus, a 2pm ribbon-cutting by, say, Martin Buchan, would take priority over a Bring and Buy sale that began at two but would go on until 5pm, the photographer thereby having a three hour window in which to cover it. The idea then was to sort them into some kind of geographical order to avoid manically zig-zagging across the region like a loon. And not forgetting, of course, there could be three events that started at 2.45pm, or 3pm, or ..

Joe awoke on that first Saturday morning with a feeling he hadn't had since he'd almost drowned. An unstoppable tide was threatening to overwhelm him, and the tension put him right off his breakfast. But he'd double-checked his new Olympus, made sure his flash batteries were charged-up and filled the petrol tank on The Frog to the very last drop. He was good to go. He stretched a leg over his bike and kick-started the engine. "Let's get to it, Joe," he said, pushing down his pudding hat. Deadlines! Schedules! Pressure! He pictured himself as a high-flying Sunday Times photo-journalist, accepting assignments that even the great Don McCullin had baulked at, and went off to photograph three Bring-and-Buy sales and a new dog-walking class in the leisure centre annexe!

Cutting edge, Joe! Cutting edge ..

Page 9

Her Majesty's Armed Forces. The obvious choice, really. Well, it was if you were Joe's Mum, who'd taken the same view as his careers teacher when it came to photography as a life-style choice. "There's no bloody money in that," she'd huffed, disappointment on her face. "But I've looked into it. You can join the Royal Army Ordnance Corps and train to be a photographer with them .. if that's what you bloody well want to do." (Oh, she'd got it all bloody well worked out!) Once she'd learned of Joe's afternoon with McVine, she shooed him off to Manchester's Army Recruitment Office where, at the ripe old age of fourteen and a half, he found himself - seven stone (wet through), five foot two on tip-toes - staring up at a gruff, bored, ironically fat Scouse recruiting sergeant who smiled impatiently and pointed to the dial on a large set of upright weigh-scales. "Come back in a year or two," he winked, patting Joe roughly on the head. "Perhaps when you can make the needle move, eh son?"

Mum's thinking was this: Joe's cousin Brian was in the Parachute Regiment and currently serving in Hong Kong. He was, therefore - at least in her mind - seeing the world and having a whale of a time. Ergo, if Joe joined the Army he would not only (a) see the world and (b) have a whale of a time, but also (c) make some bloody money and (d) *still* be a photographer ("If that's what you bloody well want to do!") She seemed to have forgotten that (e) Brian was six feet two and seventeen stone, (f) Brian was a nutter, (g) a nutter who would take great delight in killing people, and (h) had now been trained and put into the perfect position to do so. She certainly didn't take into account the fact that (i) Joe didn't actually fancy the idea of killing anyone, and (j) had never spent a day away from home in his entire life. He read the glossy brochures anyway, and (eventually) convinced himself he quite liked the idea of being a soldier, even going as far as joining the local Army Cadet unit and only crying once when they finally took him away to camp, even though it was only for two nights over Easter and less than an hour's drive from his house. He'd never felt so homesick in his life, so far from everything he'd ever known. Nevertheless, he then took to jogging around the estate and holding bricks out at arms' length in a half-hearted effort to pump up his twig-like arms. Another year later, nudging nine and half stone, he was back at the Army Careers Office, passing the medical (Cough!) and being sent on a two-day selection course up in Harrogate. He'd been rather good at writing and, twelve months earlier than usual, had taken and passed - much to his surprise - 'O' Level English Language ("Grade A, Mum. It's Grade A"). And so the Army liked him this time and said that, if he wanted, he could join up as soon as he turned sixteen. Joe tucked the letter of provisional acceptance into his sock drawer and the idea of joining the Army into the back of his mushy little brain. It was a handy Plan B - assuming he wasn't immediately snapped up by a national newspaper, of course - but it took him completely off the boil as far as schoolwork was concerned. In addition, because he would turn sixteen before the coming September term, he knew he could leave school in May, whilst exams were still ongoing. And so revision, toil and fret played no part in Joe's 'Summer of '76'. He waved a relieved tatty-bye to education and, in readiness for his early military risings and shinings, got a part-time job - and eighteen quid a week - at a local family-run bakery. He'd jog down smugly for his six am starts, breathing deep of the delicious, dawn-cool freshness before spending the rest of each morning cooped up in a tiny room at the back of the shop, helping Mr Fletcher - a diminutive, chipper Cockney, living two hundred miles from home - by oozing gloopy, melted jelly into hot, fresh dinky meat pies, and scraping burnt, black crust off battered, greasy baking tins. It hit ninety-seven degrees during that renowned summer of drought yet Joe, working just three feet from the searing oven, would have to go outside to cool down.

-

"One for you," said Joe's sister, handing him an offical-looking letter one morning. His heart leapt. Flippin' 'eck. It couldn't be, could it ..?

It was the end of August, a mere three weeks before Joe was supposed to 'take the Queen's shilling'. Excitement was mixing with nerves, and a growing disinclination to join up. With appalling timing - as his days at school grew ever shorter - he'd found out about a press-photography course and, believing in 'better late than never', had put his name down to be considered. The course was a big deal, being, in fact, the *only* course there was - the prestigious year-long

programme run by the NCTJ - the National Council for the Training of Journalists, and Joe became desperate to be accepted. He didn't get in. His exam results weren't good enough. He threw the rejection letter to the floor and burst out laughing. What a bloody irony! His dedication to photography had prevented him from getting onto a photography course. Locking himself away in the school's darkroom meant he'd devoted precious little effort to all that time-wasting tripe like revising for exams, and one of his five 'O' levels had come in a grade too low to be accepted.
Oh, ha ha, bloody ha.

So, Her Majesty's Armed Forces?
Yep, Joe was going to be a soldier.

Page 10

Joe *did* have one memory of his father that would never leave his mind. The day his Dad left home.

May 15th, 1971.

Joe knew the date was correct because he had in his possession an old diary in which, as an innocent ten year old, he'd scrawled, in scratchy blue pencil, the words

Went to pet shop. Dad left.

Simple as that, the prioritisation still painful to him every time he read it.

Young Joe didn't have a clue that things were going awry between his Mum and his Dad. Hadn't spotted a thing.

Thought it was normal not to see Dad until half eight at night, just before he got sent to bed, when this oily, drained-looking fellow would heave himself into the house, squiggle his meaty, bashed fingers through Joe's soft brown hair then flop down at the dining table for a cup of tea and a meal that had dried up hours ago. It would take Joe another seven years before he realised *why* this guy flopped, and stank of oil, and could never play with him before bedtime. It was because he'd just done a twelve hour shift in a dirty, deafening, ball-buster of a factory *and* walked the five miles there and back to avoid having to 'waste' money on bus fares. (He got time and a half at the weekends so he always worked then, too.) So no helping the kids with their homework, no Saturday afternoons at the football with Joe, no family picnics on a Sunday. Poor bloke hardly spent any time at all with his family. His parents must have worked on it, though. Joe remembered that, at least for a while, his Dad started having Saturday mornings off work. (Unbeknownst to Joe, he made up for them by working later into the evening.) He'd take Joe by the hand and they'd walk the mile into town so that Joe could choose a 'Matchbox' model car from the mouth-watering selection at Mr. Haydock's toy shop. (By sheer coincidence, it was right next door to Halkyard's camera shop where, just a few years later, Joe would drool through the window at all the cameras and lenses he hadn't a cat in hell's of affording.) The toy-shop run was fine until, one sunny June Saturday, after a boiled egg for breakfast, Joe started to develop a splitting headache. He complained all the way to the toy shop and, by the time his Dad had carried him home again, Joe was wailing in agony and the egg was all over his t-shirt.

"Keep him in the dark," said an emergency doctor who came out that afternoon and then, rather stupidly, proceded to do exactly that by telling Joe's parents he'd let them know what the problem was "When it was all over."

What *it* was was meningitis, though Joe was convinced for months after that it had been the boiled egg, and didn't eat one for another three years.

The outings came to an end, and so did seeing Dad. Mum refused him access to his children from the day he left the house.

The day I left ..

I didn't 'leave', alright? You need to know that from the start. I didn't leave her, she asked me to go. Although I'm not sure if 'asked' is the right word, now I think about it. Anyway, I'm here now, in my sister's chilly back bedroom, with a great view of fuck-all and my beautiful wife and three wonderful kids at home. And I'll bet I haven't .. aw, fuck, I haven't .. I haven't even got any photies of any of them. Not even a picture of us all together. She must have packed my stuff so quickly she forgot to put any in. Aye, that'll be it, she forgot to put them in. (Although, have we actually *got* one?) It must have taken some planning though, to have all my clothes bagged up and ready to go when I got home from work.

Look, I know I work too hard. My hours are far too long. But what else can I do? I should have seen .. ach, blah, blah, blah .. listen to me! But aye, you're right, I really should have seen it coming. But I didn't, did I? At least, not to this extent. I'd really hoped my efforts with Joe and the girls might have turned things around.

He'll be lying in bed now, my wee 'un, reading his books about space and Neil Armstrong. He's a bright wee lad, he is. He's passed the Eleven-Plus, you know. Off to the Grammar in September. And my girls will be giggling now, hiding their heads under their pillows, trying hard not to go to sleep. Don't worry, I'm not daft. I know it'll be boys that's keeping them awake, that's for sure.

And my wife. I wonder what she's doing right now. I hope she's alright. Oh God, please let me know she's alright. Look after her for me. Take her in your arms and guide her, Lord. Please don't make her sad. Give her the strength to move on and ..

Sorry? Aye, come in, sis. What about ya? Whiskey? Well, why not? Thank you. My God, that's a lot. Could you add a wee bit of water next time? Bless you.

Sorry God, where was I? Ah, yes .. the strength to move on and .. erm .. wooooph, that's strong. Erm, I hope she's not too worried and perhaps .. *perhaps*, God .. you could see your way to getting us back together again.

Soon? Please?

Page 11

Kevin took Dad's place, three years and a day after he'd gone. Mum's new boyfriend was short and squat, handsome (some would say), with a dimple in his chin and a brylcreemed head of hair that wouldn't have budged in a wind-tunnel. He rode a push-bike everywhere and whistled as incessantly (and as annoyingly loudly) as he possibly could. But everybody loved Kevin. Right old laugh, was Kevin. Salt of the earth, real ladies' man, do anything for anyone, Kevin would. He worked in the foundry at one of the town's two main factories and Mum had met him twelve months earlier, as he fitted in a part-time job at the pub at which she now cleaned. Initially a secret to her kids, Kevin was drip-fed to them over time until, before too long, he was visiting their house every other evening, bringing home a weekly Chinese take-away (how exotic!) and taking them to the pictures once a month.

Joe heard there was an autumn sale in the photographic department of the big Boot's store in Manchester. A beautiful 'electronic' Sunpak flashgun had been reduced from eighteen quid to fourteen. Bargain! Trouble was, Joe didn't have fourteen quid or any way to get it, until a mate told him that a local farmer was looking for 'spud-pickers' over the half-term holiday. "It's a fiver a *day*," Steve Stark wowed. "And all you have to do is pick potatoes." "Have a go, Joe," Kevin almost ordered. "All you have to do is pick potatoes." Picking potatoes was one of the hardest things Joe had ever done. Back-breaking and relentless, it was made all the more difficult by the first sparkling frosts of the season, which hardened the endless fields and iced the spuds into the crispy, dark brown earth. A little gang of kids - a gang of little kids - worked the soil, their breath a misty micro-system above them as they threw rock-like King Edwards into crates. Every two hours or so a red-cheeked woman would turn up with a big plate of jam butties and a warming jug of tea, and lunch was sarnies scoffed in the shelter of the farm's big barn, the alien stench of cattle crap and pig poo doing nothing for Joe's townie appetite. At the end of the first day he was so stiff he could barely straighten up. Mum ran him a bath and Joe stood in two inches of lukewarm water, trying to pump life and feeling back into his frozen toes. By the end of day two he'd had enough of rural life, but forced himself on for the sake of the flashgun. He left at the end of day three, fifteen quid in his pocket and desperate to get into Manchester before the sale ended.

"I'll come with you," Kevin said, helpful and friendly. "We'll get the bus in the morning and I'll take Donna with us for a run out." The dog? thought Joe. That's odd. Shouldn't she stay with her six new puppies? Her second litter in a year? He thought no more of it, his head a whirl at the thought of his new piece of kit, and spent half the night dreaming of shots he might take in the dark. He and Kevin caught the 67 at half-nine next morning, the family's scruffy mongrel reluctant to step on board. Once in town, they walked to the central shopping area and Kevin left Joe at Boot's whilst he carried on with the dog. "I'll just let her stretch her legs," he said, smiling weirdly. "Go and buy your wotsit and I'll see you in half an hour." Joe dashed into the shop and homed in on 'his' new flashgun like a SAM on an F4 Phantom. He blew his spare pound note on new batteries, and was grinning from ear to ear when Kevin came back from his walk.

Donna wasn't with him. He'd had her put down at the vets.

Page 12

"A complaint?"

Day six at Courier Group Newspapers and Joe was on the carpet. The Editor called him to his office and waved a sheet of crinkled fax paper, synchronised with a wiggle of his massive, bushy eyebrows. Joe had only once met Mr

McGowan, on the day of his job interview over six weeks earlier, and the grey, gruff seventy-something was still clothed, as far as Joe could recall, in the same shirt and tie he'd worn that previous day. He was still shrouded in a fog of rough shag, that was for sure, a curly wisp of which rose now from the Sherlock pipe in the corner of his mouth. (He'd picked up the habit during his time as a correspondent during the second world war, and took advantage of his time at work to fill his lungs with Golden Virginia, Mrs McG having banned his smoking in the house after a breast-cancer scare in the 1960s.)

Joe was nervous. McGowan took a deep breath and eyed him through the small gap between his half-moon glasses and the eyebrows. It must have been like looking through a busted horse-hair sofa. "Joe," he began. "I want you to realise something." His pipe clattered against his false teeth as he spoke and, in the long pause that followed, Joe wondered if he was getting a free guess. "You are the front-line of our newspaper," McGowan eventually continued. "*You* .." and he pointed at Joe with his pipe for effect " .. are the physical embodiment of our entire organisation." He paused again. He really was being dramatic.
"Yes," said Joe. (He didn't know what else to say.)
"Your presence, out on the streets .." the Editor explained " .. is the only contact most of our readers will ever have with any of our esteemed publications." Joe remained silent. (I can't just say 'yes' again, he thought.) "So you need to show more respect." The Editor folded his arms and leant back in his chair. "That's all I want to say, lad. Respect." Joe's mind whirred. *Respect*? Respect what? Respect who? What? *When*? Had he sworn at a Bring and Buy Sale? Was he rude to the lady with the seven-grand gas bill? Did he fart during a darts match? Any number of the jobs he'd photographed over the last few days went through his head, but none struck him as a time he might

have .. "You do not ask the Mayor to wear a football scarf," McGowan re-started, tilting forwards again.

"Oh, *that!*" Joe said, visibly relaxing. "You're kidding."

"You do not ask the Mayor to wear a football scarf, Joe. End of .."

"I only asked him to put .. he was at .." Jeez, what a pompous old tosser. On his first Saturday in the job, in between the jumble sales, morris dancing competitions and sponsored 'sit-in-a-bath-of-baked-beans' events, Joe had been sent to photograph the local Conservative Mayor, who was collecting funds for an annual charity appeal. That he was doing so outside Manchester United's Old Trafford football ground had thrilled Joe to bits, but the fact that he got to meet an actual *Mayor* as well .. well! Joe recalled the ermine, the gold chain, the chauffeur and the Roller, driven right up to the gates of the ground. And he was there to photograph it all. Oh, you've made it Joe, he'd thought, you've made it. (It really *was* a sheltered old life on that council estate!) And all he'd done - it being an event at Old Trafford - was ask the Mayor to wear a football scarf. And the Mayor had complained. And now Joe was getting a bollocking, six days into his new job.

The Editor's brows wiggled again and he laughed, loud and long and punctuated by the chesty cough from his years of rough-shagging. "Ah, bugger him," he said, in the strongest language Joe would ever hear him utter, and he threw the fax in the bin and leant forward on his desk. "I'm really only telling you all this because the Mayor's gone to the trouble of contacting me. Personally, I think you did a great job, but just remember two things, Joe. Two things .." He conveniently held up two fingers for Joe to count. "I know, and now *you* know, that our esteemed Mayor is a self-important fuddy-duddy who, in truth, is practically an irrelevance in the lives of most of the people in the borough. But he's a councillor in our community and he's worked long and hard to warrant his year in office so respect that, lad, will you? Just show a little more respect, alright?" Joe nodded. "Secondly .." winked the Editor " .. and despite everything, you *did* actually get him to wear the bloomin' thing, so well done, lad. Very well done indeed. That job could have been just another run-of-the-mill photo op, but you turned it into something much more fun and, more importantly, eye-catching. A picture like that in the press will do a much better job of promoting his charity than he could ever could just standing on a street corner with his rattly flippin' tin. So don't ever let *anyone* put you off trying to get the best picture you can for the 'paper."

Joe almost melted.

"People skills, Joe," McGowan continued, having had a good long suck on his Sherlock. "That's what that took, lad. People skills."

The day I realised ..

My kids didn't miss me anymore. Dawned on me after I'd got my first flat. After I'd sent them out a letter telling them my new address. I laughed out loud when I posted it. Why am I sending them *this*? I asked myself. What was the point, when it seemed they'd already turned against me? It had been three years since I'd last seen any of them, and that was a bit of a damp squib - pun intended - because I'd tried to go round to see them on Bonfire Night and my wife had already let off all the fireworks before I got there. I didn't want them staying up late, she'd said. It was 6.30pm.

How much hope can one man sustain? I've hoped until it's hurt that, one day, I'd be together again with my children. Not *living* with them - no, I can't ever see *that* happening again - but being able to get together with them, every now and again, that would be nice, wouldn't it? Not too much to ask, is it? Not at all. The nearest I've had anything to do with Joe was last year, when my wife told me he was changing schools. Not asking my opinion, note. She was *telling* me he was leaving the Grammar school and that was that. I was distraught. He'd done so well to get a place there and I'd high hopes it would lead to a career in accountancy. We'll just have to see what his new school offers. At least it's Catholic.

Anyway, the flat. I'd been waiting on the council three years by then, waiting for my name to move up the list so that I could get out of my sister's house. (My brother-in-law was getting a bit funny about me still being there, I can tell you.) It's a nice place, exactly what I need but, even though the rent's so reasonable, I know I'm going to feel it, what with paying out so much in maintenance every week. See? I'm paying for my kids and I *still* don't get to see them. It's just not fair. And I can't do a thing to change it.

So that's three years now and not a sniff of any of them. They must be so tall now. Joe must be five feet, at least.

Try not to think about it. Have a whiskey.

Page 13

Joe was outside the Town Hall, photographing the annual Armistice Day parade. He'd shot his home town's Remembrance Ceremony on several occasions in the past but, this time, it mattered more than usual. Since he'd started at the 'paper, almost everything he'd had to photograph had been posed, set-up, staged, but this job was 'real-time', with an important theme and no chance to re-create anything that might occur. The pressure made him tingle. He wore a dark tie and a heavy coat and sweated heavily as he tiptoed around the Cenotaph, cringing every time he pressed the shutter during the One Minute's Silence, but he'd covered enough of these ceremonies to know by now that the grave solemnity would soon be overtaken by the second half of the annual event, involving pubs, tear-stained reminiscence and lashings of ginger beer (with Johnny Walker and ice).

A young lad was standing Guard of Honour at one corner of the Cenotaph - his army cadet uniform at least a size too big, puttees awry, beret pushed to the back of his head - and holding a World War Two Lee Enfield 303 rifle. It was chilly that November day and the poor kid was obviously feeling it; shivering and sniffing, his red nose dripping as he stuck stoically to his post. His frozen fingers let him down and the rifle slipped from his hand, clattering noisily down the white, granite steps and coming to rest at the feet of the vicar. Joe was standing well back, trying to be inconspicuous with his telephoto lens, and he spun around just as the vicar tripped over the 303. He raised the camera to his eye and then .. a man stepped between himself and the picture. Shit, missed it! (I didn't just say that out loud, did I?) Joe side-stepped left for a better angle and noticed .. the man in front had a *camera*. There was *another bloody photographer* blocking Joe's view, getting a great shot - *the* shot - of the boy and the rifle and the vicar. Bastard! Joe dashed forward, his tie tangling with his camera strap as an anger welled inside him, but the vicar picked himself up and made a swift sign of the cross as a bubble-cheeked bagpipe player led the procession off (to the pub).

Joe had missed the picture. He was fuming. The 'other' photographer turned and proffered a thickly gloved hand. "Sorry about that," he sniffed, just about hiding a smirk. "John Bachelor .. from The News." It was quite possibly the most exciting moment of Joe's life. His anger disappeared like *that*, and he fawningly grabbed John's hand and ferociously pumped it up and down. John Bachelor? He was on a job with John Bachelor? Holy shit, he was actually covering *the same job* as a *staff photographer* on the city's daily newspaper. *Daily!* With deadlines and morning and evening editions and a circulation well over nine times that of Joe's 'papers. John Bachelor was The Big Time and Joe was in awe. Mind you, John Bachelor had just prevented Joe from getting a really good photograph. Twat!

Small scale though it was, the episode was Joe's initiation into the cut-throat world of photojournalism. He'd never experienced the fury he'd felt at being beaten to a shot, and he didn't like it. God damn it, that hurt. A necessary pain of course, and one that Joe would joyfully inflict on many another snapper as his career progressed. Still, it was another lesson learnt and Joe was *almost* pleased that it had been given by John Bachelor. He'd seen John's byline in the 'paper so many times, and couldn't believe he was actually chatting to the guy right now.

"Yeah, thirty five years I've been there." John smiled modestly, sipping tepid tea in a nearby café. "Seems like a lifetime."
"But where's the rest of your gear?" Joe pointed questioningly at John's bashed Nikon.

"That's it," John laughed, pointing at it, too. "At least for this job, anyway. That and a pocketful of film. What more do I need?"

"But .." Joe stopped and shook his head. Before he'd got onto the 'paper he'd only ever met one *actual* press photographer, so imagined they all walked round dripping in shiny cameras, with zoom lenses and flash guns and tripods and filters and exposure meters and cable releases and motor-drives and .. basically all the tasty stuff Joe lusted after, stuck as he was with the company's bare minimum.

"Well, look .." John began. "You just saw how light and agile I was back there, didn't you?" Joe nodded, reluctantly.

"Right gear for the job, Joe. That's what it's all about. No camera bag to get in the way, no heavy gear to weigh me down and a wide-angle to get me right into the action." Joe nodded again, mouth open, instantly deciding he needed a wide-angle - a lens that required a photographer to be close to his subject in order to avoid it seeming too far away. Don McCullin shot like that and Don McCullin was a war photographer. I could be like that, Joe thought, dismissing the idea just as quickly as he'd had it. He knew he didn't have the balls to go to war. Oh, well. "But what about football? Or portraits? Or night shots, or .."

"Oh, I just keep all the other equipment in the car," laughed John. "Always ready, always handy. I've got everything up to a 600 and a tripod in the boot of the Cavalier. God help me if it's ever nicked. Ha ha ha .." Joe fleetingly thought about following John home for a spot of casual car-thievery, and just managed to disguise a smile with a nod, grateful for the experienced snapper's advice. Another lesson in the bag. (The camera bag!) John walked him back to The Frog and Joe breathed in deeply as he fired up his bike, his thoughts already turning to the afternoon's Autumn Fairs. Revving the throttle, he said "I'd kill for your job, you know?"

"It's Dead Man's Shoes on the News," John chortled. "You'd rather have to!"

Mum was a new woman with Kevin on the scene. Gone were the deep frown lines, so out of place on a woman in her mid-thirties. Away was the sharp, angry snap every time her kids annoyed her. Back was the smile, and a lightness of step that took Joe back in time. The smoking was down, too. (Twenty a day now. Hardly anything.) Months went by and Kevin was brilliant, a great laugh, what with his take-away meals and his cheesy, risqué jokes. In Joe, he also found an eager ear for his long and winding tales of military life, having served two years' national service in the late 1950s. Just as well, now that Joe had got his rejection letter from the press photography college. It was time to instigate Plan B. In September 1976 he became 24305468 Apprentice Private Bancroft, J and ..

.. three fleeting months later, he was a civilian again, out of the Army embarrassed, ashamed and smarting, albeit with the rosiest cheeks he'd ever had. So much for squaddie at sixteen and boy, did the kids on the estate remind him. Their constant piss-taking, and a thump in the mouth from Mark Sladden, certainly let Joe know he was right back where he'd started. At least he'd packed a lot into his military 'career' - a lot more than *they'd* ever done, he told himself - but it took Joe quite a while to absorb that salient fact and start to hold up his head again. It didn't take too long after *that* for it to dawn on him that hey, he *had* actually had the balls to try it, and from then on he shouted it loud and long, sneering at the street kids and boring whoever he could with tales from his Army 'career', making those twelve swift weeks sound like he'd been posted simultaneously to Berlin, Belize and Belfast. It was hardly 'shots fired in anger', but he *had* travelled to London for the first time in his life, and learnt that he excelled at buffing boots (Handy!) He'd made use of his 'O' Level French on a day trip to Calais; he'd slept in a piss-leaky bivouac during a three-day fieldcraft exercise in Hampshire; he'd taken part in a passing-out parade in front of his Mum and Kevin after six weeks of basic training, and he'd learnt that the kick from firing live 7.62mm rounds from an SLR was bloody amazing. (He also got a kick from the fact that a self-loading rifle had the same initials as a single lens reflex camera.) He'd even been put on a punishment charge for not shaving off a wisp of soft, wafty bum fluff, which made him feel ever so grown up. (At sixteen, his chin was about as hairy as a honey melon!) More importantly, he'd learnt that he could hold his own against a barrack-block of twenty-nine other lads. Odd, when he thought about his experiences at the Grammar School, until he realised that, on this occasion, he was on a level footing with each and every one of them from the start. They were strangers to each other, all starting from scratch and, as might be expected, every man jack of them working class. Unfortunately, he also discovered that, as a sixteen year old junior soldier, he'd have to wait another two years before the Army got round to teaching him his 'trade' photography. "But what do we do until *then*?" he whined, and almost cried when they told him it was two years of the same. Two more years of blind, unquestioning conformity? It was Catholicism (Part Two), and he couldn't bear the thought. "Help, Mum," he pleaded in a long letter. "Get me out of here." (Leaving was permissible without cost in the first six months of junior service). Against her better judgement, Mum finally wrote to the Commanding Officer, and asked for his release. The Army joined her in trying to talk Joe into staying - even offering promotion to Apprentice Sergeant - but he'd had enough. He was out.

He was out, though, with a valuable gift. A new-laid stone on his life path. His spell in the military had taken away a timid lonesomeness and turned it into individuality, and Joe took pride in knowing he could never again be part of *anything* that treated him as a mere thirtieth of a thing. In this case, his platoon. The platoon that required him to go to bed at a specific time and eat at a certain time and continually drill and march and clean toilets and make hospital bed corners until every other dimwit in the squad could do them to the same fantastic degree as he could. The Army taught him he was a one-off. For the first time, he felt he was his own man, destined to do things his way or not at all. All well and good, until Kevin had to find him a job at his factory.

Three months after leaving the Army, Joe found himself stuck at a desk for eight hours a day in a cigarette-grey prefab, hemmed in by filing cabinets and typewriters and bored, chittery-chattery secretaries. The only good thing was that those girls, though only a few years older than he was, exuded sex and worldly-wiseness and gave him a hard-on every time he passed the typing pool. And then Joe found out that the president of the local photography society - *the President* - worked on a lathe in the machining hall. As part of his job, Joe was treated to the daily joy of having to visit several different departments in the factory - correlating 'outside-machining' figures with hard-of-hearing foremen in pounding, metallic hell-holes like the foundry and the 'something-something' test rooms (Joe had never been very good on technical stuff) - and it was on one of those walkabouts that he was introduced to the man at the top. He was thrilled to meet someone who knew so much about photography. This guy had been at it for over forty years! He knew all about lenses and ASA and everything, and it wasn't long before he was bringing in his equipment for Joe to ogle. (At this point in his life Joe had only managed to get his hands on a £16 Halina Paulette camera, which took him four months to pay for whilst still at school.) He was invited along to a meeting of the chap's society where, every Tuesday without fail - for two whole weeks - he would pop along to the Sally Army hall to meet other keen amateur photographers. It was here that he was taught another important lesson. He learnt he could never, *ever* be part of a group that got excited over photographs of rainbows, waterfalls and robins.

Page 15

Kevin moved in, and Joe's life changed forever. Although still a boy, he felt he was - without realising it, of course - the dominant male in the house. True, his voice may not have broken, and his bollocks wouldn't have filled an eggcup, but nature is nature and Joe was King of the Hill. Kevin soon put an end to that. Muscling in - physically, as it eventually turned out - he immediately began to turn their happy family home into his own personal bachelor pad, cramming it with military band records and disgusting colognes, a weird collection of horse brasses and several smelly homebrew kits. The cherry on the cake was his incessant, and God awful, trumpet playing. Every bloody evening. Parp, poop, bad note, wrong note. He was absolutely bloody useless. (In Joe's mind, no brass music would ever surpass that on Peter Skellern's 1972 hit 'You're a lady'.) There was friction between the two of them straight away, and it didn't take long before Joe and Kevin found themselves locked into a vicious cycle of shouty rows and angry, macho face-offs.

Joe's hobby had grown to the point of having his own darkroom. More accurately, his own darkroom *equipment*, which he would set up in the bathroom whenever he got an opportunity. He'd black out the window with thick plastic sheeting, place an old table-top across the bath and spend hours printing little postcard photos. Kevin put an end to that, too. A lover of long, soaky baths, he immediately ordered Joe into the loft. Ideal in theory, of course, with as much darkness as Joe could ever need and oodles of space for a permanent set-up, but it also meant sweltering heat in the summer and temperatures of minus five in the winter, with Joe constantly trekking up and down the wonky loft ladders to warm his chemicals on the stove. Kevin put an end to all of that, as well. After a particularly turbulent morning between the two of them, Joe, now seventeen, came home from work that evening to find his darkroom equipment - and absolutely everything else he owned - waiting for him in the hall. Kevin threw a scrap of paper at him, on which he'd scribbled the 'phone number of a tubby, balding, eternally-chirpy chappy called Horace who worked in the stores section at the factory. "He's got a van," he snarled. "I've told him what's going on so give him a ring. And don't forget to put your 5p in the box."

Joe's 'turbulent' morning with Kevin had finally brought things to a head between the two of them, and his arrival home that evening turned out to be much worse than he'd expected. He was being thrown out! He'd known all day that he'd pushed his luck too far with Mum's boyfriend, as one of his regular snide remarks over breakfast led to their first ever full-on fight. A milk-bottle was smashed just inches from Joe's head, and he would sport a black-eye all week from the moment his face hit the cooker. Kevin was a chunky geezer, skinny Joe no match for his thick foundry-worker arms. He was flung around the room like a bag of Cheesy Wotsits.

Joe phoned Horace, piled his belongings into his van and spent the most miserable night of his life lying frightened, angry and sad in a mouldy, spare back bedroom. "Bastard," he growled. "I'm gonna kill you Kevin, I swear it." He was so scared. How had things got to *this* stage? And what was he going to do *now*? He had to admit, he *had* been a bit of a swine since Kevin had arrived, resentful of the new man in the house, but the bastard had changed *so* much since he'd moved in. He was asking for it. (*Asking* for it? Ha! *He* was the one with the sore face and the bruised arms and everything he owned in a big pile all around him.) Joe tried to think back to when the dynamic between them had changed. Perhaps it had been as far back as that first time Kevin had stayed overnight, going up *their* stairs to Mum's bedroom (Oh, my God!) instead of shouting his cheery 'bye-byes and cycling away, whistling his annoying bloody whistling. Perhaps it was his insistence on always controlling the television channels, reaching to the set to switch over from Nationwide. Or perhaps it was the time he and Mum had a baby. Gary was born two weeks after Joe's seventeenth birthday and the 'half-brother' became the instant centre of the entire known universe. His cot was transferred into Joe's bedroom the moment it was free. It was free five days before Christmas.

Page 16

Dad. Joe knew his father was the only person to whom he could now turn. It was well over six years since they'd last spent any meaningful time together, and Joe was terribly unsure of how things might pan out, nervous about even speaking to someone who was by now, to all intents and purposes, a stranger. God, he thought, the embarrassment. I can't just turn up in front of him after all this time .. *Can I?* .. and he agonised all night long, various dramatic scenarios playing out in his head. In the end though, it was either going to be a simple yes or a no, though he felt he'd be wise not to rule out yet another thumping. Nevertheless, he made up his mind to go and see his Dad the next day.

There were two large factories in Joe's blue-collar town, their hooters sounding off in 'stereo' at eight and twelve and five. His Dad worked at the 'other one', its gates no more than 2000 energetic paces from where Joe clocked on every day. He stood outside them that wintery lunchtime, shivering, shaking and damn-near shitting himself as his Dad walked through at 12.03. He looked an awful lot older than Joe had ever remembered, and seemed extremely thin in an oily boiler suit, with a fag in his mouth and a butty box and scuffed thermos flask tucked in the crook of his arm. Joe's knees almost buckled as he stepped forward to explain his predicament. "You too, eh?" said Dad, the merest hint of amusement on his face. (Joe had completely forgotten his sing-song Ulster accent.) And then, just like that, he said "yes".

Back at work that afternoon, head fizzy with relief, Joe had another word with Horace and arranged to take his belongings round to his Dad's that night. His flat was on the top floor of a block of three-storey maisonettes, just off a busy main road, half an hour's walk from their respective factories. Climbing its echoey concrete stairs, darkroom bits in his arms, Joe's heart was pounding. Have I done the right thing? he wondered. Did I have any other option? Will it even work? He tinkled a cheesy festive bell and Dad opened the door looking for all the world like Father Christmas. "Ho ho ho," he chortled, white foam fuzzy round his chin. "Sorry, I'm just having a shave." He was stark naked save for a pair of bulging underpants that prompted Joe to 'Remember you're a Womble.' (Oh my God, thought Joe. His sausage *was* big, after all.) "Come in son, come in," said Dad. "Put your stuff down there. Fancy a wee snifter?"
"A snifter?" Joe blinked, looking blank.
"Aye, a drop of the old spuice juice. You know, a shot. A slug. A dram. Ach, a bloody *whiskey*, for God's sake."
"Ah! Oh! Er, no thanks," said Joe, having never tasted Scotch in his life. "But you have one if you want."

"Well, that's fucking kind of you," laughed Dad, and led Joe into the kitchen where a thick cloud of cigarette smoke swallowed up his son like a Newfoundland fog bank. He poured half a tumbler of Bell's and offered it to Joe anyway. "No?" he shrugged, shaving foam speckling his chest. "You sure? Lemonade, maybe? Oh well, suit yerself." He raised the glass, said "Welcome. Here's to .. well .. *you,*" and downed the whiskey in one with a smack-satisfied "Aaaaah!"

"Look, I'm going out," he said, heading back to the bathroom. "I'll be back later so why don't you get your stuff away and make yourself at home?" There was a little ahem, ahem and Joe turned to see Horace, wheezing in the doorway, three bags of clothing and books under his arms. "Speaking of your 'stuff'," Horace puffed, nodding down at his cargo. "Where do you want this lot?"

"Oh Horace, sorry," said Joe. "Thanks for bringing it up. Just put it down and I'll bring it all in in a mo." He followed Horace back to the car and the pair of them had the rest of Joe's stuff upstairs in a minute and a half.

"Right, that's that," said Horace, grabbing Joe's hand urgently. "Good luck to you, son. (And to *you* sir, he shouted to Joe's Dad.) Oh, and happy Christmas, eh?"

"Thanks a lot, Horace," said Joe. "And same to you. Although I *will* see you at work tomorrow."

"Oh, so you will," laughed Horace, flattening down his comb-over. "So you will, lad. So you will."

Watching Horace drive off, Joe's chest seemed to hollow suddenly, and his throat cracked dry and tight. He was fifteen again, back at the cadet camp, lonely, lost, homesick without a home. He carried his belongings into the hall and relaxed ever so slightly as he heard the hum of Christmas carols coming from the bathroom. Dad reappeared minutes later, togged up to the nines, suit, tie, hankie in breast pocket, the works. "Going daaaancing," he half sang/shouted, and a cloud of Old Spice hit Joe full in the face.

"Lovely," he said, eyes watering. "Have a good time then, er .. Dad." (It felt strange to say the word.) "I'll get all this sorted whilst you're out. Erm, where's my bedroom?"
"Your bedroom?" laughed his Dad, hands on hips. "Sure, that's a good one Joe. Ha ha ha .." He gave Joe a heftily playful splat, right across his shiner. "Bedroom? Hahaha .."
"What?" said Joe, his face throbbing. His Dad turned to the mirror and gave his tie one last little jiggle. "Sure, didn't you know, Joe?" he said, jutting out his chin. "This is a one-bedroomed flat. Ha ha ha .."

The day my boy came back ..

Merry Christmas! Merry fucking Christmas! My wee son's come home. Can you believe it? Joe's come to live with me at last. Cheers! Bottoms up and here's to many more! My wee son Joey's home.

Wee? Ach, listen to me, sure the boy's bigger than I am now. Well, an inch or two. Four at a push. Amazing how much they grow in six years, eh? So no, he's not a boy, not any more. Especially after he told me he was in the Army. My Joe .. in the Army! A *soldier*? Can you believe *that*? Ha, ha ha .. sure, if you'd told me that a year ago I'd have told you to piss right off, so I would. Catch yerself on, for God's sake.

And home? Hm, well .. it's *my* home, so it's *like* coming home, isn't it? And I know he'll settle right in, sure as eggs is eggs. Although, God knows *where* he'll settle, 'cos I've only the one bedroom and I'm buggered if he's going to share that with me. We'll work something out,

I know we will. It'll be alright on the night, that's what they say.

Oh Joe, you came back to me. Thank God, thank God, thank God. Sure, let me get a Bell's and I'll toast you here and now. And here's to you, oh Lord Jesus Christ. Thank you for sending me back my son.

That Kevin sounds a bastard. Have you seen the shiner he gave my boy? Wait 'til I see the fucker, I'll break his fucking jaw, so I will. (Aye, sure you will, y'eejit. Cassius fucking Clay are ya?)

But how's she let it get to this? My wife, I mean. How on earth has she let it come to this? That's what I want to know. And how's she feeling right now, her wee .. sorry, her *big* son .. out the door and a thug for a fucking husband? God, I hope she's alright. I really do.

It never happened did it, God? You never sent her back to me, did you? Wasn't to be, I realise now but, well, at least I have my Joe back. My little boy, Joe. Yes, to me he'll always be that wee fella with his hand in mine, looking up to his Da, eyes full of love or, at least, the wanting of a new toy car. Maybe I should buy him a new Matchbox toy for Christmas? Ha ha ..

Oh, he's going to love living with his old Pa ..

Page 17

Christmas morning, and Joe was shivering in a hastily-purchased three-quid sleeping bag, which he'd rolled out parallel to the skirting board, using as a mattress the two well-worn cushions from his Dad's rickety sofa. His back ached like hell and he could have done with at least another five hours' sleep. Alongside him, his camera bag, photography books and a small pile of clothes marked out a little patch of territory in what was now his 'home' though, with no spare room in the tiny flat, all his darkroom equipment was outside, sparkling in a frost-covered jumble on the balcony. He'd stopped leaving his glasses on the floor, having almost crushed them when he turned over the night before, and had to squint to see the blurry figures on his luminous watch. It was almost eight o'clock, still dark, and he could hear faint snores from his Dad's bedroom.

"Fucking bastard," he whispered. "How would you like it if I woke *you* up?" He breathed in deeply, nostrils flaring as he replayed his Dad's return home one previous evening. He'd just dropped off to sleep when the bastard stumbled in through the front door, singing loudly, drunk. "Ah well, it's Christmas," Joe had said to himself. "Ho ho ho, and all that." But he knew that wasn't the whole truth. Last night could have been Christmas, bonfire night or plain old March the anythingth. The date didn't matter, and it hadn't taken Joe long to realise there was a routine to all of this. There'd now be at least another half hour before any hope of sleep, his new 'flatmate' still not remembering that his son was trying to get some kip on the floor behind his chair. Dad's nightly bedtime ritual went like this: arrive home late, singing loudly/slam front door/struggle to take off coat/ switch on light/ pour whiskey/complain about flat lemonade/ switch on TV/light fag/smoke it on settee - sans cushions/ cough, cough/fall asleep/wake up for pee/go to bed. Knowing he'd soon have to get up to switch off the front room light, Joe had left his sleeping bag unzipped and, with the telly on far too loudly now, had sighed but knew he couldn't complain. He'd tried that the third night he'd stayed there. Dad had swirled in on a fine rendering of 'Cigareets and whiskey and wild, wild women', and slammed the door so loudly that Joe had physically jumped into wakefulness, taking a second to realise where he was.

"They'll drive you crazy, they'll drive you insane," sang his Dad, a little off the beat.
"Too fucking right," hissed Joe, scrunching the sleeping bag around his ears.
"Take warning dear stranger, take warning .."
"Shut up!!" Joe shouted, and instantly wished he hadn't.

His Dad did shut up - instantly - and, after a moment to work out where the voice had come from, yanked off the shoe he was undoing and threw it straight at Joe. Joe cried 'Ow' as it bounced off his forehead. (His Dad might have been pissed, but he was still a fucking good shot.) "Don't you *ever* tell me what to do in my own flat," he yelled, across like an arrow and full in Joe's face. Joe's arms shot out defensively, eyes shut tight, head hunched. "I'm sorry Dad," he shouted, wincing in the whiskey blast. "I only meant .."
"Night, son. God bless." Dad stood, and turned away. Point made, episode over. He shut the front room door - even switched off the light - and the evening was never spoken of again.

-

Joe rose, rolled up his sleeping bag and felt a sad space in the pit of his stomach. It was a Christmas morning unlike any he'd ever experienced. (Two years ago he'd have still been sneaking downstairs with his sisters to see what Santa had brought them.) Dad's approach to Christmas seemed a little less magical. He had no tree and no decorations bar the novelty doorbell and seven cards on the sideboard. Joe took a bowl of cereal into the front room and switched on the TV. He switched it off five seconds later, glum at the over-chirpy show presenters as, swathed in monochrome paper chains, they pulled crackers with sickly kids in hospital beds. He picked up Dad's 'bumper' Christmas Eve edition of the Daily Mail and half-heartedly flicked to the TV listings. At home - at *Mum's* home, he reminded himself - he and his siblings had already marked out a heap of Christmas programmes to watch, all ringed in red felt-tip in the Radio Times, their entire festive viewing militarily planned long before video recorders would expand their options. He remembered that Billy Smart's Circus and the Morecambe and Wise show were going to be two of their highlights that particular Christmas. Perhaps he could watch them later, at his Mum's?

He wondered if his Mum had bought him any presents. She *must* have, he thought. His ejection from the house must surely have come as as much of a shock to *her* as it was to him? He presumed they were still tucked away at the back of the airing cupboard, where they all *knew* Mum hid their gifts. He rummaged in his pile of clothes and pulled out a small, square box, wrapped in red foil paper. In it was a necklace, which he'd bought for his Mum two weeks earlier. Hope she likes it, he thought. Maybe she'll let me come back when she sees it?

A loud fart told him his Dad was finally up. He appeared around the corner, simultaneously scratching his bollocks and ruffling his hair like the winner of one of those 'pat your belly and rub your head' competitions. "Mornin'," he called, squinting against a low, watery sunbeam that now penetrated a gap in his cheap, nylon curtains. "Sleep well, did ya?" It's incredible, thought Joe. Dad had gone to Midnight Mass, had a drink or two with the priest in the sacristy,

spent a boozy hour at his sister's house and *still* got up in tip-top form. "Merry Christmas, Dad," he said.
"Oh shit, yeah!" said his Dad, in a swoosh of new cigarette smoke. "I forgot about that! Well, Merry Christmas to you too, Joseph. Fancy a wee snifter, do you? A little drop of 'Christmas Bells' to get you going?" Joe declined. Stuck his tongue out, actually, but Dad took a whiskey anyway, then held out his right hand and said "Merry Christmas, Joe. All the best, son. All the best."

-

Joe moped for the rest of the morning whilst his Dad took to ironing the suit he'd worn the previous night, sniffing it tentatively under the armpits and declaring it "Tickety boo and good to go." Without needing to get anywhere near it, Joe knew that the suit stank of slops and cigarette ends and could probably take itself off dancing all on its own if it needed to. "Are you coming to Eleanor's with me?" Dad asked, out of the blue. "I've told her you're staying with me and she'd be happy to have you over for Christmas dinner." Joe hadn't seen his auntie for years. "Oh, no thanks, Dad," he said. "It's very kind of you both but I'm going to Mum's for Christmas dinner. I've got to take her present round, anyway." He almost swallowed the words, it suddenly striking him he hadn't bought a gift for his Dad. Dad just shrugged and said "Oh well. Have a ball," and went off to pick out a clean shirt.

With Dad gone, Joe prepared to head out too. He paused, feeling guilty as he closed the front door, a glimpse of Dad's holy-water font reminding him he hadn't been to church that festive morn. He punished himself by power-walking the two short miles to his Mum's, the not-quite-light streets echoing with that shivery, silent emptiness specifically designed to make you feel lonely at Christmas. Everyone was indoors. Everyone was having fun. He'd be having fun

soon, wouldn't he? He paused before knocking nervously on the familiar old front door, smiling at the Christmas wreath that he had put up just two weeks previously. The door half opened and the smile dropped from his face as his Mum thrust herself urgently through the gap and whispered "What the bloody hell are *you* doing here?"
Joe's chin wobbled as he struggled to form a sentence. "I .. I .. it's Christmas, Mum. Merry Christmas. I've come to spend the day with you." His Mum set her jaw and pulled him by the shoulder into the house. "Sit down," she said. "And. Don't. Move." She shot from the front room and he heard her thumping up the stairs. A silence descended on the house. Where were his sisters? he wondered. At church? Ha ha ha! He was sitting in the middle of that wonderful Christmassy mess that comes from an early morning of manic pressie opening. At either end of the settee, threadbare pillow-cases bulged with newly-unwrapped gifts, the names of his sisters pinned onto their appropriate 'sacks'. They'd done well. Santa had been very kind. Joe couldn't help but think what *he* might be getting. Gosh, the tree's looking nice. And ooh, tangerines. More thumps on the stairs. The front room door swung open and Mum shut it rapidly behind her. She looked like murder. Joe smiled, then lost it again just as quickly. "Look Joe," she said, standing over him. "I'm sorry, but you can't be here. You just can't .."
"But it's Christmas," Joe whined, getting dizzily to his feet. "It's Christmas, Mum. Look, I've bought you a present." He held out the little box, pathetically.
"No. Sorry, Joe. No .. Listen, Kevin's upstairs and he's being good enough to .. er .. he's waiting up there until you go. You're real spoiling his Christmas, so .."
"But Mum!! .." Joe's eyes filled with tears and he bumped into the settee as he pushed past her and out of the front door. He ran and ran, and threw her present off the motorway bridge, his nose streaming as he bawled his eyes out. How could she do *that* to him? he wailed, snot streaking the fur around the hood of his parka. "No .. it's all Kevin's fault,"

he told himself, once he could finally speak again. He was hunched down, his back against the wet wall of a dark drainage tunnel. "I'm gonna kill that fuckin' bastard," he sniffed. "I'm gonna fuckin' kill 'im."

Back at the flat, having used a spare key under the leprechaun by the door, Joe began to drink what was left of Dad's whiskey. He cried for a long time and missed Billy Smart and Morecambe and Wise, and was so out of it by the evening that he even missed his Dad's rendition of 'Jingle Bells' at half past one.

The day we fell out ..

I wouldn't say we 'fell out', exactly. It was just a .. do they call it a misunderstanding? All I know is he really hacked me off and ok, I know I was pissed - for a change, ha ha (ach, it was Christmas!) - but, just for a moment, just for a *millisecond*, I thought I was going to whack him, so I did. I'd clenched my teeth so hard I thought my top set was going to fly out. Cheeky bastard, telling me what to do in *my own flat!* Shut up, he shouted. Shut up. Well, it was something like that. I can't quite remember now but, come on, you'd be the same, wouldn't you? being told what to do in *your own flat!*

Anyway, I was no sooner up to him than it was over. I had a flash-back, see? Back to when he was a wee 'un. There was this one time when I thrashed the living daylights out of him, just for stealing a packet of Polo mints. Hit him and hit him and hit him, I did. Whack,

whack, whack across his poor wee backside. My God, he bawled and he wailed but I just had to let him have it. I was so ashamed that my lovely son could have let me down so badly. And him an altar boy, too. It hurt me so much.

I cried then, too. For a full hour afterwards. I don't mind telling you now. Not this long afterwards. I told you I was soppy but this was a whole new anguish altogether. Now it was *myself* I was ashamed of. Me, a full-grown man, taking out my anger on a poor defenceless boy like Joe. Ach, I know my Da did it to me but that's no excuse, is it? That should have taught me how *not* to behave, instead of throwing my wee son over my knees and have him screaming 'Sorry' and crying so hard he couldn't breathe.

I was straight to Confessions that night, and I put a ten pound note in the St. Vincent de Paul box the next Sunday, but that guilt never went away.

Hurting my boy like that is something I will never forget.

Page 18

Joe's first Christmas on the 'paper was one he would never forget. Who knew that so many people/companies/organisations/charities/churches/scout troupes/offices held Christmas parties, or that every single one of them wanted to be in the local free-sheet? Not to mention all the Christmas fayres (Because that's how they're *spelt*, said the boss), the Christmas church services, the Christmas carol concerts, the Christmas 'charity deliveries of toys to the children's hospital', the Christmas .. it went on and on and on.

For the first time in his life - and much to his initial shock - Joe found himself working on the morning of the twenty-fifth, photographing 'Christmas babies', the squealing, rubbery sprogs who'd popped out since midnight on the twenty-fourth. He couldn't stand the thought of children and had to work hard to hide the feelings of pity he felt when he looked at all the gooey new Mummies and Dads. (No virgin births here. Move along.) Still, it wasn't as if there was anything else to do on Christmas Day. His Dad was taking himself off to his sister's again and Joe knew he had no hope of going to see his Mum, so working was perfect, and he ended up dragging things out until after lunch (cheese butties), developing and printing all his baby photos and making sure their captions were typed and ready for the Editor's return on the twenty-seventh.

That Christmas also meant Joe's first ever 'works do' in a restaurant, with party hats and a choice of turkey or beef or fish. A restaurant! What a wonderful world he had entered. Joe had never eaten in a restaurant before. Until this job he'd never even *been* in one (although the chip shop on his estate did style itself as the Codfather 'Restaurant'). Kids on his estate just didn't do things like eat in a restaurant. Their parents couldn't afford such luxuries, but that was alright because Joe and his mates didn't even *know* such luxuries existed, and would have moaned at having to wash and scrub up just to *eat* out when all they wanted to do was *play* out! All in all, his first 'posh' dining experience was a positive one, making him feel grown up, sophisticated and drunk, if not festive, befriended and laid. Out on the dance floor, Noddy Holder bawled 'It's Christmas', Andy somehow got off with Della, and the Editor's pipe set fire to a string of

Christmas decorations during his sentimental, overlong speech. Great fun! A mini-bus was laid on for the staff at the end of the evening, dropping them all back at the office, from where they could make their own way home. A tad tipsy, Joe, with his own back door key - the photographers always needing 'out-of-hours' access - decided he'd nip in for a quick wee and a snooze on the darkroom floor before risking going home on the Frog. He was woken at two am by squeaks and a heavy panting. Ho, ho, ho ..

"Oh Barbara, Barbara .." Well, this was embarrassing. Roused from his boozy, post-party nap by some serious huffing and puffing, it was impossible for Joe to avoid hearing what was going on. It was the boss, having sex - with Barbara, apparently - in the Editor's office. One of them whacked the return carriage of the secretary's typewriter and the stark, metallic DING made them both giggle like mischievous school kids. "Shhh .." said Barbara, adding "Oooh, I like that," (Ugh!) as a stack of old newspapers fell off the desk. Joe sat up and banged his head on the underside of the chemicals' shelf. Movement in both rooms froze and there was an agonising silence as the three of them held their breath. "What was that?" Barbara whispered. "Probably nothing," hissed the boss. "But you never know. Let's skedaddle while the going's good." Barbara whined, but the whizz of a zip told Joe her party was over. The randy buggers shuffled off through the darkness and Joe only felt he could move again when he heard the click of the closing front door. He sank back onto the towels he'd laid as a bed, then sat bolt upright again, earning a second bash on the noggin as he panicked, aware The Frog was parked outside. He remembered it was around the back but still, time for him to hit the road too, so he eased out from beneath the shelf and splashed his face again and again until he felt sober enough to get home safely. He opened the darkroom door and switched on the light in the Editor's office. It looked like a bomb had hit, and Joe felt suitably righteous as he put the desks back in order. He hadn't expected to find the used condom but felt relieved, so to speak, that it was empty. "Well well," he smirked. "You old rascal," and then he shook his head and laughed. "Who'd have thought? Bringing the missus back for a quickie at your age."

He didn't know he was still so naïve, but it began to dawn on him when the boss invited him and Andy for a Christmas drink with his wife the following weekend.

"Chaps," he said. "I'd like you to meet Doreen."

Page 19

My God, the power! Walk into a room with a camera and you had people in the palm of your hand. It was one of the first new things Joe learnt. Man, the trust these people put in you! The faith they had. They were like putty. One person, five, a dozen, it didn't matter. All they wanted to know was where he wanted them to stand, how he wanted them to pose, what expression they should paste across their eager, flattered faces. They loved it, and he loved it just as much.

"Get my good side," they'd say.
"Hey, I'm spoilt for choice."
"Where do you want me?"
"The Maldives."

Oh, the spiel, the banter. But where had *this* come from? Surely this wasn't the same Joe who, just three years earlier, would blush as he self-consciously lifted a camera in the street? The Joe who would have to *force* himself to walk up to a person and ask if he could take their photograph? (He'd stand outside the local newsagents - a bag of nerves in those early days - and wait until a suitable subject came out of the shop, then timorously approach them, camera in hand, and dare to ask for a portrait. They always said yes, back then. People weren't wary of men with cameras in those days.) "Thank you," Joe would say afterwards. "And thank *you*, Victor Blackman, for all your wonderful advice." It had really helped break down his shyness. 'Buggy-Babes' helped, too. The boss, all credit to him, had realised Joe's Achilles heel and, from his second week at the 'paper, had put him on 'Buggy-Babe' duty to heal him once and for all. It was a new feature in the 'paper, a weekly photographic montage of four young mothers and the children they wheeled around the shopping centre, written up with a short 'vox-pop' on a topical subject of the day. Every Thursday, Joe would team up with a reporter as junior as himself and approach young girls in the tawdry mall. It was guaranteed to steel the nerve! "Hello," they'd say. "We're from the Courier and we'd like to ask you a question. Would you mind? Nice picture of you and the nipper, too?" The reporter would then proceed to grill the girls on gritty topics like 'Who's better? Boney M or Rose Royce?" or "What is the best way to cook Spam?", whilst Joe took a photograph of each young mother and her baby. (He reckoned there was an average age gap of about sixteen years between the two!) The idea worked for about two months until everyone realised that the same girls pushed the same babies in the same prams around the same shops on the same day each week, and the project was quietly scrapped.

The 'Suzzie Girl' feature bit the dust a couple of weeks after that. Technically entitled 'Local Lovelies', the 'Suzzie Girl' spot was another of the boss's great ideas. Pictures of half-naked young girls in suspender belts? Hey, why not? Each week, he'd remind Joe to get the phone number of any new 'buggy' mums he'd photographed and he'd call them up and invite them to be the 'paper's next 'dolly bird'. (There never seemed to be any troublesome wedding rings around to thwart his plan.) He'd arrange his appointments and pop round to photograph them in their homes - and their underwear - and the jobs always seemed to take ages and Joe never got asked to photograph one and it was all very, very frustrating for a callow young youth like he was.

Joe had needed to 'steel his nerve' on one other occasion, the first time he covered a court-case, which involved identifying a defendant in the local magistrate's court - photography inside being forbidden - then grabbing a surreptitious 'snatch' shot of them as they left the building. More papier-mâché than paparazzi, Joe chickened out and, rather than braving a sneak shot, sidled meekly up to his 'target' - a skin-and-bone scally who'd just been convicted of shop-lifting - and asked if she'd pose for him instead. "Am I gonna be in the 'paper?" she squealed, a roll-up bouncing on her bottom lip as she tried to get it lit. "Brill, our kid. Where do you want me?" The boss followed up on *her* too, and she made Suzzie Girl two weeks later. Unfortunately (for the men of the 'paper's circulation area), "Sexy Sharon's" 'outfit' left not a lot to the imagination and convinced the Editor to bring the whole arcane, sordid seventies' practice to a stop.

"Hey, that's the girl from the court-case," Joe had said, admiring the boss's (over) revealing prints of Sharon as they wobbled in the wash water. "Ah! Is that why they call it a snatch shot?"

"So how did you get into Press Photography?"
The Queen stretched her pale and elegant neck and fluffed her dyed blonde hair. Joe stretched too, but only to conceal a zonker of a zit on his left cheek. "Oh, it's a long story," he said, for no other reason than that's what he thought you had to say when asked that particular question. "Well, we've got a long time, haven't we?" said Wendy, her lips forming a perfect, frosted-pink pout on the Ws. Joe suddenly felt warm. Wow!
"Go on," she winked. "Tell me."

-

Wondrous Wendy was a Beauty Queen, specifically the outgoing 'Miss Northwich, Oughtrington, Knutsford East and Romiley South', which meant the poor lass had just spent the past year attending functions and opening galas whilst sporting, across her fine, healthy bosom, a shiny, white silk sash which spelt out, in a light sky blue, the word NOKERS. She and Joe were backstage at the town hall for the association's annual beauty pageant, the dinner at which Wendy would hand over the unique banner to whichever lucky lady inherited her title. It was Joe's last job of the day and it looked like he was in for the long haul. It had already turned 10.30 and, eyeing the dawdling waiting-staff, he could see they were still only serving dessert.
"Well, since you ask," he said, loosening his tie. "It all started when I joined a camera club at school." Wendy gulped but smiled briefly and encouragingly, nodding as she absent-mindedly twiddled an earring. I wonder, she pondered, if I'll get as much sex now my year's finished. "I got it into my head that I wanted to be a press photographer," Joe continued. "Actually applied to get on a course when I left school but, er .. they were full up."

"So what did you do instead?" asked Wendy. "Get a job in Tesco's?" She laughed at her little joke and made eyes at a passing, curly-haired waiter.
"Nooo," said Joe, a tad miffed. "No I didn't, actually. First of all I joined the arm .. er, I got a job - a very important job - as an Outside Machining Controller at a fac .. at a design facility in Manchester." Wendy tilted her head and nodded, smiling rigidly. After a year as Queen she had become completely adept at feigning interest in conversations she was forced into with members of the public. I'm getting on well here, thought Joe. Play your cards right lad, play your cards right. "Anyway, I decided that if I couldn't get into college, I'd get into press photography all by myself. I just needed to start getting pictures into the 'papers. There was once an inter-departmental five-a-side football competition at our fac .. er, our facility .. and I took a picture of the winning team. I sent it into our local 'paper and they used it the very next week. Oh Wendy, the thrill of getting a picture published. I can't describe it, it's amazing, it's .." (Did she just stifle a yawn?) "After that, I started to look for events that were going on and took pictures of them to submit to the 'paper." Wendy eyed a tray of drinks and greedily licked her lips. I'd kill for a Campari, she thought. "It wasn't long before the 'paper was actually giving me jobs to do, which meant that, by the time the Courier job came up, I could go into the interview with a scrapbook full of published pictures."
"Fascinating," said Wendy, bringing to an end a short silence once she'd realised Joe had stopped speaking.
"Hey, do you fancy a .."
"Ooh look, they're calling me," she said, standing and smoothing down her skin-tight sequinned two-piece. "See you on stage, Joe," she smiled. "Get my good side."

Two weeks later Andy asked him out for a pint. "Come and meet my new bird," he said. "She's a belter." Joe walked into the pub and recognised Wendy immediately. He'd know those NOKERS anywhere! He was in a bad mood when he got home from the pub that night. His Dad was already in bed, door wide open, loud snores emanating from within. "Andy, you lucky bastard," Joe said, zipping himself into his sleeping bag. He reached into his undies but gave up on the idea of a fiddle. He was *so* frustrated. "Why can't I get a girl like that?"

Bollocks!

Page 21

He'd only been out with one girl. Pauline Holmes had been his first date .. twice! She worked as a typist back in the days at the factory and it took seventeen year old Joe four attempts before he dared ask her out to the pictures. Truth be told, she wasn't the prettiest in the typing pool but the others looked far too genned-up and mercenary and scared the heebie-geebies out of him. So, Pauline it was and, as he was secretly a fan of the band, he took her to see the new 'Abba: The Movie' film at the Princess Cinema in Broughton. He was scarce able to believe she'd said yes. *She* couldn't believe it when he took her to see the very same film the next night.

A scrum of press photographers swarm around ABBA, the band having just arrived in Sydney at the start of their Australian tour. It's a photo-call on the steps of the city's famous Opera House and the photographers are shouting to the singers and trying to shove stuffed 'this is so you know they are now in Australia' koala bears into their hands.

Oh my God! Joe almost choked on his Butterkist. Press Photographers! It was the first time he'd ever seen a pack of 'real' ones in action and it thrilled him to bits, even though the entire scene took up less than twenty seconds of the film. It was far too short a time for him to get his 'fix', so he decided he'd take Pauline to see the pressmen again the following evening. "Watch this,' he urged, sitting rigidly upright. "This'll be me soon Pauline, you just wait."
"Watch *this*," she said, dropping a half-licked ice-cream 'tub' into his lap and walking out of his life for ever.

It would be a long time before Joe thought about another date. There was another distraction in his life: the Yashica FR1. He wanted one as soon as he saw the ad in Amateur Photographer. The camera was jet black, sexily sleek and completely out of his reach at three hundred and twenty-five quid. Nevertheless, he tore its picture from the magazine and apologised to Farrah Fawcett Majors as he replaced her poster with his new pin-up. God, she was a beauty. There was a stockist listed, a camera shop some twenty miles from home. Joe rang and made an appointment to go and look at the camera, and was like the proverbial kid at Christmas as he waited for the day to arrive. The shop assistant told Joe that the camera could be bought on hire-purchase, which involved a deposit of £50 and fifteen monthly payments, as long as he could find someone to act as a guarantor. It took Joe a bottle of Bushmill's and forty John Player Special but he finally convinced his Dad to do it, assuring him he was on a good wage at the factory and would in no way default on his payments. Dad went with him one Saturday afternoon, signed the scary paperwork and got the camera ordered. It would be available in a week and Joe circled the calendar in bright red ink.

It was a date.

The day we bought Joe's camera ..

Joe likes photography, it seems. Not cars, not girls (not that I've noticed, anyway) .. just photography. It's such a shame, and Lord knows where he gets it from. There's not a person in our family's even owned a camera.

He asked if I'd sign some HP agreement thing and I said yes, of course I would, anything to help. Thing is, he's seemed a bit frustrated lately, has Joe. Unsettled, I'd call it. Not unhappy, not .. actually, yes .. unhappy. You see, I don't think he's really suited to that job in the factory. It's not bringing out the best in him, which is a pity. Trouble is, he keeps going on and on about people who take photographs for newspapers. I could do that, he keeps saying, I could do that, Dad. But, tell me this .. how on earth is *that* a proper job, taking photographs for a 'paper when he could be holding down the real job he's already got in that office? Factories. Manufacturing. That's where you've a future. Not taking bloody happy-snaps for a newspaper, for God's sake. Factories are solid. You're there for life when you've got a job in a factory. A lad on our darts team has been at Joe's factory since '75 and told me he'd only need to be there another year and he could make section manager. And come on, he knows what he's talking about, Stu does. He's already been promoted twice and now he's on sixty-five quid a week. Every bloody week!

Still, Joe is Joe and Joe has got this idea so .. off I went with him to a swanky photo shop near Warrington and signed on the dotted for this Yashathingy thing. He looked like a pig in shit when I did it so I hope, I just *hope*, I've done the right thing. He really believes in this photography lark, see? I can see it in his eyes. He comes to life when he talks about it. (Never shuts up, if you want to know the truth!) And he's started going out of an evening, taking piccies and sending them to our local Journal. They put his name next to one of them recently and, I have to admit, it made me really proud but .. I was *sort* of hoping it might have got it out of his system.

Page 22

Dad's signature on the hire-purchase marked a new stage in the growing relationship between the two men. It spoke to Joe of trust, and of a further willingness to help, and it stripped away a layer of tension that he felt had existed since the day he'd moved into the flat. They had been .. what's the word? .. formal .. those early days. Awkward, you'd probably say. When he'd moved in, Joe hadn't really grasped just how much he was 'invading' his father's personal space and, especially after the Christmas 'incident', had begun to work hard to respect his Dad's home, going over the top with his repeated thanks for being allowed to stay there.

"Look Joe, it's *our* flat," his Dad finally said, twisting around as he scrubbed at socks in the sink. "*Our* flat, alright?" Three words, and Joe went weak. Things were going to be alright with him and his Dad, weren't they?

-

Joe felt he should go for a jog. He'd not paid attention to his fitness lately and took himself off for a mile around the block. When he finally made it home again he was surprised to see his Dad still in the flat. (Being skint will always make that decision for you.) The TV was on - Cyril Fletcher was just finishing up on 'That's Life' with Esther Rantzen - but Dad had dozed off and a bare arm lolled over the edge of his armchair. His psoriasis had obviously been particularly bad that evening and he'd rolled up his sleeve to scratch away the agony. Joe looked at the raw, red-cratered arm and suddenly felt an incredible surge of emotion. Poor bastard, he thought. Look at the state of that arm. And the rash was all over his Dad's back, he knew only too well. But what a guy. Never complained. Just rubbed in the cream and cracked on.

Joe's breath caught. The emotion drained away and he looked at Dad as if he'd never seen him before in his life. Just who *is* this guy? he thought. This man I'm sharing a flat with all of a sudden. This *stranger*, to all intents and purposes.

And then he felt a tear. A tear for a father he'd not seen in six years. Poor bastard, he thought. Look at the state of his life. And he never complains. Just opens another bottle and cracks on.

Joe loved that Dad had signed the hire-purchase, and his old man stirred as Joe stretched over to switch off the telly.
"Hey, I was watching that," he croaked, rubbing his eyes and yawning.
"Yeah, 'course you were," smiled Joe.
"Fuck off," said Dad.

It was wonderful.

Page 23

Joe heard his name called as the boss hurried into the office. Busy filing negatives, he looked up just in time to see the Racing Post being tucked inside the bugger's jacket. Nice try, Joe thought, knowing full well the git spent his two-hour lunch breaks at the pub just down from the bookies. "Get your gear and come with me." Joe grabbed his camera bag and followed the boss from the office. For the second time, they walked in line to Focus and the boss took Joe's Olympus from his hand. "Time we had some proper bloody cameras," he muttered, somewhat shamefaced. "I'm sick of that stupid shutter dial." (Joe was never to know that the shop had given him a fifty quid back-hander to bulk-order the fiddly little cameras.) A diminutive salesman put the OM1 beneath the counter and Joe heard bells ring, choirs sing, angels rejoice on high as he replaced it with .. a Nikon FM. Oh my God, a Nikon! "Oh, and one other thing," the boss added, holding the door open as they left. "Mr Attar says he'll pay for driving lessons 'til you pass your test."

Joe couldn't believe his luck. Home later, he purred contentedly as he stroked his new baby like a kitten and played with the focus ring of a gorgeous new 28mm wide-angle lens. All this and driving lessons *as well*. Heaven! The boss filled in the blanks next day. "You're becoming an embarrassment," he said, blankly. "Mr. Attar's getting fed up with your scruffy appearance." Attar was the newspaper's Persian owner, and Joe knew what he meant. Getting around on The Frog, Joe found he was constantly turning up at posh civic functions or rotary club dinners and having to sneak away somewhere to peel off all his - usually soaking - motorcycle clothes before he could start taking photographs. Mr Attar had standards, the boss told him. Standards, and friends to impress, and Joe's squelchy-biker look wasn't going down too well in the rarified atmosphere of rich business chums and corporate management. "Tell him to book as many lessons as he needs," Mr. Attar had said. "Just get him off that ridiculous bike."

Free driving lessons? Who was Joe to argue?

-

As a youngster, it hadn't occurred to Joe to think about driving lessons. Mike Bent put him right on that one, straight away. Mike worked for the Journal in Joe's home town and had the distinction of being the first (only) press photographer Joe had ever met. In the factory where he worked, with as many employees as it had, there were retirement ceremonies and long service awards on an almost weekly basis, and Mike would come in to take photographs of all the grinning Gold clock/Teasmade/Cut-glass vase recipients. Joe kept an ear to the ground, listening for forthcoming presentations in the hope he might get a chance to see Mike at work. Spotting the flash of Mike's camera as he passed the canteen windows one day, Joe decided to bite the bullet, sneaking in and waiting until Mike had finished his work, then stepping up shyly to introduce himself and tell the pro his plans. Mike couldn't have been lovelier. Warm and full of funny stories, he was enthusiastic, encouraging and - most importantly for Joe - happy to chat. He bought Joe a cup of tea, even let him hold his battered old camera and then, after forty-five minutes, looked quizzically at Joe and said "Erm, shouldn't you be in your office?" Joe shook his head cockily and said "No, it's fine. No-one ever notices I'm missing." (The chap whose job he'd taken over had retired at sixty-five, having spent forty years fine-tuning the skill of making his piss-easy job last a week. Joe, naïve to a fault, could get the lot done in three days flat and, in the belief that his absence wouldn't be noted, would idle away the rest of the week with long strolls around the factory perimeter. It *was* noticed, of course, this absence, and he'd already had two warning letters, which he'd stuck to the dartboard in his Dad's kitchen and used as target practice.) The subject of cars came up at this point and Mike shook his head when Joe said he couldn't drive. "No?" he gasped. "Well, you'll have to sort *that* out, my friend. How are you going to get to your assignments if you ever make it onto a newspaper?"

-

What was so important about a three-point turn, anyway? And reversing around corners, keeping the kerb 'in the same position' in the back window. Joe's driving lessons were driving him mad. As were the stockinged legs of instructress Sheila, her mini dress riding up whenever she got into the passenger seat of the car. (Joe was convinced she did it on purpose, the minx.) Now that the company was paying, Joe's driving lessons had increased to three a week. Hottie Sheila would turn up, Tuesdays, Wednesdays and Fridays, in her gaudy emerald-green 'Sheila's Skool of Motoring' Morris Marina, and the pair would head off for an hour of 'biting clutch-points' and 'mirror-signal-manoeuvre' in the seedy back streets of Manchester's Piccadilly, the high-heeled hookers that tripped from the bus-station providing him with more than enough 'emergency stop' practice. Sheila finally said "I think you're ready to go, chuck," and his driving test was booked for two weeks hence. (Swatting up on the Highway Code with his Dad singing 'Carrickfergus' at 11.30 pm would forever remain one of Joe's less amusing life memories.) He passed first time, skidding only once on the city's rainy back-streets and, true to his word, when Joe got back to work, Mr. Attar had a lovely new (second-hand) Vauxhall Chevette parked up in the lay-by at the front of the office. Joe handed over the keys to The Frog - he wasn't sorry to see it go - and practically salivated as he sat on the grey cloth seat of his lovely new sky-blue wheels. Sophistication. Glamour. Girls! Oh this is it, he thought, my biking days are over. No more changing out of waterproofs, no more long nights, frozen stiff as he scootered thirty-five miles back from the furthest reaches of the newspaper's coverage area - Dad had once had to physically prise his solid fingers from the handlebars - and no more flat hair from that bloody pudding helmet. "Joe boy," he tittered. "You are on your way."

Kind of.

He picked up his new wheels at almost the exact minute petrol rationing began in England. Caused, ironically, by a decline in oil production after the revolution in Iran - the birthplace of the newspaper's owner - it meant Joe now spent more time in queues at petrol stations than cruising the mean streets looking for action, exclusives and fanny. Moreover, he dented the car's off-side wing within a week, scraped the whole left side a fortnight later and had the radio stolen in a break-in just a month after taking the reins of his 'Chevvy'. The Boss was livid, the owner of the dealership that sponsored the company cars fuming, and Joe .. well, Joe was in shock. The keys to The Frog had been handed over to a kid called Barry, a new sixteen year old apprentice who'd suddenly appeared from nowhere, crashed the bike in his first week and smashed the femurs of both legs. A couple of months later, sitting next to this strange boy's hospital bed, Joe couldn't help notice the gory, deep scar holes left by a scaffold of metal pins. "That looks painful," he skilfully observed. "Still, at least you'll have somewhere to put your pencils."

The day Joe took me for a drive ..

Well, it shows you how much I know. He's only gone and done it, hasn't he? Joe's gone and got himself a job on a newspaper and good on him for trying. So it's goodbye to the factory and hello, hello to a whole new life as a photographer.

I just pray he's made the right choice, that's all.

I worried a bit about the motorbike. I can tell you that now. I noticed a scratch on his helmet one day and the box on the back is getting a bit dented, so I know he's come off it at least a couple of times. Not that I'd say anything to the lad. I just hoped I'd never *need* to say anything! Anyway, I was glad to see the back of it and, I have to say, I was very impressed when he turned up outside the factory in his new car. I could tell the lads on shift were jealous. It's only got 8,000 miles on the clock and looks good as new. "Come for a spin," he shouted, waving me over as I clocked off in the foreman's office. "Let me take you home, Dad. Get in."

"Let me take you home, wee man." My God, it doesn't seem five minutes since *I* said that to Joe, climbing back into that old Dormobile two weeks after my wife had given birth. We sat in the back, rattling along, the three of us, me as proud as punch and itching to start our new life together. New life? New lives? I don't know, which is it? Were we one life now, or three?

New lives. New starts. Seems all of life's just a collection of new starts, doesn't it? A stream of constant departures too, even if that's something as mundane as leaving home every morning and plunging yourself into a day over which you have absolutely no control. New start, new departure, new start until .. well, until the day your starts are done and that's your lot. I wonder if my life will ever have a new start again. My God, listen to me. I'm off again. Bancroft, stop daydreaming! Ha, ha, I can hear him now, Mr. McIlvenny, my old school teacher. He must have bounced half the chalk in Antrim off my forehead. I left school at fourteen and he was at the gate to wave me off. "You'll never fit in anywhere, Bancroft," he sneered, with one last tug of my lug 'oles.

I'm beginning to think he might have been right.

Page 24

The little metal nose pieces on Joe's glasses bent backwards and fell off. He'd raised a camera to his eyes so often now that they hadn't stood a chance. He didn't care. He was thriving. He'd taken to the job like eggs to bacon and his horizons peeled back like the lid on a can of kippers. Not only was he doing a Vic and Kent - photographing glamorous celebrities and people in positions of power - he was also connecting with the man in the street; the Mr. Smiths and Mrs. Browns who stood before his lens for more prosaic reasons - an argument about an over-tall yew hedge, a diamond wedding anniversary, a gas leak.

He was taking photographs in town halls, scout halls and bingo halls; army barracks, theatres, offices; shopping centres, sports centres, unemployment centres; hospitals, schools, football grounds. He'd attended car crashes, fires, picket lines, Anti-Nazi marches and Rock Against Racism parades. He was meeting mayors and milkmen, mothers of quads, Scout leaders, Chief Inspectors, four year old cancer sufferers, 100 year old Queen's telegram recipients, soroptimists, marathon runners, plumbers and surgeons, and had photographed both Doctor Who *and* Princess Anne before the end of his first four weeks. He'd even photographed the raw-looking backside of a Texan chick who'd had the Union Jack tattooed there (it wasn't used in the 'paper, of course, but she *did* introduce him to Jack Daniel's, so all was not lost) and he'd been ticked off by Joan Collins who, he discovered, definitely didn't like the camera too close to her beautifully sculpted skin. "Oh, purrlease, darling .." she'd complained, as Joe flashed at her during a book-signing. He'd been up in three different cherry-pickers and the local fire station's 'Simon Snorkel' hydraulic platform; flown in a helicopter, ridden a speed boat and a steam train and been up on the roof of Manchester's tallest building. He'd sailed down the ship canal on a barge and been thrown around a greasy skid pan in an HGV. He was, to coin a phrase his Dad used all the time .. "Having a ball."

And it didn't matter whether he was photographing Royalty or Bertie Bloggins, he always gave every job the proverbial "one hundred and ten percent". Never before in his life had Joe been so thrilled with, well .. his life! The sheer joy of waking up and being desperate to get to work. It began to dawn on him just how lucky he was. Who else did he know could arrive at their office and be told to go and photograph some "up and coming" politician doing the hustings? "You can do this one, Joe," said the boss, handing him a press release. "Two fifteen in Urmston. There's a politician doing the rounds. Margaret Thatcher, or somesuch. Get some close-ups. Oh, and a nice picture of the crowd if she gets one."

-

Joe's creative mind was expanding, too. Thanks to the local library and a twelve week night-school course, he soon realised there was more to photography than the pure mechanics of film processing or having the right lens on your camera. There were aesthetics and there was composition; morals and responsibility; timing and intent and, rather more mouth-wateringly, a whole new world of unknown photographers, just waiting for him to discover.

In the beginning, Joe had started .. well, at the beginning. What's an aperture? Why shutter speeds are different. How does the perspective differ between a 28mm lens and a 135? He devoured the introductory books he borrowed, all the more eagerly when there were chapters illustrated with full colour shots of tasty naked models. (It was no coincidence that, at the tender age of fourteen years and eleven months, Joe finally discovered masturbation!) He was quickly au fait with photography's nuts and bolts, and began to immerse himself in bigger, thicker 'teach yourself' books, where he'd attempt to absorb page after page of 'inverse square law' and 'circles of confusion'. (Boy, did *they* live up to their name!) Realising he didn't *really* need to get so worked up about the theory, he turned to the more esoteric aspects of the medium and threw himself at - rather than into - such major works as Susan Sontag's 'On Photography' and John Berger's 'Ways of seeing'. They scared him half to death, but at least Sontag's book lead him to the next level of his education. She wrote of, among others, Diane Arbus, Robert Frank, Elliott Erwitt, Cartier-Bresson and Lartigue, all master photographers and all new names to Joe, and he would search for their books, usually unsuccessfully, in the pathetically lacking photography section at the library. "Have you got any books by Dwazknow ..?" he once asked, and the librarian almost fainted. "Je pense que vous verrez que ça se prononce Doisneau, darling," he said, his French as perfect as his sarcasm.

Sontag's book intrigued Joe with quotes like Garry Winogrand's "I photograph to find out what something will look like photographed" and Minor White's "I'm always mentally photographing everything as practice." Now *that* really got Joe's juices going. Those little pearls of wisdom rang a bell. He'd noticed he was starting to see potential photographs everywhere he went. Wherever he looked he'd throw a metaphysical frame around whatever was in front of him, sizing it up as a potential photo, or he'd stop in his tracks in sheer unexpected joy as a hotchpotch of objects or people fell into what, to him, was a perfect photographic composition.

The 'Photographer's Eye'. He had it. Could just 'see' when a photograph was right. Could *feel* it. Would know when there was no other way to improve on a composition. It thrilled him to bits, which is why he signed up for the night-school course. Tantalisingly entitled 'Tricks of the trade for the experienced amateur', it spanned twelve Thursday nights in the Green Lane adult education annexe. Joe went down there just to enquire about the course, but was convinced he should enrol after a fortunate chance meeting with the tutor. Phil's chilled vibe, scruffy beard and shy, posh voice were nice, but Joe put his name down the second Phil told him that, in no uncertain terms, would they be photographing rainbows or robins or waterfalls. What they *did* photograph - in only the third week - was a semi-professional model, the likes of whom Joe had never seen in his life; a blonde, crop-haired, perfectly made-up Heaven-sent Goddess called Janine, who sported lip-liner and blusher under a cheekily tilted fedora and introduced him to the concept of 'out of your bleedin' league, mate'. Annoyingly, during the shoot, Phil kept rabbiting on about lighting and angle, exposure, pose and shadows, when all Joe wanted to do was stare at this vision in a hat. God, she was gorgeous. Why can't I get a girlfriend like that? he thought, wanking over his shots of her for a month.

But Steiglitz? Winogrand? Frank? The course went nowhere near them until, picking up on Joe's enthusiasm, Phil lent him one of his own books, featuring chapters on many of these great 'masters'. It was an absolute eye-opener, and such a good book that Joe never gave it back!

Page 25

It didn't make the news, but the Bermuda Triangle had upped sticks, and hovered now over Joe's little piece of South Manchester, sucking him in along the way. The Burger Bar and the Camera Shop were two of its danger points, the third being a wondrous new discovery for Joe, a treasure trove of a place called 'Discount Records', mystically linked to the others by an irresistible, unseen force that would imprison him and hold him hostage for hours.

Discount Records was owned by Hippy Jim, the hairiest geezer Joe had ever met. Long lank hair, long sticky beard, long dangly moustache and long springy chest-hairs sprouting through his long sweat-stained cheese-cloth shirt, tangling with the long rosary beads he wore as a necklace. He was also the most gently-spoken, intelligent, kind and concerned man Joe had ever had the good fortune to meet, which is why he was regularly giving him a good ten quid a week out of his £45 starting pay. Joe didn't begrudge him a penny of it. He'd have given Jim the whole forty-five if he could afford it. More! Because what he got in return was priceless. He got a musical education. Hippy Jim sold the sort of music you just didn't find in other record shops. Joe couldn't go wrong with Hippy Jim on his side.

He'd named his shop 'Discount Records' because the goods he sold were reasonably priced and were records that most general 'pop fans' would er .. "discount, man! Geddit? Hee hee hee .." He spent hours proudly maintaining a magnificent 'Wall of Sound', a mouth-watering display of picture discs and 45 rpm singles that covered the entire left-hand wall of his shop. He updated it regularly and made sure only the records *he* considered 'future classics' were allowed to remain permanently on display: Magazine, Wire, The Fall, The Clash, Siouxsie, Joy Division, Devo. That was the way Hippy Jim worked, see? Made you feel you *had* to have whichever record he was recommending that day. Oh yes, he was all "love and peace, man", but his rent wasn't cheap and he had a weed habit that smacked his bottom-line pretty hard. "Capitalism, man .." he'd drawl, apologetically. "Small c, yeah?"

Hippy Jim looked like John the Baptist and in his presence you were, indeed, only one short step from God (or John Peel, as He was known to his followers on Earth). Peel was a cult, semi-sidelined Radio One DJ who, in an echo of his disciple Jim - and to put it at its most simple - played the sort of music you just wouldn't hear on other radio shows. He had an evening show that started at ten pm, which was perfect for Joe, whose long shifts meant he was always able to tune in in the car or back in the darkroom. Peel would flit, in his uniquely quirky way (and in his deliciously languid Scouse accent) from punk to poetry, reggae to bizarre Bulgarian women's choir, all in the time it took to say "And this next record's going out to Groggo and his mates at Nottingham Polytechnic." Joe would hear a song played by John Peel and could more or less guarantee it would be in Discount Records before the week was out. He'd pop in to buy it during what passed for his 'lunch-break', be that at 4.30pm or 10.45am, and often come out another five quid down as the 'Baptist' got to work. And verily, it came to pass that, from small beginnings, Joe's musical knowledge expanded and his record collection grew.

It had all been rather pathetic in the early days. He'd nicked a scratched copy of Manfred Mann's 'Mighty Quinn', and bought a 25p ex juke-box copy of The Black Watch's 'Scotch on the rocks' and a random Rubettes single at a jumble sale, but had then redeemed himself with Queen's 'Killer Queen' and 'S-S-S-Single bed' by Fox, all of which were supplemented by the must-have LPs of the seventies, the shit-but-fun 'Top of the Pops' soundalike 'cover' albums that were only really worth buying - as an adolescent fifteen-year-old boy - for the teasing, scantily-clad beauties that beamed out from their sleeves. But then came the epiphany. Joe heard 'God save the Queen' by the Sex Pistols .. and he was off. The Damned's 'New Rose' was next and then - thank you, oh, wondrous, wondrous God (Peelie!) - 'No more heroes' by the Stranglers.
Ka Boom!

He was hooked. Instantly hooked. He'd never heard anything as exciting in his life, and it thrilled him to know he'd found a genre of music that 'did' it for him. Man, the power. At least, it *should* have been powerful, but Joe was still listening to it all through the crappy little speakers that came as part of his Dad's 'State-of-the-art' Music Centre (with built-in turntable, radio, cassette player and graphic equaliser). The sound-quality was pathetic and something needed to be done about it. Fortunately for Joe, another star in the ley-line alignment of wonder-shops was Stereo Hi-Fi, a specialist Technics boutique that hand-built its own hardwood speakers. The cost of a new set-up was eye-watering - what with needing a new amp and turntable too (the equaliser deck would have to wait) - but, like the hire purchase agreement for his Yashica, Joe knew there was a way he could get his sweaty hands on it all. It was all going to be so affordable .. until his Dad mentioned paying rent.

Finally accepting Joe's need for a room of his own, Dad had put his name down with the council for a two-bedroomed flat. But moving on meant coughing up, and it was time for Joe to start paying his way.

"Sure, what can I do?" pleaded Dad, voice echoing in their empty new front room as they wandered round on a look-see. "You either pay your whack or sleep on that bloody floor for the rest of your life. And I hope you realise what a ball-ache this move is for me. I really like that wee flat of mine."

Joe's guilt lasted about four seconds - the amount of time it took him to walk into what would be his own, private, bedroom. "Oh, this is brilliant Dad," he said.

"Glad you think so. Your rent's a tenner a week."

And so Joe's new hi-fi was put on the back burner. He'd have to ease off on the record collecting, too. Maybe tape songs off the radio instead of buying new records, but he reckoned it would all be worth it in the end. He pictured all the babes he'd soon be having back to the new pad.

"Shit," he said to himself. "What if Dad brings a bird home, too?"

The day I wondered ..

.. if I'm ever going to see Joe with a lass.

Joe's meagre pile of possessions had grown somewhat in the long months since he moved to his Dad's, and boxing it all for the transfer to their new flat brought back horrid memories of being thrown out by Kevin. Joe still shuddered at the shock of finding all his belongings in the hall, and his anger made him boil when he thought again of Kevin, now nicely ensconced in his new home. New home, new baby .. new *wife*. He'd heard on the grapevine that his Mum had married Kevin that spring. Kevin is my *step-dad*? Just *what* was his Mother thinking? Disgusting!

Mum!

Joe had only tried to see her once after that disastrous Christmas morning. It had been on her birthday, nine months from the day Joe'd been told to leave the house, with not a word between them since, and he felt the time was right to bridge the gap. He spent an age choosing a birthday card and trying hard to remember her favourite perfume. (Peace-making gifts had to be just right.) Feeling it best not to tell his Dad, he set about a plan of action, though it was hard to know the best way to approach her. Going straight to the house was an obvious no-no, but what were the alternatives? Whilst she was shopping? When she went to the baby clinic? (And just when was *that*, he asked himself!) When she was .. oh, he had no idea.

He went back to his old estate for a recce and, by sheer chance, saw his Mum coming out of the hairdresser's in the row of shops on the main road. He'd never seen her looking so good. His heart leapt and, instinctively, he ran across the road, registering, just too late, the sudden look of fear on her face as she pushed her little one in front of her. "Look out," she gasped.

Kevin came flying out of the bookies next door and punched him straight in the face. "Piss off," he spat, his false front tooth hitting the exact same spot as the fist.

Joe shook all the way home. "I'm gonna kill that fucker," he wept.

The day I moved again ..

Do you like it? Love it, he replied. Which room can I have? I let him have the bigger bedroom. (Sure, my shit doesn't fill a shoe box.) And so I moved again. Got the rent book on a two-bedroomed flat just down the road from my old one. I was sad to leave it, though, I can tell you. Living there was the first time I'd felt settled since the day I .. you know .. since the day my wife and I parted. I spent the first evening in that old place just wandering from front room to bedroom to kitchen to bathroom, just because I could. To finally have so much space after all that time in my sister's back bedroom .. I can't tell you the freedom I felt.

I hope this is it, now. I hope this is my 'forever' home, even though it's number thirteen. I don't care. I've had bad luck for years and that's without being superstitious. I'm sick to death of the packing and the unpacking and the moving on again. This is, what, the fourth place I've lived in seven years? Like I said, I'm beginning to think McIlvenny was right. I was fifteen when I first moved. Me and my brother got shunted off to an aunt's house three streets from ours. (The requirements of seven older sisters held a lot of sway over two skinny wee boys.) It was an odd time, that was. Going home for meals and then walking back to Auntie Moira's to bed down. I did that all the way through my apprenticeship.

The move to Manchester came next. A room had been arranged in a boarding house run by a Swansea woman called Mrs. Bach. A real Welsh dragon, she was. Me and the lad in the front bedroom used to wonder if her first name was Helen. Her breakfasts were good though, I'll always remember that. I must have hit ten stone after stocking up on her fried bread for six months. She'd been a firm believer in 'No dogs and no blacks' but changed her mind about the Irish when Man. United gave her a ton of money to look after a new striker they'd shipped over from Fermanagh.

Glasgow next, after my firm shunted me up to the Clyde to work on one of the new liners. I shared a bunk-bed for a year with a smelly bastard called Collins. Could fart for Scotland, could Collins. Back to Manchester then and, by this time, nearly all of my sisters were over from Ireland. One of them put me up until I found a place in Stretford, walking distance to Trafford Park. And so it went until the day I met my wife, the night of that works' 'do' at the Labour Club. Once we'd tied the knot we shacked up together in her Mum's house, just up by the power station. It got a bit tight for space when Joe came along, I can tell you, but then, bugger me, the firm sent me back up to Govan and we had to live apart for another six months. I've never written so many letters as I did during that time, and I didn't know I had it in me to express love so strongly with mere squiggles on a sheet of white paper. It kept me going that the same strong love came back, only this time in her exquisite, flowing hand. I counted up once and she'd put two hundred and forty nine kisses at the bottom of one of her letters. On and on and on they went, and I felt as light as the air as I imagined her planting each and every one of them on my rough, sea-chapped lips. I'd never felt so moved in my life.

Page 27

When the boss told Joe he'd be going to London to photograph a football match, he got so excited he drove back to the old flat without thinking. "It's an FA Cup game," he told his Dad breathlessly, once he'd got back to the right place. "Third round, first leg. Altrincham against Spurs and I'm going to White Hart Lane to photograph it."

His Dad hated football. "Bunch of fucking pansies," was his favourite, if highly unoriginal, put-down, so he found it hard to share that part of Joe's enthusiasm but - not that he'd ever tell Joe - he felt so proud of his son that he wiped away a tear when he got to bed that night. Joe went down 'The Smoke' on a supporters' bus, the Wednesday afternoon of the game, suffering the incessant chants of the fans but loving the fact that, of all the passengers on board, he was the only one who would enter the ground through the 'Press' gate.

It was a dark night. Wet and cold, and a bloody boring game, to boot. Talk about David and Goliath. The northern team's small group of supporters made barely a dent against the home crowd's roar and Spurs went one-nil up in the third minute. To add insult to injury, there were a couple of 'Norf Larndon' photographers there who nicked all the half-time bacon butties from the press room *and* took the piss out of Joe's measly 135mm telephoto lens. Happily for him, it was the perfect lens to capture Alty's 89th minute equaliser and, being the only photographer at their end of the ground, it meant he had an exclusive. He stuck two fingers up at the southern snappers as he left the ground - couldn't resist it - and, by the next evening, his photograph of the goal that won the team a replay was all over the back page of The News.

"*The News*?" he raged. "How the bleedin' hell has my photograph got into The News?" He was furious, mystified and .. delighted, having sweated all the way back up north on the supporters' bus. Have I got the goal? Did I get it in focus? Was the exposure ok? What if I've missed it? Oh, please don't tell me I've missed it, probably the most important goal in the lower league team's history. The goal that's got them a home-ground replay against Tottenham Hotspur and a possible route to the fourth round of the FA cup. Oh, please ..

He arrived back at the office in the dead of night but, despite his fatigue, had piled straight into the darkroom to develop his film. He had to know. He just had to know. Pushing the ASA - the film sensitivity - to 1600 had meant his processing time was a lot longer than usual but he persevered and was 'over the moon, Brian' when he discovered he'd got a cracker of a shot of the goal. How the hell it had got into The News was beyond him.
"Nice little earner, that," the boss said, later the next day, and shoved twenty quid into Joe's top pocket. He'd printed off the pictures and sold the shots to their daily rival.

-

The twenty quid 'earner' was the ideal down payment for the hi-fi system Joe had had his eye on, and the sexy new set-up was in his bedroom just three weeks later. A lucrative new revenue stream had begun to flow.
"I do it all the time," said the boss, when Joe asked why he'd sold on his work. "Everyone does. Why wait for your photos to be published in a weekly newspaper when you can have them used in the next edition of a daily? *And* make good money into the bargain!" Delighted as he was with the twenty quid, Joe couldn't help but feel a little queasy about the whole underhand practice. "So, let me get this straight .." he said. "You do a job for the 'paper you work for - the 'paper that's actually *given* you the assignment - but sell the shots to the dailies to use first?"
"Of course," said the boss. "A foreigner! What good is waiting up to a week to get a picture in our 'paper .." he repeated " .. when the dailies will use it the next day? Far more relevant then."
"But isn't that stealing?" Joe asked. "Surely you're nicking pictures from your own employer, aren't you? Does he know about this, Mr Attar? And what would he say if he did, eh?" The boss leant frighteningly close to Joe and hissed "You little shit. No, he doesn't know and no .." and at this point he grabbed Joe's lapel " .. he's not going to find out, is he?" He pushed Joe back and straightened his tie for him. "Anyway, you're going to do alright out of it, you wait and see. You're already twenty quid up and I did all the work."

And so it wasn't long before Joe found himself at the reception desks of the News and the nationals, handing over prints from jobs his own employers hadn't even seen. The peaked-capped doormen got to know him well, eventually allowing him upstairs to their editorial departments for his first glimpse of the weird and wonderful world of 'real' picture editors and wire-machines and lupes. Poking around for a way of getting work from those bigger 'papers, it was politely explained that he'd never be commissioned whilst he was employed by another newspaper, but the desks would be "very happy" to have a look at anything he brought in.

The cash began to flow. Morals went out of the window.

Page 28

Joe was on the twenty-seventh floor of the town's one and only block of high-rise flats, trying to disguise a yawn as eighty-five year old Brenda Smethwick handed him another blurred photograph of a cat. "And this was Tibsy," she croaked. "Lovely cat was Tibsy. Jumped off the balcony, daft thing. Trying to catch a pigeon. Terrible accident." She necked a schooner of sherry and coughed so violently that a tiny ball of phlegm hit the cuttle-fish in her budgie cage.

Why, oh why did old people think he'd be interested in pictures of their pets? Or their family over in Australia? Or their bloody award-winning cabbages? Joe got stuck for it, every time. He'd go along to some old dear's house to photograph them for whatever reason and they'd collar him for half an hour whilst they guided him through their entire collection of five by three inch snaps. "Here, you like photography, don't you?" they'd say, and they'd reach for their laminated photo albums and drop them in his lap. "What do you think of these, then?" Joe never had the heart to turn them down. (Poor things, stuck at home all day and night.) Still, if he didn't get a spurt on he'd miss the start of the Girl Guides' twenty-four hour sleep-in at the Methodist Church. "Mrs. Smethwick," he said, preparing to stand. "I'm really sorry, my love, but I'm afraid I'll have to be going now. I'll be late for my next job." Oh, the look of disappointment on her face. She put a vein-bumpy hand onto his thigh and Joe saw a tumble of face powder as she coquettishly fluttered her over-mascared eye-lashes. "But I've put a casserole in," she purred. "I thought you might stay for tea and, well .. you know!" Joe almost threw up, and only just managed to turn his retch into an expression of caring regret. "I'm so sorry," he woozed. "But they'll have me guts for garters if I miss this next picture." He was out of the flat in three seconds, er .. flat, although the casserole *did* smell bloody delicious!

Hitting the call button for the seventh time, it finally dawned on him the lift was broken, and he huffed, pissed-off, and shoved the strap of his camera bag higher onto his shoulder. "Right, stairs it is," he said, and opened the door onto the chilly, concrete stairwell. Another smell hit him full in the face. God, it was awful. What *was* it? Piss? Shit? Gas? Paint? All of the above? It was only as he got down to the thirteenth floor that he realised it was glue. A small group of teenagers was passing around a bag of it, sprawled on the floor and blocking his way with a web of spindly legs. A builders'-sized tube of Uhu lay scrunched up on the landing and Joe's eyes started to water as he coughed loudly. "Shut up!" yapped one of the kids. "We're trying to get a bit of peace here."
"Sorry," said Joe, instantly wishing he'd actually said "No, *you* shut up, you zit-faced dick-head." (Always too nice, Joe was. Well, mostly.) The spotty youth used the wall to raise himself up and stood a surprising five inches taller than Joe. "Sit down, Titch," said a dewy-eyed young girl, squinting up from the floor into the weak, green light of the stairwell illumination. "Sit back down and have another wazz."
"Yeah, have another wazz, Titch," said Joe and, as he made to pass, a bovver-booted foot came out from the tangle and tripped him up. Crashing to the floor, his camera tumbled from his shoulder bag and, as its back sprang open, a roll of film went spiralling down the stairs. "Oh, for God's sake," he shouted. "*Now* look what you've done." None of them heard

him. They were all too busy laughing. Well, everyone except the frightened-looking boy who'd tripped Joe up. He stood nervously, then bent and reached to pick up the camera. "S .. sorry, mister," he said. "Sorry. I didn't mean that. Sorry." Joe raised a hand in acknowledgement and took the camera from his sticky mitt, giving it the once-over for any damage. "No harm done," he said, his voice cracking through the glue cloud, and then he realised the laughing had stopped.

"What's the camera for?" said the girl, her hair tied back in a pony-tail. A feeling of disgust was rising in Joe's gorge, but he resisted the urge to say "It's for taking bloody pictures, you half-wit loser" and instead asked "How old are you?" and then "How old are *any* of you? And what the hell are you doing .. this .." - at which he kicked the glue tube down the stairs - " .. for?"

"Summat to do, innit?" said Pony-tail. "Oh, and since you ask, I'll be sixteen on Friday."

Joe shook his head sadly. "Haven't you got anything better to do?" he asked.

"Like?" said two of them, together.

"Like .. oh, I don't know. Scouts or guides or something." The laughter began again. "You're having a laugh, aren't ya?" said Titch, who'd slid to the ground once more.

Joe shrugged. "Why? What's wrong with scouts?"

"Scouts is for tossers," said Pony-tail. "I mean Guides is," and they all burst out laughing again.

"And they won't let us in, anyway," said the young lad. "They know we like sniffing glue."

"Bit of a Catch-22, innit?" said Pony-tail, much to Joe's surprise. "Oh, don't look so shocked," she laughed. "I'm reading it for English Literature GCSE."

"You're .. *what*? So why the hell are you sniffing glue? Bright young girl like you, messing up your life."

"Like I said, summat to do, innit?" She coughed, wiped a dribble from her nostrils and leant forwards. "Actually, to tell you the truth, I'm getting a bit bored with it all. Putting on a fake 'street' accent and all that. It's all getting rather tiresome."

"I have to admit, she's right," said Titch, sliding upwards again and proffering his hand. "Sorry about all that, before," he said, jerking his head to 'before'. "I feel a bit daft now."

Joe was stunned. "None of you are actually sniffing this stuff, are you?"

"Ooh, nooo .." they said, in concert.

"At least, not any more," said Pony-tail, and she started to blush. "I mean, we *did* have a go when we first started - just a *little* go, honest - but .. well, we all know just how dangerous it is. I mean, the stink alone messes you up, doesn't it? So to actually inhale? Oh no, we learnt that lesson soon enough."

"And our parents would kill us, anyway," Titch shrugged.

"I can't believe this," laughed Joe. "A bright young bunch like you lot and you're .. what? .. *pretending* to sniff glue in a block of flats? I can't believe it."

"Keeping up appearances?" suggested Pony-tail, with a shrug.

"So, what *is* the camera for?" said the young lad, after a second or so. "Are you from the 'paper or something?"

"Actually, I am," said Joe, feeling instantly important. "I'm from The Courier. I've just been taking a picture of one of the residents here."

"Well, do a story on *us*, then," said Pony-tail, and they all looked at each other, enthused. "Yeah, do a feature on the lack of facilities for young people in this dead-end town. Show up the council. Put them on the spot. Do it, go on .. please!"

"It's not as if we haven't already tried," said Titch, kicking a plastic bag down the corridor. ("Don't worry," he apologised. "We always tidy up before we leave.") "We've delivered a petition to the Mayor, *and* tried to meet with our local MP, but no-one's interested in kids of our age-group. We're in that no-man's land between fuzzy-felt at youth clubs and getting hammered in the pub." Joe bit his bottom lip and pointed to the lower staircase. "Let's get out of this stench," he said. "Come downstairs and I'll tell you what I'm going to do." He picked up the ruined roll of film and breathed in deeply as the fresh air hit him like a Bondi roller. "Right, here's my plan. I haven't got time now but, next Friday, if *you're* not busy with your birthday .." - he smiled at Pony-tail - " .. I'll come back here and take some pictures, but we'll *pretend* you're sniffing glue, alright? None of you must actually breathe it in. And I'll try to dig out a reporter, if that's ok. No promises, I'm afraid, but let's see if we can't get your story into the 'paper."

"You'd have to hide our faces," said Pony-tail.

"*And* change our names," said Titch.

Joe laughed out loud. "No problems, er .." and he gestured to Titch to fill in the next word.

"Nigel," said Titch, flinching. "Not what I'd have chosen, but there you go."

Joe smiled again. "Alright, Titch it is. So, I'll see you here at six next week and we'll get something going, alright?" He bade them farewell and realised he was now a good twenty minutes late for his next job. His heart sank further as he got back to his car. He looked at the ruined roll of film, then back up to the 27th floor of the flats. "Oh shit," he groaned. "I'm going to have to re-shoot Mrs. Smethwick!"

-

He stopped to buy a birthday card for Pony-tail before he headed to the flats the following Friday. He'd arranged for a reporter to join him there at six, and was absent-mindedly looking up as he waited in his car, half expecting a cat to fly off a balcony with a pigeon in its mouth. By ten past six he was still alone. "Don't tell me they're not coming," he moaned, chin taut as he tried to extract an overly-stubborn blackhead. By twenty past he was getting annoyed. Shit, he'd been so excited to have found a story of his own. At half-six he reluctantly started his engine and was almost out of the car-park when he saw the top of Titch's head, bobbing along on the other side of the hedge. "Thank God," he said, reversing back to his parking space. "Just need that bloody reporter now," and he greeted the group, who were excited, giggly and full of apology.

"So sorry," said the young lad. "We've been trying to buy more glue for the pictures, but I think the shopkeeper's on to us, now."

"Well, *that's* good," said Joe, eyebrows raised. "Anyway, glad you're all here. I thought you were going to let me down."

"No way," said Titch. "This is a great opportunity for us. Where's your reporter, by the way?"

"Ah, I think he *has* let us down," said Joe, ruefully. "Sorry about that. But don't worry, I'll .. erm .. tell you *what*, I'll write the piece myself. Yeah, that's what I'll do. Oh and, by the way, happy birthday, er .."

"Joan," said Pony-tail, smiling as she reached to take Joe's card. "Aw, that's so kind of you." What a shame it wasn't her eighteenth, thought Joe. He fancied the pants off her.

"Right," he said, concentrating again. "Let's get cracking." He led them all to the thirteenth floor, and they 'staged' the seedy scene from the week before.

"Don't sniff," he said sternly.

"And don't take pictures of our faces," Joan shot back, making such eye contact that Joe's heart thumped. He crafted his story over every spare minute he had that following weekend, and held his breath as he dropped the prints and copy onto the Editor's desk on the Monday morning.

It made the front page of the next edition.

The kids of the 13th floor:
Halfway down, or halfway up?
Let down by their elders, or the future of our country ?

Words and pictures: Joe Bancroft

My God, the thrill. Joe hadn't been this giddy since he'd seen a guppy giving birth to live fry in Mrs Carline's infant class. "Free fish," he'd squealed. "Free babies, miss. Look, free babies .."

"Nice little piece that, Joe," said the Editor, tapping him on the head with the stem of his pipe. "You didn't tell us there was a writer in there, too."

Page 29

"What on earth is a cookery?"
"A kukri?" smiled Joe. "It's a sword used by Gurka soldiers. You can see it in the picture, just there," and he pointed helpfully, just there.
"Mmm, hmm .." said the Editor, turning back to Joe's photograph. A short, smart Nepalese chap was showing off a sharp, curved blade to three awkward-looking members of Rotary International. "I can't see *anything* in this picture to do with kitchen-based ironmongery." He flipped the picture over and drew a large red circle over Joe's photo-caption.

Former Gurka Sergeant Raju Koilara shows off his cookery to three members of ...

"That is *not* how you spell kukri," he huffed, dabbing at the caption with his nib. "Now go and buy yourself a dictionary, lad. And *never* commit anything to paper until you've checked all the facts."

One of the things Joe liked most about being on the newspaper was working with journalists. Real 'trained' journalists, journalists to whom such fact-checking was second-nature, not to mention interview techniques, syntax and shorthand. Journalists who typed properly - unlike his one-fingered stutter stabbing - and who understood libel laws and what to put a preposition behind. As much as he enjoyed writing, Joe knew he was - as he'd just demonstrated to Mr McGowan - as thick as two short planks when compared to these guys. Nevertheless, back in the days before The Courier, he would find stories to cover and submit them to his local 'paper as an entire package, extended caption included. He'd enjoyed writing those little articles. Reminded him of studying for the English Language exam. He knew he'd be out of his depth here though, upstairs at the office, where all the reporters had their desks and educated Cheshire accents mingled with gruff, Northern verbals, all cutting across the clatter and schwing of half a dozen typewriters and the constant ring of telephones. You could positively smell the 2.1s in History and Politics. You could certainly smell the cigarette smoke. (*And* the alcohol. There was usually more than one of them 'at it' at any given time of day. Everyone knew Gill Fuller was into her gin, and Chris Hudson never got through a day without a little help from a certain Mr. Haig.) The reporters ranged from the proverbial 'hard-bitten' to the cute and cuddly cub, with every career stage in between. One of the longest-serving members of staff was a genteel, amusingly-upright lady named Jean Davy, who Mr. Attar had personally recruited in the early days to help him start up the newspaper. As a somewhat misguided sign of his appreciation, he made her both the 'Showbiz' reporter and the 'Agony Aunt', two subjects of which she knew absolutely nothing. (She once confused a black actor in the TV sit-com 'Love thy neighbour' with a chap who sought her advice about suing his employers for racial discrimination. Boy, did that cause a mess.) And she secretly loved the fact that, every time she left her desk to go on an interview, Andy and Joe would warble the new Manfred Mann song 'Davy's on the road again.'

Jack Johnstone had thirty years behind him, the most recent seven at one of the more, let's say 'sleazy', national tabloids. He couldn't write an article about a planned extension to a by-pass without trying to find out who was shagging which councillor in order to get the proposal through the budget. The natural state of his left eye was half-closed, and he typed with his head to the right as a column of fag smoke coiled up past his nose. Fortunately, he could touch-type, which was just as well as he couldn't see his keys for ash, and his irritatingly gruff 'hak, hak' cough synchronised perfectly with the clack, clack, clack of his typing.

The unfortunately named Eric Hunt had once edited a major daily in the Midlands, and held a grudge now that he was now back 'in the 'burbs' after a rather unfortunate episode involving his publication's 'Spot-the-ball' competition. He'd colluded with the chief photographer, whose job it was to 'tweak' a footy photo and render the ball invisible, and they'd both been sacked after entering under the name of the photographer's wife and winning the £10,000 top prize. Joe would never discover that part of his boss's history!

And then there was poor old Helen Lambert. Fresh-faced and timorous, only three weeks out of college, she wouldn't say boo to a goose and the Editor had already pencilled her in as the next Religious Correspondent. (God bless her.)

They were a good bunch in a pub, though. Always the same round too, which was convenient. Guinness for the most of 'em, sweet sherry for Jean and an orange juice with a slice of lemon. (Helen, obviously.) They were intelligent, opinionated, cynical and never-failingly funny, and were happy to welcome Joe into their little group, even if he did just sit at the end of the table and duck as their bigger concepts and ponderings flew over his head. One afternoon, with the fire roaring at The White Hart, he was suddenly aware of a pause in their raucous conversation. He looked up from the beer mat he was busy tearing.

"Well?" said Eric.

"Eh?" said Joe, gormlessly. "Well, what?"

"I asked what *you* think," said Eric, pointing hard, pint in hand. "Would *you* say there've been a few back-handers in this 'New Town' building policy malarkey?" Joe shrugged and sniffed loudly. He could feel himself begin to blush.

"Well .. *I* don't know," he squirmed. "How am *I* supposed to know?" and he wriggled awkwardly, almost falling off his little stool.

"But aren't you the big investigative journalist now?" said Eric, beaming as he looked around the table for approval. "Front page stories and all that? Sex and drugs and rock 'n roll? Haw, haw, haw .."

"I think you'll find it was just glue," said Ilene Klabacher, slapping Eric's hand sharply.

"Oh yes, that's right. Glue," glared Eric. "You sure 'sniffed' out a good story, didn't you, Joe? You sure 'stuck' it to 'em, didn't you? Haw haw haw .."

"Leave him alone," said Ilene. "It was good little piece that. I've already heard the council are to form a working party to look into the kids' requests."

"Ooooh .." said Eric, his mouth twisting cruelly. "A result for the wannabe writer, eh? A big hand for the world-famous wordsmith, folks," he ridiculed, gesticulating wildly towards Joe. He put down his pint and began to clap.

"Sod off," Joe said. "I'm going to the toilet."

-

"Don't let him get to you," said Chris Hudson, splashes going in every direction as he pissed towards the urinal next to Joe. His voice echoed in the cave-like, mildewed toilet. A man farted in one of the booths.

"He's *not* getting to me," Joe lied. "I don't give a monkeys what he says."

"And neither should you," said Chris, shaking his dick. "We all know he's a knob when he's had a few."

Joe just shrugged. He'd been so proud of his front page story.

"Hey come on, you did *really* well," Chris hiccupped, patting a damp hand on the back of Joe's shirt. "Ignore old 'jealous features' there. It was an excellent little piece, made all the better by your cracking pictures. Who'd have thought a tasty front-pager like that could come from our quiet little backwater, eh? It was like something from The Sunday Times."

Joe smiled a thank you and blushed again. "Well, it's not like the stuff you guys write, is it?" he said, modestly. "You lot can knock it out in minutes, all accurate and precise and interesting to read. In *minutes*. My piece took me two days."

"Well, I wouldn't say 'minutes'," Chris laughed. "But thanks for the compliment, pal. It's just a case of 'practice makes perfect', isn't it? I mean, we're writing all the time, aren't we? Day in, day out. Plus, we've all spent bloody ages on journalism courses."

"Hmm, well I haven't even *been* to college," said Joe, glumly. "I couldn't get .."

"But you haven't *needed* to," Chris interrupted. "Look at your work. You're a bloody natural."

Joe went even redder, and a lovely warm glow spread around his entire body. "Well, it's kind of you to say so," he said.

"Don't be so hard on yourself," said Chris, wondering if he had any 50ps for the Durex machine. "Don't put yourself down, lad. You're supposed to be a thick-skinned press photographer, aren't you? Well, you're not going to get very far if you can't take a little light piss-taking like that, are you? And hey, if you wanna write, then .. write."

"Can I get you a pint?" said Joe, light-headedly holding open the toilet door.

"Very kind of you," said Chris. "But I've got to take our Sandra to the badminton. Maybe next time, eh? See ya!"

Joe marched back into the snug, his heart a-flutter. His colleague's words had completely lifted him. (Who cares if the effusiveness had been alcohol driven?) He stopped and glared triumphantly at Eric and, as his soles began to adhere to the flat, once-patterned carpet, an idea rushed up unbidden from somewhere deep in his brain. Write a book, the idea said, and the suddenness of the suggestion made him gasp. Yeah, write a book Joe, the idea repeated and Joe thought bloody hell, I will, as his juices began to stir. Yes, I'll write a book, he decided. Oh yes, that's what I'll do. He re-took his seat at the table and sent a large smile in the direction of Hunt. Articles for the 'paper? he grinned. I don't need to write articles for the 'paper, mate. I'm gonna write a *book*.

That'd show the fat twat, wouldn't it?

Page 30

The opening line would be the hardest. Of course it would. But get that bastard out of the way and the rest would be plain sailing. At least, that's what Joe told himself, having committed himself to the challenge. Chris Hudson thought he could write, and the Editor thought he could write, so write was what he was going to do. Time to get one over on Eric. "How hard can it be?" he said again, cracking open the third of a lager four-pack. "Loads of people have done it." But what would he write *about*? He tried to picture his local library, authors in order, murder, love, biography, all that jazz. Hm, well he knew bugger all about murder, and way less than that about love, so .. an autobiography? "But I haven't *done* anything yet," he laughed out loud. "I'm as far from famous as anyone can get. And who'd want to read about *me,* anyway?" For inspiration, he picked through a pile of his Dad's brightly illustrated cowboy books. (He seemed to have a predilection for someone called Louis L'Amour. 'The Cherokee Trail', 'Showdown on the hogback', 'Bendigo Shafter'. Hm, maybe not.) Then, out of the blue, a cheap, dog-eared paperback came to mind, a murder-mystery he'd found forgotten in a phonebox and read straight through one dreary Sunday evening. Nice and thin, a couple of red herrings, one dead body and the murderer revealed in ninety-nine pages flat. Ninety-nine pages? Piece of piss!

"Hey, 'Page Ninety-Nine'," he chuckled. "That's what I'll call it. 'Page Ninety-Nine,' by Joe Bancroft." It had a nice ring to it. He toasted his progress with the fourth can, burped loudly, jotted the title on the back of a take-away menu and poured out a large Jack Daniel's. "Us authors need to keep our creative juices flowing," he said. "Cheers!"

-

The TV had been on in the background, the sound turned to its lowest. Combing for ideas, he inched up the volume and flicked channels to the news. Petrol rationing followed Ulster bombing. Train strike followed riot. A man had been beaten unconscious at a punk gig ..

"And finally tonight .."

A duck had taken to following a herd of sheep in the West Country.

"Aha!" laughed Joe. Now *that* was more like it. Bright and breezy. Nice and light. The business. Truth was, he wasn't really in the market for writing anything 'heavy'. There was enough *'heavy'* in the world without him adding to it and, as for writing from experience, his new life on a local newspaper hadn't exactly brought him into regular enough contact yet with royals or fame or drama. Kent or Victor he was not! Ok, Joan Collis had moaned at him and he'd once photographed a fireman that got trapped in a drain - a lovely twist on 'kitten up a tree' - but no, a derring-do eye-witness biography wasn't really on the cards in those dawning days of his new career.

"Oh well," he sniffed. "As long as I've got it wrapped up in ninety-nine pages."

He marched himself off to his bedroom and opened up a writing pad.

The day Joe started writing ..

Oil. The word will stick with me forever. I'd had a morning off work - the factory had the auditors in - and was watching over Joe as he lay on his belly with colouring book and crayons. He'd picked up a red and was haphazardly scratching out random letters in his jiggly three-year-old hand. Daddy, he'd ask, straining his neck to look up at me, what does that say? GHJ. That's not really a word Joe, I'd tell him. Try again. KQU. No, that's not a word either. And then he wrote down O and I and L and asked What does that say, Daddy? I couldn't help notice the irony as my work-stained fingers picked up his little book. Oil, I told him. It says Oil, Joe, and his face broke into a huge beaming smile as soon as he knew his ad hoc efforts had finally resulted in a word. Four years after that and he received a postal order for a pound after a letter he'd written was published in his Look and Learn comic. Four years after that and he's passed the eleven-plus. Bright wee thing, my Joe. Gets it from my wife, of course. She was always the clever one in our relationship. That's how she got the job in the typing pool, and why she was moved on so quickly to secretary for one of the directors. She'd only been there a month when I saw her coming out of the staff canteen, a vision in a cashmere sweater. You know the rest. Works dance, shared coca-cola, cigarettes in the bus shelter. Days to lift my feet from the ground.

But me? No, writing was never a strong-point, let's put it that way. Put Declan's bike in front of me and I could have told you everything about it, but school books scared me to death and McIlvenny couldn't have cared less. These days, I only read westerns and the Daily Mail. Well, the racing tips. (How funny. I'd never noticed the 'horse' connection before. I always wished I could have been a cowboy in another life but, tell you the truth, horses scare the shit out of me.) Anyway, I digress. In the end, it was my wife that taught me how to read. The patience of the woman. I can still see her red finger nail moving slowly across a line of letters as I tried to turn the symbols into sense. Ironically, it helped me later on, when I had to read the divorce papers she sent me, but in my mind there was no making sense of those. Divorce? I said to her. But we're *Catholic*, my love. You and I can *never* be divorced. Why did she even think it? Has she never heard of 'marriage for life'?

Two weeks after his front page 'exclusive', Joe photographed a famous American 'A' list actor, who'd written an autobiography and was schlepping it round a book-signing tour of Britain. (It would have been a thrilling moment for Joe, but for the fact that he didn't know the actor, which - fortunately - amused the 'star' immensely.) Joe had really enjoyed the feeling he'd got that day as, for the first time, his 'sway' as a press photographer meant he'd been able to walk straight past a queue of over a hundred people and plonk himself down right in front of the 'stage'. (Shame he'd then had to listen to another forty-five minutes' rambling before he could get his portraits taken. Made him miss the trophy presentation at a marrow-growing contest.) The Yank had said that writing an autobiography was 'an exercise in vanity'. "But, hey .." he'd drawled. "We've all got one in us, you know?" Well, *he* certainly had, thought Joe. Thirty-odd years in Hollywood, a near-death experience involving two Ferraris and a jet-pack and as much sex as he could possibly ever, *ever* need with .. well, anyone he wanted. Joe got an immediate buzz of excitement. Perhaps 'Page 99' *should* be an autobiography, after all. The idea fizzled as quickly as it arrived. No Joe, his brain chided, you *can not* write an autobiography. Do you want to be thought of as vain? Joe knew he was shallow, but .. vain?

-

He stared hard at an empty writing pad, then lay back on his bed and shut his eyes. Hey, what if writing makes me famous? The thought made him smile. A little bit of fame and fortune would be alright, wouldn't it? I mean, who knew if the photography was ever going to provide it? (That was his true calling, though. His 'passion', in the vernacular, and he knew he wouldn't be giving up on that any time soon. Maybe for the book-signing tour and the TV interviews, then it would be back to covering those all-important cheque-presentations, bowls matches and local council elections.)

He was on a rare day off. The normally-stable advertising had mysteriously dropped across all titles that week, so management had cut the number of pages in each edition and instantly put a line through 25% of the photographers' work-load. A day off meant a lie-in, a trip to the launderette, a chance to re-stock on microwaveable 'Boil-in-the-bag' meals and an afternoon to really get 'Page 99' off to a flying start. (Although, with the autobiography idea now a no-go, Joe hadn't even taxied to the runway.) He looked to the cinema listings for stimulation. 'The Deer Hunter' had just opened at the 'pictures', along with 'The magic of Lassie', and he scratched his head in vain for animal-based inspiration. (The nearest he'd actually ever come to interacting with wild beasts was the time three slobbering mongrels followed him to school because Donna was on heat.) He threw the listings into the bin and closed his writing pad. Basildon Bond. Ah, the name's Bond. Basildon Bond. (Hasn't that joke been done?) The microwave pinged as his Chicken Supreme exploded. It drove him mad that he could never get the timing right. "Now *that ..*" he laughed " .. is an exercise in insanity." Then he said "Oooh .." and wrote it down.

-

He didn't actually want to be an *author,* of course. It was only about shoving two fingers up at Eric but, now that the seed had been planted, it was all starting to get a little bit exciting. "If we've all 'got one in us'," he said, pen ready. "Then it's about time mine came out."

Page 1

~~Dad is whippet thin, yet strong as an ox. He drinks like a fish and gets drunk as a skunk but is never sick as a parrot. He has two tattoos, one of an anchor and one that says 'Mum and Dad' in a heart shape on his left forearm. The top of a his left index finger is missing after he accidentally chopped it off in a machine. Well, it would be an accident, wouldn't it? You wouldn't deliberately ..~~

No, forget that bit, Joe sniffed.

~~For a joke he often puts the finger up his nose and, because it goes right up to his knuckle, it looks really funny. He says he looks like Dave Allen ..~~

Joe scrawled a deep black line through the opening words of his new book and threw his pen to the floor. This might be harder than he'd thought. He riffed a thumb down the thickness of his pad, alarmed by all the empty pages, crying out to be filled with his words of wit, wisdom and .. what?

"Have another go, Joe," he said. "Focus, fella, focus."

Page 1

James yawned and dropped a trashy paperback onto the floor. "Well, that was totally un-put-downable," he said, rubbing at his eyes. "What a great idea for a book. You don't see anything coming until page 99 and then .. Bam! Revelations! Surprise! The End! What suspense. What a great way to get the readers hooked. What a …" He shut his eyes, then opened them again instantly. "Hey, I could write a book like that. Ninety-nine pages? Piece of piss." He marched himself off to the bedroom and opened up a writing pad.

"Page 99," he muttered. "All I have to do is reach Page 99 and then .."

And then .. what?" His enthusiasm dipped, so he reached into a cupboard and unscrewed the top of an 'emergency' bottle of Jack Daniel's. "Then I hit them with the killer line," he rallied. "The 'who-dunnit' moment; the .."

He scratched his balls, his baggy four-year-old Y fronts allowing more than adequate access. "Yeah, but you need a plot to get to that point, don't you? And .. er .. characters, situation .. all that gubbins .." His English Language 'O' Level suddenly seemed a long time ago. 1975. Three years, already? Jeepers, where had _they_ gone? Still, it'd be just like riding a bike, wouldn't it? He hadn't done _that_ for ages, either.

He recalled the words of his English teacher, Mr King. (The first 'queen' he'd ever come across.) 'Write of what you know'. Well, all James knew was press photography, and who the hell would want to read about _that_? "Hmm.." he sighed, resting his chin on his hand. "I'm sure something will come to mind."

He downed the Jack, gave his bollocks a last long seeing-to, closed the pad and went to bed.

-

"Hmm .." sighed Joe, resting his chin on his hand. He re-read the first 294 words of his new best-seller, closed the pad, gave his bollocks a last long seeing-to and went off to bed. Sleep was impossible. "Oh, come on Joe," he urged. "You've only got to write ninety-nine bloody pages." He went back into the living room and tore the top page from his pad. Start again lad, start again. He lay back and thought and thought, but not a single idea popped into his head. The book *might* have to be about him, after all.

Page 1

'You should know ..' he wrote '.. that most of this book will be a blatant effort to surreptitiously run a memoir passed you. The autobiography of someone who isn't famous and hasn't actually done a single interesting thing in his life ..'

He bit the end of his pen and let that one sit for a minute. Not bad, he thought. A clever little intro, if he said so himself. He fell asleep before he could come up with another line.

"A flash-gun? But it's sunny!"
"HP5 or Tri-X?"
"Which lens do you prefer?"

And, Joe's perennial favourite .. "How do you become a press photographer?" "You'll never be one .." he'd answer smugly " .. if you have to ask how to do it."

Amateur photographers. The bane of his bloody life. There he'd be, minding his own business, covering an event - a fair, the footy, a march - and *Pooof*, there *they'd* be beside him like a genie from a bottle, attempting to pick his brains or casting sad, sorry eyes over his increasingly-battered photographic equipment. "Nikon? Oh, nowhere near as good as Canon. My lenses are so much sharper, and that new model's got that, that er, you know where you can, you know .." He'd smile, he'd be professional, sometimes he even tried to be *helpful* but man, he wished they'd all just go away! It took him right back to the photographic society he'd briefly joined, where the members felt that *owning* the right equipment was more important than getting good results *from* it. (The more a camera cost, the better the photographs it took, apparently!) Yet they still only used them to photograph those damned robins and sunsets and silhouetted steam trains. He knew that because he was looking at six pictures of the damned things right now.

"Thank you everybody," he shouted, stepping carefully down from a table and switching off his flash. It was the annual awards night at the local camera club and he'd just photographed a group of weekend snappers with their framed cutesy pictures and their trophies and their big, beaming smiles. "Great shots," he added, somewhat disingenuously. "Lovely robins."

"We wondered if you had time for a chat." The Treasurer smiled hopefully into Joe's face. "Perhaps stop for a cuppa? We thought you could give us a few tips, let us pick your brains so to speak, seeing as you're here." Joe breathed deeply and pulled out the crumpled list of that evening's assignments, though he knew full well this was his last job of the day. "Erm, I've got five minutes," he fibbed. "That any good to you?" Before he knew it he had a coffee, three chocolate biscuits and fifteen people sitting around him. The mundane questions about equipment (sigh) were always going to be first but, as five minutes became thirty, it dawned on Joe that he might have been a little too harsh to judge them all as he did. They were just as keen on photography as he was but .. well, just not the right types for press work, or just not interested *enough*, or maybe just earning too much money from a 'real' job. Things got a little more personal after a further hour of chat. "What was it .. " he was asked " .. that kept him so enthused about his job?" Hm, good question. He had to stop and think. Was it the variety? The chance to meet so many new people and go to places he never would have otherwise seen? The excitement of deadlines? The thrill of bylines? The kudos? The money? (No, definitely not the money.) "It's the creativity," he finally said. "Yes, that's it. I get to be creative all day long."

-

I'm a creative. The thought gave him a lovely glow as he drove home over the aquaduct. "Of course, I'll be even *more* creative when I've written my book," he smiled, and then John Peel blew his head off. He played three songs in a row that .. well, that Joe could just not imagine *ever* coming out of one's .. er, imagination. "How the hell does *anyone* create *anything* like *that*?" he gasped, amazed. "This is fantastic." And then it dawned on him. His 'way' of being creative was *nowhere near* as inspired as that of writing or music. Photography was visual. It always had a baseline, a starting point, a subject .. and it didn't matter how inventive a photographer you were, you were always looking at something to begin with - however abstract - from whence you could travel with your eyes and your mind and your message. But music and words, harmonies and plots? They came directly from the head and the heart and the soul, plucked from nothing, from nowhere, the most wondrous gifts of man to mankind.

And now that he'd created that thought, his glow went out for the evening.

The day we went for a pint ..

Now, I'm not vain (heaven forbid, vanity's a sin in the Catholic church) but I have to admit that, these days, I do like to hog the limelight. Is that how you say it? Hogging? I love to start the singing in the pub, that's what I mean, and I'm always first on the dance floor at the Irish Club. I've even taken over as Captain of the darts team, and I'm shite at darts! It's the booze, of course. I know it is, 'cos I was never like this in the old days. (Why are they called the 'old days' when they're really the days you were young?) I never drank back then but yes, put a drink in me now and I'm a different man. A *new* man I'd say, a better man, and I like the way I change. I love the confidence, the certainty I have about myself. Makes me wish I'd started drinking years ago. Might have stopped me from always being the 'little man'. Having said that, I used to see what the whiskey did to me ol' Pa and kept as far from it as I could. Jesus, the lashings I've had when that man was blootered. And he'd hit Ma, too. Poor old Ma, who used to swing at him with her rosary beads until the day she clunked him in the eye and sent him to the infirmary. "God came to me in a vision," Pa whined to the nurse.

It was the fags for me, so it was. I think I was twelve when I started smoking, perhaps ten. (Maybe eight, now I think about it!) I'd sneak quick drags of Pa's Senior Service and my sisters' fancy pink cigs when they weren't looking, and then it was twenty a day through my teens, upping it when my apprenticeship money started coming in. Seems stupid now, doesn't it? But that's what you did, back then. Smoking was good for your health they said, so it made sense, like having all your teeth knocked out at sixteen and a good set of dentures shoved in in their place. It'll save you years of trouble in later life, they told me. Fucking liars.

The drinking started at my sister's. She'd slip whiskeys round the door to 'calm me down' and I got a taste for it, didn't I? Been drinking ever since. I'm not an angry drunk, though. Not like Pa. No, I get brave. I start to think I could take on the world. Perhaps I *should* have had the odd drink whilst I lived at .. well, you know .. at home. Maybe I'd have dared stand up for myself a little bit. Too late for all that now.

I used to see my own reticence in wee Joe, used to pray he'd grow up differently and, I have to admit, I thought we were on the right track once he'd passed that swimming certificate thing. That seemed to ease a lot of his anxiety. Certainly stopped the bed-wetting, that's for sure. And, don't tell anybody but I was chuffed to bits when he set about clattering the wee lad next door. Poor Stuart Holmes. Didn't half get 'what for'. That's my boy, I thought. Stand up for yourself, Joe. Look life in the eye. Give the world hell. Shame it all fell apart at the Grammar School. Crumbled, he did. Got absolutely walked over, just like his Dad. (I was already off the scene by then, but I blame myself 'cos I wasn't there to help him.) Still, they're never quite as perfect as you think, your kids, are they?

Shit, I completely forgot what I was going to tell you. About the night I took Joe for his first pint ..

Page 33

After an uncertain, nervous start, Joe and his Dad were getting on like a house on fire, even though Dad was really old. (You know, like fifty-one or something.) They'd certainly worked out when it was safe to go for a pee in the night, having simultaneously opened their bedroom doors at three o'clock one morning and caught each other stark-bollock naked!

Dad's quirks and habits were something Joe quickly got used to. His heavy smoking, his constant drinking and the fact he could never quite rid himself of a piquant 'Eau d'oil', no matter how much Old Spice he threw at it. He kept his false teeth in a glass of fizzy Steradent on the draining board and took five sugars in his tea. His catch-phrase was "Have a Ball" and he always said "Not tonight, Josephine" as he left the flat in the evening. He wore a crucifix around his neck and held his trousers up with braces, never belts.

One of his favourite songs was 'Black Velvet Band' by the Dubliners, which he played constantly, along with Johnny Cash's 'Folsom Prison Blues' and a never-ending stream of country and western cassettes. He would go through odd periods of growing a beard without a moustache, making him look remarkably like Abraham Lincoln, and he had a poached egg for breakfast, boiled in a pan with added vinegar that used to make the flat stink like hell. He loved sterilised milk, a pint of which he'd make last two weeks, by which time it too stank something 'orrible. Saturday meant a mixed-grill dinner with two free sausages from the butcher, and the walls of the flat were full of curled, yellowing cuttings, as Dad would tear photographs from the newspapers and add his own amusing captions. Joe's favourite was a picture of Prime Minister James Callaghan, to which Dad had added a speech-bubble saying "I made Linda Lovelace gag".

At least Joe had his own bedroom now, so didn't feel they got under each other's feet as much as they had done. In fact, to all intents and purposes, they lived completely separate lives. Ships that passed in the night. Every morning, Dad would be up at 'Dawn's Crack' (as he used to call it) and out, light or dark, for the walk to work and, every evening, he'd walk back in, grease-smeared and knackered, after yet another day as a Maintenance Fitter at the factory. For his part, depending on what time he was due to start, Joe would pick out a clean shirt, knot on a multi-coloured tie and head off for a day of .. well, who knew what? Every shift was different. Every trip to the office the start of something potentially wonderful. Their worlds couldn't have been more different if they'd tried. Joe didn't understand a thing about 'maintenance fitting', and his Dad hadn't the foggiest about press photography. When his son was just hours old in maternity, Dad had looked nervously down into his cot and made a vow. He tickled Joe's toes with his nine and a half oil-grained sausage fingers and

pledged that no son of his would ever grow up with hands like those. "Hello, my little chartered accountant," he'd said, beaming with pride. And then Joe grew up to be a press-photographer! "It's my calling," he'd explained, posturing theatrically. "I didn't choose it, *it* chose me. And I'm shit at maths, anyway."
"Fair enough," Dad had said, consoled at least by the fact that Joe didn't come home covered in crap every day. "But what do you actually *make*?"

No, their worlds would never meet. All Joe knew was that it was his Dad's job to fix each and any of the huge machines that went wrong in the factory, and they went wrong all the bloody time! And all Dad knew was that it was Joe's job to take photographs that went in a newspaper, and it was the most piss-easy job on the planet. At least Joe was happy. Not rich, like an accountant, but happy. And, as a true adherent of the 'judged by appearance' policy, he *did* get Joe to wear a tie every day. 'Smart at all times' was his philosophy. "You never know who's watching you," he'd wink, with his irresistible Irish twinkle. He practised what he preached too, with his daily shaves and his suit and tie approach to nights out. Every evening, he'd wolf down a quick meal - chips with everything, fried in a pan of gritty, grey fat which never seemed to get changed - then he'd settle down for a kip in front of the local news. After that, a shave and a 'sink' bath, bending low to get his head between the wash-basin taps and rid his greying curls of another day's filth, and then it was time to tog up in his one and only suit and head off to .. well, you name it. The pub, the Irish club, a darts match, the Catholic club, the dancing .. it just depended which day of the week it was. The guy was never in.

Joe's evenings were just the same, now that he was on the 'paper. If he wasn't at a disco he was in a pub, and it was nothing out of the ordinary for him to hit at least three others before last orders. If he wasn't in a pub he was at a dinner, or a theatre or a fancy-dress party. Sometimes he went to a swimming baths, and sometimes a gym, and sometimes a football match. It was a social swirl, and he loved it. The only problem was .. everyone else was doing the swirling. It was an understandable fact of his life now that, if he *did* go to the pub, nine times out of ten it was to photograph a Crown Green Bowls competition or a cheque presentation. If he was at a nightclub it was probably for the visit of a semi-famous DJ or a 'Miss Wet T-Shirt' competition. (He didn't mind *that* so much!) The gym visit would be to cover a badminton tournament, the theatre to shoot a play rehearsal, the party to mark a moment in a stranger's life. It was dawning on Joe that he was an odd-one-out. *All over again.* The irony amazed him. He had one of the most sociable jobs in the world yet *still* did everything on his own. He went on jobs alone, he worked in the darkroom alone, he went to gigs alone, he ate alone, he drank alone, he had sex alone ..

Pull yourself together, he'd say, trying to shake the self-pity as he drove from, say, a really lively fiftieth birthday party. Don't worry about it, he'd say dismissively. Working in a job like his, he was *bound* to get a good compliment of mates soon *and* probably a hot chick or two or three, and then he'd be the envy of everyone around. But, talk about confused, Joe *loved* working on his own. The freedom, the control, the space. In fact, he couldn't see how a photographer could work in any other way. Indeed, if there *was* one thing he hated, it was being lumped together with a bunch of other photographers, as always happened at a photo-call, because when photographers outnumbered the subject it was nigh on impossible to get a shot that was different to everyone else's. They all nicked each other's ideas! No chance of that happening at The King's Head, though. He could practically guarantee he'd be the only photographer covering their Bridge tournament tonight!

They made an effort to take a drink together every now and again, him and his Dad, down at The Navigation Inn. Dad's long-time local was just along by the canal, a few yards from the betting shop, meaning Dad could peruse the racing tips then nip next door for a 'ten pence each way' on whichever horses took his fancy.
"Can't we go somewhere else for a change?" Joe would whine. "I'm sick of this bloody place."
"Oh, not good enough for you now?" Dad would stick out a little finger and affect a posh voice. "Too common for the Big Knob, is it? He who swanks around with mayors and footballers and Joan Collins. Well tough shit, kiddo. It's my local and I'm not changing where I drink, just for you. Why should I, when I've found a place I like?"
"How the hell can you like *this*?" Joe would complain, his arse sinking into the filthy, fag-scorched corner banquette that his Dad had claimed as his own. "Look at it. Smell it, for God's sake! Look at the yellow walls, look at the shitty tables, get a whiff of the disgusting toilets, look at the .."
" .. price of the Guinness? That's all you need concern yourself with, Joe Bancroft. Cheapest pint in town, this pub has, and Barry doesn't half look after his kegs." Joe had to agree on that one. The Guinness was bloody lovely. At least, it was now he'd a taste for it, but he'd never forgotten that first time on the black stuff, the night before New Year's Eve, just over a year ago. He was still only seventeen and it was less than a fortnight since he'd moved in with his Dad. It was their first night out together ..

.. and Joe's first time in a pub!

The day Joe got pissed ..

Yes, I've remembered now. What I wanted to tell you. The night my son got pissed!

Page 34

"What'll you have, son?" Dad pushed Joe forwards 'til his belly hit the bar. "What's your poison, kiddo?" Joe was bewildered, and coughed through a haze of fag smoke as he squinted at a row of spotlit optics, labels half hidden behind a boa of festive tinsel.
"God, it's smoky in here," he said, wafting his hand in front of his face.
"Of course it is," laughed Dad. "It's a *boozer.*" He beckoned to the landlord, who dashed from the other side of the bar and shook Dad's hand with gusto. "Seasons greetings, y'old bastard," he shouted, in the same Ulster brogue as Dad. "Here, let me buy youse a wee drink. A tipple for Christmas, like. The usual?"
"You're a good man, Barry," Dad winked, and gave him a thumbs up.
"Who's your wee friend?" Barry asked, nodding towards Joe.
"This, Barry .." Dad said, with just the merest hint of a crackle in his voice " .. is my son, Joe. Joe. Barry. Barry. Joe."
"Your .. *what*?" Barry's arm stopped in mid-air as he went to pick a glass from the rack above the bar. "Did you just say your fucking *son*?"
"My fucking son," said Dad, breaking into a broad smile. "My Joe, our eldest."

"Well, I'm a dog's ding-dong," Barry exclaimed, through a faggy cackle. "You kept that quiet, you sly twat. Nice to meet you, Joe. Ah yes, I'm seeing the family resemblance now. Same chin, same huge nose!"
"Piss off," laughed Dad, bouncing a beer mat off Barry's belly. "Get those bloody drinks in and less of the cheek." Barry placed a half pint of Guinness and a Bell's whiskey and lemonade (no ice) in front of Dad, and they both looked at Joe, expectantly.
"And?" said Barry, looking at Joe's blank face. "What'll you take, young fella?"
Joe panicked. He'd only really drunk alcohol once before, and tried hard to remember what he'd seen his Mum sipping at The Queen's Silver Jubilee street party.
"Erm, can I have a sweet martini and lemonade?"
Barry and Dad looked at each other and burst out laughing.
"No, you fucking can *not*," said Barry, tears streaming down his face. "Ha ha ha .. fucking sweet martini? Here, do you want me to hold your hand-bag, as well? Ha ha ha .."
"Ach, he's winding you up," said Dad, when he could speak again. "He'll have a Guinness, same as his old Dad."
"Oh, I don't .." began Joe.
"Pint of Guinness it is, good man yerself," said Barry.
"No, I .."

"Let's sit down," said Dad. "That'll take a minute to settle." They edged through the crowded pub to an empty corner seat that Joe would come to know very well. "My seat, see?" said Dad. "Everyone knows it's my seat."
Barry brought Joe's Guinness over and Dad clinked his half against its side. "Slàinte," he said, smiling happily.
"Eh?" Joe said, gormlessly.
"It's Irish for 'Good Health'," Dad laughed. "Cheers, good health, our Joe. Get that down you and here's to many more." Joe took a tentative sip and gagged. "Mdmmph!" he managed, swallowing the tiniest mouthful and splurting the

'head' of stout all over his Dad's broad-striped nylon tie. "Oh God," he groaned. "That's awful."
It took two minutes for Dad to stop laughing this time. "That'll be yer first, then?" he said at last. "Here, I'll get you something to sweeten it." He walked to the bar and returned with a glass of blackcurrant cordial. "Pop a drop o' that in," he said. "That'll take the edge off it. That's a Guinness and black, that is. Women drink it." Two pints later and Joe was pissed for the first time in his life. Trolleyed. Wrecked. Arseholed. Bladdered. He threw up the second the cold night air hit him, and had to lean against his Dad the whole wobble home.

"Will youse be wanting a snifter?" his Dad asked, the minute Joe fell into the flat. Joe honked again, only managing to bring up a tiny dribble of something white and a sultana from an earlier mince-pie. "Imgoinabed," he'd slobbered, and spun round so woozily that he fell to the floor and just about managed to crawl across to his sleeping bag.
"Floor's rolling," he burbled. "Whysafloorollin'?"
Dad leant against the door and chuckled as Joe half-heartedly threw the sleeping bag over his head. He walked into the room and set it properly across his young son's already sleeping body. "Night night, God bless," he whispered, raising a shot of Bell's in his direction. "Sleep tight, my wee darling," he added, lips quivering.

Joe felt like shit but, having had a pint with his son for the first time in their lives, his Dad was in seventh heaven.

Page 35

"Sacked" wasn't a word Joe ever expected to hear. Fortunately for him, it was preceded by the words "could" and "possibly", but it still turned him pale and made him wish he'd worn more deodorant. "I'll have no more damned shenanigans like *that*," said the Editor, knotting his eyebrows. "You'll be out before you can say Pitman's shorthand. *And* you'd have no recourse to an appeal. I just won't accept appalling behaviour like that on this newspaper."

Appalling behaviour? God, it made him squirm. Why the hell had he done it? Because he was angry, that's why. A busy Friday night - no different to any other, really - had started well with the champagne opening of a local artist's new exhibition. Two flutes to the wind, Joe had then headed thirty miles west to photograph the mother of a soldier who'd been shot in Coleraine. Sobered by her story, he'd then driven thirty miles back to get a shot at the start of an archery tournament, and then he'd gone to the annual awards evening of the County darts league.
"Hello," he chirped to the organiser. "I've come to photograph your winners."
"The awards haven't been given out yet." The chap spat the sentence as he collected tickets at the door, and his beer breath made Joe wince. "You'll have to come back later."
Joe glanced at an ornate Queen's Jubilee clock, ticking loudly behind the bar of the working men's club. Ten to nine. He nodded, smiled politely and set off for a Muslim community centre seven miles down the road. His first ever Eid festival was a delight, offering a multitude of colourful images despite Joe shooting in black and white. Re-jigging his schedule, he managed to persuade the contestants in a dominoes tournament to take a break so that he could get a picture of them all together .. and then he went back to the darts.

"Still not finished," sneezed the man, dropping a handful of change as he searched for a hanky. Joe huffed heavily and eyed the clock. Quarter to ten. He dashed off to a fund-raising disco for the Northern Branch of a Pony Rescue Society and was back at the darts by ten-fifty, by which time the awards had been handed out and the atmosphere had turned bawdy, fuelled by bitter and mild and two half-time strippers. The organiser shrugged as Joe approached.
"What can I say?" he gurned. "You're too late."
"Too late?" Joe snapped. "Oh, come on mate, this is the third time I've been back. Can't you just get some of the winners together so I can get a picture?"
"Can I buggery, lad," said the secretary. "You should've been 'ere at the right time."
"I was told to be here at nine," Joe shouted. "I was actually early."
"Too bloody early."
"Look, I'm here now," said Joe, trying to calm himself. "Can't we just get something organised? Please? All I want is about six of the winners over here with their trophies." Seventeen minutes later and Joe was fuming as, finally, enough of the piss-heads were mustered for a photograph. Unfortunately, the boisterous rabble were just too far gone to be serious. Three of them thought it would be hilarious to hold their trophies in front of their faces. One lay across the front of the line-up like a dolly-bird on a car-bonnet, one insisted on posing as if he was throwing a dart, and the other two turned and presented Joe with their bare backsides. One of *them* was the winner of the Ladies' cup! Joe had had enough. "Fuck the lot of you .." he spat under his breath and, at almost half-eleven, having given up on any semblance of control, lifted the camera to his eye and, rather than take a photograph, simply pressed the button on his flashgun to make it fire. And then, like a moron, he told the Editor exactly why he didn't have a picture to show him from the darts presentation. Too honest for his own good, Joe was. God bless Catholicism.

Page 36

Dad had a horrendous coughing fit and then, eyes shining, said "Pass me that .. er .. er .. er .." with a quivering wave of his left hand.
"*What*, Dad? What?" said Joe, impatiently.
"The, er .. oh, you know .."
"No, I *don't* know. And if you don't tell me now I'll never know 'cos I'm off out and you can get whatever it is yourself."

That was weird, Joe thought, lying in bed later. His Dad had come in from work - as oil-streaked and fagged-out as usual - and completely forgotten the word for piccalilli. Joe had had to point at seven different things on the table before Dad had nodded and said "There you go. That's it. What's the problem?" Probably just fatigue. Joe knew how hard his Dad threw himself at life. A day's hard graft, then he'd gobble down his tea, catch five minutes' shut-eye, splash a gallon of pure undiluted Brut under each armpit and go drinking and dancing until he ran out of dosh. Every single night. Joe laughed as he thought back to one particular day, when he'd flopped back home - knackered from a twelve hour shift - as his Dad cooked his tea on the stove. "What a day," he'd groaned. "I thought I'd never stop working." His Dad, topless despite the spitting chip-pan - and a sight for sore eyes in bright red polyester underpants and battered steel-toe capped boots - turned to Joe and waggled an index finger to mimic the pressing of a camera shutter button.
"Joe .." he'd smirked. "Doing *that* all day is not what *I'd* call working!" They'd laughed so much the chips caught fire.

But he *was* working. Every time he pressed the shutter - despite what his Dad might think - he *was* working, working to record a memory .. *whatever* it was. His dutiful, obedient camera just took it all in .. an event, an occurrence, a moment; a hair style, a description of late twentieth-century road-signage, a car design; a rising pop star, a failing politician, a building where a space had been, a space where a building had been. Photography was *all* about memories. Joe knew that now. My entire career, he thought, is all about making memories, good or bad. Mostly good, he realised - considering a local paper was generally about the promotion of the positive - and he almost physically swelled with pride when he thought of the importance - yes, the *importance* - of his work. He was brought back to earth when Della thrust a Post-it note at him next morning. "Ring this number," she shouted. "There's been a suicide." Panicked, Joe read the note and put his hand across his eyes. "Oh God," he groaned. "I'd forgotten about her."

-

There's no subtlety with a stomach pump, and Joe threw up the moment he saw the lime green bile in the bowl. How ironic. And how bloody annoying that she'd asked for *him* when she was taken into hospital. Carol bloody Brereton.

-

She'd made for a great feature when Joe first met her. A real battler against adversity, he'd got talking to her during the opening of a new drug-dependency clinic. This girl's going to make a great piece, he said to himself. I'll tell the reporters. No wait, I'll write it up myself.

Carole Brereton. Single Mum, bipolar, polio victim, heroine. (She'd tried the other spelling, too.) Bringing up daughter Stella on her own, despite the stigma of having been raped and the malicious (in her view) social service departments; despite her asthma, her haunting mood swings, smoker's cough and hunched back.

"Smile Cazzer," he'd said, when he visited her at her home. His interest in her warmed her, his jokes amused her, made her feel special. Three year old Stella performed beautifully, her nascent afro giving her that extra cutesy 'wow'. "Brilliant," said Joe, putting away his camera. "Some great shots there, Carol. You'll look lovely on the features page." He was sure she'd blushed, but the port wine stain across her rotund face made it hard to be certain. "So, just a few questions then I'll leave you in peace."
"Oh, do you have to go?" she'd said, scrunching up her face. (Oh shit, thought Joe. She's going to get a bloody photograph album out.) "I do, yes," he said, and pulled out a long job list just to prove how busy he was.
"Well, come back any time, Mr Bancroft," she said. "Probably after six, when I've had all my tablets."
"Joe," he offered. "My name's Joe. And call the office anytime." He gave her one of the new business cards he'd just had printed. "Always there for a chat," he smiled, surprised at his own benevolence. It was just, he felt so sorry for her. (Good God Joe, take it easy.) She *did* call the office. Or rather, Accident and Emergency did. "Can you ask Mr. Bancroft to call us as soon as he possibly can," they'd said to Della. Carole had taken thirty-seven aspirins and a miniature bottle of Bailey's (It's difficult to work out the ratio if you don't drink) and was calling weakly for him as she lay shaking on a pale-blue hospital trolley. Life's weight had finally crushed her and the pills were her call for help. Joe, for his troubles, was the only person in months who'd shown her anything like kindness and his business card was the only item on her person. Her call was really a call for Joe.
"You'll be alright, Carol," he said, tapping her arm with his fingertips.
"Eeeuuuggghhhh!"
"Just hang in there, they know what they're doing."
"You must mean a great deal to her," said a baggy-eyed nurse in a splashed-plastic smock. "She absolutely *insisted*

we call you. Now we're just going to give you some more charcoal, Miss Brereton. Open wide."

Oh God, thought Joe, I'm missing an Undertones gig for this.
The lime green bile made him sick.

Or was it just his luck with women?

Page 37

Ah yes, girls. To be more precise, girls and music, the two other interests in Joe's busy life. His musical tastes had exploded since his early days and, by now, he was just as likely to buy Kate Bush's 'Wuthering Heights' as he was The Only Ones' 'Another girl, another planet' (which, for Joe, basically summed up Bush in a nutshell!) But, whilst his rows of records grew, girls proved harder to collect. It would be more accurate to say that 'having an interest in possibly one day getting to know a girl' was Joe's second interest in life, seeing as, even at eighteen, he'd still never so much as put his arm around one. (Pauline wouldn't let him!)

He hated to admit it, but he'd once had a 'thing' for Kevin's daughter when they were both fifteen - getting as far as walking her twice around the cemetery one heady summer's evening. Kevin had taken them all to the pictures by way of introduction and Joe had fallen for Angela straight away. Ask him now and he'd be unable to tell you what film they'd gone to see, distracted as he was by her 'Avon Timeless' scent and the budding breasts that gave shape to her grown-up Mexican peasant blouse. Angela took up with the 'cock of the school' and that was the end of that.

Françoise was next. Fifteen and French, she was an exchange student who'd stayed with a friend in '77, all pouty Gallic "Ooo" lips and absolutely unintelligible English. So exotic, so .. er, foreign. With his sketchy 'O' Level French, Joe had acted as part-time interpreter for his pal, helpfully deciphering the menu at the chip shop but completely mistranslating Queen's new single as 'Nous sommes les champignons'! He was heartbroken when she went back to France, but convinced himself she fancied him when she posted over a Laurent Voulzy single called 'Rockollection'.

'On a tous dans l'cœur une petite fille oubliée
(We all have a little forgotten girl in our hearts')

She'd written 'Pour Joe' on the back of the record. Yeah, poor Joe, he thought. Très triste! But that was it. No going steady, no snogging, no funny stuff, no .. anything .. with *anyone*! It was all getting a little bit frustrating. He'd even had to concoct a fake girlfriend when he joined the Army just to convince the other boys in 'B' platoon that yes, there *was* a 'girl back home', she just doesn't write very often!

So let's face it, *music* was numero two after photography and now, in his new bedroom, it was posters for Chrissie Hynde and Strummer that began to nudge out those for Mamiyas and Bronicas although, as of 1978, he still hadn't been to a gig, afraid of punks and their upfront, aggressive ways. Besides which, he obviously wasn't a student, so assumed he wouldn't be admitted to a university to see a band. Julie Rumsey put him right on that one. Twenty-four, slim and bonkers, Julie had a shock of bright orange hair and the thickest, blackest eye make-up Joe had ever seen. She worked upstairs in the 'paper's tele-sales department, a job she needed if only to pay for her expensive 'gig' habit, seeing at least three new bands a week.

Joe had been at Discount Records one afternoon, Hippy Jim trying to convince him to buy 'Being boiled', the new single by the Human League.
"Good choice," Julie squealed, pinching his bum as she popped up from behind. "Bloody Nora," he jumped. "Where the hell did you come from?"
"I come from another dimension .." she half-sang, curling her arms around her head like a Balinese Gamelan dancer. "Wooohooo .." Hippy Jim chuckled and gave her a Winston Churchill 'V'. He loved Julie. Especially after she'd once let him go all the way when he'd been stock-taking in the back of the shop. "I'm teaching him 'the way', Jules," he said, head bobbing. "Pointing him in the right direction, you know?" Julie plucked the single from Joe's hand and pressed it hard to her ear. "God, it sounds brilliant," she said, her panda eyes opening wide. "Buy it, Joe. Buy it." He bought it. "Wanna go see 'em?" she said, halfway back to the office. "Only, they're on at Sheffield Uni next Thursday and I can give you a lift, if you like."

-

His first ever gig and he was hooked. Deafened, but definitely hooked. What a kick. What a thrill. To see a band playing music *right in front of you!* Amazing! Jostling about in the amiable crowd - it had come as a shock that there were no seats in the venue - Joe yelled into Julie's ear as they waited for an encore. "They're not so bad, these punks, are they?"
"*These* aren't punks," she laughed. "Ha ha ha! They'd hate you for saying that." The pulsing first bars of 'The black hit of space' cut off any further conversation.

The sweat had cooled by the time they got back to Julie's car, and his ears whistled all the way home. A blessing in disguise. She never stopped talking once as she drove back across the Pennines, and Joe heard barely a word.

She made a lunge for him as she dropped him near his flat, her lip-linered pucker just grazing Joe's right ear as he jerked out of reach. He knew it! Just knew it. He knew she'd make a move on him and he'd been trying to make himself fancy her all evening. It hadn't worked. "Cheers, Julie. See ya .." he yelled, slamming the car door behind him. He might have been desperate for a girlfriend but he didn't want to go out with anybody *that* old!

He signed up for the music 'papers - NME, Melody Maker and Sounds - and scoured their gig listings religiously. Quickly learning that punks weren't half as scary as he'd imagined, he was soon a regular at many of the north-west's dives and dingy shit-holes, their midnight starts fitting in nicely with his late evening work-diary. It was hard to look like a punk, though, when you worked for a weekly news-paper, especially with a Dad like Dad! "Shirt and tie, Joe. Shirt and tie." So no pink mohican, no torn bondage trousers, no purple-painted fingernails for Joe. Dressing for work, the best he could hope for was a spit of chewing gum juice to subtly spike his hair, a favoured red and yellow-striped tie, a Devo badge on his left lapel and an 'Ere we go, 2-3-4' Jilted John badge on the other. He really envied punks their 'anything goes' stylishness. One of his first 'solo' gigs was by a London band called UK Subs, who were playing at the Russell Club in Manchester. He'd not had time to change after work and had gone straight to the gig in his 'uniform' of jacket, shirt and tie. The first punk to catch sight of him screamed "Fuckin' 'ell, a Mod!" and Joe almost shat himself. He whipped off his tie and sped to the loo to 'rough himself up' a bit. He wasn't the only one that got roughed up that night. A riot ended the gig. A punk, standing right in front of him - his spiked hair half-blocking Joe's view of the band - drained the dregs of his beer and smashed the bottle straight over the head of the guy next to him. The victim dropped to the ground and *his* mate rammed his pint glass straight into the first punk's face. Joe had no idea what happened next. He was too busy cowering under a pool table, pint pots criss-crossing the club in arcs of bitter and lager as the whole place went bananas. The band dived off stage, the main lights came on and everyone scarpered as five coppers dashed in through the front door. Joe found it absolutely thrilling. Far less scary than a kiss from Julie!

-

He started taking a camera to gigs. Long before barriers separated bands and their fans, Joe's old Nikon would get him right to the front of any stage in town. Made him feel really important. One time, he was hit in the face by a singer's whipping microphone lead, and a quote from war photographer Robert Capa ("If your pictures aren't good enough, you aren't close enough") came pretentiously to mind as he rubbed at the sting. Something wasn't right, though. Joe would come away from a gig, confident he'd got a good shot or two, but totally at a loss as to what the gig had been like. He was concentrating too much on taking pictures and completely missing the music. So he stopped taking his camera to gigs. Didn't really matter. The 'paper didn't show one iota of interest in his music photography, and never used a single shot he ever took.

Page 38

Joe allowed himself a lie-in and a lazy breakfast before tackling a pile of ironing that had grown way too high. He'd been to see The Gang of Four the previous evening, and a new Split Enz album was on his turntable. It was the first of the Easter Bank Holidays and he was feeling really happy. It was Good Friday, and he felt really uncomfortable. Good

Friday was one of the most important 'Holy Days of Obligation' in the Catholic church and, growing up, Joe had always attended the important three pm service. Today he intended to miss it.

There was a hammering at the front door.
"What are *you* doing here?" said Joe.
It was Andy, red in the face with exertion. "Er, excuse me, what are you doing *here*?" he shrieked, hands in the air.
"I live here," laughed Joe.
"Yes, but you're supposed to be at work!" Andy bellowed. "And if you'd got a bloody phone we could have called you. The boss has made me drive all the way over to get you."
"But it's a Bank Holiday." Joe's forehead folded into a crease. "Everyone's off on a .."
"Mate, you're a press photographer. Press photographers are *never* off on a Bank Holiday."

At least he had an excuse for missing church.

-

It turned out to be a really busy day. Spring fayres, flower festivals, hot-cross-buns in the town square. Joe finished late, tired after a day spent catching up on jobs he'd missed earlier. Unable to shake off tradition, he'd made a surreptitious sign of the cross at three o'clock - having made sure no-one was watching - and 'gave thanks' to Jesus for dying on the cross. Yawning as he neared the flat, he turned off the main road and braked sharply, almost hitting a car that was parked in 'his' space. It wasn't 'his' space of course, but the closest to the flat of three 'off-road' parking spots and the one that Joe parked in most of the time. "Fucking Wyatt Earp," he snapped, before reversing and parking further down the road. Deciding against a can of Guinness - it *was* still Lent, after all - he put the kettle on to boil and, looking down from the flat, swore again at the car. He could see the house of the man who owned it, too. Fucking Wyatt Earp! The twat parked there on purpose, he was sure of it. God knows what his real name was, but Joe and his Dad had given him the wild-west moniker after they'd once spotted him running stark-bollock naked down the road, nothing on but a stetson and a pair of cowboy boots. (He'd come home pissed from a fancy-dress party .. apparently!) God, they'd laughed that night.

The kettle boiled and Joe made himself a coffee. He'd just sat down when there was a horrendous squeal from the street, and he jumped up just in time to see his Dad and Earp, rolling around on the grass in front of the parking area. The street lights lit them up like Madison Square Garden. "What the hell?" Joe pelted down the stairs and dashed across to the wrestlers.

"Nnnggrrrooowwmmmgggyyyhhh .. " groaned his Dad. "Aaaghghghtttttthhrrrooooiii .." growled Wyatt Earp.

The pair were pissed as farts. Their 'fight' consisted of gripping tightly onto each other's coats and rolling backwards and forwards like a couple of amorous Weebles. Joe burst out laughing. "Give it up, you two," he said, slapping them both on the back. "Pack it in, you piss heads." With a cheering crowd of at least eight other neighbours, the two finally ran out of steam and got to their feet, panting heavily.

"Bed!" said Joe, sending his Dad off like a naughty child.
"Bed!" said Earp's missus, laughing as hard as Joe.

"So, what was that all about?" said Joe, next morning. "Think you're Mick McManus, do you?" His Dad scratched his head and looked away, abashed. "I think I was bouncing on his car bonnet," he muttered.
"You .. *what*? Oh, Dad. Why?"

"He was in your parking space, wasn't he?" said Dad, shrugging his shoulders. "I'm sick of him taking your space." Joe shook his head and walked into the front room. "It's not 'my' space, though, is it?" he said. "Although, thanks for fighting for it, you daft sod. But, on Good Friday? You shouldn't be fighting on a Good Friday, should you? And drunk, too? Some Good Friday that turned out to be."

"Aye, it did," Dad beamed. "A bloody good Friday, that was."

The day I went for Wyatt ..

I'd been wanting at the bastard for a long time, and I don't know why. I mean, I don't hate him or anything. What's he ever done to *me*? Sounds stupid then, doesn't it? Why would I want to hurt, er .. what's his name? (God, my memory!) Ah, Wyatt Earp! That's it. (At least that's what we call him now.) Ach, I don't know. I've just not taken to him, that's all. I see him swanning around the Irish Club like he owns the place, and he's forever trying to park in Joe's space, but that's no reason to want to belt the fella, is it? Not very Catholic of me, not at all.

I think that last Good Friday was .. ach, I don't want to say. Oh alright, I'll tell you. I think I was frustrated. I think smacking Earp the Twerp gave an outlet to a frustration I've been feeling for a long time. Years, probably. Just building up and building up. Years and years of holding back, being nice, saying yes, getting walked on, working and working and getting nowhere .. you know what I mean?

I'm just so fucking fed up. Sorry to complain, it's just that .. it feels like life's just going on and on and round and round and I never seem to be getting anywhere with it. I haven't even had a win at the bookie's for over a year!

So this it, is it? This is how my life's going to be for .. for ever? Day after day of the same old thing, over and over and over? Jeez, I might as well just do myself in, right now. Sorry, stupid thing to say. I didn't mean it. Ignore that last bit, please. The 'S' word? God, I've never said anything like that in my life. And it would be a one-way ticket to hell, doing that. I haven't the balls to do it, anyway. Fucking hell, why am I talking like this? What's got into me? Look, forget everything I've just said, alright? Fuck me, have a drink, fella. Focus on the good things in life. Put on the happy face and get back out there.

Father Sheehan says I should count my blessings. So yes, that's what I'll do. I'll count my blessings. Well, there's Joe of course, always first on the list these days. And my daughters, though it seems they've turned their backs on me good and proper. And then there's ..

Leave it with me, will you? I'm sure I'll think of something else ..

Page 39

Clipping a new bleeper to his belt, Joe felt on top of the world. The size of a packet of fags, it made him feel really important as he paraded it around the office. He couldn't wait to show it off to a girl. Any girl. "I get to know about all sorts of emergencies now," he rehearsed. "As soon as this baby goes off, all I have to do is find a phone-box, call a central registration number, confirm who I am with a special code to an operator, wait until they play me the recorded message that someone has left and then call that person back. It's amazing." Truth be told, once the system was up and running, the only messages he received were along the lines of 'there's a horse in the canal' or 'can you get some Toffee Crisp on the way back to the office', but the thrill of the bleeper going off in a crowded place was worth all the crap it might engender. That all changed one day in May. It went off as Joe was taking pictures of a golden wedding couple.

"Fuck me, Joe .." It was Andy, screaming manically as he impatiently recorded his message. "It's Woolie's! It's going up in flames. I've just heard it on Piccadilly Radio. Get back here as fast as you can and we'll go in my car."

The huge Woolworth's store was ablaze in the middle of Manchester city centre.

Joe drove like hell to the office, Andy already revving the car. He threw his camera bag in the back and almost fell from the door as the car sped off. "Chuffin' 'ell," he shouted, excitedly. "At least *wait* for me."
"Oh, this is going to be a big one," said Andy. "The radio says it's going up like a good 'un." Joe's heart pounded. A big city centre fire? How fantastic. Much better than the three he'd photographed so far. A chip pan fire, a sabotaged bonfire - set off by a rival gang three days before November

5th - and a mechanic's workshop full of welding gases. (Actually, that one *was* a bit scary.) Getting closer, they couldn't miss the thick and angry smoke, darkening the skies above the city and drawing them in to the excitement. "Good God!" they gasped, flashing press cards at the police cordon. The store was an inferno. Flames were roaring from the shop's top-storey windows, and the noise was scarily intense. Sirens, shouting, cries, bangs, the splatter of water. The pair split up and Joe ran towards a huge Simon Snorkel fire-appliance, battering a jet of water against the building's Portland stone walls. He recognised its operator from the day he'd been given a 'joy-ride' in the machine and gave a cheery wave. God, this was thrilling. He snaked through the chaos and shot the anguished expression of another fireman, the tight marks of his breathing apparatus smoke-moulded into his face. Joe's heart thumped. He was close-up now, all Don McCullin wide-angle, right at the heart of the action. His trousers were soaked from the hoses and his nose was running with the smoke. It felt fantastic. He pulled back, got some shots of the entire building again, then went in close for more pictures of the rage and pandemonium.

On the other side of the building, ten people were dying.

-

Artistically satisfied, Joe hoofed it up nearby Oldham Road to the office of one of the daily newspapers where, as first photographer back, he was almost physically grabbed and dragged up the stairs to the darkroom. The wait for his film to be developed was excruciating, and then ..

"What the fuck is this?"

"What the fucking fuck is this?" said the picture editor, scanning desperately through Joe's negatives. "Some fucking art-school project or what? Where's the action? Where's the fucking *action?* They're saying people are dying in there and you're taking fucking landscapes?"

Joe had never felt so small in his life.

-

And then came the shame. Coverage in the following day's newspapers knocked him for six, their gut-wrenching photographs filling front and inside pages. Grainy black and white images showed desperate arms stretching desperately through grim, barred windows that trapped, and ultimately caused the deaths of, the ten victims of the worst fire in the city since the war. Subject matter notwithstanding, it was incredible press photography. Necessary, unflinching, objective. No landscapes here, not an artistic portrait in sight. Truthful. Sickening. Sad. Future changes brought in - including the removal of the murderous metal window grills - owed much to the clear and honest work done by the professional photographers at the scene that day.

Ten. RIP. How bloody awful. And Joe had treated it as a jolly. A bit of excitement. A chance to be in with the big boys. The big boys blew him away. He would never be flippant about press photography again. It was a painful lesson, as all the best are. Ten people dead, and he didn't get their pictures.

Damn!

He flicked between sadness, self-flagellation and .. envy.

Stop it, Joe. Stop it.

Ten people dead. God, the embarrassment. *You idiot,* he cried. How did the other photographers know there were people dying whilst I shot pretty close-ups and arty scene-setters? The truth cut him to the quick. He was still a boy. A boy in a grown man's world. At least he'd been taught another lesson. The work of a press photographer was a serious business, with a duty to accurately describe the outside world to an intelligent, curious and concerned public. He took it all on board and grew a little, vowing that - from thereon in - everything he photographed - from a children's painting competition to the inauguration of a new Chief Constable to, yes, a scene of major disaster - would be treated with the reverence and respect it deserved.

He got such a high from his new-found self-importance. "Shit, Joe," he grumbled. "You are so shallow."

Page 40

He could talk to anybody now. Could stand in front of any number of people and do his job. But he knew it was all an act. Like Clarke Kent peeling off his Superman suit, Joe was only too aware that, without *his* 'costume', without his 'photographer' *outfit*, he was still just shy old Joe. Still the guy who couldn't say 'boo' to a goose, the lad whose upbringing had taught him where his boundaries lay and advised him to stay behind them. Thank God for cameras, for the comfort they afforded behind that silvery, metal mask. But take away the disguise and Joe's confidence disappeared as quickly as the pop of a flashgun. It pissed him off completely, and meant he got absolutely nowhere at the new disco - the Blue Rooms - just around the corner from the newspaper office.

It was the ideal place for Joe, who could work until midnight and know he still had a full two hours to get in there and pick up a nice piece of stuff. (It was bound to happen, one day, for sure. His chat-up line was all ready to go. 'Yeah, I'm a press-photographer. Wanna see my zoom?') Until then, Joe had to endure a routine that began on his very first visit to the night-club. Buy pint/ogle at girls/go home. (A simple, energy-saving approach, although rather a waste of Germolene ointment, which he'd slather generously over his spots on the morning of any 'disco' day.)

The Blue Rooms played great music though, and that was good enough for Joe. No UK Subs, of course. Just disco, through and through. Disco, disco, disco, all night long. It made Joe smile to think that, if he *had* looked like a punk, the bouncers on the door wouldn't have let him anywhere near the joint. Here, it was all Chic, GQ, Bee-Gees, Michael Jackson. Music that grabbed him just as urgently as punk but .. differently. If punk was power, then disco was rhythm. It was impossible to stand still when records like those hit the deck at the Blue Rooms and so eventually - despite everything - Joe would find the balls he needed to squeeze onto the darkest corner of the dance floor and strut his stuff, safely hidden behind a flock of mock plastic parrots and a grove of balsa wood palm-trees. He loved the fact that he had a foot in both styles of music. He didn't dismiss punk because it wasn't disco, and he didn't ignore disco because it wasn't punk. To Joe, music was music and if he liked it, he liked it, and that was that. It began to rub when he experienced hostility from punks who were dismissive of other types of music. Bollocks, he thought, to their closed-minded categorisations and, to underline the sentiment, he made Hippy Jim squirm when he ordered Dana's new single 'Something's cooking in the kitchen'. (Thought it was really good, actually.)

-

He was assigned to a job with a new reporter. Guy Nuttall replaced shy young Helen, who got the boot for bursting into tears whenever the Editor sent her out on interview. Guy was her polar opposite. Self-assured, eager, enthused, he was the spitting image of Gary Numan and, bloody hell, even had the same initials! Struck by his encouraging demeanour - watching him effortlessly prise an eye-witness account from the reticent victim of a post-office robbery - Joe immediately decided this guy Guy was going to be his mate, and invited him to the Blue Rooms the next evening. If anyone could help him pick up girls, Guy could. They arrived at eleven pm, pretty early for Joe. They'd already had a couple at the Swan and Duck and Joe was buzzing. Guy was great company and Joe felt good vibes in his bones. Look out girls, we're coming. He couldn't walk into the Blue Rooms with his camera, but he *could* walk in behind Guy Nuttall. Two drinks in and Joe had already seen at least 560 girls that he fancied. He whittled it down to three as all the others lit up cigarettes. (He really did hate smoking. His eyes had already started stinging in the thick fug of fag smog and he knew that, even this early on, the foul stench would be sinking into the very fibres of his clothes and skin and hair. Indeed, the ever-present pong of roll-ups was the one bad thing about living with his Dad.) Still, three chicks was plenty. Guy could have any of the other 557.

Six drinks in, they both went off to the toilet. "Well, what do you think?" said Joe, angling his head to avoid a view of Guy's snaky penis.
"About the disco? You were right. It's bloody great. Absolutely *full* of talent. See that one in the black one-piece? I think she's got her eye on you."
"Naaaa .." said Joe, pulling up his zip. "Her mate's a lot fitter. That red-head in the big, ruffly blouse? She looks lovely."
"Oh well, you can have her," said Guy, magnanimously. "I'll stick with the one in black."

"Fair do's. So, you gonna make a move, then? It's half one already." Guy's Adam's Apple bobbed alarmingly. They came out of the toilets to a rolling cloud of dry ice, the crowded dance floor disappearing beyond the mist. It was like a smoke screen before the Somme offensive. "Go to it, my man," Joe yelled, coughing as the ice mixed with eye-watering cigarette smoke. He slapped Guy on the back and tried to push him forwards. "Come on fella," he bellowed. "They're bloody gorgeous. Get them chatted up and I'll buy us all a drink." Guy's shiny tonsure flickered red, green and orange under the pulsing disco lights. "Go on Guy," Joe pressed, slightly perturbed. "Pour some of that reporter's charm over them. They won't stand a chance." His new friend's reticence, and the sweat that glistened on his brow, told Joe all he needed to know. Without his notebook, Guy was just Guy. Guy was just like Joe. Joe was back to square one.

-

They bumped into each other a few weeks later. Guy was in the kitchen, adding milk to a cup of tea. They hadn't seen much of each other recently, what with one thing and another. "Alright, Guy?" Joe asked, switching on the kettle. There was no answer. "You ok?" When he looked properly at Guy he dropped his spoon. "Cripes," he gasped. "You look awful. What the hell's happened?"
"Oh, you don't want to know," said Guy.
"Well, I do," Joe chuckled. "Otherwise I wouldn't have asked, would I? What's up?"
Guy sniffed and took a swig of his tea. "Remember that night you took me to the Blue Rooms?"
"Yeah, 'course I do. Just after you'd started at the 'paper." (That night you chickened out, Joe thought to himself.)
"Remember that bird in the black one-piece, the one I thought was after you?"

"Erm .. vaguely. Why, what about her?"
"Well, I went back to the disco again the next week and she was there again, so I bit the bullet and went over to say hello."
"Aye aye, you sneaky bugger. Flying solo, eh?" Guy shrugged apologetically.
"So how'd you get on?" Joe prodded, pouring water into his cup. He grinned, leerily. "Did you - you know? - get anything out of it?"
"I most certainly did," said Guy. "I got the clap."
"The .. *eh?*"
"Yeah, she gave me VD."
"Holy shit," giggled Joe, before it dawned on him that now was not a good time to be laughing. "Sorry about that," he added, and he looked back at the kettle and made a mental note to wash his hands the instant Guy left the room. "So I guess you're having treatment?"
"I sure am," said Guy. "I have to go to the clap clinic once a week and have a bloody big needle shoved up me wanger."
Joe winced and sucked the air. "Yowch," he grimaced. "I can't imagine anything worse than that."
"Oh, *I* can," said Guy. "Stay tuned, my friend. Turns out darling Monika was a German au-pair, and she'd just got the sack for taking lads back to the house she worked at. She asked if she could shack up with me and moved all her stuff into my bedsit next day."
"The *next* day? Bloody hell, I see what what you mean," gasped Joe. "Who'd want *that* after a one-night-stand?"
"I haven't got to the worst bit," said Guy, glumly. "Second time I went to the clinic, she did a bit of washing and put some clothes over my electric heater to dry. Silly cow fell asleep and burnt the fucking flat down!"
"Whaaat?" Joe blurted. "You're kidding me?"
"Does this look like the face of a kidder?" said Guy, pointing at his pouty mush.
"Cripes .. I don't .. I .." It was no good. Joe burst out laughing, laughed so long that even Guy started to smile.

"All my records melted," he grinned. "Wanna buy a black plastic fruit bowl?"

The days I hanker for youth ..

I hear him coming home sometimes. Only sometimes, mind. (Obviously, I'm normally well gone by three in the morning.) But yes, that's when he comes in after a night at his discotheque or his .. you know .. punk-rockster concerts or whatever they're called. Sneaks in, shuts his door then straight back out for a piss. Bladder the size of a Smartie, that lad.

I often wish I could have been like that as a teenager, though I know I'm talking shite. Out at clubs doing who knows what and to who? Whom? Dream on. There's no way we had social lives like that when *I* was eighteen. And I wouldn't have known what to do if we *did*, thank God. So I'm not jealous, no. Don't envy him at all. If you ask me it all seems far too much like hard work these days. All that faffing about in dark clubs, getting yerself scundered over girls and the like. And Lord, the money he must be spending. In my day we had the dance at the IOGT hall and that was that. (International Order of Good Templars, since you ask, although we called it 'I Owe Granny Tuppence' for some long-forgotten reason!) A wee Ceilidh, once every so often, thrupence on the door, a ginger beer or two to wash down the meat paste sambos and a chance to gaze at the gals in their best plaid. Smashing! Home by ten, of course. None of this late-night tom-foolery like me laddo here. For me it was back home and father waiting by the back door with his spade ready if you were a minute after the clock-strike. Great memories!

Ha, ha, ha .. look at youse! You don't believe all that blathering, do you? *Great memories?* Catch yerself on, ya spoon! Those times were awful. No beer, no necking, no rock and roll and absolutely no 'how's yer father' until you had the ring on your finger and your name in the register of marriage. The deadline was still there, mind. I had many a lathering from me old Pa when I got in late until, well .. until I grabbed the shovel from him one night and whacked him right back. I was strong for seventeen, I was.

So I'll admit it, he lives in a different world and lucky old Joe, that's what I say. Jeez, he must be inundated with girls. Not that I've ever seen one round the flat, come to think of it. Oh, to be eighteen again. The world, oysters, all of that. Grab it, Joe, that's my advice. Grab it by the scruff of the neck and have a ball. Just be careful where you put it, that's all.

Page 41

"Hello Phil. Fancy seeing you here." The curly mop of orange hair was unmistakeable as it emerged from underneath the dark cloth of a large, square plate camera.
"Hey Joe, good to see you," said his old night-school tutor, grinning widely. "Still taking pictures, I see."
"As are you," said Joe, pointlessly pointing at Phil's impressive Cambo 5x4 set up. "Nice bit of kit you've got there."

"Right gear for the job," said Phil, his barnet bouncing excitedly as Joe shook his hand. "You know I've always said that."
"Oh, I've remembered a lot of things from that course," said Joe, suddenly embarrassed about the book he'd nicked. "So, what's new ..?"

They were at the corner of a huge expanse of open ground in the middle of town. An old hospital had been demolished and the space had been cleared for the construction of a new office block. Joe had just photographed the company chairman 'breaking ground' to signal the start of the work.
"I'm shooting for the architects," said Phil. "Compiling a series of images to show the building work in all its stages."
"The history of an erection, eh?" laughed Joe, throwing in a few descriptive hand movements to help the pun along. The joke went right over Phil's head, even over the massive ginger afro. He'd always been a bit serious, Phil had. A bit quiet. Completely the wrong person to have been a night-school teacher, having only just graduated but looking for a bit of extra cash until he could get his photography business up and running. Still, he'd brought Janine to the class and Joe would always thank him for that. They stood awkwardly for a moment before Joe sniffed loudly. "Oh well, better be off. Got a dog-show to photograph at half-past." Phil proffered his limp palm and they parted with a smile and a redundant 'keep in touch'. Joe burst out laughing as he got back to his car. He'd just remembered that night at Phil's party. What a bloody disaster!

-

"I am definitely going to get shagged tonight." Joe was convinced of it, telling himself with certitude as he waited for the bus to take him across Manchester. It was inevitable at a party, wasn't it? Sex? "As long as I don't have to take drugs," he fretted. "There's no way I'm taking LSD."

To mark the end of his tenure as a night-school teacher - all twelve weeks of it - Phil had decided to throw a party. Not a meal, not a drink in a pub, but a full-blown, university graduates' house party. Joe had never been to a house-party before, graduates or not. How grown up. How exciting. How *scary*. He'd freaked out the minute Phil had said he'd be welcome. "Come on over," he'd said. "Bring a friend. We'll be having nibbles." The invitation had come out of the blue and, to Joe's delight, Phil had told him he was the only one from their class to be asked. He spent an age trying to sort his appearance, eventually deciding on yellow cheese-cloth shirt and perfectly-ironed brown Wrangler bell-bottoms - an Army crease straight down the front - a combo positively guaranteed to pull the birds. On board the 67, he found himself daydreaming about how many people, right now, all over the world, were having sex. *Right now!* Lucky buggers. Still, I'll be one of them by the end of tonight, he thought, catching his smile in the rain-streaked window. He got off the bus and paused in front of the Hare and Hounds, daring himself to buy a packet of condoms from the vending machine in the loo. He'd never bought Durex before and felt the eye of The Almighty looking down upon him. Contraception? Oh, this meant hell and no mistake. "Sorry God," he said, pushing open the door, and he took it as a cautionary sign from above when one of his ten pence pieces got stuck in the machine. A lad in a dirty Kenny Rogers t-shirt thumped it to get him a freebie, and gave Joe a wink on the way out.

He was bored to death at the party. He'd gone alone, of course, despite the 'plus-one' invitation, and was instantly cornered in the kitchen by a tiresomely effete maths graduate called Toby. The 'nibbles' meant bowls of weirdo foreign crap, tararasemolina and humorous or something, when Joe could have murdered a meat and potato pie. The toilet was filthy and, when he'd gone in for a pee, he'd had to use the last piece of loo roll to dry the seat for fear someone would think he had been the dribbler. Worst of all, there wasn't a single spare girl in sight. Not one! What a waste of bloody time. Joe escaped from Toby and spent the rest of the night yawning in the hallway as sophisticated twenty-three year olds danced or snogged or talked about the abolition of the monarchy as they drank flat white wine and blew smelly blue smoke out of their mouths. The condoms went in the bin and Joe would hate Barclay James Harvest for the rest of his life.

The day we partied ..

I couldn't believe he'd remembered, and all the more so because I'd forgotten it myself. My birthday, of course. I came home from work to find two wrapped presents and a greetings card waiting for me on the dining table. Surprise, surprise, he shouted, jumping from behind the door. I ripped away the shiny (Christmas!) paper and there was a lovely big bottle of Johnnie Walker and forty Silk Cut. (I'd already guessed the whiskey, so I had.) That boy certainly knows the way to my heart!

Happy Birthday, you old fart, said the card. From Joe.

The picture on the front showed a man, fishing with a long, bent rod from the deck of a sea-going yacht. Hm, perhaps he doesn't know me *that* well yet, after all. I thanked him by opening up the bottle and pouring us both a nice big swig of booze. Cheers son, I said, clinking his glass. Cheers Dad, he said, putting far too much lemonade in his drink. Happy ninetieth! Ha ha ha ..

It was the start of a wee party that lasted the rest of that entire evening. Well, until the bottle was two-thirds gone and so was Joe, fast asleep with his head squashed against my box of tea bags.

I can't believe you remembered, I said. You've made my day.

I've remembered every year since you left home, he said. There was just never anything I could do about it.

Page 42

A dog pees up a vandalised horse-chestnut, the shattered remnants of the last tree in the cul-de-sac. A gull rips at a Kentucky Fried Chicken box. Slanting rain stipples a puddle. Dog ..

"Shit!" Joe threw down his pen and angrily munched a Crunchie. Keen to get 'Page 99' off to the best possible start, he'd enrolled on a 'Creative Writing' course and was trying hard to do his homework. The class of seven had been advised by teacher Kate - a scrawny, pallid wisp in purple scarf and patchouli oil - to "get something down on paper" everyday, even if it was just a description of 'the view from one's window'. "Virginia Woolf would 'practice' writing by doing just that," she'd said. Well that's all well and good, thought Joe, but Virginia Woolf's view consisted of ponds and elms and cows and smirching shadows, whereas he was staring at a dog peeing up a vandalised tree and a seagull and an .. etc., etc., etc ..

"What if?" Kate had said. "Think 'what if'. And 'what next?'" What's smirching? was all Joe could think, and it wouldn't have helped in this context even if he'd looked it up. "What if? What if? What if? Aha! What if I'd never had meningitis?" Now he was on to something. He stopped tapping his biro and pressed it to his pad.

```
It was my fault our 5-a-side football team
lost a cup final - he wrote - and I've never
got over the guilt. One morning, when I was
ten, I began to suffer a blinding headache.
By four that afternoon I was lying in my
darkened bedroom, the doctor explaining to
my Mum he'd tell her what it all was when it
was all over!! What 'it' was was viral
meningitis - how lucky to get the milder
form! - and I was off school for three
months, unable to eat, or experience bright
light .. or play football. It ruined my eye-
sight, and I had to start wearing glasses as
soon as I'd recovered. Everyone called me
Specky Four-Eyes and Joe 90 until I left the
junior school.
```

He stopped writing and leant back. Gosh, what memories. As part of a football team that had won the semi-final of an intra-school tournament, little primary school Joe had really been looking forward to playing in the final. The onset of meningitis meant participation was impossible and his team lost 5-1. He still had the losers' medal *and* the guilt that had caused him to 'win' it. It was the nearest he would ever come to being 'successful' at sport. Joe stuck the end of the pen in his mouth. Hmm, what next? he thought. "Beer," he said out loud. "This shite's giving me a headache."

-

Football? You were either a blue or a red on Joe's estate. City or United, simple as that. To declare their allegiances, all the boys ran around wearing the long woolly scarves their Mums had knitted them. Knit one, pearl one, red white, blue white, red, white, blue. And if you didn't like football you were a mong! Joe supported Manchester United, for no other reason than his next-door neighbours were all blues. Then, someone at school told him about United's famous manager and he instantly started describing himself as a 'Busby babe', even though he considered himself very grown up at seven. His parents wouldn't let him stay up to watch his team's historic victory over Benfica in the '68 European Cup Final but, next morning, having been told of the score, Joe ran up and down the street yelling "Champions, Champions," at the top of his voice. The fact that City then went on to win both the FA Cup and European Cup Winners Cup in the following season soon brought him back to earth. The 'enemy's' successes were reason enough for him to start despising true-blue neighbours Stuart and Gary Holmes, what with their gloating and their cheering and their constant jibes at Joe, but it was hard to fall out with the two friends you spent most of your time with.

"At least we've got Georgie Best," Joe would crow. "And Bobby Charlton. *And* Denis Law."
"Yeah, but we've got Colin Bell," they'd counter. "And Mike Summerbee. *And* Franny Lee."
No-one would ever know what sparked it but, one afternoon, their normally friendly sniping turned into something a little bit worse. Perhaps it was the fact that Gary had held on a little too long to Joe's 'Park Drive book of Football' - the irony of a cigarette manufacturer promoting sport not then an anachronism. Or perhaps it was that, according to

Stuart, Brian Kidd played "like a kid" and "Nobby Stiles, he's got piles" .. whatever *they* were. Joe snapped. He leapt onto Stuart's back and began to thump at his soft, plumpy shoulders. Stuart was ten to Joe's nine, and a good two inches taller to boot, but Joe was having none of it. Nobody says "Tony Dunne plays like his Mum" and gets away with it.
"Gerroff," snarled Stuart, arms around his head. "Pack it in, you divvy."
"Hit him, Stu," shouted his brother. "Kick 'im in the scridgies!"
"The *what*?" said Joe, turning to look back at Gary. The slap he received made his right ear ring for an hour. "That's not fair," grumbled Joe, rubbing the throb. "I wasn't looking."

"Ha ha ha .. " Hard to carry on a scrap when you can't stop laughing.
The lads shook hands and went to play Cowboys and Indians in Blackie Woods, a patch of scrubby, stunted trees - the *only* patch of woodland within half a mile of the estate - where Joe was once convinced he'd seen a squirrel.

Page 43

He was driving home one warm spring evening when a mouse dashed out from the verge at the side of the road. It was squished instantly under the wheels of the truck in front. Half squished, Joe supposed, as only the head and front legs were flattened whilst the rest of the mouse, its tail still high in the air, was frozen in mid-stride as if it didn't know the front was dead. It had all been so fast. Here one second, gone the next. It depressed Joe immediately and he sat in gloomy contemplation of his own eventual death for the rest of the evening.

Life, eh? What the hell was it all about?

He sipped a Jack Daniels, its rich tones taking on an even more luxuriant glow in the lurid incandescence of a red lightbulb that perpetually illuminated his Dad's gaudy, gold-framed 'Sacred Heart of Jesus'. (The colour was a replica of the safelight in the 'paper's darkroom and the exact same hue as the blood splats from the poor little mouse.) Ever the staunch Catholic, Dad would make the sign of the cross in front of the votive image and say little prayers for who-knows-who. He'd hung a crucifix over the table in the kitchen, too - just above his black wooden shillelagh - to aid him when he said 'Grace' and, just as when Joe was growing up, had a little font of Holy Water by the front door, from which he would bless himself every time he went out of the flat. For a laugh, Joe once filled it with whiskey. Just for a joke. Just to see if his Dad would notice any difference. Dad started blessing himself on the way in!

Dad was out now, at church, for yet another of the nightly 'Stations of the cross' services during Lent.

Jesus falls for the second time. Jesus is nailed to the cross.

Jesus! (Whoops!) Joe caught himself blaspheming and lowered his eyes, mentally apologising to The Lord Above. Bloody Catholicism! It totally screwed him up. He'd had it rammed down his throat from the very day he was born. Come to think of it, he wouldn't even have *been* born if his Mum hadn't converted, a stipulation his Dad had insisted upon before she could think of marrying him. He knew Dad had fallen for her hook, line and sinker, which was all well and good but, Holy Mary, Mother of God, the last thing on earth he could ever do was marry a bloody *Protestant*! They swapped rings once Mum had swapped sides and, as soon as Joe was old enough, it was Mass every Sunday and prayers every bedtime, his own set of Rosary beads at five, First Confession and First Holy Communion by the time he was six then Confirmation at eleven after years of service as an altar boy. How cute he'd been, all decked out in his cassock and his cotta, his curly hair tamed with Mum spit. He'd stand at the altar, hands joined in front, and take it all so, so seriously. He was horrified when he once dropped the spoon used by the priest to put holy wine into the chalice. Clink, clank, tinkle, it went, all the way down the three altar steps. Unfortunately, Joe then caught the eye of Pete O'Driscoll, his co-server that day, and the pair of them burst out laughing, right in the middle of the Consecration.

"He broke the bread and gave it to his disciples," said Fr. Sheehan, raising up the Host.

"Ha ha hee hee pfffff …""

"This is the cup of my Blood. Do this in memory of me."

"Tstst, tstst, tstst …"

God, the bollocking they'd got once they got back into the sacristy.

Another time, he'd been serving at evening Benediction and almost dozed off.
(It didn't help that the ceremony lasted an hour and didn't even start until eight pm.) Joe was kneeling, day-dreaming on the knee-creakingly cold, hard tiles just outside the altar gates, sending eye-watering incense smoke into the air as he metronomically swung the thurible. He was staring up at the cross, looking at the doleful face of Jesus and thinking of a conversation he'd had with a 'Proddy Dog' a day earlier. "Do you know why the symbol of the cross is so impor-

tant in your religion?" asked Darren Robb, flicking elastic bands. "It's 'cos your God is always so cross, that's why. It's to remind Catholics how angry they've made their God. Ha ha ha .."

Joe lost concentration as he tired and his hands twitched, convulsively. The thurible bashed hard against the floor on the downswing and the lid flipped open, sending burning incense zizzing half-way across to the Confessional Box. "Leave them, leave them," shouted Fr. Sheehan, shattering the calm as Joe chased after the smouldering embers. An old dear in the front pew opened her legs faster than at any time since VJ Day.

Funerals were the best, though. What other eight year old got to stand on the rim of a freshly dug grave, watching a shiny, brand-new coffin being lowered into the ground? And all he had to do was hold the bronze holy water container and try not to stare at all the boo-hoo weepy people. Easy peasy. Best of all, he got the morning off school and, by way of thanks, at least a couple of sixpences from the mourners. Brilliant! And the person in the box? Well, he never really thought about them, apart from wondering whether they were going 'up' or 'down'. Heaven or hell? he used to ponder. Heaven or hell .. or .. aagh .. purgatory? Just who the hell (so to speak) had come up with the idea of purgatory? It was, as far as he could comprehend, a kind of bizarre waiting room in the sky, full of the souls of people who had a) not lived their lives too badly to go to hell but b) not lived them well enough to go to heaven. In other words, he felt, practically *everybody* .. and Joe pictured a stretch of infinite plateau covered in white, haggis shaped blobs - souls - spattered with black blobs - sins - all waiting to be prayed for and have the stain of those sins washed away. He couldn't quite work out when the hoax began to dawn on him but now, years on, he was trying really hard - *really* hard - not to fall for all that holy, holy bunkum.

Unfortunately, he'd been so brainwashed by all his years of Catholicism that he really didn't dare *not* believe. It was far too scary to give up on God. What if He really *was* there? What if He (She?) was there right now and listening to all Joe's efforts to disown him? Holy shit! Ha, 'holy', snorted Joe. Stop it.

Good job Father Reville hadn't got his way. Joe would have been well on his way to becoming a priest by now! Reville had arrived, much to his chagrin, as Joe's new parish priest after the death of Father Sheehan. He was dropped into the murky grey of the north-west after a cushy little number in sunny Spain, where he was 'Director of Vocations' at The Royal English College, a seminary for trainee priests in Valladolid. Father Reville instantly changed every single thing his parishioners had grown accustomed to. He altered the times of the masses, he moved Confessions to a Friday evening and he insisted that many of the services' spoken responses would revert to being sung again. It meant churchgoers had to get up earlier on a Sunday, couldn't nip in for a swift absolution on the way to the pub of a Saturday lunchtime and had to allow at least an extra twenty minutes for the new priest's 'extended version' of Mass.

Young Joe took to him straight away. This new bloke was fresh, inspiring, enthused. Everything that Fr. Sheehan hadn't been. Even his sermons were interesting, delivered in a deep, Hampshire accent that somehow seemed to add gravitas to every word he uttered. At this stage, Joe still attended Mass on an infrequent basis, but started to up his visits once Fr. Reville got settled, even offering to walk the priest's Great Dane. He was far too old now to be an altar boy but, after a year or two of getting to know him, 'Rev. Rev' - as everyone had begun to call him - had bigger things in mind for Joe.

"The priesthood, Joe," he'd said to him after Mass one day. "You'd be a natural. Come round for a chat some evening." He laughed at Joe's expression for thirty seconds flat!

"Father Bancroft?" said Joe, walking home.
God, that sounded weird.

The days I pray he'll return ..

He's not one for the church any more, our Joe. Packed it in years ago, he did.

I still pray he'll return.

I mean, it's not as if I rammed Catholicism down his throat, did I? *Did* I? I know my wife always said I was a wee bit .. how did she put it? .. zealous .. but ..

I *did* want him to be a priest, though. Never told the wife that, by the way. Stuck with the 'accountancy' line but, if I'd have had my way, I'd have loved it if he'd gone on to study for the priesthood. I can still feel the lash of me Pa's tongue when he had at me for failing to get into the seminary but I swear that's not my reason for wanting Joe to try it. I was delighted when he became an altar boy, and thrilled when Fr. Sheehan took my hint about the extra-curricular religious classes, but it's just a shame it never went any further than that.

I just think it's important to practice the one true faith, that's all. Uphold the tenets of the Catechism and live like God would have you live. Is that too much to ask?

Ach, it breaks my heart that's he's turned his back on it all. And, you know, I'd have thought his mother would have insisted he keep on with his church attendance. I mean, there was a time when she was more Catholic than *I*, if you can imagine that. Aye, the time after she converted from, you know .. the other religion .. so that she and I could marry. I loved her so much for that. For her to undergo all that tuition, week after week, two years on the trot, and then that beautiful day of her baptism. Alright, I admit it, she did question my reasoning when I first broached the subject of conversion. I'm already a Christian, you know? she'd said. I'm sorry love, I told her, but Christian isn't Catholic and, until you take up my faith, you and I can never be married. My prayers were answered when she said she'd do it.

Why Joe's turned against it I cannot even begin to understand. I really must ask him, one day.

Page 44

"Come for dinner," Rev. Rev. said. "Seven?"
"Seven?" said Joe. "That's tea!"

He'd never heard of Chicken Kiev, but that's what the housekeeper served up when Joe popped to the presbytery for his 'chat' with the priest. "Garlic," said the priest, dabbing his lips with a serviette. "It's called garlic, Joe. Good for the heart as, indeed .." and he topped up Joe's red wine " .. is this." After the exotic meal, they settled in the lounge and John (Please call me John, Joe) poured them both a gin

and tonic. "So, have you thought any more about what I said?" he asked, lighting up a fag.
"You smoke?" Joe almost shouted, wafting at a swirly cloud. "Priests aren't allowed to smoke!"
John cackled, chestily. "Holy smoke eh, Joe? Ha ha ha .." He raised his glass and giggled as he jiggled its melting ice-cubes. "You'd be surprised what you're allowed to do as a priest."
"What, like, listen to Judas Priest, or Black Sabbath?" Joe teased. (Two of his cousin's favourite bands. He didn't know why he'd picked them. They just sounded appropriately satanic and naughty.)
"Led Zep too," said John, much to Joe's surprise. "Lizzy, Maiden, Rainbow. Whatever floats your boat." Joe looked at him, open mouthed. "No, *I* don't listen to them," said the priest, shaking his head. "I'm more of a Vaughan-Williams man myself but, if I wanted to, I could."
"Blimey, how do you even *know* about them?" blinked Joe. "They must be way out of your comfort zone."
"I have a parishioner .." smiled John, leaning conspiratorially forward. "He comes to Confession every week to tell me just what, exactly, he does whilst listening to records like those. Let's just say he must have a very strong right forearm!"
Joe laughed, and raised his glass in return. "Wow, you must hear some great stuff in Confessions," he grinned. "Go on, tell me something else."
"Ah well," said John, pouring himself a top up. "There *are* some things you *aren't* allowed to do as a priest." Shame, thought Joe. He'd love to have heard some of the more sordid details of his fellow parishioners. Mind you, he thought, if I *was* a priest I could hear them all for myself, couldn't I? He accepted a refill and gulped at it, greedily. He'd never had gin and tonic before.
"So?" said John, firing up another Rothmans. "Tell me your thoughts."

Joe took an extra long swig and tried to cross his legs. (They seemed to be disconnecting from his body.) "I just can't understand why you'd say I'm priest material," he said. "What on earth would make you think that?"

Jets of smoke fired from the priest's nostrils as he casually tipped his ash on the floor. "Well, you offered to walk my dog, didn't you?"

"And that's it?" laughed Joe. "If you can walk a dog you can be a priest?"

"Now, now," said John, wagging a finger. "No, listen to me. That was just a sign of an outward kindness. Of an interest in your fellow man. I know it sounds trivial, but I have enough experience to be able to spot certain qualities in a young man, and I see a lot of them in you. You're bright, enthusiastic, cheerful .."

Joe began to feel rather odd. Is he seeing the same guy? he wondered. He would never know if any of John's views were genuine, or whether he was simply trying to prop up the nose-diving numbers of wannabe priests, but he smiled anyway and said "That's nice to hear. But I'm also sad, lonely and introverted." (Bloody hell, that gin's strong.) "Not exactly upfront requirements for the priesthood, are they?"

And then, out of the blue, God spaketh unto Joe. It was his Damascene moment. "Gosh, I've had a thought," he exhaled. "You live on your own, don't you?" He got a nod from John. "And in a *free* house. And you have a cleaner and a cook, and you get a car, and you can play records as loudly as you like, whenever you like, and all you have to do is say Mass every day and pray for codgers in hospitals and tell people not to worry, 'cos God loves 'em and they're all bound for heaven. Actually yes, it sounds fantastic. Where do I sign?"

John jumped up and practically strangled him. "There is a *bit* more to it than *that* .." he growled, thumping out his fag-butt.

"Sorry, I was only joking. (Whoops!) Don't worry, I'll confess it all on Friday."

"You cheeky bastard." John sat back and burst out laughing. "Do you know? I'd have given you six hundred Hail Mary's if you'd come into the Confessional and repeated all that." He cracked open a single malt - a thank you gift from a recent baptism - and said "Here, have a drop of the good stuff."

Joe coughed heartily as he sipped the golden liquid. He'd never tasted a single malt before. "Oh, God .." he coughed. Hack, hack, hack ..

"And less of the blasphemy too," John snapped. "Please don't take the Lord's name in vain."

"God!" Joe sat up sharply, Glenfiddich splashing his knees. "I'd forgotten all about God's part in all of this. All that worship and love and what not. Do you know, John, I'm not sure I actually 'love' God. You know, like everyone says you should do? Is that bad? I mean, every hymn's about loving God, isn't it? All the prayers are about 'Glory be to God' and everything you do is supposed to be to show your love to God. It's a bloody big ask, isn't it, all this faith stuff?"

Father Reville lit yet another fag and leant over his lazy great dane to look into Joe's watering eyes. "Joe," he wheezed, smoke rolling from his mouth, "Even *I* have my doubts. I mean, who knows?"

"But you've devoted your life to God," Joe gasped. "How can *you* have doubts about your faith? Surely, a strong belief in God is a given for a priest. Anyway, God *must* like you, 'cos he's let you *be* one."

The childish remark made Rev. Rev laugh, a crackled, embarrassed guffaw, and he raised his glass to Joe and said "I'll drink to that. And God bless you for saying it. Anyway, I can't really go wrong, can I? If He's up there then I'm in, aren't I? It's heaven all the way for me. And if He's not then .. well, I've not had such a bad old life out of it, have I?"

Another tot of whiskey meant the good life carried on for a little while longer and Joe was happy with that. Perhaps he *should* become a priest, after all. His mind flipped back to

another evening, another time, some school play or something, where he'd ended up chatting to a young classmate with a lisp.
"Don't you jutht look up at the thtars and feel tho thmall?" she'd asked, apropos of abtholutely nothing.
"Oh, I don't know," said Joe. "When I see all that and know that God *still* made me then I feel absolutely incredible." Jesus, where had *that* come from? (God knows!) In the end, he decided against the priesthood. It was the Army that got Joe's first signature. At least he didn't go into accountancy.

Jesus!

Page 45

"Oh look, it's your wedding anniversary." Joe had stupidly pointed at the calendar one September day and his Dad had looked at him like thunder.
"You think I don't know that?"
"Sorry, Dad. It's just that I .."
"Don't worry," said Dad, waving away the subject. "It's just another day to me now, Joe."
"But it isn't 'just another day', is it?"
"'Course it is," Dad said, clumping down hard on the settee. "Get me a Bell's, will you? No ice."
Keen to make amends, Joe went for the drink and sat down opposite. "I'm sorry, Dad," he said. "I didn't mean to remind you."
"It wasn't a reminder," said Dad. "I can't be reminded because I've never forgotten." He downed the shot in one and Joe went to get him a re-fill. "Have one yerself," Dad shouted towards the kitchen. "You know I hate drinking on my own."

"Yeah, sure you do," laughed Joe. "Cheers."

-

"There'll only ever be your mother for me," Dad said.
Joe paused. Then, "*what?*" he yelped, screwing up his face. "You mean you've never been with another woman since your divorce?"
Dad sat bolt upright and Joe thought he was going to get a crack. "Mind your own business," Dad barked, and then he said "No, of course I haven't, you daft bastard. What a stupid question."
"Stupid?" said Joe. "Why is it stupid?"
"Because I'm still *married!*" said Dad, standing quickly. "I'm still married to your mother, aren't I?"
"Of *course* you aren't." Joe frowned and shook his head. "Your divorce came through in what .. '73? '74?"
"Doesn't mean a thing," said Dad, flicking a hand, dismissively. "I'm still married to your mother in the eyes of God, and that's that. Me and your Mum married for life, so as long as I'm still alive then I'm still married."
Joe was stunned. "I don't believe what I'm hearing," he gasped. "This is the bloody Catholic Church again, isn't it? The same church that hasn't allowed divorce for hundreds and hundred of years. The church that's caused .."
"Stop it Joe," Dad shouted, pointing sharply at him. "Just stop that right now. I know your views on the faith have changed - though God knows I pray you'll come back one day - but I won't have you saying bad things about our religion. I love Jesus and he loves me and the rules are the rules, so I stick to them and will do 'til I die."
"Good God," groaned Joe. "So, are you saying you've never had sex since 1971?" He tried really hard to hide a cheeky smile.
"How dare you," said Dad, taking a big gulp. "That'd be adultery if I did that."

"Oh, piss off," said Joe. "If that was the case your right hand would have fallen off from all the years of wanking."
"Aye well, I use my left hand, smart-arse," said Dad, and he threw a cushion so hard it knocked Joe's glass from his grasp.

The day I asked Joe a question ..

It was the most serious conversation we'd ever had, Joe and I. Our usual chats are light, fleeting, trivial, but this one made me feel exposed. I'd never told anyone before about .. you know, how I see my relationship with my wife. Still not sure how I feel now I've told him, to be honest. Of course, I couldn't expect Joe to see the *Catholic* side of things, could I? But still, it disappointed me that he felt the way he did. I'd have thought he'd have been happy to know I still felt .. what? .. attached? .. to his mother. But hey, kids today, what do I know?

One day, on a whim, I asked why Kevin had thrown him out.
"Because he's a twat," he replied.

It was the start and end of our second serious conversation.

'White Trails' was one of Joe's favourite records. Released by Chris Rainbow, a Scottish singer/songwriter with West Coast aspirations, the LP featured on its cover a painting made over a hundred years before. 'The Shepherd Boy', by Franz von Lenbach, portrayed a young lad, lying back on a sand-dune on a hot summer's day, shading his eyes as he looked up at a cornflower-blue sky. Across that cloudless expanse a modern-day graphic artist had painted the sharp white contrail of a jet plane, passing overhead on its way to who knew where. It's how Joe spent half his life. (Not the sand-dune part, the watching aircraft bit.) From as far back as he could remember he'd been an aviation nut, and would raise his eyes in wonder every time he noticed the streaking white slash of a high-flying airliner. Where was it going? Where had it been? What kind of jet was it, and from which airline? How long had it been airborne, and will I *ever* get a chance to go on one? (Nowadays, he'd think more along the lines of 'would I be ready with my camera if it dropped out of the sky?' .. but that's a press photographer for you!)

From the age of fourteen - as often as pocket money would allow - Joe would spend his afternoons 'plane-spotting' at Manchester Airport. The 500 bus would whisk him to a world of awe, and he'd while away his hours on Ringway's elevated walkways with a camera and a little bottle of pop. (Long before terror threats and 'health and safety', the public were allowed to walk along the roofs of the departure lounges, looking down at workaday 737s and BAC 1-11s, and across to huge Jumbos and VC-10s.) Joe would click away and wave at sombrero-wearing holiday-makers arriving back from Majorca, and give enthusiastic 'thumbs-up' to nervous, soggy Mancs, clutching their duty-free in the rain as they queued for 727s. Not quite an anorak (like a lot of the people around him), he was never interested in jotting down the flight times of aeroplanes, or noting their registration numbers or aircraft variants. All he wanted was to breathe deep of the pungent kerosene fumes, listen to the ear-splitting spool of the smoky engines and take arty, angled photos of the big white birds before him. It was all so absolutely glamorous.

His interest in flight had developed early, thanks to an aerodrome at the end of his estate. Its low-flying Cessnas constantly drowned out the telly as they buzzed his home, trainee pilots pulling hard back on their joy-sticks as they scraped over some of the finest social housing the council ever built. He got even closer to them when he blew the entire eighteen quid from his first bakery wage on an air-band radio, just so that he could listen in to their crackly, staccato chit-chat. He hadn't a hope in hell of ever flying in one, until ..

A man knocked on Joe's front door and asked to come in. He was a friend of a man who knew someone who knew Joe's Mum .. and he needed a photographer to take some pictures over the weekend. "I hear your lad's a bit of a David Bailey," he said, winking at Mum. "Do you think we could borrow him next weekend?" The man owned a part share in a light aircraft and had been asked to provide aerial photographs of some nearby farmland as part of a planning application. He wondered if Joe might help them out. "Paid, of course," the man added, and promptly wished he hadn't. Fifteen year old Joe almost bit his hand off. He didn't know which part of the man's sentence had been the more exciting. He'd been called a 'photographer', he'd been asked if he could take some photographs - *for money* - but, most of all, he'd been offered a free trip .. in a *plane!* Oh fuck, oh shit, oh poo!

-

He'd never forget that first bumpy take-off, the tiny plane hitting every damned rut in the aerodrome's grassy airstrip. The stomach-sickening lurch into the air terrified him, and he sweated so much he could barely grip his camera. Pete, the man, the friend of a friend, was sitting in the co-pilot's seat and smiled as he twisted back to Joe. "Everything alright?" The question crackled through a pair of bulky headphones, which hurt Joe's ears and squeezed his glasses hard against the bridge of his nose. He forced a grin and stuck up his thumb. "That's your street, down there," shouted Pete. "Bet you've never seen it from this angle before." He was right, of course. Joe never had. "Oh wow," he shouted. That seemed enough. He was sitting firmly in the centre of the rear seat and had to slide his backside to the window and dare himself to peep over the rim. It took a moment or two to orientate himself, though the council tip and the train line certainly helped, and he took a quick glimpse then edged carefully back, worried that the window might fall out and suck him to his death. I wonder if I'd click the shutter on the way out, he mused. Weeuuggh! The plane lurched to the left, its right wing rising above him as the plane slid through an air pocket. Oh my God, he was so high. At least the light was perfect, the sky completely cloudless. "Three hundred feet," said Pete. "Should be just right, but make sure you can get the whole area in your shot." Joe nodded and readied himself. "Nearly there," came Pete's voice again. "The field's on the left with the river on its right. Can you see it?" Joe licked his lips and raised his camera. "Don't take any pictures yet," said Pete. "We'll come around and you can photograph it from this side." The pilot threw the plane into a tight turn and Joe slid all the way to the right hand side of the seat. He was looking straight down at the ground. "Oh God," he whispered. "Please don't let us crash." The plane finished its circle and lined up on the field again. "Get a grip Joe," he said to himself, and raised the camera to his eye, instinctively remembering to make sure he was on a high shutter speed to counteract any vibration. Despite the headphones, he suddenly heard an almighty roar. Pete had unstrapped his seatbelt and was forcing open the passenger door with his left shoulder, a grimace on his face as he fought against a battering slipstream. The plane filled with a tearing air. "Lean over the back of my seat," Pete yelled. "Take your shots through the gap." Whaaaat? "Hurry up," Pete screamed. "This door's fucking heavy." Joe kicked into gear and stretched forward. The raging gale snatched at his breath but he battled on, framing the field and managing five shots before it slipped from his sight. "Did you get it?" Pete let the door close slightly. Joe gave another thumbs up and suddenly burst out laughing. This was bloody brilliant! There was a powerful roar as the pilot pressed the aircraft into a rapid climb, and Joe heard him say something to Pete over the intercom. Pete turned and pointed, making Joe look down. Below them, a hundred yards or so behind, was a blue and white Cessna, tiny against a patchwork of fields and terraced houses. "Enemy in sight," Pete squealed, and pushed hard against the door again. He clenched both fists in front of him and began to shout. "Da da da da da da da ..." he went. "Da da da da da .." He was pretending to machine-gun the other plane! "Da da da da da .."

"Ha ha ha ha ha .." Oh, this was bloody amazing. The pilot of the 'target' waggled his wings and Joe heard "Get you next time" over the radio. They lined up on finals and, before he knew it Joe was back on solid ground (Thank you, God), with the pilot taxiing across the airfield to park by the old control tower. "That was absolutely amazing," he giggled, and threw up all over Pete's brogues.

-

The Red Arrows' nine-plane aerobatic team were the RAF's pride and joy, and people travelled from all over the country to see them. Not Joe! Why would he, when they came straight to *him*? One advantage of living so close to the aerodrome was that it staged an annual air show, its warm May Sundays an exciting mainstay of Joe's young years, when the usual whiny Cessnas were replaced (for five exciting hours!) by Harrier Jump Jets and Jaguar fighters, Sea King helicopters and .. The Red Arrows. (Joe was not to know it yet, but he was only a few years from working for the press and actually being *paid* to cover the show. He'd shoot from the roof of the control tower and he'd fly in an RAF Hercules aircraft and, indeed, there was a day to come when he'd be *convinced* he'd got an amazing shot of the Arrows' two solo aircraft.)

Schedule and weather permitting, the team usually closed the thrilling show and enthralled Joe every time he saw them, the nine sleek hulls of their Folland Gnats streaming red, white and blue smoke over Mum's fluttering washing line. Legal or not, the traffic on the nearby high-level motorway bridge invariably came to a halt to watch the spectacle, and the jets always got a big cheer from their audience on the estate, who would pile into their back gardens and settle down for the free show with egg sarnies and bottles of home-made cider. Staying in the garden was never an option for Joe, of course, which is why, at fourteen, he came to be standing knee-deep in an itchy wheat-field, watching a plane crash dramatically into a nearby copse. He knew he'd clicked the shutter at exactly the moment the red-striped biplane clipped the trees. Alas, he also knew his 50mm standard lens was nowhere near long enough to get him a close up of the crash and had to give up on the idea of getting his first ever front page splash. His vantage point, though, was perfect. The farmer's field in which he stood was directly underneath the flight line of the displaying aircraft, the planes keeping safely away from the fee-paying crowd. It was noisy, breathtaking and, not that any of them cared, incredibly exposed and dangerous. However, and much to the aerodrome's annoyance, there was absolutely nothing they could do to stop the field filling with hordes of free-loading estate kids.

The only problem with the air-show was that it was always held on a Sunday afternoon. So was the service of Benediction. One year, thirteen year old Joe was lying in a rustling yellow field after a thrilling display by a screeching Hawker Hunter, and it was suddenly so quiet he could make out the skylarks twittering overhead. He felt a yank and heard "There you are, you little sod" as he was hauled to his feet by his Mum. With her eye on the clock, she'd hiked across the fields to find him, then dragged him all the way back to the church where he served as an altar boy, making him change into his cassock and cotta just in time for the 4pm service.

Back on the hard church floor, the smoky thurible swinging, Joe heard the Arrows rip the sky above the church steeple. He stared at the statue of the Virgin Mary and prayed hard for forgiveness as he cursed his bloody, interfering Mother.

Page 47

Joe missed his Mum. He *was* still only eighteen, after all. Much to his relief, he'd found he couldn't bring himself to hate her, couldn't even raise resentment towards her despite what had gone on in their past. He was certain it was all Kevin's doing anyway. Mum must have had no say whatsoever in the matter once that twat started chucking his weight around.

He would lie in bed and think back to the good old days, to growing up 'at home'; Mum pushing him on the metal swing in the garden, making jelly in the shape of a rabbit, applying magic plasters that she said made you 'better' when she stuck them across the scrapes on your knees. And then, hearing her at six in the morning, scrubbing the kitchen floor before work; standing hidden behind a mountain of ironing at eight o'clock at night, sewing his clothes, going without breakfast, cooking, cooking, cooking. He'd tried one night to remember the last ever time she'd touched him - the last occasion she'd taken her eldest to her side, all warm and lovey-dovey like an advert for Cadbury's fudge - but, try as he might, nothing came to his mind. No hugs, no slobbery kisses on the cheek, no motherly scruffle of the hair. He suddenly wished he hadn't gone there but, too late, a memory made him shiver. Ah yes, that was it. The last time she'd held him. The day his Dad left home. She'd taken all three kids into her arms and cried as hard as they had until .. well, until all the tears were done, he supposed. You can't keep crying forever.

The next thought surprised him as much as the first. It began to dawn on him that, after that dark, traumatic day with his Dad, he'd essentially grown up without even the *expectation* of a hug. Without the warmth that might be considered 'normal' between members of the same family. The parental split had opened up more chasms than at first appeared, and the thought that he'd simply accepted the staus quo came as more of a shock than the actual realisation. Truth was, Mum had curled in upon herself after the divorce, had saved her 'hugs' for herself, to get her through her life as a single Mum. Not that Joe would ever know, of course. "Doesn't matter," he would say, dismissively. "She was lovely before the divorce," and, to his relief, his brain would play ball again and flood him in another wash of happy memories. He pictured her, eyes wide as she put on make-up in front of the tiny kitchen mirror, recalled her cursing at the rain as she dashed out to collect the washing from the line, telling him 'well done' when he came top of the class in French, planting cabbage, football boots for birthdays, Sandalwood soap, fruit cake on Sundays. And now he missed her all the more. He really wished he could tell her about his new job. There'd be any number of times he'd arrive home from work, bursting with excitement over some great job or other he'd had that particular day, and be itching to tell her all about it. There was Dad of course but, these days, he was becoming a little deaf to all of Joe's 'amazing' stories.

"It was Peter Ustinov," he'd said to Dad one day. "Peter flippin' Ustinov was posing just for me. Just *me*."
Grunt.

"I've just been upstairs on a Jumbo Jet, Dad. Right up there in the bump. It's amazing."
Ahum.

"Dad, I've just been served a drink in The Rovers by Elsie Tanner! Elsie Tanner, Dad. Elsie bloody Tanner!"

There was *one* glimmer of hope, when Dad asked if he'd photograph his darts team, which had just won some trophy or cup or other. A small thing, but it delighted Joe to know that his job *did* mean something to his Dad, after all. In the end though, he gave up trying to tell Dad anything about his day. All Dad cared about was that Joe was happy. Joe wondered what his Mum felt.

-

He'd taken to carrying an autograph book - blue faux-leather cover, yellow and pink pages, £2.60 from a new Paperchase store in town - and decided he'd request a signature from anyone he photographed that he considered to be important. He didn't ask Elsie Tanner, but he *did* ask Margaret Thatcher, and Bobby Charlton, *and* Mohamed Ali, of all people. Good God, he thought, I'm standing in front of Mohamed .. really, really famous .. Ali. His hero Victor Blackman got into the book when he came to town to give a

talk, and Joe also asked Chrissie Hynde, Kevin Godley, Fred Dibnah, Prairie Prince and André Kertész. Good God, I'm standing in front of André bloody Kertesz.
He couldn't believe the access his job allowed him. Barely three years back the closest he'd come to 'fame' was having a row with a kid who'd been to a pantomime and insisted Maureen Nolan had bigger boobs than Linda Lusardi. (Oh no, she hadn't.) And now here he was, shooting theatre openings and gig previews and yes, book signings - his own was on the way, he was sure - with some of the biggest names he could hope for. When David Hockney signed his book, Joe was convinced it read 'Gary Lowry', and when the explorer Ranulph Fiennes wrote his name, he pressed so hard on the paper that Joe was fearful for his Cilla Black on the other side. His Dad remained utterly unimpressed with any of his son's name-dropping until the day Joe told him he was going to photograph Terry Wogan. "*Mr* Wogan," Dad had corrected, excitedly. "You're going to meet old golden-tonsils himself?" Joe made sure the DJ's signature went on a separate scrap of paper rather than into his precious collection, though when he asked Wogan's compatriot George Best for *his* autograph, he *had* to have it on a scrap of paper as he'd bumped into him in a pub on a night off. In years to come he'd look at his half-filled book and wonder why he never asked Tony Wilson, or Ken Dodd, or Eric Cantona, or Harold Wilson, or Ian Curtis, or Pat Phoenix or .. Peter flippin' Ustinov! Only one thing had annoyed him. He'd asked one of his favourite musicians for an autograph and they'd cheekily added "Keep taking the snaps!" beneath their name. Joe had scribbled through the signature in disgust. "Snaps?" he'd yapped. "I'm a bloody artist, I am."

He couldn't wait to tell his Mum.

"It's 5p to get in."
"Oh, for goodness sake," snapped Joe. "I'm not *paying* to get into a bring and buy sale. I've only come to take a picture for The Courier."
"Prove it," said a smirking old codger, nestled behind a small table in the entrance to a church hall. His dentures clacked like castanets as he counted out loose change. "Show us yer press card." Joe swore under his breath and reached for his wallet. He was hardly ever asked for his press card but, if he was, it was nearly always by one of these little Hitler doormen, enjoying a tiny bit of authority and milking it for all it was damn well worth. (Truth be told, Joe loved it, every time!) "There! Happy?" he said, shoving it in front of the doorman's shrivelled mush. "My press card." He said it as loudly as he felt he could get away with. (You never know, there might have been *one* girl in the crowd who'd have been impressed!) The doorman snatched it and drew it closer to his crusty eyes. "Ha ha ha .." he cackled. "You look like Deirdre Barlow!"

-

Having a press card was something that delighted Joe, as getting into the NUJ - The National Union of Journalists - was just so incredibly hard. It was one of the more frustrating 'Catch-22s' in those historic days of union strength. You couldn't join unless you made a decent percentage of your income from journalism, and you couldn't make that percentage without working as a journalist. It still tickled Joe that he got classed as a 'journalist', although he was feeling a lot better about himself after his chat with Chris at The White Hart. His dreams came true when, on his very first day on the 'paper, the boss asked him to sign a form which, he explained, granted him immediate membership of the NUJ.
"Immediate?"

"Of course," the boss grunted. "You're working for a newspaper, aren't you?"
Andy took a rushed ID photo, which seemed to seriously magnify Joe's already large, questionably-fashionable 1978 spectacles and meant that, whenever he handed over his press card, he was constantly having to endure double-takes from people who assumed he was trying to enter their event as Coronation Street actress Deirdre Barlow. It caused real amusement the one time he actually had to photograph her. "Oooh, you're like bloody twins," cackled Hilda Ogden at a Granada photo-call.

-

Being a member of the NUJ also meant eligibility to their annual press photographers' competition. Joe had forgotten all about his submission to the awards and was beside himself when an invitation to the presentation dinner came to him through the post. Black tie, it said.
"Dickie bow and wotsit .. " explained his Dad, not very helpfully. "Oh, you know .. er, dinner jacket!"
"I know what 'black tie' means, thank you very much," said Joe, and his heart began to thud as he wondered how long a 'Thank You' speech he'd
be required to deliver. He was getting ahead of himself. Calm down, he thought, it *might* only be an invitation. (No way, I *must* have won!) He propped the gold-edged invitation against one of Dad's model cars - the buggers were all over the flat - and sucked his bottom lip into his mouth. He was trying to remember exactly which photographs he'd submitted. He knew he couldn't compete with anyone's Woolworth's shots, but there *was* one picture he thought might give him a shot at a prize. Difficult to say, really. It was months since he'd prepared his entries.
"Oh, and partner," said Dad, picking up the invite. "It says here 'And partner'.
So who you gonna take then, stud?"

"You can be very sarcastic at times," Joe pouted. "Anyway, plenty of time to think about that," and he snatched up the invitation and waltzed off to his room.

A date came just in time. The night before the awards, Joe was bopping self-consciously in a corner of The Blue Rooms when a tap on the shoulder made him jump. (He'd recently decided on a new approach to pulling birds, adventurously - stupidly? - taking off his glasses before he got onto the dance floor. He'd hide them in his pocket as if he was ashamed of them, then grit his teeth and scrunch up his eyes in an ironic effort to look like the Marlboro man.) Seems it had finally worked. "My mate fancies you," said a scrawny blonde in a two-tone metallic tank-top, and Joe squinted just in time to catch a wink and a teasing finger-ripple wave from the most beautifully stunning woman who was .. standing next to the one he took to the dinner.
"Hi," he said nervously, offering his hand to the stunner. "Awright?" she skreaked, in a sharp Scouse accent. "This is Susan. She thinks you're lovely," and she put her hand on the shoulder of the over-made-up woman standing beside her. Three pints later and Susan was starting to grow on him. She was also trying to lick the life out of his tonsils whilst pressing her enormous breasts hard into his gasping chest.
"Can we go back to yours?" she fluttered, reapplying lipstick now that most of it was slathered over Joe's neck and eyebrows.
"God, you're keen," he gasped, gulping for oxygen. (She really *was* enthusiastic.) "But, er .. I've got an early start in the morning. You don't fancy coming to a dinner, though? Tomorrow night?"

They had a last drink, worked out where to meet as they smooched during the last dance, and the main lights came up as Joe put on his glasses ..

-

Her face woke him next morning. Or rather, the horrific memory of it, burnt into his retinas by the harsh white light of the previous evening's 'chucking out time'. Joseph of Arimathea, she must have been a hundred and seven! "Oh shiiiit," he groaned, stuffing his pillow over his head. "Why the hell did I invite her?" All day long, heart-stopping flashes of her saggy, wrinkled face bobbled up unannounced, and it was a toss-up as to what made him feel worse; the 'not-knowing' if he'd won a prize, or the 'knowing' that, tonight, he was going to be seen out with a women who could pass for his Great-Great-Grandma. Either way, he couldn't shake the bile-bubbling thought that he'd actually snogged the old witch. "Oh shit," he moaned. "Maybe I just won't go."

-

She tottered from a taxi and Joe could have sworn he saw her drop a fag end into the gutter. He tugged nervously at his Moss Bros. dicky bow and dabbed his forehead with a hankie. "Oh God," he prayed. "Please just get me through this night." He checked for ciggy-whiffs as he half-heartedly pecked her on the cheek, catching instead a full imperial gallon of knock-off Chanel No.5. "Hello Susan," he coughed. "How are you?"
"Ooh, he's a bit of alright," she said, turning to eye up Ged Dane, a passing - and very good-looking - acquaintance from a 'paper a few miles away from Joe's own.
"Oi, you're with *me*," Joe snapped, and almost physically pushed her through the main entrance.
"Nice touch Joe," Ged laughed. "Perhaps I should have brought *my* Nan, too."

-

"Would you like a raffle ticket?" A smartly-dressed young lady made a hit on them the second they got through the door. She waved a thick cloakroom book at Joe and Susan said "Oh, yes please. One each, thank you very much." The seller tore off two tickets and handed them to Susan. "Get your money out darling," she winked, and Joe nearly thumped her.

"Ten pounds each," said the ticket-seller, and he nearly thumped *her* instead.

"What?" he cried. "A tenner for a ticket? Are you having a laugh?"

"Great prizes," shrugged the woman. "Best of luck."

Susan handed one of the tickets to Joe and swiped a glass of champagne from a passing tray. "I'm just going for a .. er, a breath of fresh air," she burped, and turned on her heels, already rummaging in her handbag.

"I *knew* she smoked," growled Joe, his only consolation the knowledge that, after tonight, he'd never see her again. Cheered with the thought, he set his mind to the prize-giving and walked to a long table at the far end of the grand dining room. Upon it, set like a mini Stonehenge, framed pictures of all the winning photographs lay hidden beneath starched white tea-towels, and his heart sank. All the pictures were in a landscape format and the picture he'd hoped might do it for him was in portrait form - an upright. Damn it, he thought. Bollocks. Fuck. Shit, shit, shit. Susan returned and he knew his evening had gone completely down the pan. So he couldn't believe it when he was named 'Young Photographer of the Year'. As the prize was announced, the invited celebrity guest, a very famous TV presenter (in Manchester) pulled the cloth from Joe's entry and craftily rotated the photograph. It *was* in portrait format after all. "Aha .." squealed the boss, sitting two tables from Joe's. "I knew that'd fox you. Ho ho ho .." Joe was thrilled, even smiled at the joke as he rose to receive his award. He was even happier when Susan rose for *her* prize, having had her ticket drawn out during the raffle. "A trip to New York?" he gasped, forcing himself to give her a hug around the shoulders. "Oh my God, when are we going?"

"We?" said Susan, scrunching up her wizened face. "Who said anything about 'we'?"
"But, *I* bought the ticket," said Joe.
"Yes, but you bought it for *me*," she proclaimed. "So I'm taking a mate." (Swine)
"You tight bitch," he snarled. "We're finished." (Drama Queen)
"I don't care," she spat, planting a big maroon kiss on her airline tickets. "You look like Deirdre Barlow, anyway." (Bitch)
"Fuck you," he yelled. (Unoriginal)
She smoked, anyway. (Cow)

(At least he'd won an award. And the winning picture? His shot of the Red Arrows, taken during the Manchester air display. A nightmare Joe had that night featured Susan falling out of a bright red jet over the Empire State Building!)

The day I started squeaking ..

Bit of excitement last month. Our darts team won the Salford West Regional Knock-out 'Round the clock' competition and I asked Joe if he'd come and take a photie at the presentation evening. Chuffed to buggery, I was. That's my son, I kept saying. See that photographer? That's my son!

He seems very happy, these days. Well, as far as I can tell, but we're like passing strangers, me and him. I'm in, he's out. I'm out, he's in. We've even taken to leaving notes for each other. Get bread, back late, no milk, stop leaving the seat down, have a ball. But yes, everything seems to be going well. Job he loves, money coming in, company car. Really pleased for the lad, really pleased.

Me? Getting along, I suppose. Can't ask for anything more than that, can I? Can't claim to be in a job I love though, and I'll tell you for a fact the wages are shite. Three weeks ago the, er .. what are they called? .. oh, the unions .. put in for a three percent pay rise and it got rejected within 48 hours. Forty eight! Fucking management, sitting there in their warm, cosy offices. They haven't a clue what it's like down on the shop floor, all that shit and swarfega and noise. Oh, and on that subject, I forgot to tell you, I've got that .. er, what's it called? .. tiny tits? Ah, tinnitus. Bastard squeaking's keeping me up half the night. Well, it would do if I wasn't usually pissed by bedtime, ha ha ha. At least it stops me hearing Joe's fucking awful music!

Page 49

"Don't worry, I'm exactly the same," said Andy, halfway through a bag of chips. "It drives me mad, but I always take it as a good sign."

Andy's mad as well? thought Joe. Phew, what a relief. "So what's *good* about it?" he asked, pinching a chip from the greasy newspaper. "It drives us both mad but you think that's ok?"
"Well, it shows how involved we are, doesn't it?" said Andy. "If we're striving for better pictures it shows we're true professionals, doesn't it? Shows we care, know what I mean?" He wiggled his little finger, nose in the air.

"Actually, I think I do," Joe said, suddenly feeling better about himself. "True professionals. I like that." Andy wiped his hands on his trousers and left to photograph a lass who'd landed a dancing job on a cruise ship. Joe was glad he'd brought up the subject. "I've got a bit of a problem," he'd said. "Every time I drive away from a job I instantly think of a way I could have taken a better photograph." It was proving to be a real bugger. "Oh shit," he'd say. "Why didn't I put that guy further over, or move that group to another background, or bounce the flash off that wall instead of that one? Aaaagh!"
"That is not a problem," Andy had said, encouragingly. "It's when you *stop* thinking like that you've got a problem."

-

He'd been in rather a good mood of late. It cheered him to think of Andy's rationalization, and the glow from his photography award still lingered. To top things off XTC, one of his favourite new bands, was going to be on TV's Old Grey Whistle Test that evening.

"Two here for you, Joe," the boss said, handing him a fax. "First one's in half an hour, so you'd better get a move on." Joe sat and read the details. A well-known clothes designer was in town to film a television programme. 'The Willis Wardrobe Workout' was a new concept in TV and involved the designer (Willis) dropping in on an unsuspecting member of the public and going through their wardrobe to work out 'what worked and what didn't.' Joe had never heard of the programme .. or the designer. The second job was at a hotel next to Manchester Airport. A so-called 'Business Angel' had been interviewed by a journo for a piece about his support of new local businesses and could only fit in a 'photo session' before he flew off to his tax-haven home on the Isle of Man. Joe hadn't heard of the business angel, either!

He knocked on the open door of a house in Timperley, well aware he was at the right address by all the thick cabling that ran into the house from a nearby generator truck. "Hello, hello," said a cheery chappie, greeting him in the hallway. "From the 'paper? How lovely! Do come in. Everyone's upstairs." Joe followed the man up a staircase full of discarded clothes, catching his foot on a scraggy Afghan coat that looked like it could have walked out of the house on its own.

"Is he here, yet?" he asked, speaking to the wobbling backside above as he made his way up the stairs. "This Willis chap? The designer? The guy that's making the programme?"

"He is," said the man. "Been here ages, actually," and he pushed open a bedroom door to reveal a cameraman with a big tripod, a hair-and-make-up girl with a massive can of hair-spray and, in the middle of it all, a woman in a fit of tears.

"Not the coat," she was crying. "I've had that coat for years. Please?"

"Look, love," said a chap in grey headphones. "I've told you three times, already. You don't *really* have to throw anything away. It's just for televisual effect, sweetie. We film Willis making fashion suggestions for you as he goes through your wardrobe, and we *pretend* that he makes you throw out all the stuff he doesn't like. Is that clear, darling? Have you got it?"

"Oh alright," sniffed the woman, snatching a proffered kleenex. "So I *can* keep it, if I want to?"

"But Lordy Lord, why *would* you?" said the cameraman.

"So where is he, this Willis chap?" said Joe, innocently. "Has he gone for a wee or something? Ha ha ha .."

Everyone stopped and stared at Joe, then the man he'd followed suddenly burst out laughing. "Ha ha haaa .." he guffawed. "It's me! It's me! I'm Willis. I'm the guy that's making the programme. Oh, how funny. Ha ha haa .."

Ho bloody ho, thought Joe. Very funny. It's not *my* fault I've never heard of you, you numpty. "You didn't know did you, really?" laughed Willis. "Oh, that was a cracker, that one. What a shame we didn't get it on film. So you really haven't heard of me, eh? How astonishing. Hey, wanna do it again for the camera?"

"No, I do not," said Joe, still blushing. "Let's just get the picture done, then I can go." He kicked the Afghan down the stairs as he stomped off, and turned back as Willis called to him over the bannister rail. "Your jacket, darling .." he said. "I mean, come on sweetie. Seriously ..?"

-

There was no mistaking the 'Business Angel'. Ensconced in a swish penthouse suite at an airport hotel, he positively oozed wealth and success. Joe had never seen a watch as big as *that* in his life. "Come in," the wearer said, holding open the door.

"Mr Angel?" said Joe, in one of his less lucid moments.

"Ha ha, that's a good 'un," laughed the chap, and he held out a wide, thick hand, squeezing Joe's with a ferocity that set the watch strap jingling. "No, it's Brian," he said, in a thick, Manchester accent. "Brian Stenning. Call me Bri, if you want. All me mates do."

"Bri?" said Joe. "Alright, Bri .." and he put his camera bag on the floor and massaged the scrunch out of his fingers.

"So, what've you got in mind?" said Bri, settling into a huge, leather sofa. "Do you want me here, or in't t'other room, or what?"

"I presume you haven't got a lot of time," said Joe, sizing up the suite. "What with your flight going off, and all that."

"Oh, don't worry about that," winked Bri. He tapped his nose and nodded in the direction of the airport. "I've got me own wheels!"

-

"You don't sound very, erm, posh," said Joe, hastily adding "If you don't mind me saying," as he realised his impudence.

"Posh?" frowned Bri. "Why the bloody 'ell should I sound posh?"

"Well, 'cos you're rich," Joe naïvely said, clicking the shutter as Bri pulled a disbelieving expression. "I thought all rich people were posh." Bri set off laughing again, making such a joy of a picture that the paper would use it over a full quarter page in the next edition. "Eeeh, you daft bugger," he said, wiping his eyes. "Posh doesn't equal rich, and neither does that vicey versey. Some of me best mates are posh, and they're as poor as church doorbells."

"Mice," said Joe. "Oh, it doesn't matter. So where are you from, then? You *do* sound very local."

"I am," said Bri. "I'm from Swinton. D'ya know it?"

"Know it?" said Joe. "My Mum's from Swinton."

"Well, there you go," said Bri. "Sorry, no disrespect to your Mum, but it's not exactly Kingston-upon-Thames is it?"

"So how did you get from .."

"My favourite story .." said Bri, bending close to Joe and adding "Here, would you like a glass of bubbly?" (No thanks!) He spent the next twenty minutes filling Joe in on his life history, from scrap metal merchant to multi-millionaire via lots and lots of fortunate, timely and very, very lucrative investments. As he spoke, he leant in further and further, until his heavily-ringed fingers rested on Joe's thigh and gave it a cheeky squeeze. "I *am* very, very rich, you know .." he said, staring into Joe's eyes. "I could make you a very happy young man .." Joe didn't even wait for the lift!

-

He'd just turned onto the motorway when his bleeper went off. He pulled off at the next exit and looked around for a phone box. The first he found had the cord ripped from the receiver and he could make out the words 'Terry is a grass'

scratched roughly into the window. A mile up the road, a second call-box seemed intact, then Joe realised he had no change to pay for the call. He bought himself a roll of Toffo chews from a nearby sweetshop and headed back, only to find the box occupied by a lady who waved her watch at him and mouthed 'Twenty minutes'. The third was fine as long as he didn't mind standing in a puddle of piss. The smell was horrendous but he held his breath long enough to connect with the bleeper office and finally pick up the message. "Dame Edna, eh?" he said, getting back to his car. "That should make for a good picture." The flamboyant Aussie was holding a photo-call at a city-centre theatre to promote a forthcoming tour. Joe knew of the comedian after catching a glimpse of him/her/it on the TV a few nights back. The boss's message directed Joe to head into town and cover a photo-op, and Joe couldn't help but think back to the day he'd first seen Abba at the Opera House. Now *he* was going to photograph an Aussie on *his* patch. "Small world," he chuckled, as he checked for the theatre's address. He suddenly had an idea. "I'll get him to hold my A-Z," he said. "Pretend he's trying to find his way around Manchester. Brilliant .." His next idea was even better. As he handed the map to 'Edna' he quickly flipped it upside down.
"What are you doing?" Humphries demanded, through a forest of gladioli.
"Well, you're Australian, aren't you?" said Joe. "I thought the picture would look funnier if the map was upside down."
"Funnier?" Humphries shook his head and turned the book the right way up. "I don't think so, cobber. I do the funnies here," and he gave Joe a glare through the trademark, lensless glasses that would have barbecued a 'roo at three hundred yards. "Now, you ready?" he asked, and set himself into a rigid-grinned pose that the Editor would call "a bit staged" when he went through Joe's work the next day. Joe hated it when a great idea bit the dust, and grumbled for the

rest of the afternoon. So much for striving for better pictures.

At least there was XTC.

-

"Where's the telly, Dad?" Joe got home just in time for his music show, having called in at the off-licence for four cans of Guinness on the way back.
"We can't watch it," said Dad, looking up gloomily from one of his cowboy novels.
"What do you mean, 'we can't watch it'? Why not? And where *is* it?"
"It's on the, er .. oh, where did I put it? .. oh, the balcony. It was the only place I could think of that would stop us switching it on."
"But I don't *want* to stop switching it on," said Joe, his voice rising. "Why would I want to stop switching it on?"
"Because switching it on's just cost us two hundred nicker," said Dad, folding his arms. "The .. er, wotsit .. the TV detector van's been round and we've been fined for not having a television licence."

Joe dropped into the armchair and swore loudly.

"Anyway," Dad added. "How was your day?"

Page 50

"I've just been made redundant."
The pause lasted a smidge too long and Joe forced a nervous laugh. "Piss off," he scoffed but, when Dad buried his face in his hands, Joe knew he was being serious.

"What the bloody hell am I going to do now?" Dad said, despairingly. "Who's going to employ a knackered old fart like me?" He lit a cigarette and exhaled ferociously. (Will I have to pay all the rent? Joe wondered, selfishly.) His Dad held up a cheque for £2,000 and said "There you go. That's all the thanks I get for thirty-five years' graft. Thirty five fucking years down the fucking pisser." He necked a tumbler of Johnnie Walker and sniffed loudly. "Still, at least I get to see Uncle Jimmy now."
"What?" said Joe, still shocked. "But I thought he lived in Toronto."
"Vancouver, actually. And that's where I'm going next Friday. I've just been to the travel agent's to book a flight." And so Joe spent the next three months alone whilst Dad blew his redundancy package on Moosehead and Molson, getting his pale Irish skin grilled to a crisp in his Uncle Jimmy's Canadian back-yard.

-

Joe sat in a darkened front room one evening, reflecting on his Dad's working days. Well, this was the end of those, of that he was sure. There'd be no more work for Dad. No more oily boiler suits, no more busted knuckles, no more long baths to tease out tired shoulders. No-one needing the years of experience he'd gained as head of maintenance, now that manufacturing was more economical in China. No point in getting up at six am like he'd done since the 19 bloody 50s. No purpose for Dad, and no way of knowing how hard it would hit him once he got back from his trip. No way, thought Joe. There is no way a man can be dropped, just like that. Shit, poor Dad. "Bastards," he snarled and, three cans in, immediately planned to smash every window in the factory. Sod it, he'd petrol bomb the dump. Burn it down, that'd show 'em. "Two measly grand and my Dad's on the fucking shit-heap?" he fumed. "You turds."

"Hello from Canaaaadiiiaaa," his Dad slurred, down a distorted line two weeks later.
"Urrgghh .." Joe groaned. "It's three o'clock in the bloody morning."
"Ha ha ha .."

Page 51

Joe got a parking ticket, and whimpered as he showed it to the boss. "Only you, Joe," the boss sniggered. "It could only happen to you." His shoulders shook hard enough for coffee to splash his trousers, and he cursed as it scalded his arthritic knee.
"I won't have my licence taken away, will I?" Joe fretted, having never been on the wrong side of the law before.
"Just tell me the story one more time," smirked the boss. "I've got to get it right when I tell 'em at the pub, ha ha ha .."
Joe blushed and slammed the darkroom door. He cursed under his breath and then he laughed too, quickly covering his mouth to stifle the chuckle. It *was* bloody funny, when all was said and done. He'd been sent up to Bolton - to him, a far-away world of strange accents and funny smells - to photograph the opening ceremony of a multi-storey carpark that had been built by a company local to his newspaper. Invitees had rendezvoused at a hotel, from where they were to be shuttled by bus to the venue. Not having the time for such indulgence - and needing to get away quickly afterwards - Joe had decided to drive straight to the site but, unsure of its location, pulled up first at the hotel to ask for directions.
"Left at t'top o't street, over't roondaboot and second reet, lad," is what Joe *thought* the chap on reception said and, when he came out of the hotel after the translations, there

was the ticket, waving on his windscreen in a stiff west Pennine breeze.

"A parking ticket," Joe tittered. "At the opening of a bloody car-park. Only you, Joe. Only you .."

-

The office handyman (the motoring correspondent) finally got round to putting locks on the darkroom doors, and Della had to go the long way round to make the coffees. The installation of a new enlarger and updated developing tanks meant the whole processing set-up was starting to look a lot more professional, too. The boss had even ordered a 'proper' negative drying cabinet, so no more drying film with a hair-dryer, although the lads still had to use the office radiators to dry all their prints. (Leave them on there too long and their curled up edges would prove a bugger to flatten. Leave them on there if Della had turned up the thermostat and you couldn't get them unstuck, anyway.)

Joe and Andy spent a lot of time in that little darkroom, sweating under the red light as they took turns to use the single enlarger. They'd long since abandoned the plastic tongs used to agitate the photographic paper in the fixer, and their fingers stank of the pungent, acidic chemical. "Ah, you can't beat coming out of a darkened room with smelly fingers," Joe used to quip. (As if *he'd* know!) When they weren't printing their own work, the lads would help churn out all the re-print orders that flooded in after every new edition of the 'paper. People relied on the local newspaper to cover their events and would happily splash out a hard-earned quid to get a copy of any photograph that showed their smiley faces. Della had the job of opening all the mail and would collate a huge pile of 'reprint' orders in a large metal basket, which she'd pass on once a week to the darkroom. Most customers paid with cheques or postal orders, but quite a few included cash with their hand-written requests, cash which always seemed to vanish before it reached the darkroom. One day, the batteries fizzled out in the darkroom radio and Joe had to work in silence. No Phil Wood on Piccadilly Radio, no poppy post-punk ear-filler, no quirky 'near-the-knuckle' ads. What Joe *did* hear was the boss's voice, growing louder and louder outside the darkroom door. "Give that to me," he barked, and Joe heard a chair bang back against the wall. He put the lid onto his box of photographic paper, pulled the cord to switch on the main white light and opened the door just in time to see the boss yank a wad of pound notes from Della's hand. So *that's* where the cash goes, Joe thought, shutting the door quietly. You greedy, grabbing git. Still, as long as he spends it on porn, he smiled. The boss kept his magazine collection nicely topped up, with a quite eye-watering selection of readers' wives, hour-glass dolly birds and glossy, oiled-up lesbians. Joe locked the door and, on a whim, quietly opened the 'porn draw' for a quick flick through the glossy tits and totty.

He dropped the entire pile when he came to the gay mag.

Page 52

Joe's bin filled with balls of scrunchy paper as he wrestled to come up with a theme for his book. Still hoping to avoid an autobiography, topics had ranged from sci-fi alien invasion to machete-wielding Bay City Roller. (He'd pictured Les McKeown singing 'Bye, bye baby' as he hacked off the heads of teenagers.)

The Bay City Rollers. Now *there* was a memory. He'd never been a fan of the band, *or* of David Cassidy, *or* Donny bloody Osmond but, thanks to his two pop-mad sisters, they were inextricably linked to his early teenage years. (He did have a thing for Suzi Quatro, he had to admit, canning her can in a leather vest and tight trousers. That stirred stuff he wasn't fully aware of when he was twelve!) His sisters were both fully paid-up members of the Rollers' 'Tartan Army', wandering the streets with their 'Shang-a-lang' singing, brightly-coloured scarves and pageboy haircuts, though how they stayed upright on their enormous platform shoes was anybody's guess! Cassidy and The Osmonds lent a *little* more maturity to their musical tastes, although the ever-changing succession of their pop posters wrecked the decor in the girls' shared bedroom, its fading floral wallpaper standing no chance against a constant stream of new dream-boats from 'Jackie' and 'Fab 208' magazines. Joe felt so much more grown-up listening to 10CC even if, for its first three weeks on the Noel Edmonds breakfast show, he *did* think 'Donna' was being sung by a woman.

-

He gave up trying to write (again) and looked over at his ever-expanding record collection. His favourite song of the moment was 'Auf'm Friedhof', a thunderous screamer of a track, (screamed in German) from the eponymously named LP by the Nina Hagen Band. It astonished him how his musical tastes had grown. It didn't seem two minutes since .. now, where was it? He scanned across his rack of albums. Ah, there it was. One of the infamous 1970s 'Top of the Pops' cover compilations, a pretty, freckly, pony-tailed 'school-girl' photographed for the cover against a lurid red backdrop. (Why did they always have to be sucking a lollypop?) "Good grief," he said, reading down the track listing.

'Popcorn', by Hot Butter.
'Brand new key', Melanie.
'My ding-a-ling', Chuck Berry.

'Jeepster', T Rex.
Every track yanking him instantly back to being twelve years old again. Back to his second horrible year at the Grammar School.

-

Did you hear the one about the budgie and the cockroach?

Comedians say they thrive on the sound of audience laughter, and now Joe knew why. Just turned twelve, small still and painfully shy, he'd just made a whole roomful of kids burst out laughing, and he was in Heaven. In the blink of an eye he'd forged a shield made of humour, and he used it to protect himself from that day on. (Years later, he'd complete his suit of armour with a breast-plate made of alcohol and a camera for a visor. He felt safe in there, did Joe.) His English language class at the Grammar School was midway through a lesson in improvisation - a bit of free-association - each pupil asked to add a single line of conversation as the play-acting moved around the room, and the theme had steered, uncomfortably for Joe, onto the subject of the working class.

"Such a run-down house," said a pony-tailed girl with a Polish surname.
"And what an awful smell," shrieked the captain of the cricket team.
"And just look at the size of that cockroach," laughed the Polish girl's twin.

"Cockroach?" yelled Joe. "That's our budgie!"

It was the most spontaneous thing he'd ever said, and he would never ever know where it came from. Joe's one-liner meant he was popular all the way to the end of the lunch break and then, for that day at least, his comedy hat was put back onto its hook and he retired again to his lonely

corner of the class. His quick wit wouldn't stay down though and, now it was out of its bottle, he couldn't keep it quiet. In years to come it would stand him in good stead as a press photographer but, for now, Joe was happy just joshing and joking and bringing joy to the world. (Or at least making a few kids laugh in the playground.) One classmate, even smaller in stature than Joe, sidled up to him one rainy Wednesday lunchtime and offered him a Bazooka Joe bubble gum. His name was Roland and he'd told the class in improv that, when he grew up, he wanted to be a pharmacist. "Why assist?" Joe had quipped. "Why not start your *own* farm?" It was another roof-raiser for Class 2T, and the start of a second friendship at the school, a friendship that lasted all of three months, until Roland's parents upped sticks and hoiked him off to Glossop.
You have to laugh ..

Page 53

"Piss off, you vulture." Well that's not very nice, thought Joe, but he pissed off anyway, just in case. (The crowd looked like it meant business.) He'd been driving along, whistling to a new record by Squeeze - 'Up the junction' - when a fire engine whizzed past in the opposite direction. Making a U-turn at the first possible opportunity, Joe chased after the appliance and followed it to the entrance of an industrial estate, arriving at the same time as two ambulances and a police van. Two cars were smashed up on the junction. "Hey, 'Up the junction', how funny," he chuckled, skidding to a halt as closely as he could. He grabbed his camera bag and ran towards the scene, heart beginning to pound. One of the cars was on its roof. "Oh lovely," he said, pulling out his camera. He took a wide shot just to make sure he'd got something in the bag and then walked forward, clicking rapidly. Two people were stuck in the upturned car, cursing and shouting for help. Excellent. Better still, a small crowd was struggling to free the angry passengers. Wonderful. Joe got down on one knee to shoot at the level of their anguished faces, and that's when he was grabbed, pulled up from the smash and told to piss off, the bloody vulture. Bastards, he thought, how dare they stop me doing my job.

Respect, Joe. The Editor's words thumped home as he was slammed against the bonnet of his car. *You need to show more respect.*

Ah, yes.

-

Another time, a fire in the kitchen of a nearby hotel saw Joe rushing to the blaze, only managing to squeeze off two shots before he was grabbed beneath each arm, lifted physically from the ground and escorted, in no uncertain terms, from the building. "I don't sink so," said a chef, a burly Frenchman with a tattoo of a tear underneath his left eye. "No peectures for you, you nosey bastaaard." Bastards, Joe thought, how dare they stop me from doing my job.

Respect, Joe. The Editor's words again. *Show some respect.*

Ah, yes.

He was getting too big for his boots, see? A 'wee bit up himself', as his Irish relatives might have said. His ego had gone bananas! Now that some time had passed since his humiliating experience at the Woolworth's fire, Joe's sense of self-importance had taken hold again. He was narcissism on speed - look at me, look at me, look at me - living life through a lens, imagining he was constantly being watched and assuming people admired every little thing he did.

"I bet I look great .." he'd think " .. turning up at fires and accidents, a real snapper, hard at work."

"I bet everyone thinks I'm amazing," he'd crow as, from high up a ladder, he'd skilfully handle a crowd of fifty people.

"I bet those girls can't wait to dance with me," he'd dream, imagining himself sliding (vaguely) Travolta-like across the disco floor.

"If I wrote a book it'd be a best seller .."

My God, he thought, I'm incredible but ..

.. because it felt normal to him, he would never stop to consider where this 'Super Joe' had come from, or when the fantasy had begun, or why it was even so, but he lived his life imagining he was the centre of the universe, adored by everyone around him, the envy of all and sundry. (He could still recall the comfort he enjoyed as a kid, when he would gather his toys and books around his mattress and curl up to sleep in the remaining two feet of space in the middle. Being there, right at the heart of everything, made him feel so accepted, so in control of all he surveyed, and his cockroach joke hadn't done him any favours in that respect, showing him just what it *was* like to be the centre of attention.) His self-aggrandisement was, of course, pitiful over-compensation for what was exactly the opposite. Nobody paid him a blind bit of notice. Joe was always the guy who'd have a six-footer stand in front of him at a gig, the guy people would push past at the bar, the guy to whom people said "Sorry, what did you say your name was?" Camera or no, he really was just an ordinary Joe but, because he'd never heard of the term, he had no way of knowing he had an inferiority complex. Forged from his restrictive working-class surroundings and the circumstances that had moulded his upbringing, his submissiveness had become a fundamental part of his character. Indeed, even when he *was* given a compliment, he found it hard to accept and would fire off a trite witticism to cover his discomfort. And so, for the time being at least, and despite what he imagined in his head, Joe lived in a little bubble of his own and real life was the stuff that was going on outside it. He spent his time pointing a camera at it, and moving on. He really was seeing life, through a lens.

Page 54

"Weddings? Of course I photograph weddings." Joe had never photographed a wedding in his life. "Great," said the Major. "See you at the registry office on Saturday." Joe packed away his camera and bit his bottom lip. Oh shit! Why did I say yes? Oh, shit, oh shit, oh shit!

The Major was in the local Territorial Army regiment and Joe had just photographed her for a recruitment piece in the following week's 'paper. He'd not troubled her with the details of his own Army 'career' - particularly after she'd told him about being petrol-bombed in County Londonderry - but they'd got on well and it was their easy-flowing conversation that prompted the Major to ask, on the spur of the moment, if he'd photograph her wedding that coming weekend. Joe drove straight to the library and stuck his head into 'Tips and Tricks for Great Wedding Photography.'

'Make sure you get the all-important group shots' it said. 'Don't forget some close-ups.' 'Stay ready for those off-the-cuff moments.' Basically, and much to his relief, more or less everything he was already doing as a press photographer. He suddenly became quite excited. "Oh, this'll be a doddle," he said, slightly too loudly for the creepy-looking librarian behind. His confidence had frayed somewhat by the Saturday but, with the adrenaline kicking in, he was 'up and at 'em' and outside the registry office a good two hours before he needed to be. Library books down, this was real. He spent the spare time checking and re-checking his gear, and running the wedding book's guidance through his head. "It's just like a press job," he kept saying to himself. "Exactly the same as a press job."

Being so early meant he got the chance to watch the comings and goings of a surprising number of other weddings. Brides, grooms and their motley gangs of guests would pile in, and then out, of the registry office at an astonishing rate of knots. What a conveyor belt. Sometimes there'd be two or three sets of wedding groups, all mingling nervously in the reception and waiting areas, and then there'd be another two or three outside, battling with their wedding photographers for space in a little scrap of a park across the way. Romantic it was not! Still, being totally ignorant of wedding etiquette, Joe relished the chance to watch the differing working methods of all the other snappers, who'd jump into action as 'their' bride arrived by car or taxi, and photograph her with her father before they entered the council building. Something Joe hadn't thought about before.

"Looking lovely," said one photographer.
"And a shot on your own," said another.
"Are you wearing a garter?" leered one particularly sweaty-looking slap-head. "Show us a bit 'o leg, love. Come on."

Joe's heart picked up speed as the time for *his* bride's arrival approached. It's no different to any other job you've ever done, he told himself. You've done this a million times. A million times. A million times ..

A car horn snapped him from his mantra. The Major had arrived and, having swapped fatigues for fancy frock, she made an absolute stunner of a bride. "Morning, Sir," Joe joshed. "Wow, you look fantastic." He nodded politely to the chap who got out of the taxi with her and asked "Can we just get a quick shot with your Dad before you go in?"

"Dad?" squealed the Major, her bouquet hitting Joe straight in the face. "This is Gerald, you dip-shit .. my *fiancé!*"

Page 55

Tanned, and looking like he'd *definitely* had a good time, Dad poured himself through the arrivals gate at Manchester Airport, duty-free open already, and brought the flag down on his amazing Canadian adventure. He threw himself at his son, ripping apart the jokey 'Welcome home' banner that had taken Joe an hour to make, and shouted "I'm home," at the top of his voice.
"Well, *you* look like you've had fun," Joe laughed, and he laughed even harder when he was handed a plastic 'Moose-up-a-mountain' snow-dome that celebrated a ..

'Sunny British Columbia'

"Piss wet Manchester," he chuckled, gesturing towards the rain-splashed windows. He picked up Dad's only bag and was suddenly filled with a unexpectedly warm and pleasing feeling. It felt surprisingly good to see him again. He led Dad back to the car and swung out onto the post rush-hour M56. "So, tell me all about .." Dad's snores cut him short, and Joe turned the volume down on Simon Bates.

His Dad rose seven hours later, staring weirdly at his watch as walked into the front room. "What's the bloody time, Joe?" he asked, yawning uncontrollably.
"It's five .." laughed Joe. "In the *evening*. You've been zonked out since I got you home. Jet lag, eh? What a bastard." He was jealous as hell. He'd love to be suffering from jet-lag. From a trip to Canada. From anywhere!
"Oh hell, yeah," said his Dad, the phoney west-coast lingo, if not the accent, still in use. "I'd only just be getting up now, wouldn't I?"
"You *are* just getting up," laughed Joe, feeling happier than he'd expected now his 'flat-mate' was back in situ. "So, what'll it be, sir? Eggs over easy? Maple syrup on rye? Pint of Guinness?"
"Oooh, now you're talking," Dad said, instantly perking up. "I've not had a Guinness in .. what is it? .. three months?"
They were in the Navigation within fifteen minutes. "Jesus, that's good," grinned Dad, a white 'moustache' of froth on his top lip.
"Jesus?" said Joe, somewhat shocked. "Taken to blaspheming now, have we?"
"Ach, that's Uncle er .. what's his name? .. er, Jimmy's influence," Dad answered, shaking his head. "Mouth like a sewer, that fella. You can tell it's been a long time since he left the 'old country'." He took another swig of the black stuff and smiled. "Aye, and you're right. I'd better get out of *that* habit before I go to Confession on Friday. Rev. Rev'd kill me if I started Jesusing all over the place." Joe smiled and took a pull on his own pint. His Dad - being, of course, the most Catholic Catholic on the planet - had already admitted that he felt bad, missing Mass because he was on the 'plane! He'd be confessing *that* to the priest first chance he got.

They sank a couple more as they enjoyed a good old catch-up. "Ach, I've had a grand old time," Dad said. "But it's bloody good to be home." And then it hit him. Dropped on him like a ton of bricks. He was home .. without a job - his two grand blown - and there was a pause of several seconds as he tried to gather his thoughts.
"You don't regret spending the money, do you?" Joe began, warily.
"Do I hell," said Dad, adamantly. "It's been the trip of a lifetime."
"Will you miss work, though?"
"Will I fuck," Dad laughed. "Still, what am I going to do now Joe, eh? What the fuck am I going to do now? Jesus."

The day I went to Canada ..

I'm going to Canada, that's what I said. As soon as I saw that two grand cheque. Uncle Jimmy always said I should get over to see him, so that's what I decided to do. My God he looked old, but then he *is* pushing eighty, although you'd never know it from watching him work a room. He was the only one of our family to 'go west', as they used to say. Upped sticks and headed off to .. er, where was it? Toronto? .. while all his family called him stupid and stayed put in Northern Ireland. Two years later he crossed to Vancouver to retire, widowed, with a tasty pension and seven successful kids. It was great to see him, confusing to hear his churn of an accent, and stunning to see how much Canadian Club he can get into his skinny wee body.

Three months, was it? My God they flew, but what great months they were. He took me all over the place, Jimmy did. Huge pick-up, he's got. A Ford? A Ram? Ach, I can't remember, now. My bloody head's going. It was fucking massive though, that's all I remember. He's huge pick up lines too, the old weasel. And I think I might try a moustache like that, when I grow older. Regrets? Not a one. In fact, can I tell you something? I know this might come as a shock, but I've never actually been on holiday before, not even for a week to Southport. Never had the money. Never had the *time*, come to think of it. And ok, I'm as skint today as I was before I went, but I've more than enough memories now to last me a lifetime. And it's funny, I never saw it coming, you know? The redundancy, I mean. Hadn't a bloody inkling. Same as the other lads, really. Oh, I know Jerry Read says he knew about it six weeks before, but then he's the one who reckons Neil Armstrong started life as a welder and Princess Anne is a bloke. Eejit!

If you want to know the truth, I'm scared. What do I do now, eh? Jobs are like hens' teeth around here these days and I know that engineering is all I can do. *All?* Jeez, listen to me. Engineering is my *life*. Sorry, *was*. You only have to look at my hands. My thick, cloggy paws. How many bolts have those fingers tightened, eh? How many times have I got 'em stuck at the back of the .. oh, what are they called again? .. the hydraulics? How often ..

Sorry, I've got to stop this. I've got to stop looking back. I should only think to the future. But I'm just so shocked. I've hit a brick wall and it's stopped me in my tracks. I thought I was in a job for life. Sure, the world

was *always* going to need engineers, *wasn't it?* Seems not, and what a bloody shame to say it. But do you know what I feel most of all? I feel .. no, it doesn't matter.
Oh, alright then .. I feel lonely.

Get a grip, man. I can hear you saying it, even as the words come from my mouth. But it's true. I feel so bloody lonely. Have done since since she and I parted, of course, but now, rattling around the flat, it's truly gone and hit me. I haven't really any friends. Ridiculous, eh? The wrong side of middle age and not a good friend to my name. No-one to talk to about .. well, you know .. my situation. There's Joe of course but, come on, he's still a boy, isn't he? Not even turned twenty. And what am I going to say to a teenager, eh? So, I keep smiling. Brave face and all that.

Or at least I try ..

Page 56

Joe envied his punk peers and their freedom of expression, with their pointy hair and torn trousers and safety-pinned noses. Ok, perhaps not the safety pins, but he loved the 'in-your-face' imagery (ho ho) and especially that of the girls. All that sexy, bold eye make-up and those luscious red/purple/black lips. All that louche latex, rips in all the right places. He was a regular on the punk scene now but, even adhering as loosely as he could to his newspaper's dress code, he still looked far too square to ever 'cop off' with one of those rock goddesses. Or so he thought ..

"Helloooo," said an office receptionist - remarkably keenly, Joe thought - as he turned up to photograph the new Managing Director of an import-export company one day. "Lovely to see you again."
"Again?" he answered, somewhat puzzled by her enthusiastic welcome.
"It *is* you?" she queried, cocking her head. "I saw you at The Exploited gig, didn't I? Last Thursday? At Eric's?"
"I'm not, er .. I .. well, I *was* there," he said, taken aback. "But ..?"
"Oh, I look very different when I go out," she giggled, and pouted sexily as she thrust a hand behind her head. A gorgeous leonine mane of red hair stood to attention, but Joe was none the wiser. "Oh, you men," she huffed, and pulled a wrinkled Polaroid photo from a bulging big blue handbag. Joe knew her instantly. As soon as she passed him the picture. Well, he knew those legs, in glossy, sexy stockings, and he knew that teeny, tight bum, shrink-wrapped in a seductive black PVC mini.
"Ah," he gulped, rabbit in a spotlight. "Is that *you*? Oh my God, yes. Yes, I *do* recognise you now," he blurted.
"You recognise my arse," she flirted, and stood from her desk to stick it out towards him. He knew he was blushing and could only cough and nod as she sat back down again. "Diane," she winked, and pointed him down the corridor. Diane was all Joe could think of as he struggled to pose the awkward MD. The woman had one of those faces he just couldn't take to. She looked like she'd just shat in her shoes. "Just so you know," she said - compounding his dislike of her by refusing to fold her arms in that 'power pose' strut that all business pages like - "I hate having my picture taken." Yeah, and I hate people that won't do what I say, Joe thought. Diane handed him her phone number on his way out, and they were smooching at the back of The Blue Rooms two nights later.

"I've never been out with a punk before," he slobbered, forcing down his hard-on and mind-humming the national anthem. "Show me where you work," she ordered, pulling him up by the collar. They walked around the corner and Joe let Diane in through the back door of the office. His heart was pounding. Bloody hell, she was keen. Was this the night? At last? Diane pushed him hard against the reception desk - God, what would Della make of this, he couldn't help thinking - and they giggled as she led him to the stairwell. Halfway up he tripped and they fell together, Diane pressing down as the stairs dug into Joe's back. He was desperate for her cutesy little boobs and tried to push her up to reach them. "I've got condoms," he whispered, not believing his luck.
"Me too," she said, and the minute she said it he flopped. He was instantly terrified. The modern woman, eh? He'd read about this mythical creature in Jean Davy's column and suddenly felt completely out of his depth.
"Erm, just going for a pee," he stuttered, squirming out from beneath her. "I won't be long. I just need to .."
"Oh, come on," she barked. "You've only just been."
"I know but .."

Diane stood and followed him down the stairs. Her lion's mane was silhouetted in the orange glow of the street lights and he saw her blow him a kiss. "Sorry," she whispered, turning to go. "I mistook you for a grown-up."

Page 57

Like anything in life, Joe's job had its highs and lows. The highs were a joy; Martin Buchan on day one, a byline for a cracking picture, being contactable by bleeper, the indescribable thrill of artistic satisfaction and, of course, the press card. The lows were almost a necessity, like vital grounding counterweights; the captains of Sunday League football teams who *thought* they were Martin Buchan, no byline beneath a cracking picture, being contactable by bleeper (as the boss threw yet another job in his direction), the heartfelt disappointment of having a really good shot butchered to fit into the 'paper .. and looking like Deirdre Barlow on your press card! Yes, there were definitely times when the exotic world of press photography wasn't all it was cracked up to be. Like the day Joe had to wait two hours to take a head-shot of a newly-elected council official. (At least that was a one-off. The reporters had to sit through those interminable council meetings every bloody *month*, God help them.) And times like today, when he had the grand total of seven jumble sales to photograph. Seven, and all with the same shitty stalls, selling the same crappy rubbish to the same poor people. Even for someone as enthusiastic as he was, it sometimes got a bit repetitive.

"You won the tombola?" he'd say. "Well done! Hold up your new loo-brush cover. Smile. Lovely."

"Gather round the coconut shy. Say cheese. Lovely."

"You bought that dress for 20p? Bargain! Big smile. Lovely."

He was wandering round a church 'bring and buy' when he chanced upon a little plastic doll, no more than four inches high, with eyes closed; big, frizzy hair; a big, red down-turned mouth and two large tears running down her cutesy, freckled cheeks. She was crying, poor sweetie, having a right old blub for reasons Joe would never know. He picked her up and laughed. "I know exactly how you feel," he said, ruffling the doll's curly hair. On a whim, he gave the stall-holder ten pence, shoved her into the top of his camera bag then stuck her to his dashboard with a big blob of Wrigley's spearmint gum. Her upside-down smile really cheered him up, so he promoted her to mascot, named her 'Moaning Minnie' and, from that day on, she went everywhere he did. Her first trip was to the Big Chimney, half a mile away from the office. You couldn't miss the bugger. Three hundred feet high, it had been a fixture of the town's landscape for generations, an integral part of the brewery from whence it rose, pumping out a delicious malty, beer smell for years. Today it was coming down. And Joe was going up it. A crew of wreckers had been brought in to demolish it but, for obvious reasons - being slap bang in the middle of town - they'd had to start at the top and throw it in upon itself, brick by sooty brick, then remove all the rubble at the bottom. It was a slow, messy process and meant that, sadly, there'd be no explosive, crowd-drawing, show-biz farewell for the old landmark.

Joe picked up his weekend schedule.

```
8) Bus station. FA Cup fans leave for Wembley.
9.30) St. Ethelred's. Youth Club summer revue rehearsal.
9.30) Brunts Lane Social Club. Flower show opens.
9.30) Town baths. OAP swim-a-thon.
10.15) Brewery. Chimney.
11.00) Margarine works. Feature.
```

"Chimney?" he said to the boss. "What's that all about?"

-

"And try this out whilst you're up there," said the boss, handing Joe the weirdest looking camera he'd ever seen. He'd unearthed an old Russian 'Zenit Horizon' panoramic camera, which took in a full 180 degree view - producing a four inch long negative - that he thought would work well for dramatic wide-angle shots at the top of the chimney.

-

The base of the chimney was huge. Much larger than Joe had expected. Arriving on site, he'd had to work his way around it, navigating dusty piles of old smashed bricks and wondering how the hell he was supposed to get himself to the top. As he strained to look up the stack he bumped into a scruffy, wild-haired man, all of five feet tall, with a face covered in soot and a flat cap on his hairless head. A filthy red neckerchief provided the only smear of colour.
"Awreet?" he said, a big white smile cracking his dirty, wrinkled face. "Ast come from't paper?"
"Hi, er .. ah, yes, the 'paper. Yes, I'm from the 'paper," said Joe, nodding as he translated from broad Pontefract. "I'm supposed to be going up the chimney today."
"'Appen so. They told us you was comin'. Come round 'ere and we'll get yer up there, quick as nifty." Joe followed him to a back section of the chimney, where a long, well-worn extension ladder was tied vertically to the crumbly brick wall. Tied to the top of that was another. And another on top of that. All the way to the top of the chimney. "You're joking," gasped Joe. "Ladders?"
"Why, what did you want?" chuckled the chap. "A bloody 'elicopter?" Joe was politely invited to grab hold of the ladders and make his way up, just like that. None of that mardy-arse stuff like safety ropes, insurance, clips, helmets, harnesses, safety-net .. parachute! "Just keep going to't top an't lads'll help you over," shouted the hilarious Yorkshire comedian. "And don't let go!" Joe was already halfway up the ladders - not letting go - and focusing straight ahead, when Yorkshire shouted "That's reet, lad. All't way up to't planks."
"Planks?" Joe felt his stomach twist. "What bloody planks?" He soon found out. At the top of the column of ladders was

an overhanging platform on which the men worked - made of 'bloody planks' - that jutted out all the way around the lip of the chimney. The edge of the staging, around which Joe would have to navigate, was a good foot behind the back of his head. He suddenly felt very woozy, and made the mistake of looking down as he leant backwards. Oh, Mother Mary! Oh, shit a fucking brick, this was high. "Oh God," he gulped, glancing skywards. "Please don't let me fall."
A beaming, ruddy face suddenly appeared over the planks. "Awreet, fella?" said this second man. "Enjoyin't view?"
"What am I supposed to do now?" Joe said to the man's feet, his palms starting to sweat. "How the hell do I get up there?"
"Climb over," said the bloke, as matter-of-fact as Joe had ever heard anything uttered, ever.
"What?" he squeaked, a cold blast of wind blowing his tie into his face. He was convinced the ladders swayed six feet to the right. "Are you having me on?"
"Reach one hand over," said the man, ignoring him. "Grab't ladder again and pull tha'sen over." Joe felt sick. "Come on, lad. Get a shift on. Some of us 'ave work to do, you know. We'll grab yer if owt gus wrong, don't worry." And so Joe let go of the ladder with his right hand and stretched his arm around the plank. His hand reassuringly slapped against the side rail of the ladder above and he grabbed it like his life depended on it. (Which, funnily enough, it did!) His cameras clanked around his neck as he pulled himself up and then, right knee safely onto the platform, he let go with his left hand, hauled himself fully 'on board' and gingerly got to his feet. Thank God, he thought, thank you, God .. and then, oh wow! It was amazing. How fantastic. What a view. What an unusual place to be. What a long way down! He relaxed ever so slightly and, after a quick peep into the black gloom of the chimney, got to work. "Right lads, can you throw in some bricks, please?" Rather pointless asking, as they'd restarted work as soon as he was up on the planks, thumping the chimney away as they stood around it,

their big bashed lump hammers sending decades of filth billowing into the swirly wind. The Russian camera really proved its worth, taking in such a wide angle that Joe could get the entire circumference of the chimney top into his pictures. He even passed it to the lads and got them to take a shot of him, looking completely out of place in his jacket, shirt and tie. And then he had to get down again ..

Page 58

Two years had passed since Joe had last seen his Mum. Enough was enough, he decided. This was getting ridiculous. The pain of his eviction was long gone and he no longer felt anything like animosity towards her. Time to do something about it. (He was dying to tell her about his award!) Every now and again, over the previous few months, he'd taken to driving to the top of his old street, from where he could see her house and the bedroom window he used to call his own. He just couldn't work up the balls to go and knock at the door. (The last thing he wanted was another fist in the mouth from Kevin.) It was costing him a small fortune, as he took a fresh bunch of roses with him every time he went, but he finally struck lucky one evening when he saw his step-dad cycling off to band practice, whistling as he went (of course), with his trumpet case strapped across his handlebars. "Hit a bus, fatso," Joe sneered. He took a deep breath and drove slowly down the road, pulling up a couple of doors away from his old home. He switched off the engine and wiped a line of sweat from his brow. Don't be ridiculous, he told himself, it's *your Mum*. Just knock on the door and say hello. Come on Joe, get a grip. She hasn't seen you in ages. Just give her the flowers, give her a kiss, ask her how she's been. No big deal. Just do it.

An hour went by. He still hadn't left the car and was beginning to worry that Kevin might soon be back. The minutes had passed slowly, as had the old Cunningham couple, who seemed to take a lot of interest in the new car on their street. Joe slid low and tried to cover his face. "Bugger off," he whispered. "Nosey Parkers!" Still, they wouldn't know the car, would they? He'd never driven it down his old road before. He bit the bullet, grabbed the roses, opened the car door. At the same moment, Mum opened the front door and grabbed some roses, snipping a handful of stems from a large bush in the garden. A small boy ran onto her lawn and kicked a bright orange ball into the privets. "Fuckball," he shouted. "Fuckball."
"Be careful near that road, Gary," Mum shouted, quickly raising her head as the kid chased his ball. "Don't go near the ..

.. Joe!"

Joe stopped in his tracks. "Hi, Mum," he quaked, blushing profusely.
"What are *you* doing here?" she gasped, glancing furtively up and down the road. "I mean, nice to see you, son. How are you?"
"These are for you," he said, coyly holding out his roses.
"Lovely," smiled Mum, holding out hers. "Just like mine!"
"Yes, that's funny, isn't it?"
"Is everything alright, Joe?"
"I just wanted to see you," he flustered. "To see if I can see you. If you see what I mean."
"Oh Joe, of course you can see me." Mum visibly relaxed. "I'd love that, love. You'll just have to do it when Kevin's not around, that's all."

A big smile appeared on Joe's face. "Perhaps we could meet for coffee in town, then?"

"Yes, that would be nice." Mum smiled in return. "Ring me next week and we'll get something arranged. Kevin's always out on Wednesdays, so call at this time of the evening and you'll be alright."

When Joe rang the the following week, Mum told him that Kevin had found out about his visit. He'd slapped her so hard he'd given her a black eye.

The day I envied Joe ..

Joe asked me out for a pint and chat last Thursday. For a minute I thought he'd noticed how I was feeling - what with, you know, the redundancy and everything - and I didn't really want the fuss so almost turned down his offer. But then - to my *disappointment* (can you believe it?) - he told me it was about his Mum. He said he wanted to go and see her. See how she was getting on, and what have you. Did I mind? *Mind*? I was absolutely delighted but yes, like I say, I was so disappointed that he wasn't asking how *I* was. I didn't realise I could get so jealous. Still, I suppose he thinks I'm fine, so that's how I'll have to play it. Why should he worry about me?

I told him I was really pleased that he still thought about her. It's worried me to think he might be doing to her what he did to me but then, I suppose he's older now, more considerate, more thoughtful, more aware. He still looked so young though, sitting there at our usual table, eyes wide, approval sought. He's not looked at me like that since I was teaching him how to use a tenon saw when he was six. Like this, Daddy? he said, the teeth of the saw wobbling wide of their guide mark. Smashing Joe, I'd said .. Ha, I can hear myself now .. smashing. Perhaps a little nearer to the black line, eh? Watch your fingers, son. Blow away the dust.

Why do you ask? I asked. You're a grown man now, Joe. Why seek *my* approval when you know you can do as you please? Well, because you're my Dad, he said. You're my Dad and, well .. you know .. because of all the things that have gone on between you both in the past. Past, I said. You've hit the nail on the head, Joe. It *is* the past. It's all history now. The future, I said, that's what's important now. Your life, and your future, they're the things that count, so get out there and make it all happen. And then I felt envy again. Envy that he would get to see her. His Mum. My wife.

His hand was resting on the table. I very nearly patted it.

Page 59

Sitting in his car, hoping for that moment with his Mum, Joe had been bombarded by flashbacks from his young life. Inevitable really, they were all around him, and not just the more amusing recollections like playing in his Captain Scarlet outfit or laughing at bum-stuck post-coital mongrels, howling in pain as they shuffled down the road together.

That cherry tree over there? He'd taken pictures of its gorgeous pink blossom during the first spring he'd had a camera. The blue garage? He'd used its panelled door as an abstract backdrop, photographing the stark, gnarled shadows of a fern against it one bleak winter's afternoon. Even the nosey-parker Cunninghams had been photographed during the early days of his hobby, as had the bread-delivery driver, the rag and bone man and a three-legged cat owned by his Auntie Renee. (Not a real Auntie, just the loveable old lady across the street who knitted at lightning speed and let him watch the Apollo moon missions on her colour telly.) Inevitably, his sisters were two of his earliest photographic subjects, hamming it up in the garden or moodily lit by birthday cake candles, and then there were the kids on their bikes, the man with a limp who delivered the morning 'papers, and the group picture of all his friends after they'd finished playing 'Japs and Commandoes' one evening.

Memories. Gosh, it seemed a long time since he'd first taken a Kodak Instamatic into the street, having saved enough pocket money to buy a 126 film cartridge, twelve new shots for the taking. He pictured himself even younger, a little boy, learning to ride a bike on this very stretch of road, and then he glanced across to the former home of old Mr Hughes, the miserable fart who'd hide behind his front door and try to pinch their football if it bounced into his garden. (Dead now, Joe supposed, and he felt a sudden twinge of guilt for all the torment he'd caused.) Before the street was tarmac'd, they'd played marbles in the pot-holes, and swapped football cards whilst the girls played hopscotch and that weird French skipping thing, all twangy elastic bands and complicated rhymes. Over there, that's where Brian Strake had stuck his hand into the cooling fan of Mr Whippy's ice-cream van and chopped off the top of his finger. How exciting it had been, an ambulance dashing down their street. He remembered that, once the bandages were off, Dad taught Brian the 'finger-up-the-nose' joke and kept him entertained for hours. Other memories of his Dad were harder to bring to mind. Not surprising really, the poor bugger was hardly ever home in those early years. Joe frowned as he strained to drag up his past. He did have one dim memory, his hand in his Dad's, being led to Midnight Mass one crispy Christmas Eve, slipping on frozen snow but lovely and warm in his woolly new car coat. And he seemed to remember one boring Bank Holiday weekend, his Dad teaching him how to use a tenon saw. "Watch your fingers," he kept saying. "Follow the line, Joe. Follow the line." (It didn't do any good. He often joked that he couldn't even *spell* DIY!) And then there was .. crikey, how could he forget? That time he'd stolen some mints from the Co-op. His Dad knocked him half way to next week for that one.

It was only a packet of Polos, but pinching them earned Joe the hiding of his life. Still only eight, and egged on by his pals, he'd dithered and nervously prevaricated until his hand flicked out and grabbed a packet from the counter. An observant shelf-stacker grabbed Joe's collar and dragged him back from the door, and his Dad grabbed a belt and dragged him into his bedroom to whup the God Damned Bejesus out of him.

"Do .." Whack!
"Not .." Whack!
"Ever .." Whack!
"Steal .." Whack!
"Again .." Whack! Whack! Whack ..

Joe screamed every time the belt whipped across his backside, his knuckles white, tears soaking his 'Thunderbirds are go' pillowcase. He couldn't sit down for hours and, as if that wasn't bad enough, Dad then made him go to 'confess' his heinous sin to the priest the following Saturday morning.

"Bless me Father, for I have sinned, it is one week since my last confession."
He hated confessions. Had done since the age of six, when he'd made his initial visit to the Confessional Booth before First Holy Communion. Convinced by a stern-faced teacher that he'd go to HELL if he didn't tell the truth during those bizarre 'one-to-ones' with a hidden priest, Joe was more worried about what he might *forget* to say than what he actually admitted because "God can *read your mind*, so DO NOT try to hide *anything!*"

It was enough to put the fear of ..

But what was there to confess at six? Pulling your sister's hair? Not eating all your sprouts? Calling your friend 'smelly'? It sure was tough growing up as a Catholic in those days, all the more so when most of your mates were Protestant and didn't have to worry about burning in Hell or spending millennia skulking in purgatory.

As penance for the Great Mint Heist, Joe had been given The Big One - Ten Hail Mary's, one Our Father and a Glory Be, but he'd rattled them off in minutes and was back home in time to join his liberated Proddie Dog pals and play in their 'jumpers for goalposts' football match. Joe smiled. They'd put them down right there, those jumpers, just feet from where he'd parked his car. He pictured them playing footie, just like all kids played footie, scurrying after the ball en masse, like tadpoles tied with string. They just wanted to plant that hard leather 'casey' into the back of the net. (The fact that there *was* no 'back of the net' meant that, when anyone *did* score, the ball would roll off all the way down the road and the scorer would be made to traipse after it.) Who'd have thought he'd be driving a car over their old 'football ground' one day? They didn't get many cars down their road back then. It was a quiet road, a happy road. Safe.

A Genesis song was playing on the radio. *Follow you, follow me*. Phil Collins, singing about hope. The hope that his love would stay, 'right here by his side', and spend 'perfect days in his arms'. Joe would love to be able to say that to a girl. He laughed out loud and shook his head. "I'm such a soppy shite," he said, and then he realised he couldn't listen to a song these days without feeling it was aimed directly at his disastrous (non-existent) love life. The Electric Light Orchestra, for example. Their 'Diary of Horace Wimp' told the story of Horace, who met a girl that was small and very pretty. It sent Joe into a dream-world. If only *he* could meet a girl like that. Small. Pretty. Anything! And then there was Exile .. 'I want to kiss you all over', and Squeeze .. 'Take me I'm yours', and even - on the bad days, - Sad Café .. 'Every day hurts'. Each song - in his head, at least - specifically written to remind him of what he was missing. American rock band The Tubes brought it all home though, with their song 'I want it all now', asking what it would be like to 'kiss a real girl and think you're in love', only to 'get married, grow old and fat and die like a fish on the end of a pole' ..!

Ah, the Joe dilemma!

As desperate as he was to meet a girl, Joe absolutely hated the idea of .. well, meeting a girl. He instantly felt trapped the moment it happened, and he knew this now because he was well onto his fourth girlfriend in as many months. (Girlfriend, therefore - as a description - might have been pushing it somewhat, seeing as he'd only managed fleeting dates with each of those lucky ladies.) There'd been Pauline at first, of course. Those two nights at the cinema still meant a lot to Joe. (He'd loved seeing those photographers on the steps of Sydney Opera House!) Then there was darling Susan, the jammy nonagenarian raffle prize winner, who still made him fume when he thought of her. (He hoped she'd been nabbed by immigration at La

Guardia and was doing thirty years' solitary for *being a cow!*) The date with Dianne was a date best forgotten, and the fourth was with a solid young lass called Geraldine, an aspiring actress whom Joe had met whilst photographing an Am-Dram rehearsal of 'Oh, what a lovely war'. He watched her demolish an entire serving of Prawn Cocktail, Chicken-in-a-basket and *both* their Black Forest Gateaux at a dismal Berni Inn on the outskirts of Wythenshawe and didn't get a word out of her all evening. Gloomily watching her spear the remnants of a glacé cherry from her back teeth, he was spared any further torture when his bleeper went off in the middle of his second pint and he abandoned the poor lass fifteen miles from home.

He wasn't looking for love, just someone to share a piece of his life, and hated that he hated feeling trapped when he was so desperate to get a girlfriend.
Andy had spoken of 'the thrill of the chase'. Maybe it was all about that? And maybe, he pondered, that's why it was called 'falling' in love. 'Falling' was going the wrong way as far as he was concerned. You fall into a trap, don't you? You fall from favour, you fall for a con trick. Why wasn't it called 'climbing' into love? Rising? Soaring into love? Call it what you liked, it wasn't going to happen to Joe anytime soon, not when he freaked out near girls like he did. He was at a loss to understand that panicky feeling his dates had given him. Was it simple inexperience or was it, he wondered, because his own parents had divorced and left him with a subconscious awareness that any relationship might all come to nought? Perhaps it was the fact that he absolutely, definitely, no way in hell wanted children.

Still, to have children, you had to have sex ..

Page 60

When he'd joined the 'paper, Joe had been given a camera, pointed at the door and left to figure it all out for himself. The very epitome of 'learning on the job'. The boss *did* once throw him a few tips, though.

"Always get an upright and a landscape shot," he'd said. "And always work from left to right when taking names for captions." It was the boss's third piece of advice that brought Joe up short. It came after he heard grumbling in the darkroom one Monday morning. "What's up?" he shouted through the door. Joe closed a box of photographic paper, switched on the main white light and opened up the door. "I'm having a bit of trouble with one of my prints," he said, waving a soggy nine by six at the boss. "I can't get this guy's face right at all." The boss took the print and held it to his rheumy eyes. "Oh, well done," he said. "That's a classic." He handed back the print and wiped his hand on Joe's shoulder. "The most basic mistake in the book."
"Oh?" said Joe, nonplussed. "What?"
"You didn't put the black guy nearest to the flash-gun. Schoolboy error, kiddo. Just look how under-exposed he is. Always put the black guys nearer to the flash when you're doing a group shot, Joe."
"That's a bit racist, isn't it?" said Joe, self-righteously folding his arms.
"Rascist?" barked the boss. "Stuff racism, sunshine. It's plain common sense, as you've just found out. If a bloke's got a darker face, he's going to be under-exposed if he's standing too far from the light. It's obvious."

Working so many evenings, Joe took an awful lot of his shots using a flashgun, and he spent an inordinate amount of time checking it was charged and correctly plugged into the synch socket of his camera. His new Mecablitz flash was a beast of a thing. German made, in-built sensor, tilt and rotate head and an over-the-shoulder battery pack that weighed a ton. On a side panel, floating green bubbles showed him when the battery needed charging, and Joe watched all three like a hawk. It was one of the tics he'd developed, within a month of starting the job. A second was the cleaning of his equipment. Joe hated dust. It got everywhere. All over his lenses and mirror, into the camera back and up inside his eyepiece, and he was forever wiping them all down - a proper Mrs Mop - puffing with his blower brush, huffing long, wet breaths over the glass and delicately rubbing everything down with fine Japanese lens cloths.

A third was his constant checking of the rewind handle on top of his camera, forever monitoring its tension and making sure it rotated when he wound on his film. As long as it turned, it meant his film was going through the camera correctly and, if it didn't, it meant the film had torn and he'd have to replace it with a new one, a habit the boss was very keen to deter. He really liked to keep a grip on the film budget, and grumbled at any of his staff who went through more than ten rolls a week. Plenty as that might seem, Joe soon found that coming in under 360 shots needed careful handling, especially if one of the week's jobs was, for example, the day-long Whit Walks - involving taking scores of photographs of churchgoers in their Sunday best - or you had seven summer fairs in one afternoon, or you were faced with shooting twelve naked models for the newspaper's next calendar.

Ha ha! Fat chance! Joe had never come within a sniff of a nude shot (and dreaded the day it might ever happen), and it pissed him off that the man in the street seemed to think that bare, busty women was all professional photographers ever shot. "Page Three, mate? Dirty bastard!"

-

He was sent to cover a rather dreary-sounding HGV drivers' 'Truk-Fest' on the industrial estate. Bristly, tattooed truckers swarmed around a long line of fancy-liveried lorries, swigging cans of Bud and thumping each other on their bare arms an inordinate number of times. Joe was drawn to a bright blue monster of a Mack wagon, with a flying eagle and the American stars and stripes painted on its door and, artfully air-brushed across the expansive bonnet, the inspirational words 'Spirit of the West'. (Yeah, West *Midlands*, he thought, cynically.) "Hey lad, do you want a good picture?" smirked one of the drivers. He nudged his mate with an elbow and winked. "Have a look in the cab," he said. "Go on, help yerself." Intrigued, Joe climbed the wagon's steep steps and practically fell into the driver's spongy seat, bouncing up a foot on its luxury air-suspension.
"Hey, big boy," said a soft voice. "So what'll it be for you then, me darling?"
A huge cheer erupted from the truckers as Joe turned to see a pretty girl smiling at him from a bunk in the back of the cab. She lay teasingly across a greasy, worn mattress, a threadbare blanket across her shoulders.
"Ah, oh .. oooh, didn't see you there," Joe stuttered. "I think I've been sent to take a picture of you. The guy outside just told me to come up."
"Oh, pictures is it?" she said, her smile dropping a little as she twisted dark locks between her nail-bitten fingers.
"What a shame. Nice looking lad like you, as well. Oh well, whatever floats yer boat, I suppose. Alright, darling, pictures are a fiver. Cash only, bien sûr!" She dropped the blanket and turned full on to Joe. She had nothing on but a neck-tie and Joe almost squeaked out loud. He fumbled in his pocket but, it being the day before pay day, he could only rustle up £1.74. "Oh go on, chuck," she said, leaning seductively backwards. "Have a freebie .."

"Oh, my God," Joe thought. "Where do I aim the flash gun?"

Page 61

The Olympus XA was the sexiest little camera Joe had ever seen. A cute, black broad-bean of a thing, so small it slipped snuggly into a pocket like a Joey in a pouch. Just what the doctor ordered. The thing was, although Joe thrived in his new job - loved it, of course - it dawned on him, a year or two in, that something was missing. There was something about press photography that just wasn't .. enough.

It wasn't ..

Hmm ..

It wasn't *real* enough.

That was it. It wasn't real enough. At least, not at his level. Not working for a weekly newspaper, photographing the meat and potatoes of life in small suburban towns. It was all too staged. Necessarily, of course, to suit the requirements of the newspaper, but failing to capture the true 'essence' of the world he was looking at. ('Capturing the essence' was one of his current favourite phrases, having come across it numerous times in the descriptions of photographers he now adored.) Reading about these 'icons' - Tod Papageorge, Wiliam Klein, Lee Friedlander - had reawakened his 'photographer's eye', and he found he was continually seeing wonderful photographs in his day-to-day life and .. not taking them. So, fancying himself as the next Robert Frank - the renowned pioneer of reportage photography - he'd dashed out and bought the XA and began to take it with him everywhere. Its tiny size meant it was perfect for working discreetly, and its near-as-damn-it silent shutter meant he was hardly ever spotted whenever he took a surreptitious picture. A long-running interest in social documentary photography had begun. Joe was thrilled by the quality and style of this new 'personal' work and would panic without the comforting bulge of the camera in his pocket whenever he went out.

His Dad, on the other hand, had stopped going out altogether. Redundancy had hit him hard. (Joe had already decided it was unfair to take any more photographs of Dad with his new camera. He also thought that it might be time to stop pestering him to "get a grip".) "Ach, what's the point?" Dad would grouch, couch-slouching in bri-nylon vest and undies. "What chance has an old fart like me have of getting a new job, eh? Did you see the .. what are they called? .. the unemployment figures in the 'paper this morning?" They were both only too aware that Dad's chances of getting back into work were grim to non-existent - what with major industry shipping ever more offshore - and it was a sorry thing to say but, as the world crunched into the 1980s, Dad's hard-earned, hands-on skills were no longer needed. Worryingly too, his Dad seemed to be forgetting things more and more. "Put the snooker on," he'd say. "It's on BBC .. er .."
"Two?" Joe would suggest. "BBC2, perchance?"

-

Once he'd moved in with his Dad, Joe had been invited to join a ritual that his father enjoyed every Saturday. Each week, he would scrub up and change clothes after a morning at the factory, then head off to his mother's house for a "wee sing-song" with his parents and his siblings, a taste of the 'old country' that held the family together after their 'emigration' all those years ago. Dad had come to England first, of course, but he was only on his own for three weeks before he was joined by his eldest sister, who tried her hand as a hotel receptionist before buggering off back, homesick, to be with her family again. Unfortunately, before she could re-settle, all her other siblings - *and* their parents - followed Dad over to Manchester. She ended up being the only one left in Northern Ireland and never spoke to any of them ever again.

It didn't take Dad long to thump a smart-arse in the mouth when asked which part of *Scotland* he came from - he was very proud of his Irish heritage, was Dad - but, otherwise, he seemed to fit into the English way of life straight away. The entire family followed suit, settling happily and relatively swiftly, and their crowded new home - just across the road from the swimming baths - became known as a house of laughter, music, fun and alcohol. Eventually, each of the family members met, married and moved on, but the house remained a magnet for them all. Their "wee sing-songs" on Saturday afternoons became a literal 'gathering of the clan' as they converged with their Bell's and Jameson's, lemonade and ginger mixers.

"I've been a wild rover for many a year .." Dad always started the singing, his strong tenor tones drowning out his sisters' screechy shrieks. Grandad would sit in the corner, puffing contentedly on his pipe and nodding as the generational baton passed on, and Grandma - in house-coat and light blue knitted bobby-hat - would pointlessly offer tea from a pot she kept stewing on top of the gas fire. (It never ceased to amaze Joe just how long that woman could eke out three spoonfuls of tea-leaves.) Eventually, after the obligatory chorus of "If you're Irish, come into the parlour", the singing would give way to silliness and sentimental reminiscence, followed by outpourings of love and Dave Allen. They loved their brother's imitation of the Irish comedian, and would howl with laughter as the end of his shortened finger disappeared high into his nostril.

-

Joe had to give up on the 'sing-songs' once he started working the weekends, but he didn't really mind. They'd become a little repetitive and he was fed up of being drunk before he'd even had his evening meal. Aware though, that he and Dad didn't seem to be doing much together these days, Joe asked the boss if he could have a Saturday afternoon off one week. (He'd work late on Sunday to make up for the time.) Determined to cheer Dad up, he pulled his suit from the wardrobe and told him to jump in the bath. "We're going for a knees-up at yer mother's," he smiled, as genuinely as he could. "Get your bits washed and we'll pick up Aunt Hilda on the way."
"Hilda?" frowned Dad. "Who's aunt is she?"
"Mine, you plonker," laughed Joe. "My Aunt Hilda. Your *sister*. Remember?"
He didn't, but he did remember the music. The old Irish rebel songs came thick and fast, just as soon as the first Jameson's was downed. Some things .. no, some things you don't ever forget.

-

Joe's grandparents died within three weeks of each other and the wee sing-songs came to an end. Sentimental at the best of times, Dad never got over their deaths and, every week - until he didn't remember any more - he'd go to the crematorium where their ashes were scattered and pour a miniature bottle of Bell's over the spot he thought his Dad might now be spending his days.
Joe had gone with him once and, with the XA's silent shutter, it had made for a beautifully intimate photograph.

Page 62

Some nosy, slime-ball, curtain-twitcher told Kevin about Joe's visit to his Mum, and the bastard slapped her so hard the bruising was still visible when she met her son for coffee two weeks later. At least the shock had subsided when they finally got together for the first time. "I was so worried it would put you off coming," said Joe, heart pounding as they took their seats in the café.
"Oh, don't you worry about Kevin," Mum replied. "I'm never letting him get between me and my son again."
"Oh Mum!" Joe stood again quickly and threw his arms around her neck, the first time he'd hugged her in years. It felt so right and his heart began to soar. "I can't believe what he's done to you," he croaked. "I'm so sorry, Mum. It's all my fault." The tears fell, despite himself, and Joe clung to his Mum for so long that the waitress had to prod him with a pencil to get past.
"So, what've you been up to?" they said, simultaneously. The ice was broken and the conversation went from there.
"I hear you're a photographer now," said Mum. "Working for a 'paper?"
"I am," said Joe, proudly. "I work for The .."
"What's the money like?" she said, straight to the point. When Joe told her his weekly wage she burst out laughing. "I *told* you there was no money in photography," she giggled, waving her teaspoon in his face.

-

The chit-chat turned to Kevin, and Mum began to falter. "I'll never forgive him for what he did to you," she said, so quietly that Joe had to crane across the formica tabletop. "And I'll never forget that awful Christmas, when I made you leave the house because Kevin was waiting upstairs, but .."

A spasm of worry shot through Joe and he held up his hands to stop her.

"No, hear me out Joe," Mum said. "This is important. You'll never know how much my heart was breaking that Christmas Day."

Yours and mine both, Joe thought. "But you told me you didn't want me there," he sniffed. "Your exact words were 'You can't be here.' I remember it like it was yesterday."

His Mum took a sip of her drink and tried to smile. "I was trying to protect you," she said. "It was *me* that told Kevin to stay upstairs that morning. He was chomping at the bit to come down and throw you out again, but I told him to stay where he was and I'd sort it out. It tore me to pieces but I had to get you out of there before Kevin got downstairs. I hope you can understand and .. I hope you can forgive."

Joe swallowed hard. Gosh, he hadn't expected *that*. "Water under the bridge," he said, his attempt at being magnanimous. He flicked a wrist and forced a smile. "And probably the best thing that's ever happened to me, Mum. Made me stand on my own two feet, that did. Or at least on Dad's," he added, throwing in a laugh. He felt sad when Mum didn't follow up on his lead. But why *should* she? His parents were divorced. Dad was of no interest to her, now. That chapter of her life was over.

He bit his lip. He needed to ask about ..

"Erm, there *is* one thing, Joe," said Mum, getting in before him. She licked her lips and urgently pressed spilt sugar into the table. Joe parked his question and half-smiled. "Look, please don't think badly of me," she began. "But I love Kevin. I know he's hit me, *and* you, and I *know* he can be a horrible man at times, but I love him. And if you're thinking I should leave him, well, that's not going to happen, is it? Not now we have Gary. I couldn't even *think* of leaving him now, Joe. Anyway, he's agreed to some marriage counselling and I think that'll help us sort things out." She lifted her eyes and shrugged, almost shyly. "Please understand, Joe. It won't stop me seeing you, but I *have* to take Kevin's feelings into consideration."

"And what about *mine*? Joe snapped, distraught. He stormed from the café and ran to his car in a rage.

Page 63

Dad signed onto the 'dole' and it nearly killed him. He dove into a depression that was exacerbated all the more by the fact he now seemed to realise something was 'going on' in his head.

Joe had had his own experience of depression and the 'dole' after he'd left the Army, and felt he had a good idea of what his Dad was going through. He'd never forgotten the shame, the embarrassment or the sense of failure at having to accept those Government handouts. Once he'd left the military, there was an interval of almost three months before he could start his job at the factory and so, until that time, he'd had to walk into town every week to 'sign on'. He hated going to the 'Labour Exchange'. It brought out in him an un-grounded snobbery, an 'above-ness' that made him feel he didn't belong in that rag-tag queue of 'losers', alongside rough-looking nicotine-stained oiks in scruffy clothes, spitting tobacco and scratching their bits as they shuffled towards the counters. The men were just as bad.

"You should have stayed in the Army," his Mum had said, stirring a big pot of her 'famous' barley broth.

"I didn't *suit* the Army," Joe'd sighed. "We've been over all this, Mum. You know I couldn't get to grips with being just one part of a platoon."
"Oh, hark Lord High and Mighty," Mum scoffed, hand on hip.
"Oh, you know what I mean," Joe snapped. "It's all well and good being good at something, but if one dimwit in your squad couldn't do it then all the rest of us were kept back with him. It just wasn't for me .."

-

"Naah, not for me," said his Dad, after Joe suggested a drive into the countryside.
"Oh come on, Let's get some fresh air into you. Let's go and stretch our legs."

A long walk would have done Dad a world of good, but these days he didn't go further than the Off Licence to restock the fags and whiskey before slumping back into his knackered old armchair to doze and drink away the day. Joe couldn't get him inspired at all and then, out of the blue, his Dad came back from the 'Offy' with three packs of rolling tobacco and a large box of Brillo pads. Joe's heart rose, thinking Dad was about to do something major like hey, wash the pots. "Now *that's* a good sign," he laughed, pointing to the scourers.
"What the fuck?" Dad threw them straight off the balcony. "What did you get those for?"
"Me?" Joe countered. "*You* bought them. You've just been to Abdul's for them."
Dad sat down and scratched his five-day fuzz. "Brillo pads?" he frowned. "Why the fuck would I buy B .. aw, shit! I wanted Bells .."

The days go by ..

Well, that didn't go too well, did it? The brave face, and all that? Keep smiling, all that gumph. I just couldn't keep it up. Couldn't maintain the façade and hey, why the fuck should I? There was only Joe to delude but it looks like he's finally worked it out at last, the daft bastard.

My life is shit. It's over. I'm on the scrap-heap and I can't see a way back. I can't even afford a night out anymore. I haven't been to the .. what do you call it? .. the .. oh, you know, the Catholic Club .. for months. I don't *want* to go now, anyway. Good Catholics *they* all turned out to be, eh? Not one of them's come round to see how I am or offered to dob me a couple of quid 'til my dole comes through. Balls to them all, that's what I say.

Do you want a whiskey? No? Oh well, I'll just have a wee one, while we're talking.

I don't think Joe's meeting with his mother went too well. He won't talk about it but he came in in a hell of a mood after going to see her. I'm glad he's around, you know. He reminded me last Friday I hadn't filled in my Pools coupon. First time I've forgotten to do that since I don't know when. Mind you, I don't know why I still bother with 'em. Haven't won a sausage in years. Anyway, as I said, I'm glad he's here. I had my doubts as to how it would all turn out back when, you know, when he first moved in, but we both settled quickly and I knew I was doing the right thing when I put my name down for the two-bedroomed flat. How he sneaks the ladies in and out, I'll never know. I've never heard a single girl in all the time we've lived here. At least, I can't remember hearing one.

Page 64

Life slipped into a delicious rhythm for Joe. Constantly learning on the job, he loved the spontaneity of his new life. It was all so different to his regulated (twelve!) weeks in the Army, and the stagnating two years behind the desk in the factory. He'd resolved to get back in touch with Mum after his angry outburst and so, despite the worry of his Dad, life was good.

He and Andy seemed to be running the photographic department by themselves these days, as there was a conspicuous and frequent absence of the boss. Sometimes, they only knew he'd been back to the office when there was something new in the porno pile. (Talk about perks of the job!) New apprentice Barry was back on his feet - albeit rockily - after his bike accident (even though they still couldn't work out what he was there *for*) and there was a pleasant 'vibe' to the whole newspaper office. Advertising had slowly picked up again and print runs had been steady across all titles for quite a few weeks. Joe even got a pay rise and had the bumps hammered out of his lovely blue Chevette. The 'foreigners' were going well, too. No-one seemed to mind - or *know* - that Joe was making a decent few quid every month now, selling on stories or making extra prints from jobs and dropping them off at the offices of the Nationals when the night desks came on at ten. It looked like a good way to get a job with them. A couple more years and I'll be in there, he said to himself.

Away from work, life still revolved around girls and music. Ok, music! There was just so much of it, and all of it so absolutely wonderful. Joe could head into Manchester and get two punk gigs and a disco under his belt before he caught the last bus home at 2.30 am. Punk, disco, punk, disco, funk, rock, pop .. the beat went on, and the louder the better. Joe loved the feeling of being physically battered by music. Loved the power, the force, the energy. It wasn't an evening worth having if you didn't come home without a ringing in your ears.
"You want to be careful of all that noise," his Dad used to say - when he roused an interest - and *he* would know. His tinitus had grown steadily worse and he was now stone deaf in his right ear after so many years in the clanging, metallic world in which he'd made his living. Joe filed that with "You should watch your back, young man". Every time he went to photograph an event in a hospital, a nurse would invariably tap him on the shoulder and warn him of the dangers of carrying his heavy camera bag haphazardly over his left shoulder. "You should watch your back, young man."

A minor Royal was in town and Joe was muscling to keep his position in a restless press pack, corralled a good twenty feet from where Her Royal Uselessness would meet Joe Public. "Hey, don't you work for The Courier?" said a snapper he'd never seen before. "I hear your boss likes little boys. You should watch your back, young man."

-

"Alright, Mince?" Joe turned instinctively, though he hadn't heard the nickname in years. "Bloody hell," he chuckled. "Batman?" It was John Dayne, his one-time 'partner-in-crime', the school pal from the playground to whom Joe had

always played second fiddle. "Wow, you've changed." He brazenly patted his old chum's shiny, bald head. "Hard life?"
"Three kids," said John, shrugging his shoulders. "Three kids, a 'mare' of a wife and a job that bores the shit out of me."
Joe's jaw dropped. "But you were *Batman!*" he exclaimed. "My hero. You were going to conquer the world .. or be a pilot for BOAC, or an astronaut, or a footballer, or .."
"Fucking hell," John coughed. "Those dreams were shattered a long time ago. I'm a sales rep for a carpet company now. Have been for years." He looked at Joe's face and burst out laughing, spraying a fine spittle over Joe's new Burton's jacket. The disappointment Joe felt in his old mucker lasted less than a second, then it was all he could do to hide an awful sense of smugness. He nodded towards a café across the street and led John in for a coffee. "So where did it all go wro .. er, why did you have this change of plan, John? I thought you'd have been set for life by now." (The fact that he hadn't actually thought of him for years seemed irrelevant at this point.)
"Ha! Life .." John puffed, through his outstretched bottom lip. "What do they say? It's what happens while you're making plans, eh? Well, that definitely happened to me. I only got two 'O' levels and Liz was pregnant before we'd left fifth year."
"Liz?" Joe automatically in leant closer. "Not Liz Parker?" he breathed, excitedly. "The girl with the mega-knockers? The girl everyone fancied when we were nine?"
"The very same," nodded John. "The girl who'd go out with anyone. She wasn't called 'Park it with Parker' for nothing. And I've been paying the parking fines ever since."

Joe let a moment pass, and slurped the dregs of his cooling coffee. "Anyway," he said, trying to remain bright. "What about old Jeff Battersby? Remember him? Great kid, wasn't he? Any chance you're still in touch?"

"Batters?" said John, somewhat taken aback. "He choked to death on his own vomit in 1975."

Page 65

There didn't seem to be a day that passed without Joe photographing a sponsored event. Sponsored beard shaves, sponsored fun runs (Who the hell put *those* two words together?), sponsored knits, sponsored twenty-four hour table tennis .. the list went on and on and on. And more power to its elbow, thought Joe. Gave a lot of people something good to do, and the monies raised kept a lot of useful charities ticking along nicely.

-

A thought struck him one day. Joe realised he'd never seen the 'middle' of a sponsored event. How funny! The beginnings, the launches, the send-offs .. yes, he was always on hand for those. And the end results .. the cheque presentations, the guide dog handovers, the crocheted hospital blankets .. he shot those all the time. But what about the events themselves? What was it like, for example, twelve hours into a twenty-four hour bike ride, or half-way around a (fun?) run? Cynically, he wondered if the damned things actually went ahead, or whether the participants simply buggered off once the crowds had all gone home? Curiosity got the better of him and he set his alarm for two am one night, dragging himself out of bed and back to the Golden Lion where, fourteen hours earlier, he'd photographed pub regular Eddie Boden as he sat down to play the piano for a full twenty-four hours. The Lion had been rammed that lunchtime, crammed with cheering supporters and banners, boozers and bonhomie.

"Go for it, Eddie."
"Eat your heart out, Elton."
"Do you know 'Clare', by Gilbert O'Sullivan?"

Things looked an awful lot different in the dark of the night. The pub was empty, lights off save a lamp on top of the piano. The bar was full of sticky pint pots, the cig smoke was sinking and a cup of strong coffee sat half-drunk by C8. In the middle of it all was Eddie, still tinkling away at twenty past two in the morning. He hadn't buggered off, after all. He was, in fact, halfway through a very slow version of another Gilbert O'Sullivan song. 'Alone again (Naturally)'. How ironic. And he looked shattered. "Me bloody back's killing me," he said, giving Joe a weary, welcome nod. He was leaning forward, chest hovering just above the keyboard, his eyes blinking rapidly and his tired fingers lifting and dropping like little spider legs. Despite the tune, he wasn't completely on his own. Another pub regular sat directly behind him on the stool, a skinny lady who tapped out a rhythm on his back with her long, sharpened fingernails, a snoozing chihuahua curled up at her feet. Every now and again she'd slap a little harder and jerk Eddie back to life with a "lovely tune, that," or a "miles better than Liberace", and the sight touched Joe immensely. The dedication, the bravery, the sheer unselfishness of it all. "Eddie," he said. "You are a bloomin' hero." He took a few available light photographs and dropped a ten pound note into the bucket on top of the piano. Three weeks later he photographed Eddie again, handing over a cheque for £4,500 to Manchester Dogs' Home.

-

The vast majority of charity funds seemed to end up at the big Children's Hospital in the west of Manchester, and Joe was such a regular visitor that the nurses had taken to calling him Reginald Bosanquet and made him his own official name badge. It broke Joe's heart to enter the cancer ward there and look at the hairless, yellow children - babies sometimes - whose bodies were wracked with the disease.

How did they all stay so chirpy? he used to think. And what the hell is our government doing when a ward like this still relies on outside funding to enable it to run? If everyone got a chance to see what he could see here, he reckoned, the place would *never* be short of money again.

-

The Red Cross Society was a good cause too, and here was Joe in its northern HQ to photograph two muscly geezers who'd swum the English Channel and raised an amazing £12,000 for its coffers. After he'd taken their photograph, he noticed a poster on the wall.

Free Parachute Jump!

He signed up straight away. Why? He'd never know. (Anything you can do, cousin Brian?) The Red Cross was offering the public a chance to 'enjoy' a 'free' parachute jump, and it was only later, when he got home, that Joe started to feel a little, shall we say, queasy? (Oh, what have I done?) As much as deep water still scared him, even a swim across the Channel seemed a better option right now.

The jump was three months hence and the idea was simple. All each participant had to do was raise a minimum of £1,000 in order to qualify for their 'free' parachute jump, to which end Joe was given a sponsorship form and urged to hustle up money from whoever he could. He began to hawk the form around the office and took it with him on jobs to see if he could convince people to cough up some dosh. It was hard going, but looked promising. Training was once a week at the Red Cross office, and the boss generously allowed Joe time off to fit in with their schedule. It didn't seem hard at all, and Joe's confidence rose after each session he attended.

"Chin up and don't forget your star-shape as you exit," said their trainer. "Arms out, legs out as you jump off the table. One thousand, two thousand, three thousand, four thousand. Check canopy. That's the sequence. Off you go .."

Each of the participants self-consciously launched themselves from one of the office desks.

"Ok, elbows and knees together and roll onto your side as you land," said the instructor. "And there you go, ladies and gentlemen. That's as hard as you'll hit the ground when you jump. It won't hurt a bit, I promise."

The group's first coach trip to the jump site, up by the coast in Cumbria, turned out to be a bit of a damp squib. Sweating profusely, Joe had stayed awake for most of the night, steeling himself to go ahead with the drop. He could legitimately pull out, he figured, as he'd only managed a promise of £850 but, come the morning, he found himself on the bus, talking the talk with his fellow squeaky-bum jumpers. It was too windy when they got there, so they all had a cup of tea, got back on the bus and came home - the very definition of an anti-climax! Three months later they were back at the airfield, all bar one young lady who'd discovered she was pregnant. Joe started to wish *he* was three months gone as an ageing Islander aircraft lifted them away from the ground. He was second to jump, sitting with his legs around the backside of the jumper in front. The aircraft door was open, and a screamingly loud wind rushed in. He hadn't been able to find a decent helmet to use, and had had to borrow his old motor-bike 'pudding' from the office.

"Are we there yet?" he yelled, looking down at a distant pattern of fields. The jump master shook his head sympathetically and the 'plane continued to climb until, after a few more noisy minutes and another 2,350 feet, a green light came on above the door. "This is it," he bellowed, his words scattered by the rattling wind. "Remember your training and you'll be fine. Enjoy!!" He beckoned to the first jumper, who slid confidently forward on his bum and disappeared from the open door with such alacrity ("Holy shit!") that Joe nearly wet himself. And then it was his turn. His heart was battering. "Remember the sequence," he gasped, through panting breath. "The sequence, the sequence, the sequence .." He glanced up at the sky, barely registering the wispy, white clouds, and whispered "Please don't let me die God," as he made a teensy Sign of the Cross. Before he knew it his legs were dangling over the threshold and then he was out, slapped manfully on the back by the guy behind.

"One thouoooooooaaaaaaaaaaaaaaaaaaaaghhh …!! Fuuuuuuuuck … !!!"

The sequence went out of the window as Joe fell out of the door. He dropped like a sack of spuds and his 'star-shape' looked more like vertical front crawl as his arms wheeled desperately through the air. After what felt like three hours, the static line tensed and, still thankfully attached to the plane above him, ripped the parachute from his backpack. The sudden slow-down yanked Joe's feet high over his head and after that - after the most wondrous feeling of relief - the most amazingly peaceful calm Joe had ever experienced.

"Whoooooooo .." he screamed. "Alllllrrriiiiiggghhhttt!!!"

He grabbed his steering toggles and tugged them left and right, aiming himself towards a big white target cross on the ground. He'd been forbidden to take a camera with him, so he began to look around, committing the incredible view to memory. Wow, the sea. Wow, the fields. Wow, the …

… ground!

He got so distracted that he crashed into a field next to the target, hitting it so hard they found his specs in a cow-pat another ten feet further on. The landing hurt a lot. That trainer was a bloody liar.

And that wasn't even the hard part ..

Joe could not possibly have guessed how difficult it was to extract money from people who had earlier pledged to sponsor him. Getting people to cough up their fivers and their pound notes was a much tougher proposition than jumping out of a bumpy, sky-high aeroplane. For every three "Well dones" there was always one "prove it", and he was constantly having to 'flash' a certificate he'd been awarded for his achievement. It took him four months to scrape together just over seven hundred pounds, but his respect for charity fund-raisers would stay with him forever.

Page 66

The British Army's L1A1 7.62mm self-loading rifle was a semi-automatic weapon with a tilting breechblock and an effective range of over 800 yards. It was gas-operated, with a 20 round magazine and a muzzle velocity of 2,700 feet per second. Made in Belgium, too. Funny what you remember when there's one pointed straight at you.

Joe froze, almost (comically) putting his hands into the air as his military training bubbled up through the grey matter. A bored paratrooper lowered the gun and wobbled in the back of a camouflaged Land-Rover as it splashed through a large puddle, sending an arc of water up Joe's leg. The vehicle turned a corner and went away. Nothing to see here, move along. Just another day during 'The Troubles' in Belfast, Northern Ireland. Walking again, heart-rate finally slowing, Joe managed a smile and nodded, knowingly. "I've fired one of them," he said. "Oh yes."

He was on his first ever 'foreign' holiday - a two week trip to Dad's old Ulster stomping ground. Despite the appalling political situation, he'd been thrilled to receive an invitation to his cousin Moira's wedding and headed off pronto to the travel agents to book himself a flight. His first ever flight in a jet. Whoopee! Just don't throw up this time, he told himself. (Or jump out of it, ha ha ha ..) August couldn't come fast enough and then finally, for the first time in his life, he was breathing kerosene fumes at *ground* level, a shiny white jet towering *above* him for once on the apron at Manchester Airport. The British Airways BAC 1-11 landed in Belfast ninety minutes after take-off and, buoyed up by two on-board cans of lager and a vomit-free sweatshirt, Joe strode lightheartedly through to baggage reclaim and straight into his first Army stop and search. He gulped hard, the memories of his military 'career' flashing before his eyes. "I was in the Army, you know?" he brazened to the Lance-Corporal going through his bag. The soldier - six-foot three if he was an inch - looked down at Joe and shouted "Boo!", and the hiccups the shock gave him didn't subside until the next fright. His Northern Irish cousin Conn had come to pick him up .. on a motorbike! A Yamaha XDP 9670 .. or something. (It was a lot bigger than The Frog, that's all Joe knew!)

"Is it yourself there, Joey?" beamed Conn, in an Antrim brogue a million broad miles from the 'rellies' at home, their accents dulled by years of Manchester mixing. (Joe hadn't the foggiest idea what he'd said!) Conn tossed over a large black crash-helmet and beckoned for him to get onto the back of the bike, then kick-started the loudest engine Joe had ever heard. He didn't throw up on the way home but a bladder full of lager meant he damn- near pissed himself as his cousin hit a hundred and ten down the narrow country lanes of 'N'orn Iron'. "Conn," he kept shouting. "Slow down, Cuz! I'm dying for a wee, here. Let me oooooff!" Conn heard not a word and, even if he had, wouldn't have understood it, Joe's Lancashire accent being a world away from his own.

The bride-to-be was busy in the kitchen, elbow deep in flour and baking mess as Joe arrived at the family home. He fell for Moira the second he saw her. A touch older than he, she was petite with jet-black hair; elegant, arched eyebrows and a luscious pair of cupid's bow lips. She was shapely, sexy and .. his first cousin .. and he practically felt The Lord tap his shoulder as he ogled his relative's wondrous breasts.

"What about ya, Jophes?" she grinned, looking up from kneading a large white ball of dough. Joe could only smile back, not knowing quite what 'waddabowcha' actually meant, but felt his knees weaken at the sound of her delicious, Irish lilt. She could have been telling him his trousers smelt of old man's plop and he'd have got turned on. Moira clapped her floury hands together and reached across for a cigarette, which burnt in an ashtray beside the yeasty globe. Suddenly, Joe saw smoking in a whole new light. The sight of the streamy, grey 'kiss' being blown towards him by those soft, sexy 'O' lips meant it wasn't only the dough that rose in the kitchen that morning. (Shame she dropped her ash in the bread mix.) He snapped back to reality as Conn thrust a can of warm Harp lager into his sweaty fist.
"YershernaruumwiCalmfyewannadropyerbagin," Conn yodelled. Joe eventually deciphered the sentence as "you're sharing a room with Callum if you want to drop your bag in", and reluctantly wrenched himself from Moira and went to get rid of his rucksack.

-

He felt rather on edge, arriving back at his cousins' house after his first soggy walk around Belfast. Soldiers everywhere, check-points to queue through and the constant drone of a helicopter high above, scanning for stuff Joe didn't want to know about. He'd been shocked to see so many garish, provocative murals on the city's terraced gable-ends ..

SUPPORT THE UFF
YOU ARE NOW ENTERING A LOYALIST AREA
PREPARED FOR PEACE - READY FOR WAR

.. all illustrated with frighteningly realistic pictures of balaclava-clad gun-men in threateningly aggressive poses. One in particular had unnerved him. Underneath a picture of a camouflaged 'soldier' carrying a grenade launcher, a painted banner urged ..

KILL ALL FENIAN BASTARDS

"Conn," he said. "What's a Fenian bastard?" Conn spat his lager over a motorbike magazine and pointed straight at Joe. "You are .." he laughed, rather cruelly, Joe felt. "You're a Fenian bastard, Joey. You're a *Catholic!* Ha ha. Aye, that's what Fenian means, so it does. Welcome to N'orn Iron, cuz. Ha ha ha .."

-

Joe nearly, very nearly, went to bed with a woman in Northern Ireland. (Not Moira, obviously!) His cousin's wedding was going well. True, the Nuptial Mass had seemed to last an eon, but now the congregation was finally out of the church and back at the hotel reception. The new Mrs. McClachlan was radiant and Joe was already pissed. (The draught Guinness seemed a damned sight stronger than it did in Manchester. Perhaps it was the anticipation; each newly-poured pint left settling on the bar until it was ready to be topped up. Perhaps it was how relaxed he felt, enjoying his first ever proper holiday. Perhaps it was the fact that Joe was envious as hell of Danny 'Mad Dog' McClachlan, the man who, from this day on, was legally entitled to have sex with .. Aaagh, stop it Joe!)

Woozy as he was, he still couldn't fail to be impressed by his cousin's wedding photographer, a wee figure of a man who called them all out from the bar for a group photograph. Five foot one, in flat cap and scruffy green mac, the octogenarian (at least) had somehow magically rustled all seventy-five tipsy, rowdy guests into some semblance of a composition with just a polite whisper and a crinkly twinkle of his old Irish eyes. Raising a battered Rollei twin-lens reflex to his eye, he breathed "Tree, two, one" and pressed the little button on the front. "Tanks a lot," he smiled. He wound on the film and led off the happy couple for a close-ups.

"One shot?" gasped Joe. "*One* shot? Shit, he must be good!"
"Oh, he's de best," said a heavily-made up lady at his side. "Sure he's Paddy McDoogan, so's he is. Been the town's photographer for years. Must of taken photies of every one of us here, right from when we was wee 'uns .."

-

Joe strolled off for a breather as the group went back to the bar. Probably best to ease off on the pop for a bit. There were hours to drink yet, and they'd not even started on the wedding breakfast. He headed to the town's renowned Norman Castle, the solid, stern, square beast that guarded the inlet to the port. He'd shot round to see it on the first day of his trip, keen to connect with the place his Dad had told him so much about. As a kid, Dad had said - long before the tourist board had done it up and turned it into a vulgar Disney wannabe - he and his little pals would run around the ruin then jump from its vertiginous ramparts straight into the sea. (Just looking at the height of it made Joe's stomach churn.) Dad had never been in the sea again though, and Joe often joked that he'd throw his ashes off the top, just to get him back in the water.

Stomach rumbling, and bursting for a pee, Joe returned to The Dobbs Hotel just in time to be served a rather luminescent prawn cocktail, and found himself seated next to the made-up lady from the group shot. "Oh, hello again," she said, in her soft, Irish lilt. "Are ye having a wonderful time?" Joe managed a nod as he wolfed down his starter. "I hear you're a photographer, too," she winked, leaning breast-revealingly close to his cheap prosecco. Joe swore he saw steam rise from the glass.
"Yep," he said, urgently munching prawns and staring straight ahead.
"So how's about you take some photies of me, hm?"
Joe gulped and forced a stretched grin across his face.
"Erm .."

She'd got him back to her house before the night was out. Joe was sweating Guinness. "I won't be able to do a proper job with this," he trembled, having travelled light and taken only his ever-present Olympus XA. (I'm naked without it, he used to say.) The lovely Clodagh went naked too, dragging him up to her chintzy bedroom and pushing him onto her bed. As she ripped at his shirt, Joe noticed a framed, fading wedding photo on her bedside table, she a twenty-something bride, a man-mountain in a cheap suit and dicky bow standing sternly beside her. "Are you *married*?" he squealed, and squirmed to get out from beneath her. "Ach, don't youse worry yourself about that eejit," she drawled. "He's on hunger strike in The Maze."

Joe couldn't lift his mood after Northern Ireland. He felt sad and very confused, and it was all the fault of religion. He just couldn't see the point of it.
Any of it.

Kill all Fenian bastards? So somebody would happily blow his arse to Kingdom Come just because his version of Christianity was different to theirs? Maybe they all had different Kingdom Comes, he mused. Kingdoms Come? Kingdoms Comes? He envisaged a wondrous version of Heaven without Benediction. "Sorry," he said aloud, looking up at Dad's Sacred Heart and joining his fingertips in placation. "I didn't mean it, Jesus. Sorry." (He just Could Not shake this Catholic guilt.) I mean, every bloody war man has ever had has been over religion, he generalised. Wrong God, wrong way of worshipping God, wrong creeds, wrong vestments, wrong .. sex? Ha, *She'd* soon sort them all out! He was a year or two from knowing of an American rock band called 'Faith No More' and, when he got into them, he wrote to ask if they'd consider changing their name to 'Religion No More'. They didn't write back. There is no God, after all.

More often than not - stuck into the Jack Daniels' - Joe's thoughts would swing from religion to his other crusty mainstay: The Meaning Of Life. Was there any? Any at all? (Answers on 6 billion postcards, please.) Annoyingly for him, his Catholic upbringing would have him believe he was put on Earth just so that he could die and (assuming he'd been a good boy, of course), rise up to Heaven, where he could sit at the right hand of some Wondrous Supreme Deity and live with Him/Her/It for all eternity. So, he'd think, why not skip to the chase, God? Cut out all that time-wasting earthbound crap, make as many billions of creatures as you need and have them sit around you 'til .. well, forever. (It usually took Joe about three JDs to get *this* worked up.) It screwed him into a ball when he thought of the mystery of it all, the inexorable need for life to keep reproducing itself. Life that was alive just so that it could produce life which produces life which ..

Aaaaaaagh!!

Round and around, round and around, the very survival of life itself more important than the actual forms it took. It seemed to Joe that, now that life had sparked into existence, it was scared to death (ha ha) of letting that light go out. And he couldn't get his head around the randomness of it all, the seemingly arbitrary 'decisions' dictating that life required water, and water needed two atoms of hydrogen and one of oxygen .. and so on and so on and so on. But *who said* water was the prerequisite for life, and *who said* it had to be two to one? Just who - or what - had made those decisions?
Aaaaaaagh!!

They weren't decisions, of course. It was all 'just' physics and biology. (He'd read about it in a Daily Telegraph book review.) The laws of nature. Science inexplicably converting inert to existing .. somehow. So forget the beards, the haloes, the miracles, perhaps that 'somehow', that 'power', that 'energy', is what should *really* be called God? The cause of everything, the architect of life, life that just *has* to keep itself going, ever evolving, ever improving, at all costs. Life, in every form, from naturally-selected virus to coal-tit to Martin Buchan that, all the way up the evolutionary food chain - for its own (selfish?) survival - must fight and bully and threaten and eat and hound and control and harass and overpower and hurt and scare and .. kill. It has to, or it won't survive. But *WHAT* was *so* important about surviving? *WHY* does life have to keep going?

Aaaaaaagh!!

He knocked back a fourth and suddenly remembered the luckless little mouse he'd seen dispatched under the wheels of a lorry. For a split second he almost envied it, a furry bag of atoms that didn't know it had died because the lucky bastard had never been troubled by that singularly aggravating human 'quality' - the bothersome knowledge that it was alive. So what had been the point of its tiny little life? And what's the point of *mine*? (Shhhh!!!! Joe knew that life was sacrosanct in the eyes of the Church and shuddered at his heretical musings.) In the end, (fifth glass) he had (as usual) to tell himself to stop worrying about it all. (Lord knows, finer minds than his had had a go at it all and never come up with anything concrete.) All Joe knew was that it *was* good to be alive. To experience for himself all those mysterious laws of nature and to be amazed at knowing he'd been given a crack at experiencing life on Earth. Ok, he'd spend it all in a constant state of befuddlement - in the dark about everything from electricity to why boats float to how a human can make an immediate assessment of another person based solely on the arrangement of dead cells on their heads - so perhaps it *was* enough just to 'be'; to spread pollen (if you were a bee), to shade a hot buffalo (if you were a tree), to make someone smile (if you were Dave Allen) or help a granny cross a road (or win a trip to New York, if you were Joe!) Oh, God knows!

Bloody God!

Aiming himself tipsily at his bedroom, Joe heard his Dad snore loudly. No surprise. He'd been in bed since four that afternoon.

"Oh God," Joe prayed. "Please help me."

Half noon and Dad got up. He looked like Worzel Gummidge, shirt creased, hair as jagged as a hedgehog. He shuffled into the kitchen and lit up a fag, setting off a rack of coughs that went on for a good thirty seconds.
"You really should give up those cancer sticks," said Joe. "They'll be the death of you. Just listen."
"Nag, nag, nag," wheezed Dad, waving a puppet-mouth hand at Joe. "Go ahead with your own life, leave me alone," he sang, his favourite line from Billy Joel's song 'My Life'.
"Oh, there's a letter for you," said Joe, nodding towards the side-board.

-

"My God. There's life in the old dog yet."
"What's up?" said Joe. "Finally won the Pools?"
"Well, fuck a duck," Dad gasped, re-reading the letter. "I've a job interview, Joe. I'm going to get a new job!" He looked fit to bust, and subconsciously began to flatten his explosion of a hair-do. "Sure, I can't believe it. Who'd have thought I'd finally get myself off the dole?"
"What?" said Joe, dropping his corned-beef sandwich. "Let me see." He yanked the letter from Dad and quickly scanned it through. "Bloody hell, how's this come about? Caretaker, eh? Right up your street, that, Dad. Well done."
"Aye, made for me. This new job'll set me up nicely."
"Well, steady on," said Joe, uneasily. "It's only an interview. You haven't actually got the job yet."
"Oh, I'll get it," said Dad, confidently. "Who could resist a good lookin' fella like me?" What looks had to do with it God only knows but, good grief, thought Joe, just look at him! His Dad was coming back to life, right in front of him. Like someone had plugged him into a charger. "I'm away for a shave," he said. "Where do we keep the towels?"

Joe shook his head and passed him a clean towel from the airing cupboard. "Get *you*," he said, grinning widely. "Good to see my old man's returned. So, tell me about the job. Where is it, and what would you have to do? Is the money any good?"

Dad slathered his throat with foam and the heavy growth scritched as he ran a blunt razor up his neck. "There's a new community centre being built," he said, through a mouth half-closed. "Just off, erm .. oh, you know .. halfway to the off-licence. What's that road called? Anyway, I happened to get chatting to some council big-wig when I walked past the other day and he told me they were looking for a caretaker so .. ouch, ya bastard!" The blunt razor snagged and ripped a plug of skin from Dad's chin. "Anyway, I told him I was the man for the job and he took my details. I mean, I'm perfect for it, aren't I? All my years as an, er .. what was it? .. engineer? All my charm. All my .."

"Good looks?" Joe interjected. "Yeah, right." His Dad flicked a splodge of foam at Joe, spattering his glasses and making him laugh. The news was doing wonders for his mental state. Please let him get the job, God. Please.

-

He got the job (Thank you, God) and started at the centre four weeks before it officially opened, throwing himself into the next chapter of his working life with a vigour Joe hadn't seen in a year. Given a set of keys and the code to the burglar alarm (on a piece of paper), Dad would turn up at the centre at seven in the morning and wouldn't leave until eight or nine every night. Forget the architects, the builders, the council or the organisations who would soon be using the place, this baby was *his*. *He* would make sure the chairs were stacked straight, *he* would make sure the dishwasher worked properly, *he* would screw in all the loose light fittings and *he* would make sure all the newly-planted bushes were watered in the garden out front. He also made sure a delivery of flowers looked perfect after a florist dropped them off on the morning of the opening day, setting them out in a blaze of colour around the edge of the stage. The Mayor was arriving at two to cut a ribbon in front of an invited audience who - no doubt, thought Dad - would spill tea and drop cake crumbs and scuff the highly polished floor he'd been working on for a month. As long as they all had a good time, that's what mattered to him. His beaming smile couldn't have got any bigger when The Mayor mentioned him - by name - during the opening speech. He was gobsmacked. (He didn't know *women* could be Mayors as well.) "Well done, Mr. Bancroft," she said. "This all looks simply splendid."

The opening ceremony was a great success, and the local paper even sent along a photographer. "My son does that," said Dad to the jaded snapper as he desperately tried to get into the shot. "You know. Er, what do you call it? Pornography?" It took him three hours to clear up after the Mayor left, and just one hour for his employers to sack him next morning. With his ever-increasing forgetfulness Dad had picked up the flowers from the front of the stage and taken them home. They looked lovely in the front room and the smell was divine, but the committee accused him of theft and Dad was back where he'd started.

Oh, God ..

The day I lost another job ..

I thought they were mine, didn't I? Simple mistake. Thought the flowers were mine and took them all home, didn't I? Well, who wouldn't? The smell was glorious.

Don't worry, I'll sort it all out when I get back to work tomorrow.

Page 69

"Can we start again, Mum?" Joe called her from the office one evening. "I'm sorry about last time. I really was pathetic. I didn't mean to run off like I did."

"Of course we can," she whispered. "But listen, I can't talk right now. Kevin's not gone to band tonight. Ring me in the morning. I've got some good news."

Page 70

Andy said "Listen to this," and handed Joe the phone. The pair were in the Editor's office, larking about as they waited for their negatives to dry. It had been a hot, flat day full of summer fairs and cycling proficiency awards. Joe froze as he put an ear to the greasy, dandruff-filled receiver.

> "I'M JACK." he heard.
> "I SEE YOU ARE
> STILL HAVING NO LUCK CATCHING ME."

"Good God," he said, yanking the phone away. "Who's that?" A slow, croaky voice - a drawly Geordie accent - sent a shiver up his spine.
"It's the Yorkshire Ripper," said Andy, bemused by the look on Joe's startled face. "The one that's been murdering prostitutes all over joint." Joe put the phone back to his ear, his hand over the mouthpiece. "Don't worry, he can't hear you," laughed Andy. "It's a recording, you pillock. He's not on the other end of the bloody line!"

> "I'M NOT SURE WHEN I WILL STRIKE AGAIN
> BUT IT WILL DEFINITELY
> BE SOME TIME THIS YEAR,
> MAYBE SEPTEMBER OR OCTOBER .."

Holy hell, this was scary. The voice of a real-life murderer? "That's *it!*" Joe shouted, and his eyes lit up as he put down the phone. "Oh, fantastic, that's it!" Andy looked at him blankly. "Eureka! Ha ha ha .." Joe laughed, his excitement building. "What a brilliant idea for my book."
"Your book?"
"Oh yes, I forgot to tell you. I'm going to write a book. I've been tossing a few ideas around and well, I've just this minute decided .. it's going to be a murder mystery."
"Oooh, that sounds good. So who are you going to kill?"
"My step-dad," laughed Joe, clapping his hands together loudly. "I'm going to kill my step-dad!"

Page 71

"Fancy a drink?"
"Who, me?" said Andy, looking around an otherwise empty room.
"Well, we haven't been out for ages, have we? We never get the chance. We're always working different shifts, or having different days off, or .."
"Yeah, OK!" Andy nodded, enthusiastically. "That would be great. Let's see if we can't fix the diary so we both finish early one night."

They fixed the diary, and Andy collected Joe one dark and rainy Wednesday. They didn't know where the evening would lead them so had togged up in their best disco gear, the sleeves of Joe's new pale-blue seersucker jacket rolled up to the elbows. Andy had one last job on his work-list, the inauguration of a new Akela at a cub scout troupe, so Joe waited patiently in the car whilst he took his shots. Andy finally threw his camera bag in the boot and bounced enthusiastically into the driver's seat. "Right, let's get stuck in," he said, and reversed onto what looked like an unlit patch of car-park by the side of the scout hut. Sadly, it was an area of flooded, muddy lawn, and the car slurched to a shuddering halt as Andy tried to drive it out in the dark. "Oh shit," he groaned. "I didn't mean stuck like *that*. Give us a shove, Joe, go on." Joe sighed, got out of the car and planted his hands on the boot. "Alright," he shouted. "Put it in gear and let the clutch out slowly." A jet of filthy black water shot up from the rear wheels, hosing a perfect line of mud straight up Joe's best togs, and finishing off his glasses with a thick dollop of crap on each lens. The car shot forward and it was all Joe could do to stop himself falling face first into the morass. Andy almost died laughing, and Joe only forgave him when he agreed to buy all the drinks that evening. Forty-five minutes later, having used up every paper towel in the scout hut, the pair sat in the Fox and Pheasant,

checking out the chicks. That was as far as they'd get, of course, what with Joe sporting a crusty, brown zig-zag right up the front of his best St. Michael's shirt. He looked like some over-zealous participant in an aboriginal rain-dance ritual.
"What've *you* come as, a zebra?" said one wit as she passed on the way to the toilets.
"Oh, ha, ha ha .."

Andy put a third pint of Guinness in front of Joe and waved his own in front him. "Where are you?" he tittered. "I can't see you for the camouflage." They laughed and took a deep swig of their pints, and then Andy suddenly became serious. "Have you heard?" he said, his eyebrows knotting.
"About?" Joe asked.
"About Mr. Attar?"
"What *about* him?" said Joe, impatiently.
"He's closing down the Stockport office."

Page 72

Dad nose-dived after he lost his new job and Joe had never been so angry in his life. He was angry with Dad, angry with the council, angry with himself for not fighting harder for Dad. He'd begged and pleaded but the council had put their foot down. "My Dad's just getting forgetful," he'd explained. "I tried to return the plants the next day but the manager wouldn't take them back."
"The damage had been done by then," said a smug fuck at the town hall. "Your father had committed a theft and you're damned lucky we're not taking it any further."

"I just can't understand why you did it," he said to his Dad, that evening.
"Did what?" said Dad, dibbing out a fag.

-

The thing that angered Joe most was his lack of anger. Punk being (generally) a working-class movement, he should have fitted in effortlessly, yet it had never occurred to him to challenge the status quo. He'd simply accepted his lot. The idea of questioning society's imbalances had never entered his mind, and had very little chance of doing so now that Joe had attained his new position in life. Unlike the 'real' punks he came across at gigs, he was finding it very hard to sing of anarchy, riot, anti-capitalism and desperation when he was living out his dream. It was difficult to adhere to the 'outraged punk' ethos when Margaret Thatcher - the so-called witch, the bitch, the bringer-down of all that was known and right - worked very well for him, particularly as he'd just made thirty quid from a close-up of her that he'd sold to one of the Nationals. She barked about breaking down the unions whilst Joe had just had to use his NUJ press card to be able to get close to her.

Revolt, despair, disdain, horrendous unemployment. They called it 'The winter of discontent' but Joe had never been happier. As he ploughed blithely on, the country was going to the dogs and punks were trying their best to rail against it all. An anarcho-punk band called Crass had made one of Joe's favourite records of the late 1970s. (He loved the fact that Crass came after Chris Rainbow on his carefully curated LP rack. What wide tastes I have, he preened. Truth be told, there *was* a Cliff Richard album in between, but he decided to file that one under 'R'.) Joe made himself a cassette copy of the album and, in a crashing illustration of 'inappropriate', would play it over and over as he cheerfully drove to take photographs of redundancy announcements, factory strikes and refuse-collectors who refused to empty the bins. The Crass song 'The feeding of the 5,000' screamed (literally) of being downtrodden, unnecessary, rejected. 'Fuck the politically minded, here's something I want to say. About the state of the nation, the way they treat us today.' Powerful stuff, but the lyrics meant nothing to Joe. All he heard were machine-gun drums, agitated guitarists and a cockney-sounding singer with a really cheeky attitude. 'Not for me the factory floor, Sweeping up from nine to four' sang Steve Ignorant, and Joe could only nod in delighted agreement as he drove from Mayoral Ball to Rotary Club Dinner to Golf Club presentation. Crass sang 'Punk is dead' and Joe hadn't even got started.

And then the penny dropped. It dawned on him (at last) that the songs were about his Dad. Redundant because of a factory sell off, sacked with no chance of redemption. On the dole, the scrap heap, abandoned when he should have still been grafting for years. Now *that* made Joe angry.

Getting home late one evening, he was surprised to see his Dad had gone out for the first time in an age. "Well, that's a good sign," he said, putting a Stiff Little Fingers LP on the record player. He blew a wedge of fluff from the stylus and dropped the needle onto the vinyl, then began to stop the turntable after each ferocious line of song. He was trying to listen to the lyrics and jot them down, as well as he could, in an attempt to grasp the band's viewpoint and observations. It was about time he took his punk music seriously. A loud slam made him jump, and he rushed to the hall just in time to see Dad slump down against the wall. A fierce cut oozed blood onto his wide, round-tipped lapels. "Holy shit, Dad," Joe cried. "What the fuck's happened? Not Wyatt Earp again, you daft bugger?"
"No, no .." groaned Dad through a split lip. "It was Kevin. Kevin beat me up."

It took a while, but the bleeding finally stopped and Dad was able to stand and walk into the front room. His hands shook as he necked the whiskey Joe handed over. "Kevin?" said Joe, his own face as pale after the shock. He raised his hands incredulously. "How've you got into a fight with Kevin, Dad? What the bloody hell ..?"
His Dad sniffed loudly and rubbed the ball of a hand into a weary eye. "I think I went to the wrong house," he said, quietly. "I .. I .."
"The wrong house?" Joe yelled. "What do you mean, the wrong house? You mean our old flat? What was Kevin doing at our old flat?"
"No," said Dad, looking sheepish. "Our .. the one on .. the one .. where your Mum lives. Our old house on the estate."
Joe was gob-struck. "You *are* joking?" he screamed. "Why would you go back *there*? You've not been there for years. Fuck me, it's no wonder Kevin thumped you. And why did you even go out, anyway?" Dad breathed in deeply and waved his shot glass pleadingly in Joe's face. "No, not until you've told me everything," Joe said, shaking his head. "How've you ended up at our old house?"
Dad licked his lips and burst into tears. "I don't know, Joe," he cried. "I just went there, straight from the pub. Like I was on auto-pilot or something." He layed his hands on his son's shoulders, then dropped his head against him tenderly. "Something's wrong with me, Joe," he said. "Something's wrong with my head. I just walked straight back to the old house without thinking. Like I still lived there. Like it was home. I even tried to give your Mum a kiss and that twat smacked me straight in the mouth .."
"Oh, my God," said Joe, rolling his eyes. "That fucking bastard. I'm gonna kill him, I swear." He patted Dad's arm and sniffed back a tear of his own. There *was* something wrong with Dad, and he knew it. "Ah, come on," he braved. "You were just pissed, like normal. You just went .."

"No, I wasn't," his Dad interrupted. "I wasn't pissed, Joe. Honest. I only went out for a change of scenery, so I just had the two at The Navvy and a couple in the .. er, in another pub .. before I decided to come home. This memory shit's been worrying me lately, so I thought I'd ease off on the sauce and see if it helped."

They called the doctor next morning.

Page 73

The day eventually came for Joe to have sex, except he came in his pants and the squishy-undie flashbacks had him squirming for a fortnight.

-

In his cab, a taxi-driver had discovered a handbag, bulging with two and half thousand smackers in used fivers. To his credit, he'd painstakingly gone back to each of the customers he'd had over the last three days before eventually finding the rightful owner of the money, a glamorous forty-something ex-croupier who'd been too nervous and embarrassed to trouble the police with her problem. That all changed when she got back her money and, once she'd had the boob-job she'd been saving for, she called The Courier to let them know of the cab-driver's honesty.

Joe was sent to 'Max's Taxis' and, as he lined up his shot, all sticky-out double Gs and very happy cabbie, his idea of heaven on earth walked from the taxi office behind them. What a babe! What a vision! Joe could have sworn she walked in slow-motion, her long blonde hair swishing across her scrumptious bum like an ad for Alberto Balsam. "Oh, my God," he said, loudly enough for his subjects to hear. "Sorry, I meant the shot looks great." He fired off two last frames and dashed to catch up with the girl. "Joe," he said, breathlessly thrusting out a hand. His camera shield was working well. His confidence positively oozed.

"Samantha," she said, surprised, her voice as broad as hotpot. He ignored a cigar-shaped coffee stain down her off-white blouse, a rip in her cardigan and a large ladder in her tights. Truth be told - now that he could see her in close-up - she had an air of Charles Shultz's 'Pig-Pen' about her, a hint of grubby dishevelment that seemed to fit with the sleep that still encrusted the corner of her left eye. "Erm, do you work there?" he asked nevertheless, nodding back at the taxi-hut.

"I do," she beamed, tickled by his interest. "I'm the head of communications."

"Oh wow," said Joe, genuinely impressed. "Can I take you for a drink?" He never realised he'd get so turned on by buck teeth!

-

He took her for the drink that weekend. A rather quick drink, as it happened, Samantha needing to be back at the taxi office for half past eight. No problem, he still had a homing-pigeon feature to photograph out near Marple. "But why are you going in on a Saturday night?" he asked, carefully dragging out a half of bitter shandy. "Surely the head of communications wouldn't work on a Saturday night."

Sam blushed bright red and giggled. "Well, when I say 'head of communications', I mean I'm on the radio," she squinted, explaining that she manned the two-way system that directed taxis to their bookings. Bit of a come-down for Joe, but he was so smitten he kindly forgave her and asked for a second date. "Can I drop you off at your office?" he asked.

"Don't be daft," she said. "I'll call a taxi."

-

Their second date was a little longer - she was on an eleven pm start this time - though, by the fourth date, what with one thing and another, they'd still only managed to spend about seven hours together. Her scruffy demeanour was beginning to bother Joe - she *was* getting a *lot* of wear out of that one torn cardigan, and her chewed-up finger nails left a lot to be desired - but, hey ho, any port in a storm. He'd even taken to wondering, only half-panicked, if she now counted as a 'girlfriend'.

She bleeped him and said she was off all the next day. "Come over," she said, and Joe swore he heard her wink on the tape machine. "Mum's at work and it's the maid's day off on Tuesdays." Tuesday came and so did Joe. Right in the middle of some really heavy necking. Hadn't even got his pants off. Laughing hysterically, Samantha told him where to go. "Don't worry," he snapped, his face as red as the ketchup bottle he squashed as he squirmed to get up from the rancid, saggy sofa. "I'm out of here." In truth, he was glad of the excuse to leave. Only now could he admit to himself that Sam was .. well, Sam was smelly. Eau de mustiness. And the house was a shit-heap. (What other explanation for the two crusty dinner plates beneath the cushion with the ketchup?) Not only that, but it was in one of the roughest parts of a very rough estate. Joe was working class, but this was a new league altogether. (He never knew he could be so snobby.)
"Oh, and I lied about the maid," Samantha giggled, as he knocked an empty soup bowl from her cluttered mantlepiece.
"No kidding," he grimaced, prising his feet from the carpet, not the only thing sticky in the room that day.

"Early onset dementia ..

.. Oh, and COPD."

"What's ..?"

"Chronic Obstructive Pulmonary Disease," said a very nice doctor, frowning at Dad's hazy X-rays. "Smoke a lot, does he?"

The days off ..

Well, it seems I haven't got a job any more. How the hell did *that* happen? Maybe it was a temporary post? Was I just there to fill in for someone, whilst they went on holiday? Oh, I don't know. Still, it means I get lots of lovely lie-ins these days.

And I've a wonderful collection of tablets now. No idea where they've come from but I've got Joe to help sort them out, so that's alright, isn't it? I wouldn't know where to start.

Page 75

It took another four weeks, but Joe finally met again with his Mum. With Gary being watched by a neighbour, their get-together stretched to almost two hours, the conversation ranging wide.

"How are the girls?"
"Oh, fine, Joe. Fine. They've got boyfriends now. I can't get anywhere near the bathroom these days."

"You stopped smoking, Mum?"
"Oh, ages ago, Joe. It was costing me a small fortune. But I feel so much better for it."
"Good on you, Mum. Good on you."

"Do you still see Auntie Renee?"
"Oh, don't you know?"
"Oh no, she's *not*, is she?"
"What? Dead? No, not at all. She won fifty grand at the bingo and moved to Bognor Regis."

"Do you ever regret the fact that Kevin threw me out?"

There was a long and worrying pause.
"Will you hate me if I say no?" said Mum.
The answer shocked him. "I .."
"Alright, alright," said Mum, throwing up her hands. "That sounded harsh. Sorry." She took a sip of coffee and licked her lips. "I remember something you said, the first time we met. You said that being thrown out made you stand on your own two feet. Do you remember?"
Joe nodded. "That's what I said."
"Well, that's all I wanted for you, too. For you to be able to stand on your own two feet. You *were* seventeen, after all."
"Seems a long time ago," said Joe, smiling wryly.

"Yes, and a lot's happened since," Mum nodded. "No, what I *meant* to say was that I regret the way it happened, but I'm glad - for *you* .." she stressed .. " .. that it did. I'm glad everything worked out well for *you*, and I'm glad you *did* end up standing on your own two feet, but I absolutely *hated* the fact that Kevin threw you out. I honestly do. But trust me Joe, I had no say whatsoever in what happened that day. Kevin just got a red mist about him and that was that. He was determined to get you out of the house and, well .." She looked hard at Joe, trying to read his thoughts. "I think you're grown up enough to admit it was for the best, don't you?" she said, softly. "What with everything, and then Gary turning up as well. It's made a man of you Joe, and I'm proud. I fretted for weeks after that Christmas Day, and it was only after bumping into your aunt Eleanor that I found out you were doing alright."
Joe gulped hard. "Another coffee, Mum?"

-

Time to go home. They hugged tightly. They'd both enjoyed the catch-up and, surprisingly, Joe felt good. The air was clearing between them. The past - at least part of it - had been dealt with. "Oh, your good news?" he said, half-way out of the door. "You said you had some good news to tell me, Mum."
"Oh, I'd forget my head if it wasn't screwed on," she laughed. "Yes, good news. I've got a new job, our Joe. I start at Kevin's factory a week on Monday."

-

Yet *another* job for Mum? It occurred to Joe that, as a kid, he'd never known her *without* one. He'd never realised just how hard she had had to work. With his own life revolving around school, Man. U and wondering if Ernie really *was* the fastest milkman in the west, he simply never noticed how often she was away from home. He just took it for granted that he had to make his own breakfast every morning, and that it was his job to peel potatoes for tea and clean out the coal fire ready for re-lighting in the evening. He made his own breakfast because Mum was already out, mopping floors in a 'Pirate' themed pub from seven 'til nine each morning. He helped make the tea whilst she cleaned toilets at the sixth-form college he'd never go to. And, as he sat in his classroom, she sold shoes, school uniforms and rolls of patterned oil cloth in a two-storey general store called Potter's. She was working all hours God gave her. Just like Dad!

She liked her job at Potter's, though. She got a staff discount and first 'dibs' on any new kids' clothing that came into stock. The store was credit, rather than cash-based, meaning that Mum (like most of the ladies on the estate) could pay weekly for any purchases she made. Joe liked Potter's, too. As far as he was concerned, the fact that he never saw his Mum hand over any money for shoes or shirts or a new school blazer meant it must be *free*! He couldn't see why not. After all, even his school meals were free - his parents unable to afford the weekly cost of the 'dinner tickets'. The truth was, everything Mum had ever bought was 'free'. Even when Dad was there, she'd never had the cash to buy anything outright. Everything was on 'tick', on the 'Never Never' .. from Potter's, or the Littlewood's catalogue, or the John Mills catalogue, or the 'Layaway' scheme at the local newsagent's. Mum was constantly building up little piles of coins, stacked on the occasional pound note, with which to pay each of her credit and savings schemes. Proud and conscientious, she dreaded getting behind with any single one of them. And then there were Green Shield and Co-op stamps, reward schemes that enabled full books of stamps to be exchanged for discounts in participating stores. Joe and his sisters spent many a happy afternoon sticking the stamps into brightly coloured books, their tongues sore and dry after each of their three-monthly sessions.

Mum counted up the cigarette coupons by herself, ashamed at the chest-wheezing speed with which she and Dad racked them up.

Still, their parents managed to give them all sixpence pocket money every Friday, and Joe and his siblings would whizz off to Braithwood's 'paper shop' to buy a bag of toffees that would last them until Sunday night. They were always doing their parents' shopping in Braithwood's, buying fags for Mum or the News - a friend dropping in - for Dad, who was constantly on the look-out for a better-paying job. Once a month Mum would need tampons. She'd write 'Doctor White's' on a scrap of paper and Joe was fifteen before he knew what on earth he'd been sent to buy.

Page 76

He thought it might be a good idea to try writing whilst he was pissed, just to see if it got the creative juices flowing. Not his best idea, and not just for the atrocious handwriting that would ensue. He knew *exactly* which juices flowed once he'd had a drink. He was never out of the toilet. Drugs, then? Perhaps a little hallucinatory, psychedelic episode might free up his uninspired mind, but he only had to think of trippy Hippy Jim, and the spliffs at his tutor's party, and the sickly smell of grass at the gigs he frequented for the idea to vanish on the spot. So, "just the one, then" he said, taking a bottle of Jack from the sideboard and hunching over his empty pad, pen poised above the blank blue lines for the umpteenth time.

"Oh, I can't," he said, sitting back, exasperated. "I just *can't*. I can't kill Kevin, for goodness sake. How bad would *that* look? Sod it, perhaps I *should* write an autobiography, after all."

He scribbled down ..

Joe Bancroft - The First Two Decades

.. and the words sent a shockwave across his brain. Twenty years? *Already?* Good grief! He ran a hand over his bum fluff and felt ancient. Where *had* the time gone? It had certainly flown since 1971, when he'd left Junior School and gone off to the Grammar. He took a drink and cast his mind over his first years on earth. A few mileposts stood out, the rest already faded from his memory, like so much from so many lives over so many years. I wonder, he wondered, how many things I've already forgotten? He smiled to himself as he thought back to memories he *could* recall. July 21st, back in 1969. Completely enthralled by the Apollo space missions, he'd risen early that summer morning and tiptoed passed his parents' bedroom in the pre-dawn dark to watch Man's first walk on the Moon.
"Did you enjoy that, love?" he heard his Mum whisper.
"Bloody fantastic," his Dad replied.
Don't tell me I've missed it, Joe panicked.

The battering he got for pinching Polos was high on the list of course, as was sitting the Eleven-Plus exam and the day he rode a 'two-wheeler' bike without stabilisers for the first time. (He didn't get far, but far enough, and he spent the rest of the day trying to borrow other kids' bikes so that he could show off his new-found skill. All well and good until David Rotherham kicked a half-deflated football under Joe's front wheel and the bike stopped stock still. He went flying over the handlebars and knocked out one of his brand new front teeth.)

Bizarrely, a day he was off school with a bad cold had stayed in his memory, too. He'd been playing with the wireless - once his Mum had left the house and he could safely abandon the pretence of infirmity - and randomly twiddled the dial to a radio station playing The Beatles. Yellow submarine. He quite liked that one. He twiddled further and there they were again. The Beatles. Yellow submarine. And he couldn't understand it. How on earth had the group travelled from one radio station to another in a matter of seconds? Joe smiled at the innocence, then remembered a loss of innocence, too.

There had been a dreadful two days on the estate when, firstly, a milkman had accidentally killed a child by reversing his float over the boy's head as he lay playing marbles in a grid. Poor Mark. Could have been any one of them. The next morning, everyone awoke to find that almost every house on the street had been burgled. It must have really taken some doing. Their television had been found smashed up in next-door's kitchen, and one of Steve Bradford's football boots had been discovered in their dining room. There was a pair of bright pink bloomers in their shed and Joe never did see one of his precious Blue Peter annuals again. (Someone was keeping *very* quiet!) Everyone started locking their doors after that horrible night. It was the end of a beautiful era.

"Naaah!" Joe breathed hard down his nostrils and put down his unused pen. "No point bringing up old stuff like that," he said. "I'll stick to killing Kevin."

-

The death of Kevin ..? Kevin bites the dust ..?
Murder in the bike sheds ..? The step-dad files ..?

Settling, for the time being, on plain old 'Killing Kevin' as the title of his new book, Joe felt an immediate sense of relief now that he'd *finally* found a literary direction. He scribbled out **The First Two Decades,** wrote down the words

KILLING KEVIN

and leant back, feeling good. So his book *wouldn't* be an autobiography, after all. Thank goodness for that! "Right, you bastard," he said, rubbing his hands together theatrically. "Let's be having you, Kevin Bailey. You're mine for the taking, you slob." Except, he wasn't sure *how* he'd take him. Much as he'd love to see the whistly, fat sod bite the dust, he was at a loss as exactly how to do it. His basic primal urge was simply to run up to his step-dad and kick him right in the teeth. Knock him flying, jump up and down on his lardy-arse and give him a taste of his own thuggish behaviour.

'He died alone, spitting teeth, slithering helplessly in his own blood.' The End.

A very short book but oooh, that made Joe feel good. Got him right in the pit of his stomach. But what a shame he'd never get the chance to knock off Kevin's block in 'real life'. Even though he'd put on a *bit* of muscle since his days as Apprentice Private Bancroft, he knew that, if it ever came to it, his step-dad could still wallop the living daylights out him. So he'd just have to 'punch out' Kevin's lights on paper. Or maybe not. After a bit of thought, he dismissed that murder method as a bit, well, shit. It needed subtlety, guile, an alibi. He needed to concentrate more when he watched the likes of Kojak or The Professionals' Bodie and Doyle. They dealt with murders all the time. Murders and murderers. He *had* to get an idea from them.

-

Ringing the Yorkshire Ripper 'hot-line' became a regularly ghoulish pastime for Andy and Joe. Sadly, the police were no nearer an arrest and the horrific killing of alleged prostitutes continued across the North of England. In an effort to identify the murderer, the police decided to carry on playing the recorded message - purportedly from the 'Ripper' - which taunted the law and frightened the bejesus out of the two young photographers.

> "AT THE RATE I'M GOING
> I SHOULD BE IN THE BOOK OF RECORDS,
> I THINK IT'S ELEVEN UP TO NOW, ISN'T IT?
> WELL, I'LL KEEP ON GOING
> FOR QUITE A WHILE YET."

"Jeepers, eleven!" said Joe, putting down the 'phone. "This guy's getting away with murder. Now that's what you call a serial killer." And then it came to him. Kevin would die at the hands of a serial killer. Yes!

He couldn't wait to get back to his writing pad.

Page 77

"Read this, superstar .." said the Editor, handing Joe an internal memo.

Is there any chance that you could permanently assign Joe Bancroft to our office? We feel his artistic eye and unceasing enthusiasm are ideally suited to our team of exciting young reporters.

"Bloody hell," Joe said, breaking into a grin. "That's flattering. Who's it from?"

"The Newtown office. Cheeky buggers!" Newtown was one of the 'satellite' offices of The Courier, and Joe shot a lot of their picture requests.

"So, could you?" Joe said, nodding eagerly. "Assign me, I mean." He quite fancied the idea. Their reporters were always coming up with cracking stories.

"No, I could *not*," grumped the Editor, getting straight on the 'phone to Newtown and throwing the memo into the bin. It hit home, though. McGowan became instantly protective of Joe and started to 'up' the quality of his jobs, much to the chagrin of the boss. As luck would have it, the owner of the 'paper had decided to trial the publication of a weekly colour supplement, and Joe became more and more side-lined to work on its more feature-like articles. He was like a pig in the proverbial, thriving on the extra time he was given to spend on the jobs, and the artistry the work allowed him. Among other things, he photographed stately homes and posh restaurants, galleries and their weird and wonderful artists, quirky fashion designers, cutting edge hair stylists, even a local landscape photographer who'd just sold a piece to the Natural History Museum. "It was a picture of a bloody *field*," a mystified Joe said later to Andy. "Fine art, eh? What a load of bullshit."

The magazine closed after three months.

-

As if on cue, a job came up on an east coast daily, and Joe had his application in the post two hours after reading it. He couldn't wait to start. The interview process had to be dealt with first of course but, after so long in his job, Joe knew he'd ace it and be working there within a month. Unfortunately, the collie-wobbles kicked in whilst he was driving down the M62 and, by the time he sat down in the 'paper's reception, he was a bag of nerves, his confidence shot and his head full of the old doubt and insecurity. "Calm down," he said to himself. "What is it Dad says?" (His Dad had a method of helping Joe with his nerves. "Joe, they're all just people," he used to say. "Even The Queen takes a shit!") Much to his relief, the interview went well - picturing Lizzie on the lavvy worked wonders - and his juices were up again by the time he left the office. Truth be told, he'd actually revelled in the obvious questions he'd been asked and felt sure he was adequately up to speed and just the press photographer the paper needed. He even felt sorry for the next applicant, to whom he winked and gave a wry smile as he held open the door. The next applicant got the job, and Joe sulked for a fortnight. Envy. What a waste of energy.

"No formal training" was the reason given for his rejection. The letter was polite and encouraging, but pointed out what Joe knew only too well. He didn't have the official qualification from the NCTJ - The National Council for the Training of Journalists. Fuck, he *thought* that might come back to bite him one day. Perhaps he *should* have spent more time in the classroom, after all. But he knew there was another way. In addition to their year-long course, the NCTJ offered an 'indentured' alternative, in which a young photographer could work a two-year apprenticeship on a newspaper and study the press photography course in a couple of two-month long 'block-release' sessions. Training on the job, so to speak. There was only thing for it. He had to get himself onto that course, and raised the idea of an indenture with the Editor.
"No," said McGowan, and that was the end of that. "You'd need to work on a different 'paper to do that," he added, somewhat unnecessarily. "One that can offer you the two year indenture. And I'd start looking soon if I were you. The owner's talking about making redundancies."

Page 78

Sex! At last! Hallelujah!

Joe needed some serious cheering up after his Dad's diagnosis and, as luck would have it, had already booked himself a weekend off for a two-day punk festival called 'Futurama', staged in a dump of a warehouse in Leeds. He'd only been there an hour when he clocked a cider-sozzled beauty sitting alone, floating like a Siren amidst a flotilla of empty beer cans. (More prosaically, curled on a scrumpled tartan sleeping bag, keeping her leather-covered bum off the cold concrete floor.) She sported a mass of peaked, bright green hair and wore a torn, studded leather jacket, on the back of which were artistically hand-painted the words 'Never mind the Bollerks'.

"Great badges," Joe said, pointing at her lapel. "Fancy a drink?"

Altered Images, The Danse Society and Siouxsie and The Banshees came and went whilst they were snogging, and they had to peel themselves apart when they remembered, every now and again, that they'd actually come to Leeds to listen to music.

Karen. Was it Karen? Debra? Oh Lord, he couldn't remember her name now, but she went back to his car and stayed with him all that night, scratching his backside with her bright orange talons and, more than once, poking him in the eye with her flour-stiffened spikes. Still, at least that wasn't the *only* stiff thing that got poked that night, and Joe was delighted. And then he wasn't. For the second time in his life he experienced the immediate - and absolutely deflating - experience of ejaculating and instantly wanting nothing to do with the poor girl with whom he'd just, er, had it off. (If he ever *had* written an autobiography, he'd have liked to have said 'with whom he'd just made love', but that was never going to happen in a sharp-edged Vauxhall Chevette on a sweaty September night, with a girl who oozed alcohol and kept getting out of the car for a noisy wee beside his front offside wheel. Still ..)

The trouble was, he then had to spend the whole of the next day with her, even though he tried, he *really* tried, to convince her that all the bands that were playing on Day Two of the festival were his absolute favourites and he must, must, must not miss them. He 'forgot' to give her his phone-number when they parted and, even though he'd used a condom - he'd only needed the one - he sweated for weeks that he'd got her pregnant and scrutinised his scrotum every time he went for a pee, just in case she'd given him something .. erm, extra.
There must be something more to it than *that*, he'd think to himself in the days and weeks that followed. There bloody *must* be! Why did every writer, every singer, every poet, go on and on and on about love?

Ah, but that wasn't love, was it? That was sex.

Wanton, casual sex!

At last!

Hallelujah!

Was that *it*?

It would all be different with Tina, of course.

Oh God, Tina! The Editor's new secretary, hotter than Debbie Harry in a mini-skirt, raunchier than Kate Bush in a blue leotard and, sadly for Joe, more unattainable than Lindsay Wagner on the far side of Uranus. At least her Mum liked him. "More chips, Joe," she'd ask, every Thursday evening when Joe went round to her house for tea. "Coffee alright for you, love? Fancy an Eccles cake?" If I married Tina, Joe mused, she'd probably look like her Mum in twenty years' time. (It put him off only ever so slightly.) He'd started going to Tina's to watch Top of the Pops - along with Whistle Test, the 'other' must-see music programme of the day - after his love of music had come up in a shy conversation he'd had with her, early in her days at the 'paper. "That's the only problem with this job," he'd said. "I've missed Top of the Pops since I started here. I'm always working on a Thursday night."
"Why don't you come to my house to watch it?" she said, much to Joe's delight. "I only live on Cartmel Street. Five minutes up the road."
"That would be great," he squealed. "But I don't control the diary. You'd have to have a word with my boss."
"Oh, we can do better than that," she said, flicking her glossy, auburn hair. "I'll have a word with *mine*." She fluttered her eyelashes at McGowan and wound him round her little finger. "Oh, go on then," he frumped. "I'm sure we can work something out."

And so Top of the Pops it was, every Thursday night, with a plate of chips, a nice hot cup of coffee and the frustration of sitting opposite the most drop-dead-gorgeous girl he knew would never, ever, go out with him.

Oh, Tina!

Still, there was always Sally James.

Oh God, Sally! Even more out of reach than Tina, she was the star of TISWAS - ostensibly a children's Saturday morning TV programme, in which she would romp about in tight, shiny leggings and low-cut tops, rolling on the floor and getting her knee-high boots covered in custard and jelly. Phwoar! Fortunately, the boss had taken to going home early on a Friday evening, leaving Andy and Joe to sort out the diary between themselves and, as Andy was still seeing Miss Nockers - lucky sod - he was quite happy for Joe to start late on Saturday mornings and cover all the jobs in the evenings. Joe got to spend every Saturday with Sally.

And then .. well, then there was Sarah. The first girl Joe ever *really* fell for.

Thin Lizzy and Fleetwood Mac had both released songs called 'Sarah' (or Sara, if you were The Mac) and, in keeping with his penchant for assuming all songs were about him, Joe longed to be able to sing about a 'Sarah, coming into my world and changing it ..' and a Sara who would 'Stay with me awhile ..." but it just wouldn't work with a Pauline or a Susan or a Karen (Or was it Debra?) And then, just like magic, God sent Joe a Sarah.

A beautiful, tall Sarah, who bumped into him at the dry-cleaners and stunned him with her long brown hair and dark brown eyes.

A brainy, bright Sarah, studying dentistry at a Midlands University with a wit about her as sharp as the drill she wielded.

A charmingly droll Sarah, who offered him free dental treatment and laughed when he told her 'not until you're qualified'.

A funny, happy Sarah, whose bubbly laugh would warm the heart of the most cynical of men.

A frustratingly remote Sarah, who he only managed to see on five staggered weekends, whenever one of them could get away from work or study.

A nosy, irritating Sarah, who questioned why he drank so much. "Do I?" he replied, surprised. (The idea had never occurred to him before.) "Never noticed," he said. "It's probably 'cos I work for the press. We drink like fish, so there. Oh, and I'm half-Irish. That *must* have something to do with it. Or it could be that I just like getting pissed, like my Dad. Ha ha ha .." (He *had* actually broached the subject of his Dad's drinking, but only once. "Joe," Dad had snapped. "There's a reason the liver is bigger than the brain.")

A heart-breaking Sarah, who called him an immature philistine and dropped him like a red-hot poker.

A hard-hearted Sarah, who seemed to know the rest of the lyrics from one of those 'Sarah' songs ..
'Oh Sarah, don't let go, no no ..'

She let go.

'Now it's gone, it doesn't matter what for ..'

But it *did* matter what for. It mattered an awful lot. For the first time in his life, Joe had found a girl that didn't make him want to run away after sex. More than that, he'd actually believed he'd found someone to whom *he* mattered, too. He didn't, and it was like being smashed in the face with a mallet.

'Changed my world, Sarah ..' sang Phil Lynott.

Yes, and made it worse, Joe thought. So much worse.

He felt terrible.

Page 80

He felt fantastic. He'd finally come up with a way to kill his step-dad. Serial killer? Perfect. "Die!" he spat, rubbing his hands together briskly. Oh yes, he was on a roll. The words were flowing. He couldn't write his ideas down fast enough ..

The Factory Stabber

Faced with a take-over from a Taiwanese start-up conglomerate - he scribbled - the management of Kevin's factory bungs a wad to a serial killer, who goes round randomly knifing night-shift workers in an effort to cut down on redundancy payouts. He stabs them in the back and disposes of their bodies in the molten metal hell of the foundry.

Kevin bites the dust in chapter three.

Or does he? Reading it back, Joe wasn't so sure. "Hmm," he pondered, tapping his nails against his teeth. "But *how* would management get hold of a serial killer, eh? They're not exactly in the yellow pages, are they?" He scratched his head for an hour until, by lager three, he'd scrubbed the serial killer idea completely and was off on another tack altogether ..

<u>Mercury Descending</u> - a musician from Kevin's Factory Brass Band thinks Kevin's trumpet playing is shit (He's not wrong, laughed Joe) and envies his position as lead instrumentalist in the band. He steals some mercury from the workshop and keeps rubbing it around the mouthpiece of Kevin's instrument until he's absorbed enough poison to die.

"Oh yes, die," giggled Joe. "Die, you bastard, die."

<u>The Bookie's Revenge</u> - Kevin backs a 100-1 outsider in the Grand National and walks home with seven hundred knicker in his back pocket. It's the start of a winning streak that almost wipes out his regular bookie, who puts an end to Kev's success by offering him a cup of tea laced with ground glass, after seeming to accidentally drop a bottle from the shelf above whilst 'brewing up'.

<u>Calibre 303</u> was Joe's favourite. When he'd lived 'at home', he'd grown tired of Kevin's never-ending National Service stories. It was all "Tripoli this, and Aden that", as if he'd single-handedly supervised the security of the entire Middle East. A favourite of Kevin's oft-repeated stories was of how they used to give a 'beasting' to a soldier called Private Noblett. (The name didn't help the poor bugger, for a start.) Kevin told him how he and several thug chums bullied the poor guy throughout his entire two years' military service, and here he was, still laughing about it twenty odd years later. Joe decided that, for Page 99, he would resur-

rect Noblett and have him shoot Kevin by 'accident' with a replica Lee Enfield 303 rifle.

Boom!

The day I ..

Sorry, I forgot what I was going to tell you.

Page 81

"How's the new job, Mum?" They were still meeting in the 'no-man's-land' of the café but now Joe felt an awful lot closer to his Mum. He'd even told her about Dad's illnesses, albeit with only a pitying 'what-can-you-do?' shrug as response.

"Mrs Bailey?" yelled a waitress. Mum waved, and took hold of a plate of hot buttered toast.
"I still can't get used to your new married name," said Joe. Mum smiled fleetingly and wrung her hands together tightly. "The job?" she said, absent-mindedly. "Oh, the job's good, but .." She turned to look out of the window. Joe was silent as he watched her. "It's Kevin," she said, turning back to face him. "He's scaring me."

"So, let me get this straight .." Joe said, once Mum had finished her story.

"Kevin's getting annoyed because you're working again, so you can't have his tea on the table before he goes to Band practice?" Mum nodded, dabbed at a tear with Joe's used napkin and looked up at the ceiling. "And, because you're working, he shouts at you because you're not giving Gary enough attention?" Another nod. "And he threatened to hit you because you spent some of *your* wages on a new coat?"

"He didn't just threaten .." Mum whispered and added, almost in passing, "And I think he's been seeing another woman."

"Ah .." said Joe, open-mouthed.

"I think it's someone at Band," she sighed. "A trombonist, I think. A lad in our office has seen them together twice in the Cross Keys, and he stinks of perfume when he comes home from practice." As Joe listened, he felt a shockwave vibrate through his chest. He ran a checklist through his mind as he sipped the last of his coffee. When Mum was married to Dad, her life was taken up with the kids. Then, divorced, life meant working three jobs and flopping exhausted in front of the telly every night. (She never had time for anything else.) And now, married to Kevin, her life was back to square one, with a new baby and full-time work in middle age with no normal network of friends around her. Joe gathered his thoughts and took a deep breath. Oh no, he thought. Mum's lonely.

And what about Dad?

Page 82

Forthcoming exhibitions: Elliott Erwitt, London, from Nov. 30

"Oh my God," said Joe, waving his Practical Photography magazine in the air. "Elliott Erwitt's having a show in London."
"Elegant who?"
"Elliott, you dimbo," chuckled Joe, thumping his Dad on the arm. "Only the best photographer in the whole wide world." He'd loved Erwitt's light, humorous reportage photography ever since he'd first discovered his work, and vowed there and then to get himself to the exhibition opening. In a weird coincidence, his Mum had just handed him a letter from Tony Croft, one of his old 'squaddie' pals from the Army, which he'd posted to Joe's old home address. "Bloody hell," said Joe. "Last time I saw him he was hanging by his ankles from an assault course cargo net."

How are you Joe .. began the letter. *Don't kno if you remember me but we was in Brunswick Platoon together you was nice to me wen everyone els was given me hell anyway mate Iv left the army good riddance and my mates is havin a welcom home party for me can you come its nexst wensday I can meet you at euyston staton let me kno cheers mate see you soon i hope*

Talk about timing! Joe drove straight to Piccadilly Station, bought an Inter-City return train ticket to London for the following Wednesday and wrote a letter straight back to Tony.

What a surprise, he thought, as his train slowed down through Crewe. I hadn't expected to see *him* again. Poor old Tony. The most picked-on kid in the company, he was bullied and tormented on a daily basis. Joe was impressed the bugger had lasted as long as he had. (Hey, he thought, perhaps I could base Noblett on him?) The more loutish elements in Joe's barracks used to throw Tony's bedding out of their first floor window and, once Tony was downstairs to collect it all, they'd dismantle his bed and throw that out, too. The training staff viewed the behaviour as 'character-building' and kept their distance. Only Joe stepped in to help - he knew what bullying felt like, after all - but fortunately, as he enjoyed a foot in both camps, the 'thugs' *knew* that Joe would help and he got away with a little light ribbing instead of a dose of the same disgraceful treatment.

"Can't you give him a break?" Joe would plead.
"No sweat," they'd answer. "Arm or leg?"

-

"Tony!"
"Welcome to The Smoke, Bankers." Tony yanked Joe's bag from his shoulder. "Long time no see, mate. Fanks for comin' darn."
"Bloody 'ell," said Joe. "You've grown."

-

"Sigh that again," said Daphne, waving over one of her friends. "'Ere Caff, listen to this geezer toe-kin'. Say it again, mate. Say samfin fanny." Cath weaved across the room, sploshing white wine over the legs of a crashed-out Chinese chap, and said "Wassup, Daff?" then, nodding towards Joe, "Awright, mate?"
"Listen to this geezer toe-kin," Daphne said again. "He don' arf toke fanny."
Amused, Joe said "I think you'll find it's *you* that talks funny." He didn't mind her piss-taking. She was only five foot two and he was getting a fabulous view of her delightful melons.

"Listen 'ow 'e says fanny," giggled Daff. "Fuunny. How fanny!"
"He's fackin' Norvern, that's woy, ain't ya mate?" said Caff, pointing at him like a museum exhibit. "Where you from then, eh? Birminem? Yokesha? Scokland?"
"Manchester," said Joe, trying to reach for more lager.
"Heard of it? Manchester?"
"Course we bleedin' 'ave," said Caff and Daff together.
"We wasn't bone yesterdie," said Caff, scrunching up her face.
"Yeah, s'near Newcarsul, innit?" said Daff, throwing out her hands.

Joe skirted the girls and picked a beer from the table. "See you later," he said, his bladder flagging red alert. I'm better off out of it, he thought, his much-needed pee adding to the stench of the repulsive toilet. That Cath was very pretty but a long-distance relationship was the last thing he wanted right now, particularly after the heart-break of Sarah.

The next day, having arrived far too early for the exhibition opening, Joe was astonished to see Elliott Erwitt step from a taxi right outside the gallery. "Er, oh, Mr. Erwitt," he gasped, his heart beginning to thump.
"Hi there," smiled the American, wrinkling his kind, baggy eyes. To Joe's amazement he reached forward and shook Joe's hand. "So, where do you want me? Am I on time? Man, what a bootiful day. Lead on .."
"Oh no, I'm not from the gallery," said Joe, shaking his head. "I'm just a fan. I've come to see your show."
"Ah, so *you're* my fan," laughed the great photographer. "Well howdy, fan."
"Joe," said Joe. "My name's Joe. In fact, could you sign that in my book, please?" He reached into his bag and pulled out his copy of Elliott's 'Photographs and anti-photographs'.
"Wow, haven't seen this in a while," said Erwitt, uncapping his pen.

"Neither has my old school," laughed Joe. "I stole it from their library in 1974."

-

He half-dozed as the train took him back north. The chap across the way was reading that day's Guardian and, in his drowsy state, Joe could just make out some sort of headline about 'primaries' in the American state of New Hampshire. It was the word 'Manchester' that caught his eye.

Democrats confident in Manchester, NH

How funny there's another Manchester, he thought and, after a quick check in an old atlas, wrote a letter to the state's tourism board as soon as he got home.

I live in Manchester, England .. he wrote. *Do you know anyone in Manchester, New Hampshire, who would like a pen friend?*

Vera-Lynn Belmarsh, wearing a badge that said ..

Chief Tourism Officer, New Hampshire, Live Free Or Die

.. opened his letter, passed it to her seventeen year old daughter Vicky-Sue and instructed her to respond to 'the Limey's request'.

"Oh wow," said Joe, when her letter arrived 'Par Avion' two weeks later, with three wonderfully franked 'Statue of Liberty' stamps and just enough of a crumpled corner to let Joe know it had come a long, long way. The United States of America. How exotic.

Dear Joel .. she wrote. *Mom says you're looking for an American pen-pal. Well, here I am, buddy. Get writing!*

He'd answered her letter and put it in the post - complete with Deirdre Barlow look-alike photo - before the Royal Mail's last collection of the day, and instantly pictured himself with an American girlfriend, her freckles and drawly accent impressing everyone he showed her off to. Suddenly, a long-distance relationship didn't seem so bad after all. Hey, why not? Yeah, he'd become a regular on the Laker Skytrain and zip to the States on a monthly basis. "Oh yes," he found himself practising. "We're a real jet-set couple, Vicky-Sue and I. I go over there all the time, and Vee-Soo (yeah, at home I call her Vee-Soo) stays with me every other weekend." Darling Vee-Soo sent a photograph by return, in which she was staring up at her fiancé Delron, in his American football outfit, leaning against his bright red Chevrolet Camaro.

Joe threw the letter in the bin.

Page 83

Two years into the job and its annual rhythm was now truly apparent. Isn't it amazing that twelve months is just long enough to fit everything in? In January, photographing Hogmanay always led to Burns' night, all bagpipes, neeps and tatties. Valentine's engagement stories turned into Shrove Tuesday pancake races. Easter bonnets preceded Whit Sunday church processions proceeded May Queens and municipal Mayor makings. The rugby season followed the football season followed the cricket season - not that Joe was any use at any. (The Altrincham goal? Lucky fluke!) Bonfire night followed Hallowe'en followed Harvest Festival, and spring fairs became summer fêtes became Christmas fayres. It could have all been so repetitive, but Joe thrived on it. The boss would complain about having to cover the Annual Parish Pet-Blessing Day *again*, whereas Joe would see a return to an event as the perfect opportunity to come up with something completely different to the last picture he'd shot there.

"You know what *your* problem is?" yapped the boss. "You want all your pictures to be award winners."

"My *problem*?" Joe fumed as he drove to cover a Radio Manchester outside broadcast. "How can *ambition* be a *problem*?" What a fucking idiot. Oooh, the boss was pissing him off more than usual these days. Never at the office, humping who knows who and forever bloody moaning, when he was in the best job in the world and had been for *thirty-five* years. Joe sighed heavily as a temporary traffic light held him up outside the Canadian Charcoal Pit, then thumped the steering wheel ecstatically as an idea bubbled up and popped sharply in his face. Freelancing! Ping! Holy shit, why *not*? The car behind Joe tooted impatiently as a wash of exciting possibilities flooded his brain, and he arrived at the job with absolutely no idea how he'd got there. Oh yes, this was a great idea. Brilliant. And the only sensible thing to do too, really. Especially with the threat of redundancies in the air and Dad not being so well. If he went freelance he could arrange his jobs at times that worked for him *and* spend more time at home with Dad. It would be the perfect situation!

He photographed the roadshow and made his decision as soon as he got back in the car. He'd leave the 'paper and move on up in the world.

Yes, it was time for a change.

Page 84

Dad's coughing had kept Joe awake half the night. Hack, hack, cough, spit, hack. He was half annoyed, half worried sick. That bad chest was definitely getting worse.

Sunrise was imminent. He could already make out vague shapes and shadows, and a blackbird on the roof was just winding up the vocals. He shut his eyes against the distractions and finally reached that woozy, hazy stage when you know you're just about to drop off. Ah yes, how lovely. Tina Grayson reached down for his ..

BOOM!!!!

He was yanked back to consciousness by the most horrendous, crackling rumble, the loudest sound he had ever heard in his life. His bed bounced into the air and a picture clattered down from the wall. "What the ..?" He jumped out of bed and ran towards his bedroom door, screaming blue murder as he trod on a slice of glass from the broken picture frame. He grabbed the door handle and pulled. It didn't move. "Oh shite," he said, grasping it with both hands and wrenching hard. The door budged a couple of inches, so he yanked hard again and it slowly scraped open, the bottom pushing back the carpet underneath. "Dad," he yelled. "Are you alright, Dad?" He hobbled across the landing and tried Dad's bedroom door. Stuck fast.
"Help! Joe .." his Dad cried. "I can't get the door open."
"I think there's been an earthquake," Joe said, hardly believing what he was saying. "I think we've been hit by a tremor." He gave Dad's door one last try then ran to the front room window, thoroughly expecting a scene of utter devastation, bodies in the street, wires down, fires blazing. (These were going to be great shots!) Outside, in a pale-blue half-light, the number 28 bus was just arriving at the bus stop on the main road. Two early starters prepared to

board. A milkman popped two bottles of full-cream milk onto the doorstep opposite. A dog ran into the street and had a dump by Wyatt Earp's nearside front wheel. "Well, that's bloody weird," he said, confused, as he gazed down at a scene of complete normality. "What the bloody hell is going on?" He gave another tug on his Dad's door. "Stay there, Dad," he said, rather pointlessly. "I'll see if I can get something to jammy the door."
"Well hurry up," whined his Dad. "I'm bursting for a crap."

-

Collapsed foundations, said the civil engineering report, when it finally came out several months later. The entire left side of the block had dropped by two point seven inches. (Official.) Dad's arse nearly collapsed too, what with the effort of holding in his morning constitutional. In the end, Joe had had to squeeze an old Tesco bag through the tiniest sliver of a gap at the top of the door, and Dad had to live with his contribution for the next forty minutes. Somebody called the fire brigade, of course, and an ambulance and three police cars screeched up the road, all blues and twos and attracting a nice little crowd down by the car-parking spaces. Having next tried unsuccessfully to open their front door, Joe knew he and his Dad would now be stuck until the firemen got to work, so he dressed, stuck a plaster on his foot and went to get his camera. The cracks across the walls were unbelievable. Two-finger width and more. Torn wallpaper, skirting boards splintered, dust everywhere. He took some shots of the internal damage and picked up everything that had fallen to the floor. Debbie Harry had torn across her left shoulder, and his 'Young Photographer' award had broken at the corner. He went to the window again and jumped back as a firemen suddenly appeared on the other side. "Alright, lad?" he shouted through the glass. "Anyone hurt? Anyone need assistance?"

"No, we're alright, thank you," said Joe. "Just stuck! What about the other people in the flats? Are they ok?"
"Oh yes, we've got 'em all out," replied the fireman, pointing down to the street. Joe looked over to see 'Mouth on a stick' and 'Fanny Craddock' yacking ten to the dozen, clutching yellowed, flowery dressing gowns to their skinny old bodies.
"You said 'we'," said the fireman. "Who else is with you?"
"My Dad," said Joe. "He's in the next bedroom." He nodded to his right and the fireman descended his ladder and went to check. He moved back and climbed up to Joe with a big smile on his face. "He's alright," he laughed. "Though I don't think I was supposed to see him pissing in a whiskey bottle! Anyway, we'll get an axe to your front door and have you out in a few minutes."

-

Safely down on the street, Joe and his Dad were instantly collared by 'Mouth on a stick'. They *thought* her name was Mildred, but only ever used their cheeky nickname for her - out of her earshot, of course - as she never, ever stopped bloody well talking. "What do you think of this for a game of soldiers?" she babbled, a hairnet and rollers cutting into her furrowed brow. "I blame the council. Knew this would happen, you know. Told 'em ages ago. I've felt movement before, see. Heard it as well. Eeh, I'd just boiled an egg for breakfast, an' all. Well, that's gone to bloody waste, hasn't it? Smashed my favourite vase, too. My cat's still up there, you know. I was supposed to be making sausage and mash for my son today. He's coming round for his tea .."
"I was doing beef bourguignon .." said Fanny Craddock, butting in. Ethel (possibly) got *her* nickname because she fancied herself as, well, Fanny Craddock. Sadly, her cooking, which she tried to palm off on Joe and Dad on a regular basis, came nowhere near the standards of the one-time famous TV chef. It was, in fact, absolutely bloody awful.
"Blimey, look at that," said Joe, desperate to escape. The brickwork at the corner of the flats had snapped in half like

a pack of bourbon biscuits and he walked off with his camera to take a close-up.

"Oh, hello again." He turned the corner and there was Mike Bent, the photographer from the local paper, snapping the same damage from another angle. "Joe Bancroft," he added, holding out his hand. "Met you once when you were taking pictures at our factory. How you diddling?" It took Mike a moment to place him, then his face broke into a broad smile and he took Joe's hand, rather softly, Joe thought, and shook it once before letting go. "Yeah, I remember," he nodded. "Didn't you want to be a photographer?" He looked down at Joe's camera and nodded again. "So how did *that* turn out?"
"Very well, actually. I got a job on The Courier. Been there over two years now."
"Oh, that's wonderful," said Mike, genuinely pleased. "Well done, you. I do hope whatever I said was of some use."
"Sure was," said Joe, turning to face his Chevette. "That's my company car, right there. I wouldn't have even thought of driving lessons if it wasn't for you. So how are you, Mike? Alright?"
"Oh, so so," said Mike, twiddling his wrist. "Some days up, some days down, you know how it is."
Joe smiled unsurely. "Erm, yes .." he said, hesitantly. "Erm .. it?"
"Eh?"
"You said 'you know how *it* is',"
"Oh, sorry. The cancer," said Mike. "Sorry! How on earth could you know?"
"Oh God," said Joe, involuntarily. "I mean .. gosh, how, what ..?"
"Spread to my neck now," Mike said, all matter of fact. "I'll be starting treatment again next Monday."
"Mike, I'm so sorry," said Joe, feeling breathless. "I .. I .."

"How's about a pint, then?" said Mike, changing the subject. "I should be able to have a drink again once the chemo's over. Say, in about three months?"
"I'll give you a bell," said Joe, brightening. "Ring the office, shall I?"
"Perfect," said Mike.

-

When Joe rang the office, they told him Mike had died. "Peacefully," they said. "You know? Like you'd want to."
"I don't think I'd want to at all," huffed Joe, slamming down the phone.
The council eventually put the flats back together. Mike was gone forever. He was 53.

Page 85

The Factory Stabber

"Let's have another go," said Joe.

Kevin's body was the ~~fourth~~ fifth they'd found in the factory that month. Well, his feet were. The rest had been melted, burnt, entirely obliterated in the foundry furnace, a fiery, ~~red-hot~~, molten, ~~steaming~~, hell-hole bubbling at ~~ten~~ a thousand degrees in the bowels of the ~~food-manufacturing~~ diesel engine factory. Was it the heat that forced away the murderer before he could throw in the ~~legs~~ feet? And was this the fate that had befallen the other four missing factory workers? Just two of the questions for Chief Inspector Desmond Calculator, the leader of a team of crack ~~rozzers~~ cops assigned to the case. They already knew it was Kevin's body. The huge, rough steel-toe-capped boots had 'Fuck off, these are Kev's' written on the underside and .. Aha! The glint of a knife caught Calculator's eye. Reaching over for a closer look, he noticed congealed blood across the blade and handle. Hmmm, he hummed. Had this victim been stabbed before being boiled to buggery?

Hmmm, had he? thought Joe, as his writing ground to a halt. And was stabbing the best idea? He sat back and scratched his neck, then pictured Kevin and shuddered with anger. He was incandescent after what his Mum had told him. "Perhaps I should just shoot the bugger with a crossbow tipped in arsenic," he growled, surprised at his own vindictiveness. He'd have to change the book's title, but he liked the idea very much.

Straight to the point ..?
Take a bow, Kevin ..?
The Archers ..?

He'd work on that later. It'd still be bam, splat, brains everywhere, of course, and he'd still chuck the body in the furnace. (Why waste a hot blazing cauldron?) It would be a beautiful irony. It really *was* Kevin's job to keep that baby bubbling a full twenty-four hours a day. "You'll play a part in your own death," laughed Joe. "Perhaps there *is* justice in the world, after all."

He went for a pee, absent-mindedly steering a rogue pubic hair down the stained porcelain with his stream of steaming urine. "Drowning!" he suddenly exclaimed. "I could drown the bastard in the Ship Canal. Knock him off his bike when he's coming home from practice and hold him under 'til his lungs filled with shitty water. Oh, that'd do it, matey. I like that." He zipped his pants and pulled up short as he turned to leave the loo. "Hang on a minute," he said out loud. "This *is* still just a book, isn't it?"

A ruffle of fright made him shiver.

"Oh, come on. I couldn't *really* kill him, could I? *Really?*"

Mercury Descending

For the fifth time that evening, the Gladsdyke Factory Brass Band struck up the opening chords of 'The Floral Dance.'

"Stop, stop," shouted Alf Stoodge, frantically waving his conductor's baton at the musicians. He glared at Kevin, seated right below him as Lead Trumpet and watched as, sweating heavily, he took his gleaming instrument from his swollen lips.

"What the bloody 'ell's going on wi' you, Kev?" he asked. "That's the fourth time tha's missed th'openin' note, ya plonker. What's the marrer wi ya? Buck up, lad. Buck up."

Kevin nodded and wiped his brow with a soggy hankie.

"Sorry Alf," he sniffed. "It'll be right next time. Carry on."

Alf raised his baton, kicked off the tune again and shouted "Fuckin' 'ell" at the top of his voice. "Go 'ome," he blared at Kevin. "Go 'ome an' come back when you can play't bloody trumpet proper."

Kevin rose unsteadily to his feet and tripped over his music stand as he made his way to the door.

"Right you are, Alf," he said, his voice a whisper. "Aye, there's definitely summat up wi' me tonight."

"Bloody right there is," said Joe, laughing loudly. "You're dying of mercury poisoning, my friend. That's what's up with you! Hee, hee, hee .." He was back at the writing pad, Dad snoring squeaky, peepy whistles in the back room. Joe took a mouthful of Jack and stopped suddenly, holding the drink tight inside his pursed lips as he theatrically wiped the rim of his glass with a tissue. "Careful, Joe," he said, after gulping down the drink. "Don't want to get poisoned now, do we?"

-

There were two things five year old Joe enjoyed on the odd occasion that Dad made it home from work before his bedtime. Grabbing hold of him, Dad would pick him up and throw him high into the air, then rub his scritchy bristles against Joe's face. Not too hard, of course. Just enough to set Joe off in a fit of tickly giggles. The other thing was Dad's little phial of mercury, which he'd bring home from the factory and empty into Joe's cupped hands, where it exploded into a million quivering, silver spheres of slithery bedtime fun. Joe would chase the little balls around with his fingers, delighting at their magical ability to merge back into one big ball after being jiggled apart. It was only when he got to study chemistry that he discovered just how effing dangerous this had been! (Thanks very much, Dad!) Still, this idea was a great idea. Killing Kevin by poisoning him with mercury. Slowly, slowly, bit by bit. Smearing it on the mouthpiece of Kevin's trumpet, his envious factory workmate would knock him off and take his place as Lead Trumpet in the band.

Couldn't go wrong.

Page 87

Joe's head was all over the place. He was worried sick about his Dad, mad as hell about Kevin, pissed off with girls (lack of), irritated that he couldn't find a newspaper that offered the two year block-release course, desperate to get going on his writing and somewhat peeved that The Dead Kennedy's new single 'Too drunk to fuck' had been banned by Radio One (although, fair do's, he could understand why).

His Dad was taking more and more to his bed, sleeping longer and longer and positively rattling with all his new medication. Joe tried hard to inspire him, tried to get him talking, walking about the room, making jigsaws .. but all to no avail. A bizarre plus - at least as far as Joe was concerned - was that, thanks to the dementia, Dad was forgetting that he smoked. So, as well as the disgusting pong that forever permeated the flat, Joe was spared much of Dad's irritating habits of taking an age to make a roll-up then having to constantly re-light it because it only contained three strands of tobacco. He almost wished his Dad would start smoking properly again, just to give him something to do.

Joe hated Kevin even more now. Why should that bastard be healthy and fit and swanning around town like he owned it? Why couldn't *he* have the Alzheimer's and the COPD and let Dad be the one that was out and about?
Life was so unfair ..

"Who's she?" said Dad from his bed one slate-grey Sunday morning. He was pointing at a faded sepia portrait on his bedroom wall. It was a photograph of Joe's Granddad, pictured looking off to the side of the camera, wearing a thick, high-collared overcoat during Home Guard duty in the Second World War.

"*She*?" said Joe, feeling adrift. "She's your Dad, Dad. That's who she is."

Page 88

Dad had always loved music. Always singing, always dancing, always listening to cassette tapes and tuning in to his crackly 'wireless'. Joe wondered if listening to old songs might help his memory. "Hey Dad," he said. "How's about I make you a compilation tape? You can listen to your favourite songs when I'm not in."
Cough. Hack. Hack .. "Good idea, Joe. Sure, I'd like that, so I would."

"Brilliant," said Joe, clapping his hands together smartly. It was the first time his Dad had been enthused about anything in ages. "I'll get a note pad and we can jot down what songs you'd like. Have a think while I look for a blank cassette."

"Billie Jo Spears," said Dad. "Blanket on the street. Er, floor? Ground!" It had been one of his absolute favourites, a sweet little sway-along song that made Joe think ruefully of the old 'western' novels that his Dad had read and collected over the years. He'd not so much as gone near one in ages. "Good choice," he said. "What next?"
"Billie Jo Spears."
"Alright .." said Joe, looking up. "Which song now?"
"Blanket on the ground."
"No, you've just *said* that one, Dad." Joe shot the words sharply. God, the dementia really *was* getting bad.
"I know," said his Dad, a wry smile beginning to appear on his ever-thinning face.
"Ok, fair enough," sighed Joe. "If you want it twice you can have it twice. Your tape, your choice. So, what next?"
"Billie Jo Spears," said Dad. "Blanket on .."
" .. the ground?" Joe slammed down his pencil. "Alright Dad, stop taking the piss." Dad laughed. He laughed, for the first time since .. well, Joe couldn't remember. A memory crashed into his head. Came from nowhere. He remembered hearing that laugh as a kid. He'd be upstairs in bed - six? seven? eight? - and he'd hear Dad roaring with laughter down in the front room. He was watching Dave Allen, his old Irish favourite, and howling and crying with laughter. Joe reached out and squeezed Dad's hand, the 'Dave Allen' one, the one with the missing finger-tip. The finger of fun that had made so many people laugh for so long. Memories.

"Let's see if I can guess what song you'd like next," he said. "Is it Billie Jo Spears, by any chance?" His Dad burst out

laughing and Joe jumped up off the bed. "Alright, have it your way, mister," he said. "You're gonna get ninety minutes of Billie Jo Spears and you can like it or you can bloody well lump it." He liked it. So did Joe, the first time. Second time was alright too but, by the time he'd heard it for the ninth time, he was going round the bend. "Oh Dad, please," he whined, and then he stopped. Dad's toe was tapping and his shortened, stumpy finger was beating the gentle rhythm of the song on the side of his armchair. It was a wonderful moment and suddenly Joe felt very excited. He went to his Dad's room and brought back the picture of his granddad. "Who's this, again?" he said, holding up the picture.
"Nurse, cup of tea? Please."

Memories. Had he left it too late to speak to Dad about his own? "Hey Dad," he said, anxiously. "What did you like most about being an engineer?"
"A what??" said Dad, still tapping his foot.
"You were an engineer."
"Shhh! I'm trying to listen to Billie."

Funny how he remembered who was singing. Such was the power of music, eh? Joe knew only too well how a few notes from a song threw you right back to the time you first heard them. 'Chirpy chirpy cheep cheep'? Always reminded him of his early days at the Grammar School, timorous wee thing that he was. (A memory he'd rather forget.) 'Billy, don't be a hero'? Ah yes, spotty, and conscious of his appearance for the first time in his life, fourteen year old Joe had tried a new 'look', dividing his hair into a centre parting and having the whole class laugh at him when their form teacher said "Look everybody, Oscar Wilde."

'God save the Queen'? The first time the Sex Pistols smashed into his consciousness, no more than four years back.

Joe leant down and rubbed the back of his head. It was only now becoming apparent that the two of them had never really chatted about Dad's past. Had he missed his chance? Would he *ever* be able to talk to his Dad about 'the good old days'. Were they gone for good? Damn it, why had they wasted so much time larking about like flatmates do, playing silly jokes on each other instead of ever getting down to a heart-to-heart talk? Or worse still, living completely separate lives, working, passing each other at the door, leaving notes ..

Gone clubbing. Happy New Year!!

Gonn to Cathollic club, having a ball
(Spelling had never been Dad's strong point)

Well, that's what flatmates did, wasn't it?

A snore told him his Dad had fallen asleep. "Thank the Lord above," said Joe, urgently pressing 'Stop' on the tape player. He brushed Dad's hair flat and went for a can of beer, then stopped as a tear rolled down his cheek. He stretched across his Dad and pressed 'play'.

-

Joe came home one afternoon to find the doctor's surgery had delivered an oxygen bottle to the flat, and Dad was sitting in his armchair, inhaling deeply. One drag on the mask, one on his cigarette. "Oh my God," Joe yelled. "You can't smoke near *that*, you idiot. You'll blow us to kingdom come." His Dad took a last sneaky puff then squashed the stub into the ash tray in his other hand. "You numpty," said Joe, wafting away Dad's smoke. "Honestly, what would the doctors say?"

He was just back from Mike's funeral, where he'd stood on the rim of a grave for the first time since he'd been an altar boy. The proximity to death had scared him. Dad, he thought, throwing soil on top of Mike. What if that was Dad?

"Let's get you sorted out," he said, carrying Dad's ashtray to the kitchen.
"And there'll be no more of *this*," he scolded, waving it back at Dad. "Not if you want to see your grandkids."
"I haven't got any grandkids," Dad shouted, breathless and crackly beneath his mask, like a Spitfire pilot in a dog fight. Joe half expected him to add "Bandits at eleven o'clock."
"Well, you know what I mean," said Joe, flapping a hand. "*If* you get some. From my sisters. Not from *me*, obviously. There's no way *I'm* having kids."
Dad stretched the mask from his face and stuck out his chin. "So how's the Bancroft name going to continue?" he moaned. "Our whole family tree will come to a stop, right here."
"Oh, I think there *are* other Bancrofts in the world," said Joe. "Not to mention all my cousins. Eugene, Ian, Brian? They've all got kids *and* they're all boys. So the family name will continue for a long time yet, don't you worry."
"More than can be said for me," said Dad, twanging the mask painfully back onto his bony face.
"Oh now, Dad," said Joe, genuinely shocked. "We'll have less of *that*, if you don't mind."
"Eugene?" said Dad. "Who's Eugene, again?"

–

The area around Dad looked like Emergency Ward Ten, what with his oxygen tank - perched on a trolley like a market stall holder's - and his mask and all its tubing, plus a

cabinet full of wipes and spittoons, and a whole table full of tablets and pills and inhalers. The flat smelled like an old folks' home, Dad's memory was going down the pan, his coughing was getting worse and Joe was forever washing socks and pyjamas and Y-fronts. Thankfully, an ever-so-patient district nurse had begun to visit, dosing Dad up and wiping him down twice a day. "He was telling me about his naval career," she said to Joe one day. "How he helped sail his ship into Sydney harbour."
"*What*?" said Joe, astounded. "He's never *been* in the bloody navy. And he's certainly never been to Australia. He's making it all up, just to impress you."
"Ah, confabulation," said the nurse, looking back kindly at Dad. "Making things up," she added for Joe's sake. "Yes, perhaps you're right. It happens all the time with dementia patients."

(The day I docked in Sydney Harbour ..

Well, what a day that was. We'd been at sea for months, operational in the Middle East and Timor before sailing down the east coast of Australia for an official visit to Sydney. I'll never forget our arrival, docking under the bridge - this was long before they'd built that pointy thing - and disembarking for 36 hours' shore leave. Best days of my life .. I think.)

Joe felt instantly depressed. "Pint?" he said to Andy down the phone. "Just a quickie? Just for a chat?"
"I'm off out," he called to Dad.
"Ah, Eugene!" said Dad, raising a pointed finger. "Your wee cousin Eugene.
I remember him. Of course I do. Joan's lad, wasn't he? Fireman. Baker. Electrician?"

Joe met Andy at the King Albert. "You look a bit strained," Andy said, clinking his pint against Joe's. "How's it all going?"

"The dementia's definitely getting worse," said Joe, glumly. "He's even started calling me 'nurse'."

"Well, you will wear those tight, white dresses," chuckled Andy, before promptly clearing his throat and looking down, chastised. "Sorry. Just trying to cheer you up. Get that down you and we'll have a sesh, eh?"

"No can do," Joe said, shaking his head and half-smiling. "I'll have to get back and check on him after this one. But thanks anyway. And thanks for listening to me, Andy."

"You haven't bloody *said* anything yet," laughed Andy, trying to keep the mood buoyant. "Come on, I'm all ears."

Joe told him about Mike's funeral and how he was worrying more and more about the possibility of Dad dying.

"Naaaaah, don't talk like *that*," said Andy, slapping him on the back. "Your Dad's got years in him yet."

"Hmm, but I don't actually think he *wants* them," said Joe, pushing out his lip.

"That's the trouble, you see. I think he's given up. What with being made redundant and all that. Accused of theft, losing his memory, health going down the pan .." He almost added "alienated by his kids and divorced for years" .. but he kept that bit to himself. "I just think he feels like he's lost all his worth."

"Well, it's up to you to make him feel valuable," said Andy, suddenly serious.

"How often do you tell him you love him?"

"Love?" said Joe, shocked at the word. "I .. well .."

"Never!" said Andy, pointing into his face. "I bet you've *never* told him you love him, have you?"

Joe lowered his head. Love? His Dad was his flatmate, not someone he should *love*! And then it dawned on him. No, his Dad was his Dad, and he *did* love him. That moaning old, cantankerous bastard he called Steptoe? Yeah, he loved him. That farting, piss-head, chain-smoking Irish ballad wailer, who always scratched his balls when he watched Pot Black? Yeah, he loved him. Loved him to bits, he realised. He cried all the way home from the pub.

-

There'd been a moment, a few weeks earlier, when Dad had really seemed to rally. Actually called out for a boiled egg, remembered how many sugars he took in his tea, called Joe Joe and smoked three fags in a row. Which was lovely. Grasping the opportunity, Joe sat down with a coffee beside his father and said "Can I ask you something, Dad?" The question that had niggled him for years. Just *what* had caused his parents to split up, leaving him and his siblings, to all intents and purposes, without a father? He'd just never had the balls to raise the subject. "Well, it's now or never," he thought, glumly, and never had 'never' felt so heavy a word. "Can I ask you about your divorce?" he said, biting the bullet. "How it all came about. Why you had to leave home. All of that. I mean, only if you *want* to talk about it," he threw in, almost chickening out.
"My what?" said Dad, and he took off his mask as if to hear more clearly.
"Your divorce," said Joe, half shouting. "I was asking you about your divorce."
"Oh, *that* .." said Dad, twanging back the mask. "Well, what do you want to know? Fire away!" Really? thought Joe. It's going to be *that* easy to find out? Good God, he thought, I should have asked him years ago. And so Dad told him all about the divorce. It took him twelve seconds, and he was as lucid as he'd been in a long time. "I was never there for you all," he explained. "Your Mum hated that all I ever did was work. 'You never spend any time with the kids' was her favourite line. But she wanted, she *needed,* all the extra money I got from doing overtime. Get us a cup of tea will you?"

"And that's *it*?" said Joe, tipping sugar into a new brew. "That's all it was? Just that you were always working?"
Dad shrugged and reached for his tea. "That's it," he said. "Nothing more exciting than that, I'm afraid. I did try to ease off on the long shifts for a while, took us all on a coach trip to .. oh, what was that Zoo called - do you remember? .. took your sisters roller-wotsiting once, but then your Mum just moaned all over again. 'We're skint, we're skint. Stop missing shifts.' I couldn't win, could I?"

No you couldn't, thought Joe. You poor bastard. But how sad. That's *all* it was about? Just money?

There was a long coughing stint, and then "I still love her, you know."

Joe felt like he'd been kicked in the testicles. "You .. *what?* I don't understand." He gasped, hand to his forehead. "How the hell can you say *that* when you acted like you did? That just doesn't make sense."
"Acted like what?" said Dad, sitting bolt upright. "What do you mean?"
"Well, when you - you know - left us in the lurch .." Dad swallowed hard and seemed to disappear into his own body. "When you stopped coming to see us all," Joe added quietly, after a moment or two. "Me and the girls. We never understood why. You just disappeared from our lives when we were all so young. You'll never know how sad we all were when Mum told us you didn't want to see us anymore." There was a cough, then a hack, and then silence. "Are you alright, Dad?" Joe was afraid he'd spoken out of turn. "Look, don't answer that," he said, waving a hand in front of his face. "It's alright. I don't need to know about that. It's all in the past, now. All in the past."
"Your Mum told you *what?*" Dad asked, almost whispering. "That I didn't want to see you anymore?" Joe swallowed hard, his fingers twisting together. He nodded, a sadness

tightening his chest. "Your Mum said I didn't want to see you any more?" said Dad, his voice rising. He fell into a coughing fit that lasted forever.

Joe's eyes pricked and his throat began to thicken. "It's alright Dad," he managed to say. "I don't need to know why. Don't worry. I'll go and put the kettle on again." Dad made to get up from his chair. "Dad, Dad, sit down," Joe flustered, as a wave of pink washed across Dad's pallid face. "Take it easy, man. Sit down." Dad breathed heavily, pushing his oxygen mask hard into his face until he eventually calmed and took a drink of water. "Your Mum told you I didn't want to see you any more?"

Joe nodded and forced back a sob. "She said you'd had enough of us, you said we were nothing but trouble, and you were glad to see the back of us. I just wanted to know why .."

Dad's head lowered, and there was a long, still pause before he spoke again. "She lied," he said, in a voice the sadness of which Joe had never heard before. "She told you a lie, Joe. I'd have done *anything* to keep you all in my life. But she banned me. Forbade me from ever seeing you after the split. Told me I wasn't welcome at the house. Said she'd get a .. a .. court order? Aye, that's it, if I ever came anywhere near you .." His voice tailed off and he swallowed hard. Joe was stunned. His own mother had done *that*? "So much for always loving her, eh?" Dad cackled. "What a stupid bastard I am." He breathed out hard, had a good cough, shook his head.

Joe's head was spinning. "You were still in love with her, even *after* she said ..?"

"Well, I didn't *know* she'd said that," said Dad, forcing an embarrassed smile across his thin, tired lips. "I didn't know *that's* what she'd told you, did I? As far as I was concerned she just told me to stay away."

"But why would you concede to *that*?" Joe snapped, angrily. "Why didn't you fight to see us, Dad? Why didn't you *make* Mum let you see us?"

Dad exhaled, then breathed in deeply. "Because I love her," he said, his voice building in strength. "Ha! Love ..?" He paused for a moment, took in some fresh oxygen and turned to look straight at Joe. "Loved .."

Joe waited until his Dad had composed himself, after being the most animated he'd been in a long time. Finally, "I don't understand," he said softly, scrunching up his face. "You didn't fight to see us because you loved Mum?"
His Dad smiled, a sad, humilated smile. "Sounds crazy, doesn't it? Mixed up, stupid .. ridiculous." Joe could only nod his head. It sounded absolutely fucking preposterous. "That's love for you," said Dad, holding up his hands, theatrically. "What can I say? I loved that woman so much that, if leaving you all alone would make her happy, then that is what I would do."
"Oh, good God ..." Joe stopped, couldn't think of a way to continue the sentence. "I don't believe it," he finally said. "I've heard of making sacrifices, Dad, but to give up on any hope of ever seeing your kids again. I .. I just don't know what I think about that, to be honest."
His Dad had another toot on the oxygen and a few seconds of energetic throat clearing. "What is they say? Patience is a virgin?"
"Ha, they probably do, somewhere," said Joe, smiling despite himself.
"Well, that's all I could do really, wasn't it? Wait. Just wait, and hope that there'd be a time when I got to see my kids again. I did, I .. cough, cough, cough .. I did the best I could for you all, Joe. You know I've been paying maintenance every since the divorce was finalised. I haven't been able to get any decent money behind me in years."
Joe took in a deep breath. "It must have been a big day, then .." he said. "That day I suddenly reappeared in your life."

It took a few seconds, but Dad eventually blinked back a tear and rubbed his eyebrow. "Aye lad, it was," he said. "Best day of my life. Thank you, son."

"No Dad," said Joe, wiping away a tear of his own. "Thank *you*."

-

Joe made yet more tea and placed it gently on a table at Dad's side. "Hey," he said, trying to lighten the mood. "You didn't half have some fun in Canada, didn't you?"

"Canada?" said Dad, burning his lips on the tea. "What the hell are you talking about, Joe? I've never been to Canada."

The day I lost my love ..

Is it possible to switch off love? Flick it away like electric light? There, and then gone in a heartbeat? Because that's what happened to me, and the love I had for my wife, when Joe told me what she'd said. It was killed within a single sentence, hurled into the darkness like a stone thrown down a mine-shaft, and it was as if I'd never known her, the mother of my three dear children.

It took me a second to comprehend him. My mind's not what it used to be, have I told you that? She said *what*? I had to ask him twice, forcing his words down through the dying grey cells of my brain until they landed upon a patch that could comprehend them. She'd blamed it all on *me*? Cut me off from my kids and then *blamed me*? I have never felt so sick in all of my life. How *stupid* was *I*? What an idiot! To suffer all those years of desparate loneliness when I could have done something about it.

God, I hate myself. I hate her.

What a fool. A fool who was fooled.

I'm ready to go, now. I've had enough.

Page 89

<u>The Bookie's revenge</u>

Derek Snodgrass was one unlucky bookie. Ever since The Grand National, he'd been taken to the cleaners by that bastard Kevin, who'd put 70 quid on the winning 100 to 1 outsider, and had been on a winning streak from then on. He was creaming in the cash on accumulators, yankees and ..

Hm, I must check out how many ways you can make a bet, thought Joe, who'd never placed one in his life.

.. and Snodgrass was more out of pocket than he'd ever been in his life.

"Oi, listen, mate," he said to Kevin one day. "Have you ever thought of taking your business elsewhere?" Kevin looked hurt and, choosing to ignore the question, turned back to his crinkly copy of The Sun and continued drawing circles around the names of horses.

"Aw, come on," pleaded Snodgrass, stepping out from behind his protective plate-glass counter. "Do us a favour, will ya? You're costing me a fortune."

Kevin sniffed snottily and held his newspaper up to the bookie's nose. "A ton on Simply Smashing in the two-thirty at Kelso," he drawled. "If you don't mind. There's a good little bookie."

Snodgrass' face turned purple, and he snatched Kevin's tenners and stormed off back behind his window.

"Bastard," he snorted, under his breath. "I'll give him smashing."

And then he had an idea. Cup of tea. Ground glass. There ya go, Kev. Have a brew. Bob's yer uncle and Kevin is a dead man.

Ooh, smashing, said Joe, pleased with his afternoon's work. He reached for a glass of his own and filled it with a can of refreshing, rewarding Guinness. "Cheers, Mr Best Seller," he said to his smiling, mirrored reflection. "And cheers to you, Kev baby. You'll be dead soon, mate. You can bet on it."

Life on the remaining 'papers ticked on, although Barry, the young addition who'd been about as useful as a chocolate chip pan, was given the boot and a two hundred quid pay-off. The boss instantly appeared ten years younger.
"You don't think they were .. you know .. 'at it' .. in the dark-room?" Joe asked Andy one afternoon. "You know, pink pork sausage and all that? You don't think ..?"
"I have no idea what to think .." said Andy ".. and, quite frankly, I don't want to, seeing as I'm about to have my lunch. Now sod off and get to that bloody supermarket."

Supermarket dashes. Joe loved them. They were routinely offered as the top prize in many a local competition and involved the winner being given one minute to charge around a supermarket with an empty trolley, filling it for free with as many things as they could within the permitted time. Joe would chase around after them, firing off shots as chickens and turkeys and boxes of Quality Street went into the trollies. (That's if the winners had any sense. Many a time, Joe had seen complete idiots spend far too much time ramming cornflakes or multipacks of crisps into their trollies - cheap stuff that they could buy at any time and that, more importantly, took up valuable space in their trollies.) Quite often, if he got the chance, he'd have a quick word with the 'trolley dasher' and put in an order, so to speak. "Get me two chickens and a big bag of frozen chips," he'd say " .. and I'll give you a fiver in the car park." Kept their freezer section stocked nicely, that did.

The 'dasher' today was rotund, red-faced, forty-five-ish. Crisps, Joe thought, straight away. This one's a muncher, if ever I saw one. She was so unfit she only managed two aisles before flomping down on the floor to get her breath back. Before she could move again, the supermarket manager grabbed her trolley and pushed it to the next aisle.

"What was it you wanted, Delores?" he shouted over his shoulder. "Tapioca pudding?" He filled the trolley with so much crap that the total bill - which his supermarket had to cover - came to only £19.50. "Congratulations, my love," he said, a wannabe Bruce Forsyth if ever there was one. "Look at all the tins you've won. Now, where've you parked your car, darling?"
"I haven't," whined Delores. "I've come on the bus!"

-

The only thing spoiling life at work was the talk of closure and redundancy. It just hadn't gone away and the rumour mill was in overdrive. With recession in the air, advertising was dropping again and everyone was convinced Mr Attar was going to shut another of his titles. "It'd be you, you know," Andy said over coffee one day at the Wimpy. "You'd be first to go. You were last in, so you'd be first out if they had to get rid of a snapper."
"Just as well I'm thinking about going freelance then," Joe said, stoically. The news popped Andy's eyes wide, a greedy mouthful of burger rendering him unable to reply. "Redundancy would give me just the kick up the arse I'd need to do it," Joe continued. Andy gulped quickly and mopped mayo from his moustache. "Didn't you say you'd been made redundant before?"
"Almost," Joe nodded. "Back at the factory. I could do that old job really quickly so I used to skive off at lunchtimes and take photos just for practice. On the day I got accepted here the manager hauled me in and told me he was laying me off. I waved the newspaper's letter of acceptance in his face and told him to stuff his job. What do you think of that?"

Andy smoothed his moustache and leant back carefully on his chair.
"I think history's about to repeat itself."

303

A shot rang out, and Kevin was dead.

Good start, thought Joe, even though it had taken him twenty minutes to conjure up.

Private P.U.Noblett, Serial Number 1056 ..er, oh, he'd make up the rest later .. formerly of the Royal Electrical and Mechanical Engineers, threw the old Lee Enfield 303 rifle into the canal and wriggled two fingers into his big ears, both still ringing sharply after the single fatal trigger-pull.

"Told you I'd get my own back," he smirked, prodding Kevin's flabby body with a well-polished shoe. "Nice work, Noblett," he added. "Always were a good shot, weren't ya. Even you .." and he prodded Kevin's corpse once more for luck .. "Even _you_ said I was a good shot. The one decent thing you ever said to me."

Noblett held a grudge. Had done so since National Service in 1957, ever since he'd met and instantly hated Kevin, his barrack-room ...

"Er, barrack-room .. what?" said Joe, chewing his nail. "I can't call him a barrack-room buddy, 'cos they hated each other's guts. Barrack-room fellow platoon member? Too long. Er, barrack-room .. comrade? Barrack-room .. oh, I know .. with whom he shared a barrack room .."

.. ever since he'd met and instantly hated Kevin, ~~his barrack-room,~~ with whom he shared a barrack-room on a damp, rambling, army camp near Camberley.

"Rot in hell," said Noblett, wiping his hands. "That's the last time you'll bully anybody, Bailey. You made my life as hellishly hell-like as you possibly could."

Yes, I like that, thought Joe. Too many 'hells', perhaps, but the subs could sort all that in the edit. He put down his pen and went to check on his Dad. They'd moved the telly into his bedroom and he was slumped, hands tucked into the belt around his dressing-gown, staring blankly at the black and white World Snooker Championships.

"And for those of you watching in black and white, the pink is next to the green."

"Who's winning?" he asked, chirpily.
"Eh? What?" said Dad, startled. "Oh, erm .. Aston Villa, I think."

Oh hell, thought Joe. Let's get back to killing Kevin.

Page 92

Knowing what he now knew, Joe felt very odd about meeting his Mum for their usual café rendezvous. She was sudddenly a difffferent woman to him, hard-hearted, cold, malicious, and he felt a sullen fake as he coolly echoed her 'hello' and brushed his cheek with hers. There was already a tense, added edge to their get-together. Mum had said Kevin was growing suspicious of her frequent outings.

"Are you alright, Joe?" she asked, cocking her head.
"Tired," he said, with a non-committal shrug. "Dad. You know .."

They took a seat across from an old chap who was fishing for biscuit in the dregs of his brew. "So, what's new?" Mum said, tidying up her fringe.
"I'm going to kill Kevin," Joe answered. It was out before he could stop it. "I mean .. in a *book*," he added, urgently. The look of horror on his Mum's face! She jumped back so sharply that the lady on the table behind hit herself in the mouth with her Bakewell tart. "I'm going to write a murder mystery," Joe explained, adding a few "ha ha has" to prove he wasn't *really* plotting a homicide. "Well, I *want* to .." he said, head to one side. "It was just .. well, let's say, I have a point to prove to someone, that's all. So, a hobby, a pastime, an exercise."
"Thank God for that, Joe," said his Mum. "I thought you were serious when you said that. Bloody hell, that gave me a shock, that did." Joe pulled an apologetic face and, as the waitress arrived, asked Mum if she'd like her usual brew. "I think I need a Dubonnet after that," she chuckled, and absent-mindedly wiped a drop of ketchup off the menu.
"So, where are you up to with him?" Joe asked, sniffing loudly. "Is he still seeing that woman? The one who plays the trombone?"
"I think so," said Mum, shrugging. "But she can have him, as far as I'm concerned. I've had enough of him. He can bugger off, the .. the .. bastard."
"Mum! Language!" Joe said, annoyed to catch himself smiling. "Well, don't worry. I'm going to have him knocked off, so to speak, so you can gain some .. what's the word? .. vicarious .. pleasure from me doing him in with the written word."

Mum's eyes widened and she smiled a 'tell me more' smile. "Go on," she said conspiratorially, stirring sugar into her second coffee. "How are you going to kill him? I mean, how *would* you do it if you were to write it?" She was like a naughty little schoolgirl, being let in on a playground secret, leaning forward, eyes wide, urging Joe for more.
Joe took a slurp of his own coffee and paused, teasingly. "Well .." he started, and then he was off, unable to keep it all in. The smelter melter, the mercury lip-balm, the ground glass gargle and the bullet through the brain. "I'm working on some other ideas, too," he fibbed. "But rest assured, Mum, whichever way I do it, I'm going to finish him off good and proper and when the book's published we'll both be able to take a little satisfaction from his .. well, his proxy kinda death. What do you think of that?"
"How can ground glass kill you?" said Mum, looking a little sheepish as she realised what she was asking. She bit her lip and lowered her head, like she was in the Gunpowder Plot or something.
"Tears your stomach apart, ground glass," said Joe, all matter-of-fact. "It'd be a nice slow death for the rat-bag."
"Ooh, yuck," said Mum. "And the mercury one? That would just poison him slowly, I suppose. But where would you get mercury from?"
"Well, your factory, for a start," said Joe. "They use it to make tilt-switches or something. Don't ask me. You know I'm useless at anything technical."
Mum nodded and took a little drink. "I *do* like the shooting one," she laughed. "It'd be just what Kevin deserved. He's always going on about Tripoli this and Libya that and just how tough he was during National Service, so it'd be great if it all came back to bite him on the bum."
"Ha ha ha .. yeah," laughed Joe. "Bam! One shot through the head and ..
Oops!" The waitress was looking at him very strangely. He realised he'd been raising his voice, getting carried away with his devious schemes. "Anyway, just desserts, eh?" he

whispered. "Oh, and let me know if you've got any other ideas."

-

Minutes passed. Silently. Mum shifted uncomfortably and pushed the salt cellar around the table. "What's on your mind?" she finally asked, eyebrows raised, head tilted.
"Nothing," croaked Joe, feeling his legs turn to jelly.
"Come on, son. They don't call it 'Mother's Intuition' for nothing."
A picture of Dad came to mind and he thought he was going to cry. He cleared his throat and went for it. "I wanted to ask you about your divorce," he said, eyes lowered. "About the split from Dad, and all that. Only if you want to, of course."
Mum nodded and breathed in deeply, then clasped her hands together on the table in front of her. "I knew this day would come," she said. "And why shouldn't it? You're a grown man now. You've got a right to know, haven't you?"
Joe gave a little shrug. "Only if you want to tell me," he repeated, pathetically.
"I *do* want to," she said, half extending an arm across the table. "I mean, I want to, and I *don't* want to, if that makes sense. And if - *when* - I tell you, you'll realise how stupid your old Mum has been. What a mess she's made of her life."
"Oh no, don't," said Joe, suddenly panicked. "Look, it's fine Mum. Forget it. Dad's already told me that it was all to do with money. How you hated him working all the time but couldn't do without the money. How .."
"See? It was all about me, wasn't it?" Mum said. "See how selfish I was, all those years ago?"
"But that's ridiculous," said Joe, an weird urge to defend her bubbling up in spite of Dad's explanation. "Look how hard you worked to bring up your kids. You sacrificed everything for us, Mum. You worked your fingers to the bone for us lot."
"In other words, just like your Dad had been doing all along," she said. "So why did I have to go and break us all

up, eh? All *that* meant was that *I* didn't get to see my kids either - yes, just like your Dad - because *I* was always working, too. I missed out on you all growing up as much as he did, and all because .."

"Because ..?"

Mum breathed in deeply again, and frowned. "Do you know Joe, I can't remember anymore. Isn't that ridiculous? I .. it was .. I suppose I just wanted more of your Dad for myself. I know he was working to keep us all in house and home - and without his hard work we'd have had neither - but I just .. I can't explain it .. I wanted my man with *me*. I wanted him at *home*. I wanted him for *myself*, just a little bit more than I got. Does that make sense, Joe? Am I rambling?"

Joe squirmed at her honesty. "But why did you keep him away from *us*?" he said, trying to control a tremor in his voice. "Why did you ban him from coming round? Why stop *us* seeing our Dad if it was all about you?"

Mum blushed and reached over to pat Joe's face. "Spite," she said. "Your old Mum was a spiteful, horrible .."

"Spite?" said Joe, cutting in. "I don't understand. What was there to be spiteful about? You'd just sent our Dad packing and .."

"I couldn't believe he'd actually *go* .." said Mum, holding out her hands. "That's why I was so vindictive. You see, it got to a point in our marriage where I felt I was living with a stranger, so I told him he'd be better off moving out. The trouble was, he took me at my word and *went*. Left me alone - with three young kids - whilst he went swanning back to bachelor life on Easy Street. I thought I had him in the palm of my hands Joe, but he called my bluff, didn't he? He upped and went, just like that. So .. right, I thought, if you can leave your kids *that* easily then you're obviously not that bothered about them, so you're not going to see them at *all*. That's what I thought, and that's what I did. Stopped him from seeing you altogether."

Joe felt sick. Oh Mum, if only you knew ..

So that was how it was. Dad had left home without a fuss because the main thing on his mind was Mum's happiness. If being without him made his wife happy, then he'd leave. Poor Dad, he thought. All those years without your family. All those years without your kids. And poor Mum, all alone in the prison of your new house - your supposed pride and joy - with three kids to bring up and a husband who was never there because ..

Oh, how sad. How very, very sad. But at least, now, he knew.

"I did my best, Joe," Mum said, sadness coating her words. Joe nodded. "Dad's very happy that I went to live with him," he said, keen to move on.
"Yes, I can imagine," Mum answered. "I must get the girls to contact him. It's about time, isn't it, Joe? The poor fella's suffered enough, hasn't he?"
Joe snatched a breath, caught a sob and turned it into a sharp cough. "I was young," Mum almost sighed. "I'm sorry, that's all I can say."

Joe had gone into the café under a storm-cloud of brooding anger, and wondered now where it had all gone. The 'sky' had cleared and he felt surprisingly calm. It was too late for rage, he decided. Far too late for that. Water under the bridge. You live and learn. No use crying over spilt ..

God, was everything in life a cliché?

His parents had cancelled each other out. The rage at his Mum was negated by the exasperation at his Dad. It was one-all at the final whistle. A score-draw on Dad's pools coupon. He thought back to being five, and idolising his per-

fect Mummy and Daddy. Well, they weren't perfect any more, were they? He shook away the image and decided to call it quits. It was time to get on with his life. "Thanks Mum," he said, placing his hand on hers.
"Thank *you*, Joe," she said, patting his cheek once more.

-

Joe paid their bill and helped Mum on with her coat. "I'll keep thinking," she said. "You know, about .." and she dropped her voice and leant towards his ear " .. about killing Kevin."
"Like I say, just an idea," said Joe, hugging her outside the door. "See you in a couple of weeks?"
He drove back to the 'paper, pressed down by a disturbing disappointment in his parents, yet feeling relieved that all the pieces had finally clicked into place. When he got back to the office they told him he was being made redundant.

Page 93

"I'll bet you didn't think I'd be home quite this soon," said Joe, holding a tepid cup of tea to his Dad's lips. "Life's full of surprises, eh? Redundant, just like you!" He'd been given a month to work his notice, begrudging the 'paper every single minute of it and feeling rather alarmed that 'going freelance' had actually now been forced upon him. How dare they get rid of *him*, the great Joe Bancroft. His meeting with the Editor had been particularly upsetting. "Please," he'd pleaded. "Can't you just keep me for a bit longer? I'm sure the circulation will go up again, soon."
"Oh, are you?" said McGowan, eyebrows raised. "And since when have you been an expert in ABC figures, Joe?"

"Eh?"

"B.C.," added the Editor, helpfully. "Audit Bureau of Circulations, lad."

Joe had never heard of it. "But you know I won the Young Photographer of the year' award, don't you?" he whined. "How can you get rid of a photographer that's won an award like that? And the Newtown office wanted to have *me* as their own photographer!" The Editor gave up trying to light his pipe and, exasperated with his young employee's ego, put his hands flat down on his desk and groaned. "Look Joe," he said, nostrils widening. "And .. don't take this the wrong way, lad .. you're good, of course you are, but you're not *that* bloody good that we can't do without you."

Joe was cut to the quick.

"Awww," said Tina, sad faced as she shrugged.

"Journalism," said McGowan, with a synchronised jerk of eyebrows and shoulders. "It's a jungle out there, Joe. You should know that, by now."

Git, thought Joe, turning to leave.

-

The 'send-off' he endured on his last afternoon at the 'paper was one of the most depressing functions he'd ever been to. Della was sent to the supermarket for ham and cheese sandwiches, and four bottles of cheap plonk were lined up next to a stack of white, plastic beakers. "Help yourselves, everybody," the boss said, to the three people that had bothered to turn up. "Well, it's publication day," he shrugged, looking back at Joe. "Everybody's busy. Oh, and have you got that A-Z we gave you?" Joe necked a full beaker of vino collapso and started on a second. (Getting pissed wasn't going to cause a problem today. He'd already handed back the keys to his Chevette.) "I left it in the car," he said. "Do you want me to go and get it?"

"No, stay here and enjoy yourself," the boss said, ironically. "I'll go for it myself." He waltzed off through the front door and Joe never saw him again.

"Sad day," said Andy, for want of anything else. "You sorted anything on the freelance front?"

"Yeah, it shouldn't be too bad," said Joe, perking up ever so slightly. "The 'paper's letting me keep my Nikon and the News said they'd take anything I could give 'em."

"Oh well, that's encouraging," said Andy, squishing his beaker against Joe's.

"Cheers to that, and here's to the newest freelance on the block."

"Hmm .. just need to buy a car now," said Joe. "Can you lend me five hundred quid?"

A dribble of reporters began to shuffle down from their desks. "Sorry to see you go," said one.

"Best of British," said another.

"Nice working with you."

"As one door closes .."

Cliché time again. He got the works. "Good luck in the future, onwards and upwards, world's your oyster .. " All the stuff you get from people you'll probably never ever see again. Joe wondered if his Dad had gone through this on the day *he'd* been given the boot. Then he wondered *why* he'd wondered, because he knew it had been completely different for his Dad. On *his* last day at work, Dad had simply gone to the wages office, picked up his two grand cheque and put his time card in the clock for one last final 'ding'. Ding! You have finished your usefulness here, Mr Bancroft. Now please fuck off and don't come back. Part Two, sniffed Joe. Bastards. Oh Dad, Dad, Dad. What am I going to do with you? he thought. Perhaps it *won't* be so easy after all, freelancing whilst you're at home. Perhaps I should wait until ..

Guy Nuttall waltzed into the front office, a big, beaming smile on his face.

"Someone looks pleased with themselves," said Joe, with just a twinge of envy. "Won the pools, or summat?"

"Next best thing," said Guy, pouring out a drink. "I've got a job with Radio Manchester. I'm joining their Outside Broadcast Unit. Hey, they're still recruiting, if you're interested. Why don't you apply for a job?"

"As *what*?" said Joe, pulling a face. "The world's first 'radio photographer'? Standing in front of a microphone describing a picture in my hand? 'And on the left is a man with a gorilla on a lead ..? No, I don't think that would work, you pillock, but good luck with the new job. You'll be able to replace all the records your German bird melted." Joe couldn't resist a little laugh, however mean it sounded.

Eric Hunt came down the stairs, a fag in his gob and an empty whiskey glass in hand. He splashed it full of murky Reisling and wrapped his arm tightly round Joe's shoulders. "Joe, Joe, Joe," he said, smoke puffing like The Mallard. "Why the sad face, chuckles? Don't look at this as story's end, kiddo. Look on it as a great opportunity. Just think of all the wonderful writing you'll be able to do now you've got so much .. er, leisure time on your hands. Ha ha ha .."

"Well, I've got news for you, Erry Cunt," said Joe, haughtily folding his arms. "I've already started writing a book, and this 'leisure' time is *exactly* what I need to get it knocked into shape. I've already had interest (even if it *is* only from my Mum, he thought) and I just might invite you to the launch if you behave yourself."

Cunty pulled back his arm and raised his beaker. "Well now, *that's* the spirit, sunshine," he winked. "I think we've turned you into a newspaper man at last."

At last? On his last day on a newspaper? Joe splashed out on a taxi home, and that was the end of The Courier.

Page 94

There was talk of a home for Dad. Or more home help. Even an offer of 'respite' time for Joe, from a social worker who seemed to think Joe had looked after his Dad for almost twenty-one years. "No, *I'm* nearly twenty-one," he said. "Give the break to someone who deserves it."

He spent the first few days of his 'leisure time' moping around, washing socks, eating Mars bars, watching telly in Dad's bedroom. Conversation had long gone between the two of them, Dad muttering gargled nonsense as he pissed into an adult nappy. Joe did *try* writing his book, but the timing was totally wrong. He wasn't in the mood. He didn't even want to write about death, not when Dad was so ..

Eh?

Nurse! Nuuuurrrse! Cup of tea? Cup of tea, nurse? Nuuurrrsse. Tea, nurse. Cup of tea? Tea? Tea? Nurse? Nurse? Tea, nurse? Nurse? Nuuurrrssse! Tea? Pleeeeeeaaaassse!

Page 95

Like peas in a pod. An aunt's description of them both, as she'd squished their faces together at one of their old family 'sing-songs'. It was the first time Joe had felt Dad's bristles against his cheek since he was five years old. His chest filled loudly at the memory, his Adam's Apple tightening at the involuntary spasm.

Oh, Dad.

Joe couldn't see it, though he'd tried, this 'peas in a pod' thing. Couldn't see much at all in the way of a family resemblance. Well, perhaps the curly hair. Oh, and the chin, of course, there was always the chin. (Joe liked to think he had a strong jaw. Still stuck it out whenever he was trying to impress a girl.) Their builds were certainly similar. Joe was just as skinny as his Dad, though a good five inches taller. Perhaps he'd see more of a similarity when he was older. Quite hoped so, actually. His Dad had been one good looking old fart, he'd give him that.

Had been.

Oh, Dad.

"Stop it, Joe," he said to himself. "Snap out of it." And then he realised he *was* just like his Dad after all. He too was a completely soppy, sentimental bastard! "And that's gonna be my legacy, is it?" he said, his lips narrowing as he looked across at his snoozing father. The word stubborn came into his head. Ha, yes! Dad had certainly been stubborn, too. Proud? That, as well. Definitely a proud man, was Dad. I wonder if he was proud of me? he pondered. And then he was off again, all emotional and moping and sad.

Oh, Dad.

A low setting sun splashed a warm pink light through the room, until a cloud covered it over and the shade dissolved to nondescript blandness. A perfect 18% neutral grey, thought Joe, an exposure technique from his studies popping up without him thinking. He went for his Nikon and began to shoot pictures of Dad in a thin, surreal glow that made his sleeping face seem soft and peaceful.

Click. A moment recorded, a moment instantly gone.

What a guy, thought Joe. The jaw still manly, the chin chiselled, the sideboards long and curly.

Click. Another slice of time, and already in the past. Photography was so ephemeral but then .. so was life. A cold panic gripped him as he faced up to the unthinkable.
Oh, Dad.

And then he smiled, as he thought back to an early memory. He wasn't to know, when he moved in with his Dad, that he'd have such an eager model for his lens tests. He'd only have to say "I want to try this wide-angle, Dad," or "Help me with this flashgun" and Dad would be there, hair slicked, clean shirt, jaw set as Joe fiddled with his latest bit of kit.

He clicked again and the sound of the shutter woke his Dad, who slowly turned and, spotting the camera, poked out a white-furred tongue. "Harvey Smith," he croaked - an in-joke about a horse-rider who'd once gestured crudely at some show-jumping judges. Dad stuck up two bony 'V' sign fingers before turning away with a long, throaty crackle.

"Ha ha ha .." laughed Joe. "Harvey Smith to you, too." He hadn't heard that one in ages. Good old Dad. Still in there. Somewhere.

Joe clicked again and again, focussing on Dad's watery, Irish eyes of blue, until he'd used all thirty-six exposures on the roll. He'd always felt an inexplicable sense of melancholy when a record faded out at the end of a song, and he felt that sadness now, watching Dad ebb away on that flat Manchester afternoon.

Page 96

Dad died, and that was that.

Complications from pneumonia, all that jazz. The usual stuff. Joe was too sad and shocked to really hear what the doctors had told him. All he knew was his Dad was dead and there he was, stiff already, pale and shrivelled on a grey-framed bed in Ward Fifteen.

Joe felt wretched. This is stupid, he cried to himself. How can you feel so sad when you've seen something coming for so long? He took some solace from the fact that he'd prayed for his Dad - no, *with* his Dad - the night before he'd died. Held his hand, looked down at his pale, unconscious face and quietly recited the Our Father. " .. Forever and ever, Amen." His Dad had made a little grunt as Joe finished the prayer. Had he *heard*? "Yes, forever and ever," said Joe, rising to go home. "That's how long I'll love you, Dad."

And it was only then, only in that darkest of moments, that Joe realised his Dad had loved him, too.

-

Bubbling away amongst all his emotions - amongst the sadness, the loss, the regret, the fear, the loneliness - was an unbounded feeling of relief. It mortified Joe to feel it but he had to, just to make sense of Dad's absence. Watching him suffer his painful physical ailments was hellish enough, but it was the Alzheimer's that had really broken Joe's heart. Dad's horrendous dementia had dragged on and on and erased the man Joe loved. Erased the man Dad loved too, Joe supposed. Wiped them both away in the eyes of the other and replaced them with two confused and frightened strangers. It didn't take Dad's body, of course. Left that for those Dad left, if only he'd known he was leaving. Now it was all over, and Dad was gone for good.

-

Joe drove straight to the Navigation - his first time there in a year - bought their usual round and made his way across to 'their' place in the corner. "Sláinte," he said, quietly raising his pint, and then he stopped himself and put down his drink. "Good health? Stupid bastard." He necked his pint in one and tipped Dad's drinks straight into the fading fabric of the threadbare seat. It pooled in an oily slick and sank into a spot his Dad would never grace again. He got back into his car and turned on the ignition. 'The Number one song in heaven' was the first tune that came on the radio.

>.. the number 1 song in heaven
> So why are you hearing it now?
> Perhaps you're nearer to here than you imagine ..

It was a throbbing disco cracker and Dad had loved it. Every time Joe played the record (he had the 12 inch remix in transparent red vinyl), his Dad would prance around the flat, singing along to Sparks and assuming, Dad being Dad, of course, that the title meant it had something to do with Jesus and The Church and all the drivel that Joe suddenly hoped was very, very, very, very true. He cried all afternoon and pored over the portraits he'd taken that distant Sunday afternoon. "Bye Dad," he said, sadly. "Bye."

Having drunk enough to sober himself, his head was suddenly filled with the million and six questions he'd forgotten to ask his Dad. It was back to that. Just *what the bloody hell* had they talked about in their short, sweet time together? *How* had he missed his chance to get to know 'the man'? His *friend*, he realised now. And yes, he *did* love him. He really did. Shit, had he ever even *hugged* him?

Too late.

-

He poured a very large bourbon and floated back to his bedroom. "Right, you're a goner, Kevin," he said, looking for a pen. He wanted revenge. Needed it. Someone had to bear the brunt of the terrible loss he was feeling that night and that healthy, living, breathing, adulterous, cowardly, bullying, shit-trumpet-playing, wife-beating, brylcreemed tit of a twat would do just nicely. He pulled his writing pad from under a pile of photography magazines and .. dropped it back on top of them.

He didn't want to think about Kevin today.
Today was all about Dad.

Page 97

True to his word, Joe took Dad back to Ulster and threw him off the top of the castle. He'd warned his cousins he was coming and packed lightly, squeezing Dad's ashes and a change of underpants into a dark green rucksack.

"What's in the bag?" said the security oberleutnant at Manchester Airport.
"My Dad," said Joe, straight-faced.

The castle looked no different from the time Joe had gone over for the wedding. Not that he was expecting change, of course. It had looked the same for over eight hundred years. There was the usual gale force nine at the top - or at least it felt like it - but, undeterred, he made his way across to the furthest corner of the parapet and took Dad's urn out of his backpack. It was cheap and plastic, in a sickly beige, with Dad's name typed officially on a label across the front.

Contains the remains of ..

He warily unscrewed it for the first time, had a little sniff, poked at a tiny chip of bone that was sticking out of the powder. Then, he dipped his hand as far as it would go into the crispy, grey grit and rubbed his fingertips gently together. "You're home, Dad," he said to the urn. "Back in Northern Ireland." First time since he'd left, Joe realised.

It was quiet at the castle and Joe had the rooftops to himself. He tried to picture Dad as a seven year old, running around the top here, playing hide and seek and dangling his legs over the edge. He leant over the low wall to look at the sea and the long drop instantly frightened him. "Bloody hell," he said to the urn. "And you jumped in from *here*?" Checking he was still alone, Joe said a little prayer (still hedging his bets) and slowly, gently, tipped the ashes over the wall. As if on command, as if respecting Dad's life-long aversion to the sea, a swirly gust came up from Belfast Lough and caught hold of the gritty bits, blowing them away from the waves and all over a group of Japanese tourists who'd just appeared in the stairwell. They were coated in a fine dusting of Dad and, as Joe watched, they used their guidebooks to swat away the last little grains of his father.

Joe laughed through the tears, couldn't help it. "Tokyo next, Dad," he sniffed. "Have a great trip."

-

It had been nice to see his sisters again. Nice they'd turned up for the funeral, even though they'd never got round to visiting Dad when he'd needed them to. Joe consoled himself with the thought that his Dad probably wouldn't have known them if they *had.* And fancy that .. they'd drunk the pub dry of Draught Guinness. Now *that's* what you call a wake! "Sorry love, the barrels are empty," barmaid Brenda had said. "You'll have to go to't Pig and Whistle if you want more."

Joe couldn't wait to tell his Da .. ah!

He'd have laughed so much.

-

Joe was numb for a month. Is that it? he kept thinking. Is that all there is? You're here and then you're not, your one crack at life done and dusted before you know it? Oh, my God.

He rattled around the flat, stroking Dad's empty chair and glancing at the front door, expectantly. The surgery came to collect their oxygen bottle but told Joe he could do what he wanted with everything else. It all went straight in the bin. The flat was too big now, too empty after Dad's death, so Joe put himself on the housing list for a move to a smaller flat. He'd planned - always planned - to start saving for a house but well, you know ..

It was time to start working again but, until he got a car, he'd have to use the buses and stay local. He took to scouring his weekly 'paper for events that he might be able to photograph and started supplying the News with filler pix and diary stories. Putting down The Journal one evening, he smiled wryly to himself and shook his head. Fuck, it was just like being sixteen again. All that searching through the 'papers? All that coming up with picture ideas? Just like starting again. The effort was worth it, though. Within three weeks he'd earnt enough to buy himself a (second-hand) push-bike. (Bald tyre, torn seat, fifteen quid.)

Page 98

It was only gale force eight - or at least it felt like it - the day Joe cycled to the top of the motorway flyover, stretching far and rising high above the Manchester Ship Canal. He couldn't get a word out when he got to the top.

"I've watched you pedal all't way up," yelled a grinning, middle-aged policeman, setting out a wobbly line of traffic cones. "I haven't the heart to send you back." And so it was that Joe was able to photograph a lorry that had blown over in the strong wind.

His transfer to a smaller flat had come through quickly - two bedroomed accommodation was always in demand in his area - and his new place faced the flyover. He'd been using Dad's old binoculars to watch the traffic that struggled through a clattering low-pressure system. The lorry blew over and Joe was at the entry slip road within twelve minutes. It took him another twenty to fight his way to the top of the cordoned motorway, where he identified himself to the bobby as a 'freelance' photographer (he still had his press card, thank goodness) and then located the driver of the overturned wagon, fortunately unhurt and trying to get at his flask of tea, jammed between the pedals on the now-vertical floor of his cab. Joe yelled to him through the gale. "Just stand here please, right in front of the wagon." The driver grimaced as a fierce gust hit him in the face and the caption in that night's News described the driver as 'still managing to smile' despite his accident! Joe was thrilled he'd made it back to the News in time for the 'paper's evening edition. Now *that* was what press photography was all about. (It *had* helped that the wind had been at Joe's back all the way into Manchester. The speedy freewheel down the bridge was one of the best experiences he'd had in ages.)

But oh, it felt good to be getting published pictures again and, before he knew it, the News was commissioning him to take photographs on a regular basis.
"I'm a freelance!" he cheered, clinking a glass with nobody. "Hurray!" Three weeks like that and he'd earned enough this time to buy a (third-hand) Ford Escort. (Bald tyres. Knackered gear box. Fifty quid.)

His new picture editor - I'm working for a *picture editor*, Joe would squeal - was a gem. A real rough diamond who'd worked all over the world and took "no shit from no-one", he drank gin and tonic from the start of his shift (6.30am!) and would have a fag on the go at every desk in the photo section. One day Joe handed him a photo from a sponsored beard shave, having captioned the willing victim as 'formerly hirsute'. "What the fuck's 'hirsute'?" yelled the picture editor, knocking back a Gordon's.
"Hairy," Joe jumped. "It means he was hairy."
"Well, fucking *put* hairy," he barked, flicking ash all over the print.

-

Sitting in the Photographers' Room - the photographers had their own *room* - Joe felt all his pay days had come at once. It was certainly the end of his days in the darkroom. Being commissioned meant that, after each job, he now had to hand over his film to either Jim or Neville, two of the incessantly complaining darkroom technicians who would (eventually) develop and print it. That left time for Joe to chat to all the photographers he'd always held in such high esteem. To John Batchelor of course, and to Eric, and to Bill, and to Foxy. He could take home free copies of the 'paper and there was even a staff canteen, with subsidised rates and Manchester tart on Thursdays.

Feeling a lot better about life, Joe treated himself to a trip to the cinema one evening. When he came out, his new (very old) £50 Escort had been stolen from the car park. "Oh, for fuck's sake," he cried. "I don't believe it!" He had a tripod in the boot that was worth more than the car.

Page 99

Joe tried very hard to keep up the momentum he'd started with the News, but it wasn't so easy when - *yet again* - he had to travel round the city by bike and by bus. The (new) boss was sympathetic but could only hold his hands up. "What can I do?" he said. "You're no good to me without wheels, chummy." And so it was back to rummaging through the weeklies for upcoming events and filler stories.

Joe froze when he opened that week's 'paper ..

Local trumpeter found dead in band hut

Kevin Bailey, the 59 year old Lead Trumpeter with the Cadistone Factory Brass Band, was found dead in the band's hut in the early evening of Wednesday the seventh.

"I thought he was asleep," said Bernie Wallwork, the cleaner who opened up the hut that evening. "He always was a dozy so and so."

Joe almost shat himself.

What? Kevin was dead?

He read it through again, just to make sure.

Oh my God, yes! Kevin was dead.
Kevin is *dead* …?

"And I didn't get to do it .. " he screamed, scrunching the 'paper into a ball. He was absolutely furious. "The bastard's gone and died, without me killing him," he yelled. "Life is *so* unfair."

He hot-footed (cycled) straight to his Mum's, only stopping to buy another bunch of the same red roses he'd offered her that long-ago day. "I'm so sorry," he lied. "How did it happen?"

-

The inquest results were revealed two weeks after the autopsy. Cause of death, mercury poisoning.

Holy Shiiiiiiiit!

It took Joe an age to find his old writing pad. "Oh, please, please, please .." he rattled. "Where the bloody hell is it?" To his everlasting relief, he found it under a stack of Creative Camera mags and, heart hammering, hastily ripped out the page on which he'd written that first early draft of Mercury Descending. He tore it into as many pieces as his shaking hands would allow and flushed them down the loo with a poo that hadn't gone away the first time. Then, in panic mode, he rang his Mum once more. "Coffee, Mum? *NOW??*"

"Come to the house again, Joe," she said, surprisingly chirpily. "The bastard's gone now. I can do what I want."
"No!!" Joe was whispering, paranoid as hell. He curled his hand around the mouthpiece of the telephone. "I'll see you at the caff, as usual .."

-

"Have you seen the autopsy report?" he said over a cappuccino, his voice still low.
"Mercury poisoning, wasn't it?" Mum said, almost smiling.
"Yes, but .."
"You know it doesn't work, don't you?" she said, stirring her coffee.
"It? What?" said Joe, confused.
"Rubbing the mouthpiece of a trumpet with mercury. Waste of time. It just slides off. Gets you nowhere at all." She played her coffee over the underside of her spoon. "See?" she said. "It all falls off. Just like that. All those lovely little balls of .."
Joe's stomach knotted and a cold bolt of electricity shot through his body. "Oh my God, Mum," he coughed. "What have you *done*? You've not been .." He caught his breath and whispered so quietly that he almost mouthed the words. "You've not been giving *mercury* to Kevin, have you?"

"Got it from the factory," she smiled. "Just like you suggested. Horace in stores was a pushover."
Joe went white and turned dizzy. And then he felt sick and missed a heartbeat. "I don't believe what I'm hearing," he gasped. "But how did you ..?"
"Popped it into his meals," said Mum, nonchalantly. "A few drops, every meal. Soon adds up."
Two policemen arrived at the same time as Joe's buttered toast. "Mrs Bailey?" said the taller one, looking straight at Joe's Mum. "I'm arresting you on suspicion of the murder of Kevin Bailey."

-

She was out after three years. Extenuating circumstances, domestic abuse .. a good solicitor.

Joe was, by now, a regular freelance for the News (and anyone else who'd have him) and he had a decent car and two goldfish and a life. He never did get onto the press photography course and quietly relished the fact that, technically, he wasn't qualified to do his job. These days, he knew he wasn't the greatest photographer in the world, but felt he was good *enough*, and that was good enough for him. He was currently 'between' girlfriends, but finally knew *good* sex at last.

Out on a job one day, he bumped into Eric Hunt and it brought to mind, for the first time in a long time, the 'book' the bastard had sparked in him. He decided he'd give it another go and, on a rare night at home, grabbed a Jack and ginger, marched himself to his desk and sat down at his word-processor.

But what on earth would he write?

A murder mystery?
"I am *not* going down *that* route again!"

A love story?
"Ha ha ha!"

An autobiography?
"Oh, do behave!"

He leant back in his chair and tipped a whiskey at a portrait of Dad, which he'd framed and hung above a sign that said 'Have a Ball'.

"Ah, forget it," he said, knocking back a glug.
"A book? In ninety-nine pages?
That is *never* going to work."

The End

With thanks ...

I've had a lot of encouragement from many people during the writing of this book, and I want to say a big 'Thank You' to them all ..

So, merci beaucoup Lesley W, Viv P, Jacqui B, Jon H, Adrian P, Colette S, Caroline D, Adam R, Kate C, Ed B, Matt Mc and last, but in no way least, my good friend Nelly!

Thanks to my Mum, too .. and The Red Arrows, Joy Division, The UK Subs and all the other fantastic bands that have kept me going over the years. And a big 'well-done' to the designer of the Olympus XA!

I also want to pay my respects to Stan Royle, Steve Bent, the victims of the 1979 Woolworth's fire in Manchester and, of course .. my own wonderful, lovely **DAD.**

One another thing ...

1978 was a very different time to today, especially for an eighteen-year old growing up in working-class Manchester, so I hope you bore all that in mind if you bumped into a concept that displeased you or a word that made you feel uncomfortable.

(And I'm sorry about all the fucking swearing!)

This book is a work of fiction, although it involves a lot of my own memories. Where this is the case, I have changed the names.

Thanks for taking the time to read my book.
I hope you enjoyed it.

Printed in Poland
by Amazon Fulfillment
Poland Sp. z o.o., Wrocław